# DOUBLE BLIND

## DAN ALATORRE

GREAT OAK PUBLISHING
FLORIDA

# *Double Blind* © Dan Alatorre

Edited by Jenifer Ruff

**Published by GREAT OAK PUBLISHING, FLORIDA**

## OTHER THRILLERS
## BY DAN ALATORRE

**NOVELS**
**The Gamma Sequence,** *a medical thriller*
**Rogue Elements,** The Gamma Sequence, book 2
**Terminal Sequence,** The Gamma Sequence, book 3
**Double Blind,** *a murder mystery*
**A Place Of Shadows,** *a paranormal mystery*
**The Navigators,** *a time travel thriller*

**HORROR ANTHOLOGIES**
**Dark Passages**
**Dark Voodoo**
**Dark Intent**
**Dark Thoughts**

# *CONTENTS*

# *ACKNOWLEDGMENTS*

A book this good is the result help from many friends,
most of whom—despite me telling them—don't seem to
know how valuable they are to me.

# CHAPTER 1

The killer clutched and re-clutched the big knife, his heart pounding as he eyed his prey.

Twenty feet away, a lone, paunchy truck driver, his shirt wet with sweat, wheeled a third dolly of boxes onto a desolate loading dock. In the distance, past the dark warehouses and empty train cars, a boat horn blared. It cut through the foggy night, signaling another departure from the Port of Tampa. Maybe tourists heading to the Caribbean, maybe car parts heading to Mexico.

The killer didn't care.

What concerned him as he crouched behind the warehouse dumpster at McClain Oil was his first victim—and how he would proceed with the murder.

His .38 would do the job the fastest, but the noise might attract attention. He glanced around. There was not another soul on 22nd Street. But a gun was less satisfying. He'd learned that with raccoons and stray dogs. And you never know; some brown-noser accountant might be working late in one of the warehouse offices.

No, it needed to be the knife. He *wanted* it to be the knife.

He lifted it and gazed at its long, serrated blade, flipping it to admire the smoother, sharper other side. The honed edge glinted in the warehouse lights. Through his latex gloves, he gripped its thick hilt and ran his thumb along the small metal hand guard.

Beautiful craftsmanship in such a large knife.

Using the knife would be more . . . personal. He'd feel the blade go in, piercing the trucker's shirt, sliding through the soft fat and dense organs; then he'd feel the warm, thick wetness of the blood.

Bliss. The very thought of it made him shudder in anticipation.

He licked his lips, peering over the edge of the rusty blue garbage bin.

With some effort, the truck driver bent and slid the dolly from under the boxes, pausing to wipe his brow. He pulled a cell phone from his back pocket, his considerable belly heaving as he pressed the button.

With each passing minute, the killer's hate of this man—this stranger—grew, intensifying into a rage so he could summon the courage to go through with his plan. He needed to hate this man, to despise this stranger enough to kill him, stabbing and stabbing—and then instantly switch it off . . . and enjoy the bliss. The serenity, as the trucker kicked and clawed, fighting for his fading life.

The killer squeezed the knife handle, breathing the hot night air in quick gasps. Sweat formed on the back of his neck.

He would not chicken out. Not this time.

"Dispatch, put me through to O'Connell." The trucker rested against the dolly, his phone pressed against his ear. He moved his head back and forth, looking skyward as if trying to get a better signal. "Mac? I decided to unload the freight myself." He closed his eyes and covered his ear with his other hand. "I don't care about procedures or contract rules right now. I'm three hours late as it is. The dock workers will be here in twelve hours and I need to be in Tallahassee in ten, so what do you suggest?"

He nodded. "That's what I thought. Look, there's nobody here and nobody comes to these warehouses after hours. If some petty thief happens by and wants to boost three pallets of car parts, I say let 'em."

He ended the call and shoved the phone back into his rear pocket. "Moron."

The man grabbed the dolly and tipped it backward, rolling it off the loading dock and onto his vehicle. Inside the truck, the light of a single caged bulb illuminated the plywood enclosure and a few stacks of boxes. He scribbled on his manifest, snapped shut the steel lid of his clipboard, and reached toward the light's pull chain.

Instead, his eyes met a .38 caliber pistol pointed at him.

His jaw dropped as he backed away, raising his hands. "I don't have a lot of money. About two hundred dollars in the cab, but it's yours."

The killer glared at the steel clipboard, raised high in his victim's trembling hand. The truck driver followed the killer's eyes, glanced at the steel case, and opened his fingers. The clipboard clattered to the floor.

The driver swallowed, his eyes wide in the dim glow of the overhead bulb. "Okay?" his voice quivered. "Two hundred bucks, and it's all yours. It's right up front in the—"

"You misunderstand." The killer stepped forward, impressed with how calm his voice sounded. "I'm not here for your money."

The man's eyes darted about the space, his breath coming in gasps. "The freight? It's not a big load but – but it's yours. Hubcaps." He swallowed hard. "Nice stuff. I'll—I'll even help you unload it."

"Nope." The killer took another step, shaking his head. "Not that either."

"Then . . ." The blood drained out of his face.

"Are you from Atlanta? That's what the sign on the side of your cab says. Messenger Freight, Atlanta."

The rush came upon the killer, welling in his gut. This was no raccoon or stray dog. The tension of glorious anticipation swelled in his neck and shoulders as he moved forward, closing the distance between him and his terrified prey.

The gun had done its job. He dropped his other hand to his belt and slid the knife from its sheath. Its beautiful power mesmerized him, but only for a moment. He gripped it firmly, eyeing the man he intended to kill, smiling as he eyed the man's soft torso.

The trucker stepped back, shaking his head, stumbling over the few remaining boxes in his vehicle. "Don't do it. Please, just take the stuff."

"Or are you based out of somewhere else? I'd like to keep this local if I can." The killer's voice was calm and even, not displaying an ounce of his desire to jump and slash.

"Please. I have a wife and kids. I have a little girl."

The killer eyed the knife, admiring it. "That's a shame. To think of some other guy raising your kid. Smacking her in the mouth when she gets out of line. Or maybe worse."

The man whimpered, dropping to his knees and clasping his hands together. "You don't have to do this."

The killer snapped upright. "Don't tell me what I have to do!" His voice boomed loud, blasting off the plywood walls. The trucker flinched, turning his head. The raw hatred of the killer was boiling upward, ready to become unleashed. "You don't know what I have to do!" He screamed, his mouth turning into an ugly grimace. "You don't know!"

He stepped back, almost staggering. Taking a deep breath, the killer steadied himself.

He raised the knife, staring past it to the truck driver's eyes. "Only I know what I have to do. Oh, and I do know. I do."

The itch that couldn't be scratched, the impulse that churned within him, the adrenaline, it was all becoming too much. He wiped his forehead with the back of his hand, trying one last time for control, savoring the moment, not wanting it to pass too quickly.

"Would you . . ." His voice fell to a whisper. "Like to say a few prayers?"

The trucker groaned, unable to form words. "I—"

"Too slow." The killer lifted the pistol and leveled it at the man's torso. "Do you believe in fate?"

The shot was deafening inside the closed area of the vehicle. The noise of the blast bounced off the plywood walls as the flash from the muzzle turned the killer's vision white.

The trucker fell backward, shrieking in pain, kicking and flailing as he held his gut. He crashed onto an empty wood palate, sending a bounce through the vehicle's floor. Blood appeared on his fingers.

The killer chuckled, the release of energy surprising even him. The rush was upon him now, an uncontrollable energy that owned his every move. He fought it, wanting to go slowly, forcing himself to not leap upon the man and cut him to shreds.

"Now," the killer shuddered. "The knife."

He raised the blade slowly, his hands shaking with anticipation, his eyes fogged with delight.

The trucker opened his mouth to scream.

Instead, he clutched his hemorrhaging gut, kicking in pain. A gob of spit swung from his mouth as he writhed and groaned on the dirty plywood floor.

"Yes," the killer said. Twirling the big knife in his fingers, he smiled as blood seeped over the trucker's hands. "I think . . . in here. What do you think?"

The trucker gurgled and coughed, spitting blood.

"Yes." The killer lowered himself to the floor, crawling forward to the dying trucker. "Yes, you're right. It's time."

The rush returned. His pulse throbbed in his ears as he squeezed the knife and plunged it into the trucker's belly. Past his hands, past his protests, into his warm, soft guts. The trucker's screams filled the air as the killer pushed the blade in deeper, warm blood meeting his waiting fingers. The serrated edge rumbled across tendons, sending vibrations up the killer's arm. The sensation electrified him. He yanked the blade out and plunged it in again, shouting in ecstasy over the cries of his victim. The sensation was fantastic, each nerve ending alive. He thrashed and swiped, sending small wet chunks of flesh to the plywood floor as the carving continued. He was enraptured in his task. Each thrust of the knife gouged out new and bigger pieces in his bloodlust-filled rage.

The excruciating moans of the trucker were met with the joyous cries of his assailant. Faster and faster, the killer chopped his way into his victim's torso, spilling blood and kidneys and intestines in a thick, frothy soup. He raged again, screaming as he plunged the knife one final time, driving it as hard as he could inward and upward into his victim. His arm disappeared up to the elbow, coming out soaked in thick, warm blood.

Sated, the killer sat back, pushing himself to rest against the plywood wall. His chest heaved as he caught his breath, blood covering his arms and abdomen. Splattered bits of his victim stuck to his cheeks and shirt.

The trucker lay as a mess on the floor, wheezing slowly as death came over him. His hand reached outward, clawing at anything. At nothing. At life.

The killer swallowed, drawing a deep breath. "You were good, my friend. A worthy first." He sniffed, throwing his head back, clearing a stray hair from his eyes. "In fact, I want to remember this occasion."

Exhausted, the killer crawled over to the dying man, placing his face next to his victim's. "A souvenir, I think."

The trucker groaned and clawed, twisting his face away.

Nodding, the killer patted the man's shoulder. The dying eyes never moved, the open mouth dripping blood and drool.

"An ear, you think? Is that a good commemoration?"

The eyes stared into space, unfocused but not yet dead.

"No? Not an ear? A finger, then."

The killer pushed himself to his feet and bent over to grab the dying man's hand. He brandished the knife and let all but the last limp finger slip from his grasp.

A low moan escaped from the trucker's lips.

"Why, thank you." The killer smiled, firmly holding the pinky, and brought his knife under the man's palm. He forced the blade through at the knuckle, slicing. It caught for a minute, jerking the hand upward as it snagged on the joint. A few solid pulls and a bit of rough sawing, and the finger came free. The killer held it up to the dying man's eyes.

"I'd have rather had an ear, I think. But this will do."

He strolled to the rear of the truck, admiring his souvenir, rolling it back and forth in the palm of his hand. His rush relieved, calmness came back to him.

"I didn't see a wedding ring, either, you liar. And I bet you don't have any kids. But that's okay." He chuckled. "It was my first death, too. Neither of us knew what to expect."

He jumped off the back of the truck, peering back into the plywood crypt. "It was a good death. For me, anyway. And even though your pretend wife and daughter won't miss you, you're about to be famous."

The faint gurgling lessened until the man fell silent. A final weak twitch from his leg, and he was done.

Sweat brimmed on the forehead of the killer, his pulse returning to normal. "Thank you." He shuddered, releasing a final sigh of satisfaction. Straightening himself, he took a deep breath and walked into the darkness. "Thank you very much."

## CHAPTER 2

Sweeping his hand over her cheek, Sergio Martin tucked a strand of soft, amber hair behind the woman's ear, bringing his face close to hers.

The phone in his pocket buzzed.

He winced. "Do you believe that crap?"

The beautiful redhead pulled him close, brushing her nose against his. "Ignore it."

"Yeah. Can't." He dug into the pocket of his blue jeans. "Duty calls."

"Are you sure?" She leaned back on the couch, placing an elbow on the armrest and winding a finger into her hair. "Things were getting interesting."

Sergio stood, patting his pocket. "I'm pretty sure I can't ignore this one. It's my work phone."

"Lousy timing."

"Would there have been a good time to interrupt this?" He pulled the phone from his pocket and mashed a button. "Detective Martin here."

Plucking an empty wine glass off the end table, the woman sauntered across the living room to the small kitchen.

Sergio pressed the phone to his ear as he flicked on a lamp. "Warehouse district south of Ybor." He scribbled a few notes on a pad. "22nd Street. Got it. How many bodies?"

His date leaned on the counter and took a sip of her wine.

"Okay." He shoved the pad in his back pocket. "Can you call Detective Sanderson for me? Tell her I'm leaving my house right now and I'll be there at the scene in about fifteen minutes." He ended the call and slid the phone back into his pocket.

"Okay if I let myself out?" The woman swirled her glass, turning its contents into a tiny, bubbly whirlpool. "I've had a few drinks and don't feel like driving."

"Stay as long as you like. Finish the bottle." Sergio grabbed his gun and wallet. "My wife won't be back until tomorrow night."

"You got yourself a deal." She picked up the bottle of Asti and refilled her glass. The golden bubbles raced upward but the foam didn't go past the rim. As Detective Martin picked his car keys up off the end table and headed for the door, she raised her drink and winked. "Hurry back."

He smiled. "Lady, you're about to see record-speed police work." Yanking open the front door, he darted out, pulling the door shut behind him.

\* \* \* \* \*

The blue strobe lights of half a dozen police cars flickered off the fronts of the warehouses on 22$^{nd}$ Street. As Sergio stepped out of his sedan, he waved to the attending officer.

"Lieutenant Breitinger is up there, Detective." The cop pointed to a raised loading dock.

"Thanks." He clutched his notepad and glanced at the cop's nametag. Fuentes. Sergio made a mental note. "How's it look?"

"Messy." Fuentes shook his head, pointing to a truck. Messenger Freight was stenciled on the door. "The body's inside there. I wasn't the first one here, but I got a look. Never seen anything like it."

"No?"

"Nope. Talk about hacked up. It was brutal. I'm happy to be stringing police tape tonight."

Sergio rubbed his chin. Fuentes looked shaken by what he saw; his face was a little pale. "Okay. Sounds like a long night ahead. I'll see about getting some coffee to you guys in a bit. Let me know when—"

Light spilled onto the scene as the rumble of a big engine approached. Detective Martin lifted his notepad to shade his eyes from the car's headlights. A burnt-orange Camaro with black hood stripes bounced over the patchwork asphalt.

"—when Detective Sanderson gets here."

Fuentes chuckled, recognizing the car. "Looks like she's here."

Carly Sanderson put down the passenger window as she drove up to the men. "Good morning, Marty." She nodded to the cop. "Morning,

Officer Fuentes. Or is it still night? I'm not really sure." She lifted her wrist and glanced at her watch.

"Twelve thirty goes either way, Detective." Fuentes said.

Sergio leaned on the car door and spoke through the open window. "The boss is over on the loading dock, and the vic's in the big truck over there." He patted the orange roof of the car. "You can leave the General Lee right here, Daisy Duke."

Sanderson got out of her car and gathered her dark hair into a ponytail. She eyed Sergio's sedan. Even in the dim lights of the warehouses, the dent in the rear panel was visible. "Right. My car's the one to make fun of." She strolled past Sergio and Fuentes. "There's half a dozen coffees in the back seat, Carlos. You and the guys can help yourselves."

Officer Fuentes smiled. "Thanks, Carly."

Sergio lifted the crime scene tape for them and walked with Carly across the parking lot. She was dressed up. White silk top and black slacks.

No high heels; her shoes were practical flats—all cop.

*Guess she swapped them out in the car.*

When they reached the worn concrete steps of the loading dock, Sergio shoved a hand in his pocket. "How's your Friday night going?"

"Probably the same as yours." Carly climbed the stairs and waved a finger under her chin. "You have some lipstick on your . . ."

Sergio wiped his face with the back of his hand, then quickly followed his partner up the steps.

A few cops lingered at the back of the truck. They parted as Lieutenant Breitinger stepped out and moved past them onto the loading dock. He put a hand on the truck frame and shook his head. Behind him, camera flashes filled the van with blasts of light like a summertime electrical storm.

Breitinger glanced at the detectives. "Good morning. Nice of you to join us." He pulled a handkerchief out of his suit pocket and wiped his mouth.

Sergio raised his eyebrows. "Is it that bad in there?"

The lieutenant took a slow, deep breath. "Worst thing I've seen in twenty years." He sniffled, wiping his nose with the hanky and glancing over the street of warehouses. "Some palm trees around here are driving my allergies nuts, the stupid things. It's November. They should stick to blooming in summer like everything else."

"Yeah." Sergio eyed the truck. The uniformed officers there didn't seem too happy at what they'd seen inside, either.

Carly pulled a notepad from her hip pocket. "Do we have a name on our vic yet, sir?"

"Yeah. Victor Franklin. Local short run driver. Shot once in the gut and then hacked to pieces with a long blade knife."

Segio flipped open his notepad and slid the pen from its leather clasp. "Was it a robbery?"

"No, and I want you guys to pay attention to me on this. Over here." The lieutenant placed his hand on Sergio's shoulder, pointing to a spot on the loading dock away from where the uniformed officers stood. Carly and Sergio walked with him there.

Their boss lowered his voice. "Whoever did this is one sick individual. They didn't rob the guy and they didn't just kill him. It doesn't look like the murderer got interrupted, it looks like . . ." Breitinger chewed his lip. "The killer took his time. He hacked the guy up like he was enjoying it."

Carly nodded. "Think it's part of something bigger?"

"Let's hope not." Beitinger grimaced, dragging the hanky under his nose again.

A young uniformed officer shouted from the far end of the loading dock. "Lieutenant, the coroner's here."

Breitinger waved at the cop, then turned his attention back to the detectives. "Stay on it, keep me posted, keep it tight. Report to me only, until we know what's up." He stepped away, walking backwards as he spoke. "Find this sicko. Fast."

"Got it, boss." Sergio crossed from the loading dock to the truck. The vehicle floor swayed slightly with his weight as he stepped aboard. Carly followed, bouncing it again.

The bulb in the truck lit the gruesome scene, a picture right out of a horror movie. A middle-aged man lay prone on the floor, massive pools of blood surrounding him. His eyes stared at the ceiling, his mouth hanging agape and crusted with blood. His chest and abdomen were flayed apart, soaked red with blood to the point where it was impossible to tell where his shredded clothing stopped and his ripped body began. A small blowfly crawled over his forehead and across his eye, pausing briefly before crossing the man's cheek and disappearing into his gaping mouth.

Standing in the back of the truck, Sergio exhaled sharply and forced himself to swallow so he wouldn't gag. The streams of drying blood nearly reached all the way to his feet. The putrid stench from the severed intestines and hacked organs hung in the air, reeking like an overused porta potty on a hot day at the fair.

Carly held her hand over her nose and mouth. Nobody would be drinking any coffee at this crime scene.

She pulled on a pair of latex gloves and squatted, examining a bloody footprint. Large sole, with a pattern. A man's running shoe. She raised her eyes and glanced at the walls of the truck. Blood splatter coated nearly everything. "From the looks of this mess, we're in for a long night."

"Yeah." Sergio put his hands on his hips, sighing. "But our killer left behind a ton of evidence."

"He's new at this." Carly glanced at Sergio. "Or he didn't care."

"Well, happy Thanksgiving, partner." Sergio tucked his notepad under his arm and reached for his gloves. "Can't wait to see what this maniac does for Christmas."

# *CHAPTER 3*

The jogger moved quickly, leaping from the aged sidewalk to the brick-paved street and back again as he raced along 7th Avenue. The cords from his earbuds bounced off his lean chest with each stride.

And the killer's eyes followed.

The digital clock on his dashboard read 6:22 P.M. It'd be getting dark soon.

He tapped the steering wheel, taking a deep breath. *Too soon?*

He'd enjoyed the first time immensely, so proud of himself for watching and waiting in the warehouse district until no one was around. Like a spider with a fly, he held his eagerness in check, staying patient two nights in a row until everything fell into place.

The right time of night, the right area, the right victim.

And how he had relived the moment, his eyes closed as he lay on his bed, going over it again and again, night after night, recalling each thrust of his knife—and creating more and more delight inside him until he overflowed with ecstasy. His first kill had been satisfying and exhausting on every level. Better than he had imagined, and for days he walked around in a state of bliss. The sky seemed bluer, the grass seemed greener; everything was right with the world.

And then it faded. The nights of bliss became nights of frustration as the incessant itch returned. The aching hunger churned inside of him, welling up until he knew he had only one option, only one way to satisfy the urge that loomed inside of him and dominated his every waking thought.

He fought it; he pressed his fists against the sides of his head and squeezed his eyes shut, curling into a ball and screaming for hours—but there was no escaping the throbbing, pulsing urges that coursed through his body and oozed from every pore. He knew that now.

*Again. I need it again.*

He buried his shame about using the gun the first time, needing only darkness to come so he could set that aside and relive the attack. No embarrassment came then, and with each day the shame of his incessant desire for blood grew smaller, while the urge to find blood again grew stronger.

As he sat in his car on 7th Avenue, he glanced at the passenger seat. His tools were there, just beneath, wrapped in a beach towel, ready. The knife and the gun . . .

*Coward!* He slammed his hands onto the steering wheel. *Shooting that trucker first.*

But it was the only way. He knew that. He couldn't risk a struggle. He certainly couldn't risk losing a fight. He took another deep breath and let it out slowly, calming himself. He closed his eyes, remembering. He had only wanted the cutting, the blood—*the power*—of taking the life out of another human being and wearing the warm, wet proof on his hands.

*You wanted the icing. You didn't want to work for it.*

He squeezed his eyes shut and shook his head, pushing the thoughts away. He had his knife and he had his gun; he could do whatever he wanted. He glanced at the clock. 6:25 P. M. The jogger might still be on 7th Avenue. He reached down and started his car, pulling out of his parking space and handing the attendant ten dollars as he drove off the lot.

Gripping the wheel, the killer leaned forward and searched the sidewalks, cruising at a slow crawl. 7th Avenue was often brimming with tourists, shopping and dining along the well-lit streets of this part of Ybor City, but a cold snap seemed to have kept them indoors tonight. After a moment, he was at the corner of 22$^{nd}$ Street.

The wider road allowed for better visibility, even as the sun went down and the streets turned dark.

He licked his lips. *If he's here, it's definitely a sign.*

The killer drove along 22$^{nd}$ Street for a few minutes, then realized his mistake. The jogger had been moving fast. He'd be out of this area by now—if he had come down this street at all.

He rushed into the parking lot of a shuttered business and turned the car around, racing back to 7th Avenue. Maybe the man would run back along the same route he'd taken. There were no hotels in the other direction, and he didn't look like he lived in south Ybor. He was dressed too nice. New-looking shorts; a clean, dark blue running shirt. A short, stylish haircut for his dark locks.

He looked . . . businesslike. An out-of-town young executive, maybe, doing deals with the mayor's office or the air force base. And if that were the case, he'd be staying near the hotel end of the strip.

*Of course he was from out of town. Who else jogs in Ybor City? And on a night when the locals were staying in?*

He nodded, impressed with his logic, breathing faster as he passed under the traffic lights. He bounced his left heel on the floor, venting his nervous energy. The streets were all but empty. The killer would be able to spot his prey from a hundred yards, maybe more.

*The legs.*

His heart jumped. The jogger had the thin legs and wiry build of a distance runner—the ones dedicated enough to run miles and miles on a business trip, even on a dark night in the cold.

He replayed the brief glimpse of the jogger in his mind, remembering. The man hadn't been sweating. Even in the cold, a runner sweats. The man had just started his run.

The killer's heart raced.

The jogger would still be out here somewhere.

He smiled and leaned back in his seat, relaxed and confident that fate had indeed delivered a fly to his spider web. All he had to do was drive around long enough to find it.

\* \* \* \* \*

It took nearly twenty minutes, but the reflective epaulettes of the shirt and the shoe stripes bouncing along in the dark were the trademarks of a runner.

The killer grinned and pulled to the curb, dousing his headlights. This fly had wandered to a distant part of the web. North of touristy Ybor and straight into the bowels of Seminole Heights.

His fancy shirt and expensive running shoes would stick out here, too—if anyone were around to notice. But no one was.

Or it could be someone else jogging alone in the night, traveling along the redevelopment sites of Seminole Heights. But either way, a runner eventually stops running, and a fly in a spider web eventually stops struggling.

It was now just a matter of time.

*Or it could be a local and they might almost be home.*

The killer's breath caught in his throat as he considered that possibility. The anticipation that had been building inside him for close to an hour, now turned to disappointment and dread. The thought of going home and lying awake in frustration—again—after being so close . . .

He narrowed his eyes, staring at the dark figure, waiting and watching. His foot bounced off the floor of his car as he shifted uncomfortably in his seat.

The figure passed under a lone street light in the distance.

It was his jogger. The dark blue shirt and shorts, the clean haircut, the earbuds dangling on his chest. This was the guy.

The swelling in his gut returned. It was a sign, that he'd found him again. A gift.

And a gift must be opened to be appreciated.

Moving out of the light, the bouncing reflectors on the shoes slowed to a walk, and the epaulettes bowed as if the jogger needed to catch his breath or tie a shoe.

This was no part of town to be wandering around in at night. In a few months, when the rehab was done and the crumbling "historic" houses had been restored, sure; but right now? Why, even foolhardy young newlyweds and the *avant-garde* artsy types weren't crazy enough to live in this part of Seminole Heights yet.

*The poor jogger needs a lift back to his hotel, is all.* The killer popped open his car door. *No telling what kind of person that stranger might meet out here.*

The killer walked toward the lone street light, holding his sweatshirt tight to his body. In his belt, pushed around behind his back, the knife rested in its sheath.

Under his folded arms, he held his .38.

He walked quickly, gripping an old tube sock he'd balled up in his hand, taking turns eyeing the vacant buildings of the construction site and the jogger who walked ahead of him. The street was deserted. All he needed was an opportunity. Rows of empty houses undergoing rehabilitation might provide—

"Hey, buddy, you got a light?"

The man's voice came from ahead. Startled, the killer stopped in his tracks and stared at the stranger.

The jogger approached, holding a pack of cigarettes. He patted the thigh pocket of his shorts. "My lighter must've fallen out while I was running."

The killer's surprise turned to amusement.

*A runner who smokes?*

The killer smiled, heart pounding, as the stranger came closer. Twenty feet away, then ten, then nearly side by side. The man was sweaty, but no less well-groomed. His dark hair remained nearly perfect, and the dark blue clothing hid any signs of sweat. The only evidence that the man had been doing physical activity of any kind was the streaks of sweat gluing down the hair around his ears, and a lightly glistening brow.

The killer snapped out of it, shaking his head. "I don't smoke."

"I shouldn't. Bad habit."

"Yeah." The killer nodded. "But not as bad as mine."

He raised the .38 and shot straight into the jogger's chest. Outdoors, the blast was nowhere near as loud as it had been in the cargo truck, and the muzzle didn't flare.

But the bullet hit him just the same, sending him careening backward onto the sidewalk. The jogger's head hit the concrete with a loud *crack!*

The stranger clutched his chest where the blood spot appeared, lifting his head and straining to get a glimpse. He groaned, pulling at the fabric of his shiny blue shirt, tearing it, no doubt in an attempt to relieve the pressure in his chest and the searing, scorching burns from the bullet.

The killer stepped over him, placing a foot on each side of the jogger's flailing torso. He lifted the tube sock and rolled it into a ball, stuffing it into the jogger's mouth.

"Here. Smoke that."

The man gagged, his eyes darting around, seeming unable to focus on the choice between the hole in his chest that pumped out his blood, and the sock in his mouth that cut off his air. He kicked and struggled, grabbing at his shirt, his muted groans muffled by the makeshift gag.

The killer smiled in satisfaction. The improvisation was working better than he'd hoped. "Shh, don't cry. Don't fight it."

The man's scream got past the sock this time, a desperate howl that ripped through his mouth and nose and into the vacant street.

"Oh, not from that." The killer pointed to the man's chest. "From this."

The knife flashed in the glow of the street light as the killer brandished it. He held it to his face, staring past the blade and into the jogger's wide, terrified eyes. The sock came free, falling open on the stranger's cheek as he struggled to gather enough breath to scream.

The killer dropped his knees onto the man's chest, driving the wind out of him with a large *Oooofff* and the crackling snap of a few breaking ribs. He raised the knife high, gripping it and gritting his teeth, the power of life and death now his and his alone to deliver.

The killer put a hand on the jogger's shoulder, pushing himself backward and letting his knees slide to rest on the sidewalk so he could see the widening pool of blood as it spread over the stranger's shirt. There, straddling the jogger like a child on a rocking horse, he lifted the knife even higher over his head. The power churned and boiled within him. Lifting his other arm, he threw his head back and turned his face to the dark sky.

The rush was upon him.

He heaved himself forward, driving the knife down and into the jogger's guts, ripping and tearing, slash after slash, with all the joy he knew would be waiting for him there. The power surged inside him, filling his veins with electricity and sending his brain into an ecstatic overload.

When he finished, he rolled off the dead man, exhausted and satisfied, resting on his back on the sidewalk. He drew deep breaths, his stomach rising and falling as sweat gathered on his forehead. He closed his eyes, working to calm the racing pulse that throbbed in his ears. Gasping and wet with the warmth of new blood that covered him like a blanket, he gazed into the glassy eyes of the dead jogger lying next to him. There on the sidewalk, they were like bedmates at a child's sleepover.

The killer took a deep breath and exhaled sharply, nodding with content.

"Thank you."

## CHAPTER 4

Sergio handed the menu back to the waitress and smiled across the table at his partner. "I swear, sometimes I think you're a guy."

Carly checked her phone before dropping it into her purse. "You know I'm not a guy. I just eat like one."

"Which is awesome." He inhaled the spicy aroma of fried hot wings that permeated the restaurant. In the kitchen, a steam cloud surged upward from the deep fryer as another basket plunged into the oil. "I'm not sure there's anything worse than a partner who eats healthy."

"Why didn't we come in one car? I'd have picked you up."

He snorted. "I can't be seen in that rolling Halloween decoration you drive."

"I'm going to let that slide because I know you make jokes when you're stressed, but what images of yours are you trying to protect? Like you're some low paid, flunky cop?"

"Hey." He tapped the glossy table top. "I like my car."

"Somebody should. At least fix the dents."

The waitress returned with a tray carrying a wooden plate stacked with a dozen pieces of celery on it, a tiny plastic tub of bleu cheese dressing riding shotgun, and two enormous plastic glasses of ice water. She slid the plate onto the center of the table and set the drinks on either side. "Your wings will be ready in just a moment."

Sergio eyed her nylon shorts as she walked away. "So what are your plans for the weekend?" He picked up his water and looked at Carly. "Packing Kyle and the boys into your not-compensating-for-anything muscle car and driving up to your mom's for Thanksgiving?"

"Mm-hmm. You?"

Sergio shrugged, sipping his drink and setting it back on the table. "Not sure yet."

Carly's phone pinged. "It's the day after tomorrow." She smiled, picking up the phone and pressing a button. "When do you start making your plans? It's not like—"

Her face dropped.

Sergio leaned forward. "Is that work?" He patted his pockets. "What's it say? I left my phone in the car."

"Yeah." She blinked, scrolling over the text message. "Yeah, it's work." Taking a deep breath, she bit her lip and stared at him. "Our case from last week just took a bad turn. They found another body hacked up the same way. Shot and then stabbed."

Sergio slumped back in the vinyl bench seat.

His partner shook her head and reached for her purse. "Looks like I know what we're both doing over Thanksgiving now."

\* \* \* \* \*

Wednesday morning at the station, Detectives Sanderson and Martin headed towards their lieutenant's office. Breitinger met them in the hallway, flanked by two uniformed officers and several people in suits.

"Let's use the conference room."

As everyone else seated themselves around the long table, Breitinger held up a folder. "This is the forensics from your murder last week. The one in Ybor on 22nd Street." He dropped the file onto the table. "The victim was shot with a .38 caliber revolver and brutally stabbed multiple times with a large knife. He also lost a finger off his left hand."

The lieutenant slapped another file onto the table. "This is your murder from last night. Shot and stabbed in the same manner. Ballistics says it's the same .38, and the M. E. says it looks like the same type of knife wounds." He pushed back his suit coat and placed his hands on his hips, staring at the folders. "Now, we either have a heck of a coincidence or some nut job is hacking up innocent victims for the holidays."

A brown-haired woman in a dark gray suit scribbled notes on a legal pad. "Detectives, do we have any indication of gang violence in the area? Or drug vendettas?"

Carly glanced at Breitinger.

"I'm sorry," he said. "This is Dr. Stevens, a forensic psychologist. I've asked her to sit in."

Carly shook her head. "No ma'am. From what we saw—and from what the lab reports indicate—each victim was attacked by only one assailant, and both cases appear to have been done by the same person."

The doctor nodded, adjusting her glasses and continuing to scribble on her pad. "Any connection between the victims?"

"We're running that down now." Sergio folded his hands on the conference table. "But it doesn't look like it. The trucker from the first murder was a local, and the second victim was visiting on business. Both appear to just have been at the wrong place at the wrong time, and so far we haven't produced any witnesses."

"Our suspect—our sick nut—is also using one of these." Breitinger held up a sketch of a long knife. "This weapon is serrated on one side and has a smooth blade on the other."

One of the uniformed cops whispered, "Holy cow."

"Yeah." Breitinger rubbed the back of his neck. "It's designed for hunting. And our guy is doing just that with it."

"Detective . . ." the doctor glanced at her notes, then eyed Carly. " . . . Sanderson. Is the knife custom-made?"

"We don't know yet," Carly said. "The hilt and the stop guard created marks on the body, but so far there are any number of manufactured blades it could be."

Sergio shrugged. "People get stuff off the internet from all over the place. The murder weapon could be a knife from a Bavarian hunting catalog and made in China. We just don't know yet."

"What about the finger?"

The uniformed cop seemed to regret his question as soon as it left his mouth. Breitinger scowled. Already committed, the officer swallowed and lowered his head, peering at the detectives. "I heard the first victim lost a finger. What about the second guy?"

"Harriman here has asked to be assigned to the case." Breitinger put his hands back on his hips. "I'm debating the idea."

Carly eyed the young officer. "Mr. Pomeroy had all his fingers. Unless it was a piece of an internal organ, the killer didn't take a second trophy."

Harriman nodded.

"Boss," Sergio sat back in his chair. "What about going forward?"

"Going forward?"

"If word of this gets out, there's gonna be a media storm. We won't be able to—"

"Then make sure word doesn't get out." Breitinger leaned on the conference table. "This is serious. Without something like a war for the national news to feed on, they'll be happy to give a serial killer at Thanksgiving wall to wall coverage. Screw that." The lieutenant stood and paced around the room. "Right now, we have two murders by this maniac. But if we get three, it'll explode. The whole town will go crazy and reporters will swarm in from all over. I've seen it. No one will feel safe. That means instead of our local businesses enjoying a nice, bustling tourist season over the holidays, we'll have a ghost town. Interest in the mayor's Seminole Heights revitalization project will dry up. Aside from which, this guy is a serious danger to the general public." He glanced at Carly. "He might be working Seminole Heights right now, but it's not like he couldn't get in his car and drive to Brandon next."

He rubbed his chin. "No, we're going to get ahead of this thing. I'll make a pre-emptive call to the mayor and tell him we're committing all our resources to tracking this sucker down. And then we're actually going to track this sucker down." He went to the door and opened it. "And you two," he pointed at the detectives, "are gonna be working twenty-four seven, leading the charge."

Sergio slumped back in his chair.

The meeting over, Breitinger headed out the door followed by his staff and the doctor.

His partner shook her head, rising. "Looks like I know what we're both doing over Thanksgiving, Christmas and New Year's now."

\* \* \* \* \*

The flaxen blonde rolled over in bed and picked up her phone. Seeing "Harriman" on the screen, she slid her finger across the phone and answered. "Hey, baby."

"Hey, I did it. I talked to the lieutenant like you said."

"Mmm." She rubbed sleep from her eyes. "How did it go?"

"I think he's going to put me on the case. At least he's thinking about it. I got to sit in on a meeting this morning. That's a good sign."

She sat up. "It is! Oh, baby, I'm so excited for you." Now awake, she pulled the covers around her naked torso and pushed her hair out of her eyes. "Baby, that's really great. I told you. I knew you could do it."

"I am pumped," Harriman said. "This is a big deal, sweetie."

"Oh, it really is." She smiled. "I'm very excited for you."

"Anyway, I gotta run, but I just wanted to tell you. Love you. See you tonight."

"Okay, baby. I love you." She ended the call and stared at the phone, still smiling. "That is awesome."

The nude, dark-haired man next to her rolled over and groaned. "Who was that?"

"Nobody." She laid her phone face down on the carpet and kissed her boyfriend. "Go back to sleep."

\* \* \* \* \*

"Come on, come on!" Mr. Dilger tapped his fingers on his desk, glaring at his youngest daughter.

"I'm telling you, it's not here."

"Susan, it has to be." He ran his hand through his gray hair. Finally, he jumped up and stormed to her desk. "We can't misplace invoices for five hundred thousand dollars and think it's okay."

She shook her head, rifling through the stack of papers. "I don't—I didn't. Dad . . ."

"Find it!"

"It's not here!" Blushing, she pushed away from the desk. Her chair rolled further than she intended and crashed into the empty desk behind her.

Her father scowled.

She lowered her eyes—and her voice. "Look, I'll drive to Lakeland and then stop by the warehouse on the way back, okay? Jerry or Carlos will have a signed copy, I'm sure."

"And if they don't? I can't be—we can't be—asking Latin American companies to trust us with millions of dollars of merchandise and then say, oops, sorry, we can't even keep track of a simple piece of paper!"

"Henry." Mrs. Dilger sat at her desk on the other side of their home office, her voice calm and steady.

"This is why, Susan." He jabbed his finger at the stack of receipts. "This is why—"

"Henry."

He stopped, red-faced and nearly sweating, to face his wife.

"It will turn up, honey." She removed her reading glasses and clicked off her computer. "They always do. Now stop raising such a fuss and let's think about dinner."

Her subtle southern accent—Texas, technically—worked on him. He took a deep breath, more for show than need. "I'll . . . go to Lakeland. And the warehouse."

"Dad, I said I'd go."

"And I'm saying I'll go. Your mother's right." He winked. "As always. Now stop this nonsense and figure out something important. Like dinner."

Mrs. Dilger stood and went to her husband's desk, shutting his computer down, too. "We have the Bradfords coming tomorrow. I thought it'd be nice if we had dinner tonight. Just the family."

He whispered to his daughter. "You see that? The mayor. I bet his staff doesn't lose—"

"Henry."

"Okay. I'm finished."

Susan checked her phone. "Well, if Dad makes those two stops for me, then I can get Sherry at the airport and still be back in plenty of time for dinner." She peered at her father. "Is that okay, Daddy?"

He smiled. Such was the family routine. Hot tempers extinguished as quickly as they flared up. "Daddy" always got him, too, and his youngest knew it like no one else.

He sighed. "Okay, I'm off to Lakeland."

"And the warehouse," Susan said.

"And the warehouse," he echoed.

"Good. It's all settled." Mrs. Dilger caught the collar of her husband's oxford shirt and pulled him in for a kiss. "Drive safely and be careful. The news says there was a murder in that area."

"Okay." Henry bent lower to open the bottom desk drawer. He pulled out a large revolver and placed it in his briefcase. "Now I'm off."

"Daddy." Susan went to her father and stood on her tiptoes to kiss him. "Goodbye. I'm sorry about the invoice."

He hugged her, patting her on the back. "Don't you worry. We all make mistakes and we all have to learn. Jerry or Carlos will have a copy, like you said."

She went back to her desk. His wife walked him to the garage and down the steps to his Mercedes. "Be careful. I know how you and Jerry get to talking. If it gets late, just come home. Don't go to the warehouse."

"I'm not afraid of any ol' boogeyman." He opened the door and slid into his car, laying his briefcase on the passenger seat. "With what I'm packing, the boogeyman had better be afraid of me."

* * * * *

Jerry Contreras talked too much. It was one of his best and worst features. On a good day—in the old days, that is, when Dilger & Contreras Imports was a startup—he could talk the paint off the fender of a fire truck. These days, after twenty plus years of gabbing, he was mostly full of old stories.

Just the kind his boss and former partner liked to hear.

Henry Dilger had saved his life, Jerry would tell any employee who'd listen. Not just once, but twice. The first time, Jerry said, was when Henry overheard the old Central American fruit broker wheeling and dealing on the old Tampa docks, and offered him a job on the spot. There was no company yet, but Henry was a man of vision, and he knew the right salesperson would open doors. After some wrangling—Jerry was smart enough to see closing deals for Henry wasn't as good as being part owner of the company he could help Henry build—the partnership was born.

But as often happens with success, money can bring temptation. Jerry loved to drink almost as much as he loved to talk. For a salesperson, one usually happens with the other. So as he sipped Maker's Mark all night with reps from Panamanian coffee producers and Guatemalan sugar cane growers, Henry crunched numbers in their tiny office.

Eventually, the booze caught up with Jerry. Calling in sick became not being able to get out of bed, but not before Jerry asked Henry to buy him out. After ten years building Dilger & Contreras, an early retirement and a cruise sounded like just the thing for the old fruit broker, then a move to St. Pete where he'd walk on the beach and live off the interest. Except he drank it up in less than two years. Literally being found in a gutter, the police picked him up after he'd been beaten and robbed and left for dead. By then the cops knew him, having taken him in on several DUIs and more than one drunk and disorderly when he refused to leave a bar at closing time.

"That's when my friend Henry saved me the second time." Jerry shouted to the warehouse crew. "I was dead, boys." He nodded at Camila. "And girls. Dead. I'd spent three straight days passed out drunk in bed, and the doctor said if I'd have been there a few more hours—hours, mind you!—I'd have been dead. But my friend Henry came looking for me."

"You called me," Henry said, laughing.

"Doesn't matter." Jerry walked along the loading dock and wagged a finger at the gathered employees. "And do you know what he said?"

The warehouse crew said it in unison: "You have your old job back at your old salary. You don't even have to come to work, just get yourself cleaned up!"

The crew laughed and cheered, Henry right along with them.

Jerry smiled. "Oh, you heard it before, huh?"

That sent them into another round of laughter.

"And he meant it, too." Jerry pointed at Henry. "This is the greatest man you'll ever meet. My friend Henry."

The employees applauded as Henry stepped forward, a can of Coke in his hand. "Well, I don't know if I'm quite ready for sainthood, but thank you." He grinned at Jerry, then to the crowd. "Thank you, everyone. The company has my name on the door, but I never forget who does all the hard work around here."

"We're paying for that new Mercedes," Camila said with a laugh.

"For my big house on Lake Carroll, too, yes. And I want to help each one of you get those things. But right now, don't let me keep you from your families. Or for you younger rascals—where did Camila go?—don't let me keep you from your after work fun."

The employees hooted and hollered.

He glanced at his watch. "And if I don't get out of here soon, my wife will be so mad, I won't have any after work fun for a month. Goodnight!"

He waved and shook hands with the crew as if he was a politician. Stepping down from the makeshift stage of the loading dock, he headed to his car and then on to the warehouse in Seminole Heights.

# CHAPTER 5

As he approached the open warehouse door, Henry Dilger's first impulse was anger.

*How could my employees be so stupid? They can't remember to lock a simple door?*

He shoved open the door and turned on the lights, passing through the reception area and into the back office. The sweet aroma of fruit and coffee beans greeted him as he turned on the next set of overhead fluorescent lights, illuminating three desks and another door marked Carlos Diaz, Manager.

That door, of course, was locked.

Henry flipped through his keys with one hand, holding his briefcase in the other, and looked for the one with the green plastic cover. The key to the Lakeland office had a red cover; the key with the green cover unlocked the Seminole Heights office.

*When they locked it, that is.*

He held the keys up to the light, spotted the green one, and brought it down to slide into the lock.

Carlos' office was relatively tidy compared to his own, even though Henry did his best to plow through whatever papers hit his desk each day. Nearly all the orders were placed electronically, of course, but when it came to getting paid, Latin American banks wanted a signature in ink. And for each day the money sat in their bank instead of his, he was burning cash—about forty-one dollars a day on this particular bill of lading.

He sat down at Carlos' desk, laying his briefcase on top and opening the drawer to pull out the binder labeled "original signed invoices." At first glance, there didn't appear to be more than twenty invoices in there. He slid his briefcase over and set the binder on the desk, opening it and skimming the first document.

A noise caught his attention; it sounded like a broom falling over. Something wooden, but not heavy. He held his breath, staring at the office door. Had he locked the front entrance behind him when he came in?

They didn't keep cash on hand at the warehouses, but a burglar wouldn't know that. A drug addict wouldn't care—a stolen computer could be turned into quick cash at the right pawn shops, and Seminole Heights still had plenty of those.

Henry stood and went to the door of Carlos' office, glancing out to the reception area. The front exit door was shut, with a healthy and permanent dirt stain on the linoleum floor in front of it. Years of truckers walking across the crumbling asphalt parking lot and into the reception area had left its mark. But nothing looked out of place.

He glanced toward the break room. The lights were on.

An uneasy feeling surged in his stomach. Henry hadn't paid attention to the break room on his way in. He'd been focused on finding his signed invoice and whatever excuse he'd give his wife for letting Jerry keep him so late in Lakeland.

*I know how you and Jerry get to talking. If it gets late, just come home. Don't go to the warehouse.*

He stood in the hallway, holding his breath, staring into the break room. The edge of the ancient refrigerator was visible, and next to it, a big wall clock with a Bank of Tampa decal on its face.

The noise was probably nothing, he told himself, but it still had to be checked out.

For a fleeting moment he thought about going back to the office and getting his gun.

*I'm not afraid of any ol' boogeyman.*

He glanced at Carlos' desk. The briefcase rested right on top. It would take about three seconds to get to it.

In the corner of his eye, he thought he saw something move. A shadow in the break room, barely moving, almost imperceptible. As if someone shifted their weight as they stood making coffee, just around the corner out of sight.

Henry swallowed hard. It could also be a burglar all hopped up on meth, hiding and thinking there was easy cash somewhere on the premises. Who knows what those guys could do? He'd heard horror stories at the chamber of commerce meetings.

He stared silently at the break room floor, the lurch in his stomach growing. Nothing moved. The office was quiet. The only sound came from the big clock on the break room wall as it ticked away the seconds.

Henry questioned himself as he stood in the hallway. Had it even really happened? Had he seen anything? Or was it just a trick of the light?

He took a slow step, easing his foot forward on the linoleum. Maybe he could rush in, shouting like he'd done with that punk in the convenience store that one time. Maybe he could catch the burglar or drug addict off guard, scaring them out of their minds.

Yeah . . . and then what? Hope they run off the premises? In the convenience store—which was easily ten years ago—there had been video cameras and a clerk to call the cops. The teenager causing the ruckus was unarmed and smart enough to leave—and even then, the kid left slowly. The burglar in Henry's warehouse might have a gun.

Henry crouched slightly, halting himself between steps. Sweat formed on his brow.

*Go back and get your gun. That's what you have it for.*

The break room shadow moved. Henry jolted upright, throwing himself into the wall. Fear and adrenaline surged through him as he whipped around, hoping he could reach his briefcase before the burglar reached him.

The old refrigerator groaned and kicked on its condenser, causing the fluorescent lights in the break room to flicker. A low hum emanated from the break room.

Henry leaned against the hallway wall, drawing a huge sigh.

*That's all it was. The stupid refrigerator.*

He shook his head, his heart rate returning to normal.

*That's it. We're getting a new fridge on Monday.*

He shuddered, walking back into Carlos' office. The binder sat waiting for him, its invoices neatly filed by date. He sat in the chair, leaning back and shaking his head. A nervous laugh escaped his lips.

*I almost had a heart attack over a refrigerator.*

He flicked the nervous energy out of his hands, deciding not to buy a new one. Still plenty of years left in this one, even if it was a little noisy.

Henry flipped through the invoices. In less than a minute he had the right one. He breathed another sigh of relief and rubbed his stomach, popping open his briefcase and slipping the invoice inside. He clicked off each set of lights as he made his way down the hallway—after turning off the break room lights first—and headed for the exit door.

*This time, it gets shut and locked.*

With a hand on the knob, he pulled it closed behind him and dug for his keys. The lights of the loading dock were just bright enough to help him find the green cover. He slid the key into the deadbolt and glanced at a faded sign on the door. NO CASH ON PREMISES.

*Maybe a new sign would be a good idea, though.*

With a solid clunk, the thick deadbolt slid into place. Henry gripped his keys and his briefcase, stepping onto the asphalt parking lot.

He stopped. A car had parked near his Mercedes. A dark sedan, a little further back on the lot than his car, and under a tree, but it wasn't there when he pulled in. He'd have noticed.

The slight fog on the windshield of his Mercedes proved him right. There was no such fog forming on the glass of the dark sedan. It had only recently arrived.

He swallowed hard, the knot in his stomach surging with adrenaline again. Behind him, the soft crunch of shoes on crumbly asphalt reached his ears. A stranger approached from the alley. A man, wearing dark clothes.

Henry's heart raced. He glanced back at his Mercedes. He could run to it and try to lock himself in. The panic button on the key fob would be useless out here; no one was around to do anything, anyway. He gripped his keys and stepped toward his car, trying not to appear scared.

*The gun.*

Would it be faster to get his revolver out?

He lifted his briefcase with one hand and pushed the shiny brass latch with the other. With his keys in his fist, he couldn't maneuver the latch fully, so the case didn't open. He kept his back to the stranger, hunched over his case, moving quickly toward his Mercedes. His heart pounded as he grabbed at the latch.

The stranger increased his pace, coming closer. "Hey, come here."

Fear shot through Henry. He raced toward his car.

The stranger ran toward him. "Come here!"

Henry clawed at the brass latch, gritting his teeth and forcing it open. The papers spilled out of the briefcase, along with his gun. Henry stumbled forward, trying to catch everything, tripping over the revolver and sending himself sprawling face first into the asphalt.

Bits of gravel ripped into his hands and tore through the fabric of his suit pants, slashing his knees. His head and neck jolted as his jaw crashed into the rough ground, snapping his mouth shut and cracking teeth. His chin stung hot like fire. The pain from his scrapes and cuts surged as Henry rolled onto his back, wincing.

The stranger was upon him. The steel of the man's weapon glinted as he raised it. Henry recognized the shiny profile of a .38. It loomed big in the bronze glow of the argon street lights.

The stranger chuckled. "You are making this too easy."

Heart pounding, Henry lifted his head and scanned the ground to find his revolver. It had skittered away, coming to rest just under his car— and out of reach.

Henry stretched out his hand, groaning as his fingertips brushed the side of his gun.

The .38's metal hammer made a solid click as the stranger cocked it. He raised it toward his victim. On the ground, Henry lifted his hands to block the view, squeezing his eyes shut.

The gunshot blasted through the quiet night, hitting its victim like a baseball bat to the stomach. The breath went out of Henry and a huge burning sensation filled his gut. He gripped his bloody stomach, pushing his heels into the asphalt as he strained to move away from his assailant. Pain burst forward in his abdomen like a searing hot steam cloud. He grunted, unable to draw a breath.

The stranger stood over him. "That's part one."

Reaching behind his back, the man pulled out a large, double edged hunting knife with a serrated edge on one side. He dropped to one knee and stared into Henry's eyes. "Here comes part two."

Then he raised the big blade.

## CHAPTER 6

"Come on, come on."

Exiting the crowded shuttle that took him from the Southwest Airlines gate to Tampa International's main terminal, Tyree mumbled to himself as he walked. He threw his duffle bag over his shoulder and stared at his cell phone, running his fingers over the beard stubble on his jaw.

No internet signal.

With only ten percent battery power remaining, he didn't want to wait too long.

"Jenny, over here!" A young man called out over the crowd of travelers. "Kids, there's Mommy!" Pushing a stroller, the man and his children raced over.

Tyree held the phone up, as if that would somehow get a signal faster. He spotted a Chick-Fil-A kiosk across the lobby.

*Dinner is served.*

The woman in front of him stopped short, smacking his elbow and knocking his phone out of his hand.

He winced, awaiting the crack of expensive cell phone screen hitting cheap airport utility carpet. As if in slow motion, his phone sailed through the air—and into the baby stroller.

Right into the head of the small child inside.

The two other children wrapped themselves around their mother as the couple embraced. "Honey, I missed you!"

"I missed you, too. All of you. And where's my little Joey Baby?"

Little Joey Baby was turning red, deciding whether to cry at high volume or a full out, ear-piercing scream.

Ear-piercing won.

The mother picked up her baby, fuming. "What happened?" The man's face was blank.

Tyree cleared his throat, reaching for his phone. "Ma'am, I believe that's my—"

She wheeled around. "Who are you?"

"I'm—"

Inspecting the tiny bump rising on the infant's head, she gasped. "What did you do? What kind of man hits a defenseless baby?"

"That's, no, I—I was using my phone and I—"

49

The woman reached into the stroller and held up Tyree's phone. She gasped. "Were you taking pictures of my child? You pervert!"

"Pictures! No, I was—"

"Why are you taking pictures in an airport? Are you some kind of, of *terrorist*?"

Other nervous passengers in the packed terminal repeated the daunting word.

"Terrorist?"

"Terrorist!"

A uniformed airport employee pulled out a radio. "Security, we have a situation here. Code zero."

"Hey, no." Tyree held his hands out. "There's no code anything. We don't have a code here. No code."

"Johnny!"

"Sir, please back away from the children and stop posing a threat."

"A what!"

Her radio crackled. "Code zero at Gate E. Alert team responding."

"Johnny Tyree!" A petite, pretty blonde in sunglasses pushed through the crowd toward him. Her smile was as bright as sunshine. "I thought that was you."

It took him a moment. Like getting a friend request on Facebook after ten years of not interacting with someone, eventually the woman's face registered and her name drifted forward from the foggy past.

"Susan?"

The gathering airport mob grew louder.

"Hi. He's with me." Susan plucked the cell phone from the red-faced woman's hand. "Johnny, we—oh, a baby! Johnny, is it yours?"

Tyree blinked. "Mine?"

The mother huffed. "It certainly is not!"

Susan lowered her sunglasses and peered at the woman. "Oh. And it looks just like you, ma'am— what with that red, puckered face and all. Who says all babies are cute? Dare to be different, I say. Take your ugly baby out in public."

The woman's jaw dropped.

"You're so brave!"

Turning to her husband, the woman shouted. "Are you going to just stand there?"

He opened his mouth.

"You deserve a medal." Susan grabbed Tyree's elbow, leading him away. "Or a stocking cap. For the baby."

Tyree chuckled.

She glided through the crowd, speaking over her shoulder at the flustered woman. "You know, your baby looks just like my great uncle Merle. He died of nose wart cancer."

"What!"

Laughing, Susan took Tyree's wrist and led him to the baggage claim escalator. As they descended from sight, she waved, shouting, "Hey, they can't all win pageants, am I right? How courageous of you for bringing that out."

51

Finally safe, Tyree let out a deep breath. "Susan. Good grief. What was that?"

"That was me saving your butt, mister. How are you?"

"Me and my butt are both intact."

At the bottom of the escalator, she turned and glanced back up. "Looks like we're in the clear."

She was dressed casual—flip flops, a t-shirt and tight jeans, like any Florida girl—but there was a youthful beauty he didn't remember her having. And a woman's figure.

He held out his hand. "Thanks for doing that."

"Is that the best you can do?" Susan threw her arms out, beaming. "Give me a hug."

*Southern girls.*

She wrapped herself around him and squeezed like she was welcoming home a long-lost family member. As her hair brushed his chin, the delicate scent of lavender and vanilla reached him. She was warm and soft and enthusiastic. Quite the contrast from how he'd been feeling a few seconds earlier.

Susan stepped back, removing her sunglasses and looking him over. Her blue eyes twinkled in the setting sun as it streamed through the massive airport windows. "I like the beard. It's a good look. What are you doing back in town?"

"Oh, Frank asked me to look into something for him."

"Your uncle?" She flipped her head, tossing her golden locks over her shoulder. "How is he?"

Tyree shrugged. "Frank is Frank. He doesn't really change."

"I remember him. Well, I remember hearing about things when you lived with him." She swung her arms like a child, glancing downward. A hint of red appeared on her cheeks. "Back in high school, you never invited me to any of your wild parties."

That was the difference. She looked more like her sister now.

"You were underage. Frank's not really my uncle, though. More of a family friend. He took me in when Mom was having a hard time." His face grew warm. The old wound still burned. "Anyway, I can't believe I ran into you here. It's really good to see you."

"I was actually waiting for Sherry's flight." Susan's eyes stayed locked on his. "But it's been delayed. I was trying to get an update when I heard a commotion."

He remembered Sherry quickly enough. Long hair, long legs, and a great smile—features just like her sister's, just in a taller package.

*Has it really been ten years?*

"Anyway, she's delayed until tonight. This wasted a drive—until now."

"Yeah. Who knew there'd be baby-picture-taking terrorists here?"

"No kidding. What will you be doing for Frank? I thought he ran a church."

"He does, kind of. Frank does lots of stuff." Tyree shoved a hand into the pocket of his wrinkled cargo shorts. "I'll be doing investigative research for him. Internet stuff, mostly."

"Ooh, sounds very secretive."

"It's just hard to explain. Anyway, he wants me to do some projects for him and see how I like it— since I'm not with the sheriff's office anymore."

"Wow. The marines, and then a cop, and now a mysterious researcher. You've been on some adventures." The smile beamed forth again. "All I did was go to work for my dad. Sherry did, too. And Mom still works there."

A thickening stream of people moved past them. "We should probably move," Susan said. "It's only a matter of time before ugly baby momma comes to get her baggage. We shouldn't be here when she does."

"This is all I brought." Tyree hooked a thumb into the strap of his duffle bag. "I try to travel light."

"Wow, you're good. I need more than three suitcases if I'm only traveling for a week. You must not be staying long."

He shrugged. "I'm not sure. It's a test run, but if it works out, who knows?"

"Really?" A large grin stretched across her face. "Well, in that case, we'd better have you over for dinner. Unless you have plans with Frank."

"I'm not even sure he's in town. When I spoke to him yesterday, he was in Brazil or something. I think he'll be here this weekend. But I should go by his place."

"Perfect." She nodded. "I'll pick you up there in an hour."

"What, tonight? Hey, I don't—"

"Shush. You just said you don't have plans and you just got back into town. I insist. Besides, Mom and Sherry will want to see you, and Dad doesn't just let any old business start up around here unless he checks them out first."

Tyree chuckled. "He's that big, is he?"

"He seems to think so. And if you don't come to Mom's house, you'll be eating fast food, right? Well, Ruby is making jambalaya."

Tyree shook his head. "When did you become so assertive?"

"I'm a control freak, just like Dad." She took his hands. "Will you come?"

It was hard to say no. Frank's place had always been a mess, even on a good day, and jambalaya sounded good. His stomach was already booking reservations for dinner at the Dilger house.

Plus, Susan was more charming than he remembered. And more persistent. It might be good to spend his first evening with friends.

"Okay, you have a deal. But I need to swing by Frank's place and pop my head in the door. Maybe shower."

"Done." Susan dug car keys out of her tiny purse. "I'll even drop you off. Does he still have his place in Town 'n' Country?"

"The townhouse, yeah. And a little office in the business park near there." Tyree walked with her as she led to the parking elevators. "Which is where I might be staying."

"In an office park?" Susan chuckled, pressing the elevator's call button.

"Yeah. It'll have electricity and running water." He sighed. "Frank's place might not."

"That sounds like a story," she said. "You can tell me the rest of it on the way. Let's go."

## CHAPTER 7

Tyree waved as Susan sped away in her convertible. "See you in a bit!"

Digging in his pocket, he produced a key for the small office and let himself in.

Frank's townhouse had been tolerable—but no electricity or running water. Tyree flipped a light switch in the office. A few fluorescent bulbs flickered and came to life, displaying a couch and a desk, an old computer, and stacks of . . . stuff. Piles of brochures for a Panamanian church, several wooden crates, rows of cardboard boxes—and a large plastic bin of used bicycle parts. The whole place was like an episode of *Hoarders*.

A metal folding chair rested in front of the computer, and next to it sat a standard desk chair circa World War II, with a thin padded seat.

*All the comforts of home—if home is a cabin in the woods built by the Unabomber.*

In the back of the office, a tiny bathroom contained a sink and a shower. He turned on the faucet and let the water run over his hand for a moment. It produced hot water—hot enough, anyway.

Pushing aside the folding chair at the desk, he opted for the padding of the World War II seat. The computer may have been the only thing not buried under an inch of dust. It worked. He opened a browser and that worked, too. The computer might be a near-antique, but the internet would be accessible, at least. Tyree nodded. The office would be home for a few days.

He leaned back in the creaky chair and folded his hands behind his head.

*It could be worse.*

The chair shuddered, then something popped.

Tyree toppled over backwards, crashing into the corner of the desk and spilling onto the dingy floor. A giant stack of magazines managed to break most of his fall on the way down, sending a cloud of dust into the air.

He sat up, rubbing his head. "Okay. Folding chair from now on."

In the far corner, a tarp covered something big. He squeezed between the stacks to reach it and lifted a corner of the musty canvas.

His jaw dropped. "What's this?"

A massive motorcycle glistened in the flickering light. The winged logo of a Harley Davidson "fat boy," on a machine that looked as shiny as the day it left the showroom floor, beamed at him from the side of the gas tank. He ran his fingers across the hog's stainless-steel handlebars and over its long, black leather seat, as he bent down to inspect it closer. It had new tires and polished chrome.

Across the front wall, a space had been left free of clutter. Obviously, that's how the Harley got in and out.

*Good old Frank.*

Tyree rubbed his chin. It might be a good idea to let Frank know he'd arrived safely. He went to the couch, pulling his cell phone from his pocket, and sat.

From behind him, a booming voice rang out. "Hello."

Tyree jolted upward from the couch, launching himself into a stack of boxes. He wheeled around to see Frank standing in front of him.

"Did I startle you?" The large man laughed.

"No. A little." Tyree tried to catch his breath. "God!"

"No, not God." Frank came forward and gave Tyree a bear hug. "Not yet, anyway. But it's on my to do list." He patted Tyree hard on the back. "Good to see you."

Tyree managed to emit a word from the anaconda-like grip Frank had on him. "Yeah."

When Frank released him, he tried a few more. "I thought you were in Panama or something."

"I was. Ecuador, actually. I think."

"You *think*?"

Frank threw his hands up. "I was blindfolded and everybody spoke Spanish. Or Portuguese. One of those two."

Tyree rolled his eyes. "Frank, *you* speak Spanish."

"Ah. It was Portuguese, then. I said I was blindfolded."

"How does a blindfold—why were you—" Tyree shook his head. "No, don't tell me."

"Oh, you should have been there, boy." Frank's eyes twinkled with mischief. "With your brains and muscles, we'd have made a heck of a team."

"Yeah? Fighting the good fight?"

Frank raised a fist, shaking it. "I am always fighting the good fight."

"I'll keep that in mind next time you tell me to go to my boss and tell him he needs to stop taking payoffs. That little move didn't go over so good."

"What do you mean? Of course it did."

"No, I got fired."

"Which freed you up to be here with me." Frank smiled. "It all worked perfectly."

Tyree's jaw dropped. "You—you wanted me to get fired?" He pointed to his chest. "I liked that job."

"Yes. And no." Frank put a hand up. "I mean, yes I wanted you to get fired, and no, you didn't like that job."

"Oh, for—" Tyree put a hand to his forehead. "I should have guessed it. You know, I ought to walk out of here right now."

"Good. I'll go with you." Frank sniffed. "It smells in here. What did you do?"

Tyree blinked. "I—"

Frank was already to the door. "Come. Walk with me." He exited, leaving Tyree to scurry behind to catch up.

"I can't believe you got me fired."

"I didn't. You did that. I was in Panama." Frank limped a little, raising his arms and twisting back and forth, before continuing his walk. As he neared a small oak tree, he stopped and pointed. "Check it out—a cardinal." Frank laughed, a booming, blustery noise that came from deep inside his cavernous chest and bounced off whatever was nearby. "I've known a few of those in my day!"

Tyree raised his eyebrows. "What, like with the Pope, or—"

Frank stopped walking and stared at Tyree. "Cardinals are birds, Johnny."

"Well, yeah, but I thought you meant . . ."

Frank sighed deeply, gazing at the tree and the round nest within it. "Is this not a regal bird?"

"Uh, I'd say . . ."

Frank frowned.

"Yes, he is." Tyree nodded. "The cardinal is regal."

"Indeed, he is! And good luck, or so say the Native Americans." Frank eyed the crimson bird. "Look at his magnificence. Such beauty. He flies with grace, and he protects his territory. He is smart, possibly the smartest of all birds, and aggressive, but only when he needs to be. Do you see?"

"Yeah, I see."

"No, do you *see*?"

"I . . ." Tyree shrugged. "I guess I don't."

"Of course you don't. I have not explained it yet!" Another booming laugh. The cardinal probably felt the tree shake.

"Johnny, can you imagine that bird being anything other than what it is?"

He knew better than to fight anymore. "No, Frank."

"And can you imagine," Frank paced back and forth on the sidewalk, "it would be right if it tried to be what it was not?"

"How can a bird be what it's not?"

Frank wheeled around, pointing skyward. "Exactly! It cannot. And neither can you."

"Nope. I'm not a bird."

"Are you sure?" Frank raised an eyebrow. "Because when one man looks at another man, he either sees a chicken or an eagle. Which are you?"

Tyree had had enough. "Frank."

"I will tell you. You are an eagle, and a glorious one at that." He danced on the sidewalk, swooping his arms out. "In the military, you rushed in where others feared to tread, saving a dozen school children caught in a firefight. As a deputy, you stood up and told the ugly truth, even when you knew you would be hurt by it."

Tyree rubbed his chin.

"You cannot be other than what you are, any more than that bird can." He pointed at Tyree, stabbing at the air as he spoke. "You have God-given talents. I cannot stand to see you wasting them."

"Frank, I liked being a deputy. I helped people, and that made me feel good."

"I know." He hunched over, stroking his chin. "It was difficult for both of us, to see you leave. But you were needed here."

"For what, exactly? Computer research, on a dusty old—"

"For your life's work. Or at least the start of it."

Tyree placed his hands on his hips. "And what would my life's work be?"

"It's difficult to say right now." Frank frowned. In the distance, a black van rounded the corner and approached the two men. "Start with dinner and go from there. I have to catch a plane. And do not let your feelings get in the way of your duty."

Tyree's jaw dropped. "How did you know about . . ."

The van pulled up to the curb and the rear door slid open. Frank stepped inside.

"I am everywhere, child. And nowhere. Just ask the Panamanians. They're looking for me in Ecuador right now." He bellowed, enjoying himself. "And the next time someone gives you a cell phone, check to make sure they didn't rig it to spy on you. Technology can be a bitch!"

The door slid shut, and the van drove away.

## CHAPTER 8

Tyree debated asking for another serving of jambalaya, since he'd already eaten two, but Mrs. Dilger seemed very pleased with his enjoyment of her main course.

*Can't very well insult her.*

She scooped up another big spoonful of the cajun rice dish and plopped it onto his plate. "My goodness, where do you put it?"

Tyree picked up his fork and opened his mouth to reply.

"I can see where." Susan patted Tyree's bicep. "You're a lot more solid than you were in high school."

He nodded. "The marines will do that. Not so much the sheriff's office."

Dinner was better than he expected— considering dinner was originally going to be comprised of a chicken sandwich and French fries—but it was more than that. It was good to be in the company of friends.

Mrs. Dilger set the serving spoon back on the big platter and pushed it into the center of the large dining room table. "Susan says you've had quite a few adventures since I saw you last. You must tell me some." She reached for the crystal stemware holding her wine and took a sip. "And again, I'm very sorry Henry didn't make it. He would have enjoyed seeing you. I know he would have enjoyed hearing your stories, but when he and Jerry get to talking, they lose all track of time."

Tyree waved his hand, swallowing. "It's fine."

"Dad does this all the time." Susan threw her napkin on the table, pouting. "Some family dinner. Half the family didn't come."

"John is practically family." Mrs. Dilger glared at her youngest daughter. "And I'm very pleased he agreed to come. Henry will just have to hear about your antics next time." She turned her eyes to Tyree. "There will be a next time, won't there?"

It wasn't really a question. He glanced at Susan, who was now smiling at him. She hadn't done anything overt, but he couldn't shake the feeling that she was flirting with him. Even at the airport.

He brought himself back to reality. "Uh, yes. Of course there'll be a next time. Absolutely."

The house phone rang. Susan jumped up to answer it—an old wall phone with a spiral cord. In

Florida, it was smart to keep one of those around for when hurricanes knocked the power out.

Susan held the big receiver to her ear and played with the cord. "Hey, we were just talking about you. How was your flight?"

From the elegant dining room table, her mother watched carefully as the one-sided conversation unfolded.

"Oh, okay. I'll tell her," Susan said. "No, don't worry about it. Dad didn't make it back in time, either."

Tyree busied himself with the rest of his jambalaya, not wanting to appear to be listening in.

"I know. Bye." She hung up, returning to the table with considerably less enthusiasm than she left it with. "Sherry says her flight was fine but she's tired. Zack's picking her up at the airport. She'll see us in the morning."

Mrs. Dilger pursed her lips and cast her eyes downward, speaking softly. "Did she mention when the rest of us might meet this new boyfriend of hers?"

"Must've slipped her mind."

"Oh. Well." Mrs. Dilger seemed frozen in her thoughts, but she thawed quickly. "We'll have our guest all to ourselves then, won't we?

"Uh, Mom, if you're getting tired," Susan rose from the table. "I can show him the rest of the house."

Tyree took that as his cue to stand as well, completely unsure of what to make of the situation.

He quickly swallowed his last mouthful of jambalaya.

Smirking, Mrs. Dilger glanced at him. "Subtlety was never her strong suit. I'll see about making some coffee." She placed her napkin next to her plate and got up, strolling across the dining room and disappearing into the kitchen.

*It doesn't matter if Susan's flirting or not, you can't guess wrong about something like this. Not on your first day back in town.*

He shoved his hands into his pockets. "Trying to keep me all to yourself?"

"No comment." She strolled to a large room with thick white carpet and a lot of couches—and a TV bigger than Frank's townhouse. "Let's sit in here. I think Ruby got dessert. Do you like cheesecake?"

"Man, jambalaya and cheesecake?" He patted his belly, gazing around the room. "If your mom wants to adopt me, I could be persuaded."

"Hmm." Susan lowered herself onto an overstuffed sofa, tucking a leg under herself.

The room was ornate but not overdone, like a magazine cover of a really fancy hotel lobby. Fresh flowers rested in vases, on tables that appeared to serve no other purpose than holding the flowers. Mahogany bookcases lined the walls and chandeliers decorated the ceiling. The white trim work and off-white paint gave the whole room a light, sunny feel, even at night. A few family photos adorned the walls and tables. Sherry with the swim team; Susan and her softball team. On the table in front of that one, a large trophy displayed a batter getting ready to swing for the fences.

"What's that room?" Tyree pointed to an adjacent area with desks and filing cabinets. "Looks like an office."

"That's the secret headquarters of the Dilger and Contreras empire." Susan got up and strode to the entry, leaning against the door frame. "My and Sherry's desks are these in front, and Mom's is that big one in back. Dad's is through there, so he can shut the door."

The office area was definitely office-like. It didn't look like it belonged in *this* house. Plain walls, no chandeliers, no-nonsense furniture.

"What's this?" He leaned over the closest desk, peering into a box that looked like a present someone had been unwrapping. A gun rested inside.

A big gun.

"Mom wants us all to carry those now. She's scared from the news."

"Yeah?" Tyree raised his eyebrows. "How do you feel about the idea of carrying a gun?"

Susan shrugged. "I've always carried a gun."

Mrs. Dilger brought a silver coffee service into the room. "A .38 is a nice, light weapon for a woman's handbag, but I prefer a .45."

Tyree's jaw dropped. "Wow, you carry a .45?"

"No, I prefer it for her." Setting the gleaming metal tray on an end table, Mrs. Dilger lifted the coffee pot. "I carry a magnum."

"Good grief, that's a freaking cannon." Tyree shook his head. "Why do you need so much firepower?"

A thin smile crossed Mrs. Dilger's lips as she glanced at her guest. "So I kill what I shoot at."

"Boy, you Texans don't mess around, do you?"

"Former Texan," Susan said.

Mrs. Dilger poured a cup of coffee. "Once a Texan, always a Texan."

\* \* \* \* \*

Sherry grabbed her bag as it came around on the luggage carousel. The lines at the baggage claim moved quickly when flights got in late. By the time she took her suitcase outside to the pickup area, her boyfriend's new Cadillac was pulling up to the curb. Zack called to her through the open windows. "Taxi, ma'am?"

She smiled as he popped the trunk from behind the wheel of the big shiny car.

"Perfect timing." With a quick heave, she tossed her bag in the trunk.

"Well . . . I might have been waiting down the street for an hour." He grinned. "I sure didn't want to miss you tonight."

Sherry opened the passenger door and slid inside, giving him a quick kiss. "You're sweet."

"Welcome home." He pulled her close and put his hand on her cheek, admiring her beauty. He kissed her again, slower and softer, letting his lips linger on hers. "Now, where to? The Dilger mansion? My place?" He sat back and rested an elbow on the frame of the open window. "Or are you hungry?"

"Definitely hungry." She buckled her seat belt and ran a hand through her hair. "Let's go to your place and I'll show you how hungry I am."

* * * * *

The ringing phone dragged Sergio from a deep sleep. It seemed like he'd just shut his eyes five minutes ago.

With his eyes barely half open, he reached over the slender back of the waitress from the wing house, pawing the nightstand until he was able to locate his phone.

"Detective Martin here."

"Bad news, Marty." Carly's voice was rough. She must've been asleep, too.

Sergio propped himself up on one elbow and cleared his throat. "Yeah? What's up?"

"One of our patrol units in Seminole Heights just found a body in front of a warehouse parking lot. The victim was shot and stabbed, so our killer's body count climbs from two to three. Breitinger's losing it. He wants a meeting as soon as possible."

"He's thinking serial killer now, for sure." He closed his eyes. "Oh, man. This is bad."

"Yep. I think we just went from working twenty-four seven to eight days a week."

"Great." Rubbing his forehead, Sergio stifled a groan. "Where are we meeting?"

"Crime scene first—Dilger and Contreras, some sort of shipping outfit. Then we need to get over to

Breitinger's office. The chiefs want us all on the same page before the press catches wind of things."

Sergio snorted. "Good luck with that."

"Mm-hmm. How soon can you get dressed and meet me outside?"

"Why would I meet you? I thought we were going to the scene."

"Because I'm in your driveway. I thought you'd appreciate an extra ten minutes of sleep."

"Well, partner." Sergio nodded, stretching. "That is very much appreciated, but I'm not actually at my house at the moment."

Carly huffed. "Oh, for . . ."

He rolled out of bed and headed to the bathroom. "Sorry, dude. I'll meet you at the scene. Text me the address."

\* \* \* \* \*

Sherry rolled over on the bed sheets, gasping in the dim light. "Wow, you were an animal. You've never been like that before."

"What can I say, darlin'? You excite me." His heart still pounding, Zack jumped up and went into the bathroom, clicking the switch. He squinted in the sudden brightness. Light spilled over the foot of the small bed and onto a desk in the corner. It was littered with little bottles, a candle, and a burned spoon.

"Wait." She sat up, pulling the sheets under her chin. "Did you take something?"

He laughed. "Yeah, you. Twice. But I have one more surprise for you."

His surging pulse caused his hands to quiver. Anticipation welled inside him.

"You're using again! Did you use an enhancer for the sex, too?" She pounded the mattress. "You said you weren't going to do any of that crap anymore."

"Hell, I said a lot of things." He opened the small vanity's cabinet and grabbed the new shower curtain, unwrapping it from its packaging.

"No. You promised." She shook her head, tears welling in her eyes. "Oh, how stupid of me." She put her hand to her forehead. "I thought you'd changed."

"Oh, I have." He emerged from the bathroom, still naked and sweating, the shower curtain over his shoulder and his .38 in his hand. "I've changed a lot."

He raised the gun and fired.

Sherry's head whipped backward as she dropped onto the sheets, her arms sprawling outward on the mattress. The long, tan legs bounced once as the bed's box springs absorbed the impact of her body, and then they were still.

Zack shook his head, gazing at her. Even as Sherry lay naked on the bed dying, she was still beautiful.

Blood pulsed from the gaping wound between her breasts. Her head lay on the rumpled sheets, her mouth open and slack. A slight gurgling noise came from her throat.

Silent tears fell from her eyes, her face as vacant as a statue. She moaned softly as the life eased out of her, barely audible over the rumbling of the thick plastic Zack arranged beside her on the bed.

Her chest lifted and fell a few times, but only barely, moving less and less with each weak breath; then it stopped completely. A few small bubbles of saliva and blood gathered at the corner of her mouth. Her soft eyes stared at nothing, unfocused and unmoving.

He wrapped his hands around her ankles and lifted her legs onto the sheet, then moved to the other side of the bed to grab her arms. With a few hoists, she was onto the shower curtain. Zack loomed over her, dripping with sweat.

"I said I had a surprise. This is just part one."

Reaching to the desk, he opened the top drawer. He removed a large, double edged hunting knife with a serrated edge on one side.

"Here comes part two, darlin'." He raised the big blade, chuckling. "Were you surprised?"

## CHAPTER 9

The killer spied two flashlight beams bouncing along toward the section of dark houses slated for renovations. Near a massive pile of old roof shingles and busted drywall, he crouched low between two small bungalows, waiting. Watching.

"See?" The teens held hands, making their way across the sparse lawn. "All these houses are empty. We can go right in." The beam from the boy's flashlight bounced off the walls and ceiling, casting enough illumination to see well in the room—and to be seen.

Holding his breath, the killer inched toward a window opening, peering into the home. The girl's flashlight lit a wall. A construction foreman had left spray-painted notes for the workers. Apparently, a new countertop was needed in the kitchen.

"What if somebody comes by?" Her soft voice echoed through the house.

"Who's gonna come?" Shining his light over the walls and ceiling, the boy roamed down a hallway. "Nobody's gonna find us in this section."

The killer smiled.

*I could not agree more.*

The prospect of claiming two targets at one time filled him with anticipation. He'd taken to cruising the streets of Seminole Heights, but after a few weeks it now seemed too dangerous. The papers had reported the killings, and the chief of police had promised increased police presence, in standard police cruisers and unmarked cars. Paranoia now made every passing vehicle an undercover cop and a waiting prison cell.

Instead, he took to parking and watching, and when that felt too visible, simply walking around.

Tonight's victims were correct. Almost no one came to the housing reconstruction project after work hours. When it got dark, the place was a virtual no man's land—except for an occasional jogger or a lone service worker, cutting through the barren neighborhood on their way home.

Or teenage lovers, looking for a place to have some fun. He licked his lips, his heart pounding as he eyed the teens.

*Two.*

The welling in his stomach made his whole body want to twitch with nervous excitement.

"Hey, Mariana, come look at this." The boy had wandered into a room near the front of the house.

Instead of joining him, she sang his name. "Leo, they got a big tub in here."

One flashlight meandered to the other and lit a small room on the side of the house.

With no doors to stop him, the killer moved from his hiding spot by the pile of construction debris on the side of the house. He crept into the family room, carefully placing each foot to avoid kicking over a paint can or a piece of waiting duct work. Next to a rectangular hole where a window would normally be, the spray-painted instructions said "window."

*No wonder this project is taking so long.*

The killer's racing pulse throbbing in his ears, his insides surging with energy. He gripped his .38 and crept down the hallway, guided by the glow of the flashlights and the chatter of the two young lovers.

\* \* \* \* \*

As Officer Mateos waved to the parking lot attendant across from the 7th Avenue movie theater, dispatch came over his vehicle's radio.

"Unit one eighteen, possible two-eleven in your area."

Mateos grabbed the handset. "One eighteen. Go ahead."

"Unauthorized access in a construction area. Flashlights in a vacant house in Seminole Heights, in the vicinity of Comanche Avenue and 13<sup>th</sup> Street. Break."

"Copy that, dispatch, Go ahead."

"Be advised, possible four seventeen."

Mateos frowned. *Possible person with a gun in Seminole Heights.*

"I'm on it, dispatch. Unit one eighteen, out."

He squeezed the steering wheel of the cruiser, a flash of adrenaline charging through him. *Seminole Heights, playground of our newest serial killer. Maybe this is the guy.* Then, more realistic, sobering thoughts came to him. *Or maybe it's a drug deal, or a civilian vigilante trying to keep the streets safe from our guy, or a drunk idiot trying out a new birthday present. . .*

He flipped on his emergency lights and stomped the gas pedal.

\* \* \* \* \*

The killer slinked along the hallway, the intensity building in his gut as he enjoyed listening to the young couple talking. He kept his hand on his .38, ready for the overwhelming rush he knew would come when he let them know they weren't alone.

*Two. Such a prize.*

He carefully edged around the corner, moving a fraction of an inch at a time, to peek into the bathroom. Leo and Mariana sat on the edge of the newly installed roman tub, their flashlights pointed at the ceiling.

Mariana swung her feet as she spoke. "Dominique don't have that on her phone. She—"

The killer stepped into the bathroom doorway. "Hello."

Leo gasped, lurching backwards and falling into the big tub, pulling Mariana in with him. She screamed.

"Oh, no reason for all that." The killer stepped forward. "Safety patrol. You two are on private property."

They struggled in the tub, wrestling to get untangled and hoist themselves out of the deep basin.

"We weren't doin' nothing!" Leo rolled sideways and lifted himself up.

"No, I'm sure you—"

Bright light flooded the window. The killer winced and raised his hands to shield his eyes.

The gun glinted in the light. Leo's eyes went to it. A short gasp escaped his lips. His jaw hung open, his arms at his side.

The killer leveled the weapon at the boy.

With a raging grunt, Leo burst forward, slamming into the killer and driving him to the wall.

The deafening gunshot filled the bathroom, ringing in the killer's ears and echoing through the house. Mariana shrieked. Leo fell backwards as the beam of another flashlight raced over the lawn toward the house. He crashed to the floor. Above his hip, a dark red stain seeped into his shirt.

Screams bounced off the walls of the enclosed room. The killer fell into the hallway, his ears ringing. He pushed himself to his feet and limped toward the family room. In the front yard, a male voice barked commands.

The killer ran from the house, Mariana's cries echoing from behind him. "Help my boyfriend! Help him! Please!"

* * * * *

The officer grabbed his shoulder radio. "Unit one eighteen on foot at the scene. Shots fired. Suspect is down. I repeat, suspect is down. Request ambulance."

"Help my Leo!"

Mateos ran to the front door and sprinted down the hallway, gun drawn. "Police! Put your hands in the air!" His flashlight lit the bathroom. Leo lay kicking on the floor, blood covering his shirt. Wincing and groaning, he clutched his side. Mariana hovered over him in tears.

"Is there anyone else inside the house?" Mateos shouted.

Mariana nodded. "The man with the gun!"

"Where is he?"

She pointed toward the family room. "That way."

Mateos whipped around, flashlight pointing where his gun would shoot. Across the backyard of the next house, a dark figure ran away.

"Stop!"

He bolted out of the house and across the grass, his equipment bouncing and thumping with each furious stride. Adrenaline fueled him. He gritted his teeth and pushed himself to run faster over the uneven ground of the construction site, racing past stacks of roof trusses and piles of debris.

The figure reached a sedan parked on the corner, opened the door and disappeared inside.

"Stop!" Grabbing his shoulder radio, Mateos called out instructions as he ran. "Second suspect fleeing," he huffed, "in late model sedan. License number—"

His feet went out from under him and he smashed into the dark drainage ditch. Pain raced up his leg. He glanced across the grass as the sedan's tail lights flared.

"Stop!" Mateos rolled around on the ground, clutching at his shin. He yelped, pounding a fist into the cool dirt. "No, no, no!"

The car sped to the next corner, squealing its wheels as it turned left and disappeared into the night.

## CHAPTER 10

Susan pulled her convertible to the curb outside the small office unit. "This one, right?"

"Right." Tyree rested his arm on the open window frame, his windblown hair only slightly out of place. "Thanks for the lift. And dinner. And the whole thing at the airport. Today turned out a lot different from what I was expecting."

She put the car in park and tucked a leg under herself, resting her hands in her lap. "What were you expecting?"

"You're looking at it." He hooked a thumb at the office. "I was planning on a lot of hours in front of a computer screen, being bored out of my mind. Reviewing ledgers for financial fraud isn't super exciting. Instead, I, well . . . I had a great time."

"Yeah?" She lowered her head slightly, gazing up at him with those sparkling blue eyes. Even at night, the beautiful lines of her face and her golden hair shined.

"Yeah."

She leaned toward him, bringing her face close to his. "Know what would make it even better?" She pressed her lips to his, sliding her hands along his shoulders and caressing his neck, her fingers slowly stroking his hair.

He let his lips linger briefly against the warm, wet softness, then gently eased away. It may have been a mistake, moving too quickly, but it didn't feel like it.

He took a deep breath and let it out slowly, heat rising to his cheeks.

Susan leaned back, biting her lip, a finger resting at the corner of her mouth.

It still might have been a mistake, but his brain was now flooding with other thoughts.

*It might be best to end the night on a good note.*

"Yep. That was even better." Smiling slowly, he opened his door and stepped out.

"Got plans for Christmas yet, Johnny?"

He shut the door and leaned on the windowsill. "That wasn't it just then?"

"Nope."

"Well, no. No plans. You?"

"Eh. I'm more of a Halloween girl. But the Dilger house will have a big tree and all the decorations. Plenty of parties, too. Bigwigs. Could be good for your new investigation business—if you're planning on still being in town."

"Wonder if I can get an invitation?"

"Maybe I can put in a good word for you. I know the owner." She put the car in drive and pulled away from the curb.

* * * * *

Zack pounded the keys of his newest disposable cell phone, trying his best not to let his excitement get him a speeding ticket. He pressed the phone to his ear with one hand while he squeezed the steering wheel with the other.

"Hello?" she said.

His pulse raced, excited to tell her and still pumped up with adrenaline from his task. "It's done."

"Really? When?"

"A little while ago. I'm on my way to dump it right now."

Her voice grew excited. "I wanna meet you at your place."

"Darlin', I gotta dump this thing first—like we talked about."

"Do it. Fast." She breathed hard into the phone. "Then I wanna see you. At your place."

He chuckled, trying to keep under the speed limit and stay in his lane. "Can't wait to hear the details, huh? You little freak."

"To hell with the details. I want to see where it happened. I want to be on that mattress while it's still warm from her. I want to be with you. There, right now. How's that for freaky?"

His stomach jumped. "Wow. Okay. Let me get rid of this . . . package."

"Hurry, lover."

The call ended.

He licked his lips, pressing the gas pedal harder as he raced toward Seminole Heights.

\* \* \* \* \*

Zack opened the door of his small apartment and let his girlfriend in. She strode straight across the front room, pausing at the bedroom door. In the near darkness, she whispered. "Tell me."

"Just like we planned." He brushed past her. "Brought her here like usual, had a little fun, and then boom. Done."

The light from the front room illuminated half of the bed. Reflected light allowed the rest of the room to be visible, a painting done in silent grays and black. She gazed at the murder scene, holding the door frame like she might fall down if she let go. "On that mattress?"

"Yeah." He pointed. "Right there."

A long, slow breath escaped her lips. "You picked up all the sheets and took everything with you?"

"Mm-hmm."

"Wow." She entered the room, creeping around the bed, her eyes searching the floor and walls. The shade was pulled closed. "It's so crazy, isn't it? My heart is pounding." She glanced at him, breathing hard. "Did you get a rush like this when you did guys for Carmello?"

"What, when me and Lentner used to whack a drug cheat? Kinda, I guess." Zack leaned against the wall. "Sometimes we used a gun when we had to go show a cheapskate what was what. Usually not. We used a lot of baseball bats back in the day."

She stepped toward the desk in the corner. Drug paraphernalia littered the top. A baseball bat rested against the side panel. She picked it up and slid her fingers over the shaft. "Like this?"

Zack shrugged. "Not that one, but yeah."

A gasp escaped her lips as she gazed at it. "I'm tingling. I wonder if we should have used this on her?"

"A little Louisville Slugger action, a golf club— whatever was handy. Piece of pipe. You bang up your cheat so he gives up the stash. Lots of hits to the ribs and knees, so he can still tell you without passing out."

She undid the buttons on her blouse. "Would a bat . . . kill someone?"

"Oh, yeah." Zack pushed himself off the wall, moving toward her like a hungry animal. "The head shots do. A few solid whacks to the skull and he's gone." He slid his arms around her waist, pulling her hips to his. "You put a beating on him first, though, to send a message. You don't want other buyers thinking they can get away with shorting you. Then the bat goes into the bath tub, you turn on the water, and leave the body to rot." He kissed her, hard and hot. "Except in Miami. Back in the day, they'd hacksaw off the guy's head and hands so no one could ID him, and leave the body in an orange grove."

She stepped away from him and set the bat on the desk, slipping out of her jeans and balling them up with her blouse. She tossed her clothes into the other room. "Before we get down to business, Mr. Bischoff—the sheets and shower curtain, all that got burned?"

"Up in smoke at the incinerator at the junk yard." He pulled his shirt over his head, eyeing her. "My friend Rico over there, he don't ask no questions."

"So." She slid a hand along her thigh, gazing at the bed. "The place is clean."

He stepped toward her, nodding slowly. "Yep."

"Except for any blood splatter."

"What?"

"Turn on the light and check the walls."

Zack frowned, flicking the light switch. Light flooded the room. "I don't see—"

She grabbed the bat with both hands and swung it hard into his belly, doubling him over and sending him crashing to the floor.

As he lay groaning, she strolled to her clothes and pulled a pair of latex gloves from her jeans pocket. "Now, you said—what? A few whacks to the ribs and knees, was it?"

"No!" He held up a hand, gasping.

She gripped the bat and landed a shot to his side. The impact of hard wood on soft flesh made a muffled cracking noise. He cringed and groaned, holding his ribs. She put her foot on him and pushed him over, taking a swing at his other side. When he curled up, she started in on his shins and thighs. When he rolled over, she laid the bat to his back.

After a few dozen solid thumps, she stood over him, breathing hard. Blood oozed from his mouth, dripping in strings to the floor. She flexed the bat in her hands, feeling its weight, lining up her shot.

"'A few solid whacks to the skull and he's gone.'" Grunting, she heaved the bat downward and connected with the back of his head. The impact shot into her hands and up her arms. Flecks of blood landed on her cheek.

His body went limp. She gritted her teeth and landed a few more head shots to seal the deal, only stopping when the blows turned soupy and splattered blood everywhere.

"And then," she panted. "I toss the place, right? So it looks like a drug deal gone bad when the cops come. With your record, it definitely will." She took a deep breath and wiped her forehead. "I'll get right on that."

She entered the bathroom and leaned over the tub, turning on the water. Chunks of hair clung to the blood-stained bat. Once the rubber stopper was placed in the drain, she dropped the bat in.

Checking herself in the mirror, she lifted her chin to peer at her neck and chest. Barely any blood splatter. Nothing a wipe down here—and a quick shower at home—couldn't take care of.

Entering the front room, she pulled the cushions off the couch and threw them on the carpet. The few books Zack owned were casually flung into the corner, along with some papers. In the kitchen, she opened the cabinets and drawers, gently placed the pantry and fridge contents on the floor, emptied the trash can onto the worn linoleum, and went on to the next room.

When she had done what she thought was an adequate amount of "tossing"—upending the couch table—she heaved the TV into the wall and let it smash to the floor, then shoved over the floor lamp. The bulb popped with a bright flash, like the paparazzi had taken a picture of her grand finale.

She strolled through the debris to the bedroom. Zack had managed to crawl a few inches since she saw him last, leaving a short trail of smeared blood, but he wasn't moving anymore. She stared at him and watched for his chest to move.

Nothing.

"Sorry about the mess, lover." She chuckled. "Good thing we aren't in Miami."

Three loud bangs on the front door sent her spinning around. An angry man's voice boomed through the apartment. "What's going on in there, Bischoff? I'm calling the police this time!"

She froze, holding her breath, but only for a moment. Casually as she could, she picked up her shirt and jeans and snapped off the lights. Slipping into her clothes, she slid open the bedroom window and crawled onto the air conditioning unit before calmly walking to the parking lot and driving away.

# CHAPTER 11

Warm and happy inside, Tyree turned the doorknob to Frank's office. The room was dark except for the glow of the computer shining around the man sitting in front of it.

Frank glanced over his shoulder. "Oh, you're back. Good. Now we can get started."

The place was practically empty. Just about every box and crate had been removed; the dusty rows of magazines and church brochures were gone. It was as if magic elves had come while Tyree had been away at dinner, removing all the clutter and debris that had gathered over the years.

Only the desk, the chairs, and computer remained—and the Harley.

Tyree stood at the doorway. "Hey, you cleaned up."

"Hmm?" Frank didn't look up, clicking away at the keyboard. "What do you mean?"

As he stepped toward the desk, Tyree's eyes darted around the dark room. "The place looks a little different from when I left."

"Oh, that." Frank leaned back in his chair and swirled around. "Well, you can't run a respectable business in a dirty old warehouse, can you? Clients might care about appearances."

"We have clients?"

"Well, prospective clients."

"Guess that wasn't a factor before." Tyree made his way toward the desk. "Some of that stuff looked like it had been here quite a while."

"Yeah, well . . . that stuff had places to go and people to see, so it went." Frank returned to the keyboard. "So it went and it saw. The Nicaraguans can't wait forever for their AR-15s, you know."

"What?" Tyree pressed his hands to his face, sighing. "Please don't tell me you're running guns out of here."

"Okay. I won't tell you."

"Frank . . ."

"We're not." He smiled. "Anymore."

Tyree shook his head. "I thought you ran a church."

"Different people pray to different things. Who am I to—"

"*Frank.*"

"Yes. I do run a church. And some other things. Like a startup research company that does investigative work." He patted the metal folding chair next to him. "Come here, I'll show you how to launder money."

Pursing his lips, Tyree stared at the computer.

"Come on."

Tyree stepped to the desk and peered over Frank's shoulder. "What about that big bike over there?"

"The Harley? That's for you," Frank said. "You're going to need a way to get around. I can't be giving you rides everywhere."

"Why do I get the feeling it was part of some dark, back alley trade?"

"It was, but so what? The whole thing was perfectly legal as far as I knew."

"Oh, for . . ."

Frank faced Tyree. "We run a legitimate investigative service here. You work for that business, not other things I'm involved in, but let me assure you, everything I do is legal. Your job will be here, doing skip traces on cars and asset tracking, stuff like that. Not guns, and not overseas missions—unless you want to."

"I don't. I'm not even sure I want to do investigative research."

"That's why you'll be perfect for it. With your library background and police work, you'll—"

"The library? Frank, I was ten years old when I worked there!"

"Still counts." He waved his hand, turning back to the keyboard. "Anyone who can learn the Dewey decimal system can find a stolen car with a computer."

Beaten, Tyree sat down next to Frank and stared at the screen. Frank had brought in a new computer.

"And if you can find a missing car, you can find anything. It's all the same process. See this?" Frank clicked a green rectangle. The personal information of William Hampton Darlington appeared. "We start with the credit card statements, cell phone bill, and social media. Most people are clueless about how much information they put out into the world, so we can track them just about everywhere. They don't think they're leaving a trail, but they are."

"Who are we looking for tonight?"

"These two guys. Darlington and this other goofball, Ted Barrow. The first one apparently wanted to hide some money, so he set up a shell company called Sterling Enterprises that magically has lots of assets now. Every time Sterling gets a new toy, his other company, Glasgow Incorporated, pays for it. Sterling gets an eighty-thousand-dollar car, Glasgow writes an eighty-thousand-dollar check—and often had an eighty-thousand-dollar loan.

Tyree folded his arms. "Seems kind of obvious."

"I never said these guys were smart. Glasgow declared bankruptcy, so now the banks and lawyers want the assets found. That's where we come in."

"Can't they find it themselves? Banks can pull credit reports."

Frank nodded. "They can, but they like to keep their hands clean. They don't want to look at credit reports, or have to physically drop by in the middle of the night and drive away with the Jaguar."

"The assets would be on the company's ledgers, though."

"It's cute you think shady companies would keep accurate books, but you're partially right. At tax time, the money has to be shown as coming from somewhere. That takes us to lesson two and the fun stuff."

"There was a lesson one?"

"Pay attention." Frank clicked another window. Sterling's general ledger came up. "We do boring stuff like going through these. Now, the IRS makes banks tell them about cash deposits over a certain dollar amount. Since most folks doing shady business don't want an IRS problem, too, they hire an accountant to help hide the funny transactions. The CPA goes to jail if the books don't add up, so the boss has to hide it somewhere that's okay with the accountant. Usually, that's a five-on-four."

"Pretend I don't know what that is," Tyree said. "Because I don't."

"I'll pretend you aren't whining as much as you are." Frank got up from the chair, kicking his legs as he walked. "Let's suppose you are a restaurant owner and I'm selling you five cases of wine, but you only pay for four, and I'm 'giving' you the fifth one. You pay for the delivery with a company check, but you've got one case of wine that is not on your books. That, you sell for cash—and since case number five never hit your general ledger, the cash can go in your pocket."

"I'd have to drink a lot of wine before the cash added up to anything worthwhile."

"Ah, but it works the same way with everything. You're buying five pallets of bananas? You pay for four. Five truckloads of computers from China? You only pay for four."

"But what about the guy selling them to me? Does he have to declare the fifth pallet?"

"Of course. His records are going to show that he sold you five. Or that one got stolen."

"So how do you get to look at his general ledger?"

"You can ask."

"Does that usually work?"

"No. So then you have to be sneaky. With bananas, you may have to represent yourself to be a fruit inspector." Frank chuckled, sitting down at the computer again. "Since we are not the police, we are allowed to use a little deception to get a look at the client's books."

"Sounds less than legal."

"Johnny boy, ninety-nine percent of this job can be done completely by the book."

"It's that last little one percent that gets everybody in trouble, though."

"Look, every once in a while, you have to make a decision that's not strictly black or white." Frank stopped clicking computer icons and eyed Tyree, a solemn look coming over his face. "When some new, young deputy finds out about a kickback scheme that's been going on in the sheriff's department for twenty years, nobody expects him to walk into his boss's office with a city prosecutor and a grand jury subpoena and tell them it's over. You're here because I'm never going to worry about the decisions you'll have to make in the gray places."

Conviction had its moments, and this was one.

Tyree nodded. "Okay."

"Now," Frank spun his chair and returned to the screen, "let's look at the second file. This one's even more interesting."

Stretching, Tyree yawned. It hadn't exactly been interesting yet. "How long do these cases usually take?"

"We can wrap up most of these in a few days, but you'll be burning a lot of computer hours. That's why I got you this new set up."

"Terrific." He recalled his earlier disaster with the office's ancient seating. "How about a comfy chair?"

"Absolutely. Get one for yourself, too."

## CHAPTER 12

Speaking in soft but firm tones, Detective Sanderson squatted in the hospital waiting room and tried again. "Ms. Moreno, you're doing great. You're helping a lot. Now, just do your best. Tell me what you saw, as best as you can remember it."

Mariana squirmed on the vinyl chair. "How's Leo? Is he going to be okay?"

"The paramedics think he's going to be fine, and we'll have the update from the doctors soon. He was lucky."

Wrapping her arms around herself, Mariana's gaze went to the ceiling. "Lucky . . ." She blinked a few tears from her eyes.

"Yeah, lucky. It could have been a lot worse. If the assailant is who we think it is, he's killed a few people. Have you seen that in the news?"

The girl nodded.

"The gunshot almost missed Leo. Your boyfriend is a big guy and he fought back. He did well."

"That was very brave of him." Sergio stepped into the waiting room, flipping his notepad shut and sliding it into his rear pocket. "Both of you were very brave." He leaned against the wall, arms folded.

Mariana shook her head. "We thought we heard something. Then this guy, he just comes in and starts saying stuff, and Leo jumped up." Tears ran down her cheeks. The words caught in her throat. "And the guy shot him. And I just . . ."

Carly put a hand on the girl's shoulder. "You did the right thing. You helped Leo."

She glanced at the detectives, her eyes wide. "I didn't. I was scared. That guy with the gun . . . I didn't know what to do."

"No, you helped. You stayed with Leo until the paramedics arrived. You helped him stay calm."

"He could have been killed."

"But he wasn't. And he's going to be all right."

Sergio pushed off the wall and came around to face Mariana. "That guy with the gun is still out there. He's going to hurt more people. Can you tell us anything—anything at all, about what you saw or heard?"

"The gun looked so *big*."

"I know," Carly said. "You were scared. Did you notice anything about the guy? Did you see any cars parked near the house when you went in?"

She shook her head. "We went in through the back of the house. There wasn't any doors or windows, so we just walked right in, you know? To be alone. Then we heard some noises and the guy was just right there."

"I get it. What about his face, or clothes? Could you see any of that?"

"It was dark. We were using flashlights. I mean, don't you guys do scientific stuff and use DNA on hairs and things? I'm sure you can find something."

"We can." Carly looked the girl in the eyes. "And we will. The killer definitely has a trademark routine, but he hasn't left a fingerprint at a crime scene yet. We're going to look at that house inch by inch, but you're the first witness we have who's seen anything."

"But that's just it. I didn't see anything."

Sergio tapped his partner on the arm and stepped away, moving to a nearby hallway.

Sanderson stood up. "Okay, Mariana. Sit tight and we'll see what the doctors have to say. Do you have someone coming to pick you up?"

"I called my mom. She's on her way."

"Good. We'll be back in a minute."

Carly followed Sergio into the hallway. He glanced over his shoulder and lowered his voice. "I think we cut her loose. She was too scared to remember anything but a big gun."

"I know. The boyfriend said the same thing. It was too dark in the house."

"Same with Officer Mateos." He flipped open his notepad. "Subject is male, average height, average weight, average build. The hoodie hid his face and hair. No discernable accent or no discernable tattoos or body markings. Couldn't get a make on the car, either. It was too far away. A dark gray or black sedan, possibly dark blue." He chuckled. "I'd give him crap, but he broke his shin falling into a ditch, so . . ."

"So we got nothing. Again." She put her hands on her hips, staring down the hallway. "Who ran our call to the other scene? The warehouse?"

"A couple of uniforms, with Roberts and Gianelli. We'll get caught up with them in the morning."

"Christ. Average weight, average height. That's just perfect." Carly frowned. "We're looking for roughly half of the three million adults in the greater Bay area. No problem."

"It's worse than that, Carly."

She glared at him. "Really, Marty? How can it possibly get worse? The whole city's pinning their hopes on us catching this guy and we have almost nothing to go on. How does it get worse?"

"The news is running with the story. They're calling our guy the Seminole Heights Serial Killer."

She put her hands on her hips and stared at the floor. "Great."

"And our newest team member, Harriman, called me from the station. He's getting slammed with calls from all over." Sergio flipped his notepad shut. "Apparently, everybody in the western hemisphere has seen our suspect—except our witnesses."

* * * * *

Officer Harriman held his hand near Lieutenant Breitinger's closed door. After a few seconds, he took a deep breath and leaned forward, knocking three times—then immediately winced and stepped back.

Breitinger's voice boomed from inside. "What idiot is trying to bother me?"

The door swung open. Sergeant Deshawn Marshall sat in a chair next to the lieutenant's desk, an array of papers and pictures spread out in front of him. "Can't you see we're busy in here?" Breitinger's face was red. "Don't you know what a closed door means?"

Harriman swallowed. "Yes, sir. I just thought—"

"That's your problem, newbie. Let the detectives handle the thinking. That's their job. You already have a job, unless I'm mistaken. Or did you resign earlier this morning?"

"No, sir."

"Then get back to your desk and answer those phones."

"This," Harriman nodded, holding up a page from a phone message pad. "This—"

"I don't care." He grabbed the message, glaring at it. "I know your mom's related to some big shots in town, but we play everything straight here. No special favors."

"Marge Harriman is my aunt, not my mom, sir."

"So you got the name but not the money, huh?" Breitinger grumbled, reading. "I attached you to the case. That means you get to sniff around a little, but most of the time you need to be right here answering phones and fielding leads, do you understand? Let the detectives run the show or so help me you'll be checking parking meters for the rest of your short career."

"Got it. Thanks, chief."

Breitinger shut the door and went back to his desk. He crumbed the note and tossed it at his trash can—and missed. "Oh, for . . ."

Sergeant Marshall took a sip of his coffee. "This is just a guess, but are you feeling a little stressed, Jacky?"

Breitinger growled.

"You were a little rough on the kid. That's Marge Harriman's—"

"I know who he is. I don't care who he's related to, he needs to work his way up the ranks like everybody else."

"Oh, come on. He *is*. And he's especially trying to impress you. Hell, he's practically working around the clock, taking calls from every mope in town that's convinced they've seen the Seminole Heights Killer. We're averaging over a hundred calls an hour on that case alone, everything from tourists who think the killer's stalking them to people convinced they've seen him going through their neighbor's trash. That boy's handling most of it—and doing a pretty good job, too. So maybe lighten up a little."

Breitinger sighed and rubbed his eyes. "Yeah, maybe."

"Maybe? You are one tightly wound white man."

Stifling a laugh, the lieutenant shuffled the photos. "Shut up."

"Nothing wrong with a little initiative." The sergeant sat back in his chair. "We were young once too, you know."

"I was, maybe. I think you were born old, Deshawn."

## CHAPTER 13

Sergio and Carly hustled across the busy downtown street towards Café Cubano as a cold front enveloped the Tampa Bay area.

A gust of wind threw her suit jacket open. She secured her purse to her shoulder and held the short jacket closed. "If you don't have a date tonight, come over and we'll work on the case."

"I don't have one yet." He hunched his shoulders against the chilly breeze. "But the day is young. Maybe I'll meet a nice waitress at lunch."

"You know, one of these girls might eventually figure out you're lying about being married so you don't have to see them again."

"Never happen."

"Why don't you settle down?"

"What are you, my mother? You know why."

She rolled her eyes as they made their way up the sidewalk. "Yeah, because you don't want one girl, you want all the girls."

Small leaves and bits of paper rolled along the street in the wind. The big flags in front of the Marriot snapped and whipped. "You know there's only one girl for me."

"Too bad she's married."

"Yeah. Getting to use Kyle's jet ski makes up for it." They crossed the last street and stepped onto the curb. Sergio checked his reflection in the restaurant window, fixing his hair. "You know, I like Kyle and all, but if there's ever a worldwide killer virus and he succumbs, I'm totally hitting on you."

"Noted. Do I get a say in any of this?"

"Depends. Do you bury him with the jet ski?" He yanked open the café door and let her go in first. "Think they're here already?"

"I'm sure of it." She waved at a few men in the back and headed to their table.

* * * * *

Detectives Roberts and Gianelli waited in a corner booth.

"Don't worry about anybody here seeing your file notes and evidence pictures," Roberts said. "The waitress will make sure we have plenty of privacy."

Sergio waited for Carly to take a seat at the booth, then sat beside her. Giannelli rested his elbows on the table and rubbed his eyes. "Your case is driving me nuts. What do any of these victims have in common?"

"They're all dead," Sergio said. "And what do you mean 'our' case? This mess belongs to all of us now. Breitinger made you a big sloppy part of it the other night when we were at the hospital and you got to run down Leo."

Carly pulled a folder out of her bag. "Guys, can we focus?" She slid some reports onto the table. "What links all these people?"

Gianelli shook his head. "They're all victims of the same serial killer, that's it. They were all unlucky enough to be at the wrong place at the wrong time."

The waitress brought two beers. Sergio glanced at Detective Roberts.

"What? I just got off duty after working eighteen straight hours. I don't care that it's 11:30, I'm having a beer." He lifted his glass and took a sip.

Sergio turned to the waitress. "A Coke for me and water for my partner, please. We'll flag you down when we're ready to order some lunch. Thanks." He eyed her dark skirt as she walked away.

Carly dug the crime scene pictures out of the folders, spreading them out. "I don't see a lot of connections, aside from being vulnerable in some way. Our guy is an opportunistic killer. The two high school kids were paying attention to each other, not what was going on around outside of the room. Probably the same thing for the jogger because he was from out of town. Definitely the trucker. He was unloading stuff onto the dock when our guy surprised him."

"You know, that's been bugging me." Gianelli tapped the picture of the trucker. "The killer took the trucker's finger, but didn't take souvenirs off anyone else."

Roberts shrugged. "You want to remember your first time."

"We don't know it was his first time. He might be transitory. Stops here for a few weeks, does his thing, then moves on. But I agree, it's a little random." Carly dug through the photos. "Maybe he just didn't have enough time to get souvenirs during the other murders."

"I'll tell you what I see," Roberts said. "Serial killers tend to start small and build their way up. They get their urges satisfied and they go away for a while, and then they come back. This guy, he's exploded onto the scene. The Pacific Killer in California had seven victims in about a year."

Gianelli slumped, rubbing his eyes again. "But that guy claimed to have killed over three dozen victims."

"When we catch our guy, we'll see what he claims, too, okay? But look at what was actually found in that case. Their killer averaged slightly more than one every two months, for about a year. Our guy has already tried five and been successful on three occasions. It would have been five if our uniform hadn't been called to a B and E."

Carly looked at Roberts. "What does that tell you?"

"That what people are fearing is correct." Roberts pounded the table with his finger. "That this guy is completely out of control."

She frowned. "It tells me he's going to get sloppy."

"How so?"

"He got away clean with the trucker. Same with the jogger. But he nearly got caught when he was attacking the high school kids."

Gianelli shrugged. "Luck."

"Good luck for him so far, and bad luck for us." Sergio sat forward. "Look, nobody thinks the increased police presence is helping—"

"It hasn't had time." Carly said. "The bodies are—" she glanced over her shoulder and lowered her voice. "The bodies are stacking up. Something's wrong about this guy and about these cases. It doesn't add up. It's too . . . concentrated."

"I'm fine with that." Roberts swigged his beer. "Throw a net around Seminole Heights and—"

A tray of glasses crashed to the floor. Sergio flinched, hunching his shoulders. The waitress, her eyes wide and her jaw agape, backed away from the table as the blood drained out of her face.

He followed her gaze. Scattered over the table were crime scene photos, displaying the victims at the scenes, gutted like fish and staring with dead eyes.

*Oh, no.*

Civilians weren't used to seeing such things. He stood, reaching out to her. "Ma'am, I'm sorry . . ."

The young woman turned and ran to the kitchen, holding her hand over her mouth. Sergio stood near the broken glass and spreading puddle, no idea what to say.

One by one, the cell phones at the table buzzed.

Gianelli was the first to react. "Can you believe it? They found another body."

"And Breitinger wants us in a meeting, now." Carly dug in her purse and handed Roberts some gum. "Guess you're not off the clock after all."

\* \* \* \* \*

The conference room was packed with people: the detectives and uniformed officers working the case, Sergeant Marshall, Dr. Stevens, and a group from the mayor's office. Breitinger stood in front of a whiteboard, scribbling some names.

*S. Dilger*

*H. Dilger.*

"Ladies and gentlemen," the lieutenant said. "I don't have to tell you how serious this is. We have two more victims this morning."

*Two.*

A ripple of shock went through Sergio. Around the room, the gathered crowd buzzed with the news.

Breitinger put the cap on his dry-erase pen. "This morning, a construction crew discovered the nude body of a young woman in a vacant house they were set to start work on. That victim is Sherry Dilger. Before that, one of our uniformed patrol officers discovered the body of Henry Dilger a few blocks away. The second victim is the father of the first victim, and he was found lying next to his car in the parking lot of their shipping business in Seminole Heights. Both victims' injuries are consistent with each other and with the injuries in our other cases." Breitinger slid his hands into his pockets. "That means our guy has gone into overdrive. He went from a regular deranged dangerous homicidal psychopath serial killer to a super killer. We need to shut this guy down."

A young officer in the back raised her hand. "What about the increased police presence, sir?"

Breitinger waived her off. "I've already put a hundred extra officers on the street. We have squad cars twenty-four seven up and down the areas, but—"

There was a knock on the door. Officer Harriman stuck his head in. "Sir, you asked for this." He handed the lieutenant a small piece of paper.

"Have a seat, Harriman. This involves you, too." Breitinger glanced at the note. "Okay, that confirms it. The Dilger family runs a business from their home in Carrollwood and has a few locations around the area. They have a warehouse and office in Seminole Heights, which is where the father was found, and another warehouse operation in

Lakeland. They also have two satellite offices. One is in New Port Richey and the other is in Sarasota. I want each of you to head a team up and get out to these locations and interview every employee, especially anyone terminated in the last year or so. Get work schedules and verify those against time cards. We've already contacted the respective agencies, so they know you're coming. Odds are, with the family connection, our killer is some employee with a grudge who decided to make a point."

Breitinger wrote on the whiteboard. "We still need to see if there's a connection between the trucker and the shippers, and between the out of town businessman and the local shipping business. Any connections at all." He pointed to Sergio and Carly. "Sanderson and Martin, we have a couple of uniforms headed to the Dilger home to give the family the news. You need to head over there. Everybody else, you'll have your assignments in five minutes, so get ready to clear out."

Sergio made his way toward the door with the others. Breitinger turned to Dr. Stevens. "Ma'am, will you stay behind a moment with Sergeant Marshall and me, please?"

She nodded, moving to the conference table. "I'd like to ask the lead detectives a few questions, too, if I may."

"Sure." Breitinger glanced at Sergio. "Sanderson and Martin, hang back. You, too, Harriman.

The trio moved away from the rest of the meeting attendees filing out the door.

"Have a seat, everyone." Breitinger took a chair, interlocking his fingers and placing his hands on the table. "Here's the deal. My instinct is to flood the streets of Seminole Heights with every cop in the state of Florida. Dr. Stevens has a different idea. You two are the leads in this investigation. I'd like you to hear what the doctor has to say."

Dr. Stevens adjusted her glasses. "I fear that this individual, seeing so many police in the area he has been frequenting, will simply go away. Not stop, but move on—say to Orlando or Miami—creating a whole new murder spree and causing needless additional deaths. I believe that since he has chosen, for lack of a better word, the small area of Seminole Heights, that we instead give the impression of more opportunities to satisfy his depraved needs."

Sergio cocked his head. "I'm not following, Doctor."

"Bait," Carly said. "She means adding targets out there."

"Wait. We *add* targets?"

"Potential targets." Dr. Stevens sat back in her chair. "I feel we've been working backwards, looking at clues to see what adds up. I think we need to force a break in the case. Disrupt the killer's leverage."

Carly nodded. "What did you have in mind?"

"Instead of flooding the street with police, we flood it with potential victims for him."

"What, go out there and dress up like people he prefers to attack?" Sergio ran a hand through his hair. "What is that, so far? We don't see a pattern. But with this shipping guy and his daughter, that does start to add up. The trucker might have a connection to a shipping business, and the jogger was an out of town businessman, so he might have a connection with a local businessman."

"I don't disagree," the doctor said. "And I would recommend looking into all that. But the high schoolers have zero connection so far, am I right?"

Sergio opened his mouth but halted himself. She had a point.

"In fact, the whole thing until this morning looked completely random, would you not agree?"

"Yes," Sergio said. "Yes, it seemed that way."

Carly looked at her notes. "They have a connection. We just haven't figured it out yet."

The doctor stood and went to the whiteboard. "They are connected by being victims of a serial killer. If your investigation leads to something, then fine. Meanwhile, people are dying. We can't predict why, and we can't predict when. But we do know where. I think if we put out enough bait, he will bite."

Sergio sighed. "There's no way the mayor's gonna go for that. No way."

"He already has," Breitinger said. "Last night he told me he'd implement whatever we come up with. Frankly, I don't see where he has much choice. This town is turning into serial killer central." Breitinger stood and went to the whiteboard, rubbing his chin. "But why not take an 'all of the above' approach? An increased, visible presence in the touristy area, and then for our bait, we get a bunch of undercover cops. That's still a higher police presence, it's just not as visible. Bait is bait. We can have people posing as vagrants and joggers—hell, they can dress as street sweepers for all I care. If he's hungry, he'll bite."

"And victims." Carly folded her arms and rested them on the table. "We have to have a few blocks of people just walking around casually and looking unsuspecting. Undercover cops?"

"Right," Breitinger said. "Then we also have to have lots of hidden squad cars nearby, and rapid response teams. How hard would that be? You know the area. There are empty buildings all over the place. A response team could be less than sixty seconds away from any of our assets at any time."

Carly sat back, pressing a pen to her cheek. "That's a big operation, boss."

"And it's high-risk." Sergio shook his head. "Sixty seconds might be too long. If this guy comes up close and pulls the trigger, then boom! No more asset."

"It's very high risk. We'll need to take every precaution."

Visions of another dozen victims—this time his friends on the force—filled Sergio's head. "Sir, I'm not sure we know what precautions to take. We don't know if he's talking to them or ambushing them or what. We don't know any of that stuff."

"Sure we do. These have each been a lone victim. That's what he looks for. Even the high school kids together were isolated. We'll have our undercover personnel emulate that. Walking in isolation, appearing vulnerable—as best as we can manage that. They'll be wired for sound and have a response team in constant visual and radio contact. We'll take nothing but volunteers for that part." Breitinger stared at the names on the whiteboard. "We'll put a ton of bait on the street, then we'll find out if this psycho bites."

"Great." Sergio dropped his hands to his sides, an uneasiness welling in his stomach. "I've always wanted to be bait for a serial killer."

## CHAPTER 14

Tyree took his turn at the computer while Frank left for another odd, clandestine meeting.

His uncle had been right. Skip tracing wasn't too difficult—but only because people were so stupid about the public information they put on social media. A bozo in Miami bought a Ferrari and drove it to Jacksonville—and then decided to stop making payments.

But not before he posted pictures of himself with it.

From there, it was a simple matter of notifying the Miami bank and getting an authorization. A private investigator friend of Frank's in Jacksonville boosted the car in the middle of the night while the skipper was sleeping. It literally took less than twenty-four hours and three phone calls.

In return, Tyree earned a ten-thousand-dollar fee. He had to split it with the PI in Jacksonville, but five grand for a couple of phone calls was easy money.

Most deals weren't like that, and they disappeared off the electronic bulletin board quickly. Before realizing it, Tyree had pinned a few—and gotten beat out of a dozen more after spending hours on leads someone else was already wrapping up.

It was borderline addictive, though; almost like a game. In the dark office, it was easy to work long hours without realizing it, too. He knew he'd worked more than a day, but he hadn't bothered to check just how much more until his cell phone lit up with Susan on the other end.

\* \* \* \* \*

Ruby answered the door at the Dilger residence, somber and quiet. "Hello, Mr. Tyree."

"Hi, Ruby." He stepped inside, for some reason being careful to not make a noise. "How's everyone doing around here?"

Shaking her head, Ruby led him toward the living room. "Worse than you'd think. Susan's in there screaming and breaking things, and Mrs. Dilger is upstairs locked in her room."

"Yep. That's worse than I expected. But I'm not sure how I'd react if my dad and sister . . . well, I don't know how I'd react."

"Let's hope you don't find out." Ruby stopped at the entrance to the living room. Susan's shouts filled the air. "She's in there. I'm staying out here."

Tyree stepped over a broken lamp. "Fair enough. Thanks, Ruby."

Susan stood in front of a flower vase, berating someone on the other end of a phone call with a string of expletives. She slammed the phone onto the table and grabbed the vase with both hands, raising it above her head.

Tyree stepped up behind her and snatched it away. "Hey, slow down. This isn't *Real Housewives Of New Jersey*."

She wheeled around, red-faced, raising her fist at whoever stopped her from smashing the vase. When she saw who it was, she lowered her fist, but not her demeanor. "Johnny, they aren't giving me the time of day!"

Tyree slid the vase back onto the table. "Who's not?"

"The police. They say they're working on 'things.' Well, what the hell 'things' are they working on? And why can't they tell me when they're going to catch the guy who—"

"Okay, okay. Let's sit down." He took her hand and pulled her to one of the white couches. "The police are doing their job. They have a ton of stuff to look at and it all takes time."

"They aren't doing enough."

He nodded. "I know it seems like that, but I have a little experience in these things. It's not like on TV. It can take days to put the information together, sometimes weeks, and the families . . . well, the families get to go crazy the entire time. I get it."

"As far as I can tell, they are sitting on their asses." She folded her arms and frowned. "We know people, you know? The mayor ate here the other night. We hire lots of off duty police for warehouse security and for events. You'd think with all my dad's done for them, that . . ." Susan's words caught in her throat. Tears welled in her eyes. "My daddy, Johnny. And my sister." Her shoulders slumped and her hands fell to her lap as she finished the thought in a whisper. "They're gone. And nobody cares."

The tears fell freely now, dropping in silence from her bowed head as her shoulders bobbed up and down.

He pulled her close, putting her head to his shoulder and patting her back. "Don't be silly. Everyone cares. Everybody who loved them has a broken heart today."

A lump formed in his throat. He hadn't seen either Sherry or Mr. Dilger since he'd gotten back, and now they were both gone. It was as though he missed a window somehow, and now it was forever closed. He felt guilty for it.

And he had no words.

Susan wrapped her arms around him and sobbed into his chest. He stared, speechless, over her flaxen locks. Tears and mascara stained his shirt.

He knew there was nothing he could say at a moment like this because he'd tried before. The eight-year-old girl whose body they finally found in the lake—there were no words for her mother. No well-intentioned phrases from a sad deputy sheriff could stop her tears or fix the gaping hole that had been torn in her heart. Not in days, not in years. Not ever.

He stood in her doorway and delivered the awful news that plunged the young mother into hell, never to return. She cried, and he cried with her.

Cops don't do that. Except they do.

He knew.

There were other times; different, but they were all the same. A drunken stranger veered over the white line and killed a man's whole family, both children and his wife. What could a cop possibly say to help fix that? Another time, two young brothers snuck their dad's rifle into the woods. One came home. The tiny body of the younger boy was like a bird in the leaves. He was too small to be so still.

There had been too many times he had to face a family member and deliver bad news, and not once were any words from him ever good enough.

"Johnny."

He peered over his shoulder to the gaunt, pale woman that had been Mrs. Dilger a few days before. Her warm eyes were now dark, ringed by lack of sleep and puffy from crying. She was worn out and frail, as if a gust of wind could knock her over and shatter her like the broken lamp at her feet.

Tyree stood. "Yes, ma'am?"

"I'm sorry. I didn't hear the door. Thank you for coming." Her eyes were blank, looking at him but appearing to not see him at all.

He folded his hands. "Yes, ma'am."

Susan touched his arm. "Johnny, you were a cop. Can you go down there and talk to them?"

"Oh, I don't—I'm not a cop anymore. The police have their procedures and I'm sure they're following them."

"Please, Johnny," Susan said. "They aren't telling us anything."

Mrs. Dilger folded a handkerchief and dabbed it under her red nose. "We have friends in high places, Johnny, but they don't seem to be much help in . . . this." Her gaze went to the floor.

The room fell silent.

Tyree's cheeks burned with the shame of not saying yes immediately, but he doubted the police would tell him anything. Besides, he was no longer a deputy, and even when he was, it was back in Texas. The Tampa PD would not like him sticking his nose in.

"Please. There must be something you can do." Mrs. Dilger's voice was barely a whisper.

He looked into her red, swollen eyes. The pit of his stomach seemed to drop right through the floor.

There *were* words that would help.

"Yes, of course I'll talk to them for you." He squared his shoulders. "I'll go right now, and I'll find out what the hell is happening."

He walked across the living room.

"Johnny, wait." Susan ran to her phone and pushed some buttons. "I have a friend on the force, but I can't seem to get my calls returned right now. Maybe you'll have better luck."

"People can get funny when something like this happens to someone they know. Even cops." He punched the name and number into his phone. "Don't worry. Your friend will talk to me."

\* \* \* \* \*

The assistant duty officer shook her head. "I'm sorry, I can't talk to you."

"What?" Tyree dropped his hands onto the counter. "Susan said—"

"Susan's a friend. But really, I can't talk." Jayda took off her headset and pushed away from her desk, grabbing a stack of reports and taking them to a nearby filing cabinet. Behind her, phones rang nonstop. "The lieutenant wants that case locked up tighter than a drum. Nobody gives any information to the public without his express say so—and he ain't giving it."

"I'm not exactly the public."

"So you said. Breitinger says no information goes beyond these walls except for what he allows or what the lead detectives will share." She raised her eyebrows and lowered her voice. "And at the rate the bodies are coming in, those two don't have time to catch their breath."

*She wants to help, but feels like she can't. Maybe she knows somebody closer to the case who I can loosen up.*

"Have they established an information officer for the case?"

She'd see that as a backward step, and one that wouldn't be regarded as helpful to her friend. Information officers pretty much only tell people what's already in the newspaper, or what's about to be.

Jayda eyed him carefully. "Look, you said you're a friend of the family, so I really shouldn't say anything. Families tend to go ballistic at times like this, especially families that have dinner with the mayor. You know what I'm saying?"

A male officer put a stack of papers on the counter. "Jayda, here are some more reports. I know how much you've been wanting these."

"Like a hole in the head."

He stepped back. "I'm sorry. Am I interrupting something?"

Jayda nodded at Tyree. "This man is here on behalf of the Dilger family. He'd like five minutes with Detectives Martin and Sanderson."

"Oh, they're way too busy for that, but maybe I can help you. I'm Mark Harriman. I'm working with them on the case."

The two men shook hands. "Thanks," Tyree said. "I appreciate the help."

"Let's talk over here." Harriman stepped to a row of chairs by the hallway. "So the Dilgers hired you? Are you a private investigator?"

Tyree folded his hands in front of himself, widening his stance. "I'm a friend of the family, but yes, I work for an investigative research company."

"Normally, I'd guess Carly and Sergio wouldn't be happy about potential interference in a case, but I'll be honest—right now they'd probably take any help they could get."

"Let's work it both ways, then. If I find anything useful, you'll get it ASAP. And if you find anything that will help the family—"

"Within certain boundaries."

"—I'm not asking you to break any rules. But the Dilgers don't like waiting to read the morning headlines to see the progress on the murders of their family members. Waiting and not knowing is torture on any family in a situation like this. If you can spare them that little slice of hell, it would go a long way."

"I like to help people," Harriman said. "Especially . . . influential people."

"The Dilgers certainly are that."

"They certainly are."

Tyree pulled out his phone. "So let's trade phone numbers and see what we can do for each other."

"Shouldn't I call Susan directly?"

Tyree cocked his head. "Who said anything about Susan?"

"I read the paper, too, Mr. Tyree. The society section has Susan Dilger all over it."

Looking Harriman right in the eye, Tyree spoke firmly but without emotion. "Right now, you can call me. If Susan wants that changed, I'm sure she'll let both of us know."

"She has a way of being direct, or so I've heard." Harriman took his phone from his pocket. "What are you looking into first?"

"This." He tapped on his phone. "Making a connection to the case was my goal for the day."

Harriman smiled. "Well, then I get to help you first. We—hold on."

A group of officers walked through the lobby. Harriman glanced down the hallway and stepped into a vacant interrogation room. "Come over here."

Tyree followed.

"We got a letter indicating that the books at Dilger and Contreras weren't quite up to snuff."

"Really? I haven't seen anything like that in what I read."

"We didn't release that yet. Probably bogus, but it's got to be checked out. Meanwhile, with a new victim popping up every two days, the mayor has pulled every available resource onto the serial killer."

"So other stuff is falling by the wayside."

Harriman bristled. "It's prioritization of assets. A necessity. But you said you're a friend. If you start there . . ."

Tyree eyed Harriman. "Think the killer links to the business somehow?"

"They don't see any links yet. That's why they aren't pursuing oddball tips. We get hundreds every day. That's my primary job these days, sifting through the lead pile to see what gets top priority."

"What gets it right now?" Tyree asked.

"Let's just say it requires putting a lot of cops on the street without looking like there are a lot of cops on the street." Harriman slid his phone back into his pocket.

"Which is why there's no time for running down leads about bookkeeping discrepancies or returning phone calls." Tyree frowned and shook his head. "Class act."

"Hey, be nice." Harriman scowled. "We've never had a serial killer like this before. No one has. It's got the top brass and all the politicians going crazy, wanting results *yesterday*. Looking into a what's likely a bogus tip takes a whole day of time we don't have, buddy. And meanwhile another body comes in. You can see—"

"I can see politicians making bad decisions. But don't worry, I'll look into it for you." Stepping toward the door, Tyree wagged his phone at Harriman. "And you keep me posted, too. Anything that can help the family."

"You'll be the first to know."

## CHAPTER 15

The phones would not stop ringing. The office sounded like a swarm of angry bees.

"Yes, ma'am." Sergio wrote notes on a pad as fast as he could. "Yes ma'am. Thank you." He hung up and stared past Carly, to Harriman on the other side of the desk cluster. "You do this all day?"

The phone in front of Sergio rang again. His head throbbing, he stuck his tongue out at it.

"All day for a few weeks now." Harriman used his shoulder to hold a phone to his ear while he typed on the computer. "It gets easier after the first few days." Letting the phone drop into his hand, he hung it up and kept typing. "No, wait, it doesn't."

Harriman's phone rang again.

Sergio groaned and tore the note from his pad. His oncoming headache was announcing itself like a marching band. "Okay, well, we need to get some food, I think." Stretching over the desks, he slapped the paper onto Harriman's pile. Next to him, wearing a headset, Carly typed on a keyboard. Sergio pulled the earpiece away from her head. "What do you say, partner? Hungry for some wings? A sub?"

"Barbecue."

Sergio wagged his finger. "I'm sure of it now. In a prior life, you were a guy. Barbecue it is. Harriman, come on."

"I'm not sure I'm allowed—"

Grabbing his Buccaneers windbreaker from the back of the chair, Sergio pulled it on. "You're detailed to us now."

Carly stood. "It'll be all right, Mark."

\* \* \* \* \*

They sat at a small, outdoor table on the front porch of Kojack's Ribs. Harriman picked up a menu. "I'm still not sure why we chose a place so far away."

"How soon do you want to be back at those phones?" Unrolling his paper napkin, Sergio let his fork fall onto the red-checkered vinyl table cloth. He glanced at Carly. "Man, I've never seen them ringing nonstop like that before."

"That is a fact." Carly dug a pair of sunglasses out of her purse and put them on. Kojacks' had been converted from a small house to a small restaurant a few decades ago, and the crushed oyster shell surface of the parking lot bounced the afternoon sun everywhere. She gazed over the packed lot to the busy street beyond.

A young man in an apron set glasses of water and a small basket of rolls on the table. "I'll be back for your order in a second."

"Oh, we're ready." Sergio plucked the menu from Harriman's grasp and handed it to the server. "Three rib baskets, one Coke."

"Cole slaw or fries?" the young man asked.

"Fries all around. Thanks."

As server departed, Harriman glanced at Carly. "So, you guys been partners long?"

Carly's gaze remained fixed on the street.

"Yep." Sergio patted the table like a drum, glancing over his shoulder. His stomach rumbled. Beyond the porch, a window allowed a view into the hickory-scented kitchen. "It's been about four years since we started working together."

"Wow," Harriman said. "Four years."

"You know, that office is too noisy to be productive." Carly rested her elbow on the back of the chair and put her chin on her hand. "Kyle took the boys camping for two weeks in Tennessee. Maybe I should take advantage of a nice, quiet, empty house for a few hours to get my thoughts straight."

"Camping!" Sergio chuckled. "You missed that for this? I feel for you."

"What? They're doing the Pemberton Winter Leadership Challenge." She said. "Besides, camping's not so bad."

"'No so bad.' There's a ringing endorsement. Hey, when my friends suggested we go camping, I made a list of the things I'd need. First, new friends."

Laughing, Carly picked up a dinner roll and threw it at him.

\* \* \* \* \*

A red plastic basket of discarded rib bones and uneaten French fries rested on the table next to Carly's elbow. "Look, some of the stuff doesn't add up in this case, but some does."

"Okay." Sergio reached over his own basket and grabbed one of her fries, stuffing it into his mouth. "Let's talk."

Harriman sat quietly as Carly took a notepad from her purse and wrote on it. "We have victim number one, a local trucker. Shot and stabbed, he loses a finger. The next victim is a jogger from out of town. Shot and stabbed, no souvenirs taken. Let's hold off on vic three for a second. The next two are a high school couple, but he doesn't kill them."

Sergio grabbed another French fry. "The cop surprising him is the only reason that didn't happen."

"Bear with me." Carly drew a circle around the names on the pad, leaving out the Dilgers. "All those murder victims look like random targets. Then the next two are father and daughter. And she's naked. We haven't seen that before."

Sergio shrugged, his cheek stuffed with French fries. "He didn't kill a woman before."

"He almost did," she said. "The high school kids. But there, he thought he was getting two victims for the price of one."

"So that's what he wanted again?" Harriman asked. "With the father-daughter?"

"Maybe." Carly chewed the end of the pen, staring at her notes. "In a family business they both worked at, it makes sense they'd be together at the office—but they weren't. The dad went there for some invoices and the daughter wasn't supposed to be there at all. They didn't have a meeting scheduled. The crime scene investigators say she wasn't killed at the warehouse, and that she was definitely moved to where she was found. On top of that, she was naked in that house up the street. Now, was our killer going to do that with the high school girl? I can't see it. Why undress her?" She tapped the pen on the pad. "That's what doesn't fit. It takes time to remove clothes from a dead body. It's messy. There would be blood and urine . . . If he shoots our two high schoolers, Leo and Marianna, like he did in the prior attacks, what did the killer intend to do with them after that? Take his time stabbing each one in turn? Okay, and then what? Was he going to move the body of a high school girl up the street, like he did with Sherry Dilger? Even at a hundred pounds, that load gets heavy."

"And noticeable by people in the area," Sergio said. "Yeah, I see what you mean. What about his car? Maybe he planned on—"

"He's not been planning, really. Not like that. Our guy has been opportunistic. He waits. He watches. Then he strikes. He probably figured he'd shoot the high school kids and then he could take his time with stabbing them. Two for one, like you said. But he couldn't have been planning on moving Marianna after he killed her because he fled the scene—whatever he was going to move her with, he'd have left behind or carried out with him. But there was nothing left at the scene that would move a body. And Officer Mateos didn't see much, but he saw the killer flee the scene and chased him across an open yard. Mateos didn't recall seeing anything in the killer's hands. From that distance, he might not have been able to see the knife or the .38, but he would have been able to see something that would be used to help move a body."

She leaned back in her chair. "The killer could have stuffed a lawn and leaf bag in his pocket. It would be bulgy but not visible from a distance. But when he didn't pull off his two-for-one murders with our high schoolers . . ."

"He was still obsessed about it." Sergio grabbed a handful of fries and stuffed them into his mouth. "Father-daughter gives him another shot at the two-for-one."

"That's just it. Do they?" Carly tossed the pen onto the table. "Sherry Dilger was moved and she was naked. She's different from every other victim for those two reasons. Now, does the killer take the time to force her to remove her clothes? That's a lot of patience. Or were they lovers? Either way, that has to tell us something."

Sergio nodded. "Don't rule out nude sunbathing."

"Not at night, Detective," Carly said.

Harriman stared at the notepad. "Sounds like we need to talk to the crime scene investigators again."

* * * * *

"Your case is pretty high profile, Detectives." CSI lead investigator Freedling closed his office door as the two detectives and officer Harriman sat. "I want to help as much as possible. I live here, too."

"Thanks for seeing us on such short notice." Carly read from her notepad, pointing at it with a pen. "Our victim, Sherry Dilger—we have some questions. The fact that she was nude bothers me."

The investigator pulled out the case file and opened the folder on his desk. "More than that. We looked everywhere. Her clothes were not at the crime scene or anywhere near it."

Sergio raised his eyebrows. "Maybe there's the souvenir."

"And it's a different souvenir," Harriman said. "Because this victim is his first female kill?"

Freedling peered over the file. "The evidence suggests she wasn't wearing clothes in that house."

Sergio cocked his head. "What?"

The investigator turned the pages of the file. "The blood found at the crime scene overall was appreciably less than we would expect a live body of her size and weight to emit. The victim's stab wounds bled much less, and we noted a lot less blood gathered on the floor of the vacant house where the body was found. Now, less blood from the stab wounds could be a result of the killer shooting her and waiting longer to stab her, but the blood around the body was appreciably less than what we'd find in that case. The evidence suggests she was dead when she got there."

Carly glanced up from her notepad. "She was killed somewhere else and moved to the vacant house? Are we certain?"

"Yep." Freedling grabbed another folder. "Also, her wounds didn't have fabric fragmentary evidence. In other words, with each prior victim, as the knife stabbed, it carried clothing fibers into the body. The serrated blade was the primary culprit there, but it can happen in trace amounts with any knife. In the case of Ms. Dilger, the knife did not. Her wounds indicate the same serrated blade, but with no fibers in the wounds or in the body, we have to conclude she was already without her clothing when she was attacked."

Carly looked at the Freedling. "Were there signs of a sexual assault?"

"No signs of rape, but signs of recent intimacy." The investigator leaned on the desk. "It's very likely she undressed voluntarily. We have no defensive wounds on her hands, and no indications anywhere on the body that she struggled. No evidence of being drugged into submission. That indicates he knew her. A boyfriend, maybe."

Sergio frowned. "She came in from out of town and was supposed to get picked up by her boyfriend at the airport. Nobody's seen or heard from him since. She was supposed to go with the boyfriend to his apartment, but we don't have an address yet."

"Her cell phone records show a lot of calls to the number she used from the airport," Carly said. "But it seems he preferred to use a disposable cell phone."

"All the finest people do. Nothing suspicious there." The investigator closed the folder. "His apartment may be your murder scene for Sherry Dilger."

"And that makes her boyfriend our serial killer?" Harriman asked.

Freedling nodded. "It's very possible."

Sergio stood. "We finally have the break we wanted."

"Detectives." Freedling gathered the folders and picked them up, stacking them on the corner of his desk. "It's also possible the boyfriend was another victim of the serial killer—and you just haven't discovered his body yet."

\* \* \* \* \*

Dr. Rodriguez elbowed his way through the operating room doors at Tampa General and walked toward the wash basins. A nurse caught up with him. "How's the patient?"

"Alive—barely." Rodriguez pressed the foot pedal to engage the faucet. "I've never seen someone beaten so badly."

"The police want to talk to you about him. Officers . . ." she glanced at a beige business card. "Santos and Rainfield. Should I ask them to wait in your office?"

"Sure. Bring them on back." He pulled off his bloody latex gloves and plunged his hands under the water. "Let them know there's no rush, though. If he doesn't die, Zack Bischoff's probably going to be in a coma for a long time."

## CHAPTER 16

"Can I help you?" Sergio walked to the duty desk with Carly behind him, reading the message from Breitinger. They had a visitor—the nephew of a friend of the lieutenant's.

Tyree introduced himself and shook their hands. "I work for a private security firm. Maybe we can help each other by sharing information."

"Well," Carly said. "There's a whole procedure . . ."

Sergio groaned. "Hey, meet the Digi-Cop 9000, the latest advancements in human – cyborg relations." He clapped Tyree on the shoulder. "Yes, we will work with you. My phone's been ringing off the hook with bogus leads. The last one saw the killer going through his trash—in Miami. And on top of that, now I have to get ready for a fishing trip where I'm the bait."

Tyree scratched his chin stubble. "Funny, my old job felt a lot like that at times."

"Yeah?" Sergio smiled. "What was your old job?"

"Law enforcement."

"And now you're a P. I. Making more money?"

Tyree shrugged. "Nobody does our jobs for the money."

"Boy is that ever true."

"Procedure says I'm supposed to check in with the local law enforcement," Tyree said. "So I checked in. Mark Harriman says he's the contact person, so I'll be calling him if I discover anything in my investigation that pertains to yours. But he seems like a bit of a showboat, so I thought I'd stick around and meet the principles to let you know I won't be messing up your deal."

"Showboat, huh?" Sergio chewed his lip. "Yeah, maybe. Any idea where your case is taking you?"

"Lakeland, for starters."

"That tip about the trash in Miami is already starting to look better, isn't it?"

"Mark's our point man right now," Carly said. "And we'll have him follow up on any family connections. If you turn up anything, please call him. He'll keep us posted. And thanks for checking in. A lot of P. I.'s don't."

Sergio handed Tyree a business card. "Regular business, run through Harriman. If you think I need to know something, call me directly."

"Good luck on the fishing trip." Tyree headed for the door. "Try not to get eaten."

\* \* \* \* \*

In the Tampa PD parking lot, Tyree straddled the Harley while making a call in the bright sunlight. A light wind brushed his hair back and threw a few leaves around.

The phone rang a while before Ruby answered. "Dilger residence."

"Hi, Ruby, it's Tyree. Is Susan around?"

"No, but Mrs. Dilger is. Would you like to speak with her?"

He opened his mouth to say no, but halted himself. Why hadn't he called Susan on her cell in the first place? "Uh, sure that's probably better, anyway."

It wasn't. It was harder to talk to Mrs. Dilger. Susan had appeared devastated, but Mrs. Dilger had been destroyed. It made sense, too—she'd lost a husband and a child. There's no way to measure another person's pain, but the eyes of the mothers he had to deliver bad news to over the years, they always seemed to be hurting the most.

That's why he called the house. Inside, he knew he had to.

As much as he didn't want to give bad news to either of them *at all*, in this case he might have to do it twice—with whatever news he learned. And who exactly should he be reporting to, anyway, about the possibility of funny business happening at

Dilger and Contreras? Who was the boss now that Henry had—

"Johnny?" Mrs. Dilger's voice was as listless as it had been when he left the house. He hated the thought of telling her something might be up with the books, and likely at Henry's doing, but . . .

*But that's what they need you for now.*

He closed his eyes, trying to think of a way to deliver the news without causing more hurt than was absolutely necessary. Experience told him the best way was to do it quickly and without emotion, like taking off a band aid.

Experience also told him there was no best way.

He took a deep breath. "I just spoke with the police and . . . well, ma'am, they got a letter about the company recordkeeping not being completely above board. They don't think it's legit, but—"

"Johnny, I trust you." Her voice cracked. She'd been crying. "If you think you need to look into something, look into it. I have nothing to hide."

"You might not, but a business—a shipping business—I might turn up things that are embarrassing or uncomfortable for you or the family."

She didn't hesitate. "If you have a successful shipping business, there are always people who think you might be also involved in running drugs or making payoffs. There are a lot of temptations in this line of work, and good companies fall prey to it all the time. Henry wasn't involved in that sort of thing, I can assure you."

Tyree tucked his free hand into his pocket and hunched his shoulders against the chilly breeze. "Well, whoever gave that tip to the police did it for a reason. Maybe a competitor is looking to hurt your business. It's worth checking into."

"Then by all means, look into it. If we have things to clean up, tell me and we'll get them cleaned up. My husband *was* the business, Johnny. If he or anyone else did something wrong, the sooner we get it corrected, the better. If there's nothing to this allegation, we want that known, as well."

"Yes, ma'am."

A few officers walked out of the station and down to their patrol cars. To any outside observer, life was normal in Tampa. You'd hardly know a killer was running amok and that the citizens were afraid to be outside at night in what used to be paradise.

Mrs. Dilger sighed. "Let's make things official. I'd like to hire you to look into the murder of my husband and daughter, and anything related to their deaths, including the business. I want the facts, whatever they are, so that my family and our business can move forward with a clean slate."

"Okay. I suppose we should discuss a fee."

"There will be no discussion. I want you working on this full-time, your top priority. I read online that private investigators earn about two thousand dollars a week."

"Well, yes, for basic stuff, but there are expenses and overtime hours, and all sorts of—"

"I'll pay you ten. Will that be adequate?"

"Ten thousand dollars a week?"

"Yes."

"Holy cow. I should've left the sheriff's department a long time ago."

A firmness returned to her voice. The one he recognized from the other night. "I'm willing to pay a premium because I want you focused fully and completely on our situation, but I'm paying for more than just a private investigator. I'm paying for information and confidentiality. Whatever you find, you bring to me, and you bring all of it. No matter how uncomfortable the news, bring it here and bring it right away. I don't want to read about it in the newspaper."

Tyree shifted on the seat of the Harley. "Everything will go straight to you unless I'm required to give it to the police."

"If you're required to give it to the police, you give it to them. But I don't want to be surprised. You tell me first."

*This must be those gray areas Frank was talking about.*

He nodded, more to himself than anything else. Frank's gray areas would not be scarce in this line of work. "I don't think I see a problem there, ma'am."

"Good." The sadness in her voice betrayed her façade of strength. "When can you check out that letter?"

Holding the phone away from his face, Tyree glanced at the time. "I should probably start by looking at the books and talking to the employees."

"The books are kept here, but only digital copies and summary reports. The original ledgers and receipts are all kept at the branches."

"Can you tell the folks out in Lakeland to talk to me when I get there?"

"Everyone will be instructed to tell you whatever you want to know. If anybody doesn't, you tell me."

"Yes, ma'am." He hauled his keys out of his pocket and slipped a big silver colored one into the ignition of the motorcycle. "Thank you."

"No, John, thank you. This needs to be taken care of and if the police won't do it I'm thankful I have the resources to be able to."

"Actually, you have the resources to be able to hire somebody much more competent than me."

"I suppose I could, but I don't really want a gun for hire. I want a friend that I trust looking into something that's very important to me and my family, and who will protect us. I'm not sure I get that if I hire someone else."

"Okay, but we need an understanding." Tyree sat back and drew a breath. "If Henry was connected to some sort of bad situation that cost him his life, I can't—I won't—cover it up. We need to be clear on that."

"Henry ran the company, but he didn't do it alone. We were a team. There's nothing wrong with our books, as you'll see tonight."

"Tonight?"

"When you get finished talking to the employees and checking the ledgers on site, come look at the books here. Make sure everything ties together. If a serial killer is connected to my family, the financial records will be the best place to find out how."

## CHAPTER 17

Sergio frowned as he strapped on the bulletproof vest. "I can't tell you how much I hate this plan."

In the police parking garage in downtown Tampa, Carly and Harriman helped him dress, using an oversized flannel shirt to hide the bulk of the protective gear. Several groups of SWAT team members worked with the other officer volunteers, wiring radio communications under the vests and checking equipment.

"Carly, I swear, if I get killed, you are going to have to deal with my mother. Because I won't do it."

"Right. You'll be dead."

"You think that will stop her? She'll come to my grave every afternoon just to yell at me." His lighthearted comments did little to ease his nerves. In a few minutes, he could be face to face with a raging homicidal maniac. "She wanted me to be a dentist, you know."

The SWAT team technician wrapped an earpiece around Sergio's ear.

Harriman stepped back, tapping Carly on the shoulder. "Is he okay?"

She shrugged. "He makes jokes when he's stressed. Just ignore him." She handed Sergio a tiny medallion. "Here."

"What's this? A good luck charm?"

"Sort of. It's supposed to be St. Jude."

"Am I going to a children's hospital later?"

Carly smiled. "He's supposed to be the patron saint of lost causes. I figured it couldn't hurt."

"Terrific." Sergio stuck the medal in his pocket and forced himself to take a deep breath. "Let's hope we don't need him, then."

"I got him from a street vendor. For all I know it's a Pokémon game piece."

"Probably just as lucky." Sergio held his arms out, looking over his outfit. "Well, how do I look?" He stepped toward the waiting van.

"Good." Carly walked with him. "Remember, what matters here is what your killer likes. Do what the SWAT guys said. Act as vulnerable as possible. Doc Stevens is going to be reviewing the data as we go, so we'll eventually get closer to what our guy wants in a vic."

Harriman trailed them. "The lieutenant says it might be a few weeks before we get it right."

Sergio fought a shudder. "Weeks! Terrific."

"Hey," Carly said. "You don't have to go every night. I'm going tomorrow and about fifty other people volunteered to go, too."

"Yeah, yeah." He stepped into the van. "At five or ten a night, I'll still be bait once a week. That's still too often for my comfort level."

The other team members took their seats on the benches that lined either side of the van interior, checking their equipment. The knot in Sergio's belly grew. He didn't believe they'd actually encounter the killer this way, but he couldn't shake the possibility that they might. He'd seen the bodies. Each had been unable to fight off their murderer because they'd been surprised somehow, and he needed to be smarter about that than they'd been.

*Focus. Nothing will get you killed faster than not keeping your head in the game at all times.*

The bulletproof vest would stop a bullet much larger than a .38. It would stop a knife. The SWAT teams were seconds away, watching his every move.

All this, he knew.

But he also knew mistakes happen. A little more than four years ago, his partner Franklin had been wearing a vest the night a tweaked out drug dealer decided to hold his girlfriend and kid hostage and burn his trailer to the ground with everyone in it. The gunshot should have hit Franklin's vest, but it grazed the collar and nicked the carotid artery in his neck. He bled out in seconds.

Everyone was there. Cops. Ambulance. Everyone.

It didn't matter. Franklin was just as dead as if he'd been all alone.

*All alone, walking down a street where a serial killer has been on a rampage.*

Sergio wiped his sweaty palms on his jeans. Cops think just like anyone else. They read the paper and see the news. The badge doesn't make them immune to the world's evils—they carry the badge because of those evils. Because they decided they'll stand in the space between good and bad.

He gritted his teeth. *That's why you're going to go out there now.*

"Listen up, team." The SWAT sergeant held up his radio. "We'll be nearing our location in a minute, so let's go over the procedures one last time. Detective Martin, when you get out and start walking, stay to the assigned streets. We will be in constant radio and visual communication. Your collar microphone will pick up your voice even if you whisper. If you don't think you can speak safely, click your hand switch. We'll ask questions you can answer yes or no. Your code name is 'Walking Boss' for this operation. What's your safety phrase, sir?"

"Crash cart."

"That's right. If you get in any trouble for any reason, you say that and we come running."

Sergio sighed. *And scare our killer away for good if it's a false alarm.*

149

"Tonight, you are acting like a resident of this area," the sergeant said. "You live here. You're going for a nice, leisurely walk. Act like you're the age of that trucker and walk slow. Vulnerability is usually the key for these guys."

The van came to a stop. Sergio took another deep breath. The knot in his stomach would not subside.

Carly patted him on the shoulder. "The safety house is right on the corner. I'll be in the van listening a few blocks from here, with a ton of other cops."

"Yep." Sergio flung his hands a few times, trying to vent the stress. He looked into her eyes. "That doesn't matter if he walks up and pops me."

She stared directly back at him, unflinching. "No, it won't. So stay safe."

"While I appear vulnerable. Got it. I should have gone to acting school."

The sergeant grabbed the door handle. "Ready?"

Sergio nodded.

"Command, this is unit two," the sergeant barked into his radio. "We are in position. Do I have an all clear to commence?"

A man's voice came over the speaker. "Unit two, this is Command. Stand by. All tactical teams for unit two, report. Are we all clear?"

The lieutenant held his radio up so everyone in the van could hear.

*"Tactical squad Alpha. We are in the corner house, Walking Boss, and we have eyes on. You are good to go."*

*"Tactical squad Beta. Eyes on. You are good to go."*

*"Tactical squad Charlie. Our street is clear. You are good to go."*

"Roger that, team. Unit two commencing." The sergeant glanced at Sergio. "Okay, Walking Boss. Remember, walk slow."

Sergio nodded. "Until the shooting starts."

The sergeant opened the van door. Sergio lowered his head and stepped through the opening, easing a foot onto the asphalt below. The cool night air sent a shudder through him, emptying him inside. Three or four blocks away, in the setting sun, the serial killer's hunting ground awaited. Sergio's heart pounded. The van door clicked shut behind him and the vehicle pulled away.

He rubbed his belly as the van disappeared around the corner. *Stay cool. Do your job.*

The voice of SWAT team sergeant crackled in his ear. "Stop watching us, Detective. Start walking toward the assigned area."

Sergio moved to the sidewalk. Each breath was a fight through his tight chest.

*Relax. Nothing's even going to happen tonight.*

"That's better, Walking Boss. You don't have to look around too much. We have people doing that for you. If you get an itch, we will see you scratch. Keep submissive-looking, eyes down."

Sergio nodded again, his heart thumping in his ears.

"Let's try the hand button. One for yes, two for no. There's a green car up ahead. Do you see it?"

Sergio squeezed the hand button until it clicked.

"That's perfect, Walking Boss. I'm receiving that signal. Try to relax. It'll probably be a long night of nothing happening."

Sergio walked onward, keeping his eyes on the sidewalk. "Let's hope so."

"Reading you loud and clear. Okay, let's take a nice leisurely walk to our control area. The next unit is lining up to make their drop."

\* \* \* \* \*

It took about five minutes for Sergio to reach the designated area. The drop off point couldn't be too close to the target zone, or the suspect might see it happening; too far away, and it would take too long to reach on foot. Buses were planned for the next phase, but the logistics hadn't been worked out yet. It didn't make sense to get off a bus with a group of people when the bait was supposed to be appearing alone and vulnerable. That could mean walking until the undercover asset was clear, and that might not be in the area filled with hidden cops.

Sergio walked down the sidewalk, keeping his eyes low and hunching his shoulders against the chill. The knot remained in his stomach. The neighborhood ahead looked dead. No lights in the houses, few lights on the streets, scattered debris.

Darkness came over it like a thick blanket, but it was a blanket that didn't shut out the cold.

*"Charlie team to unit two. A group of pedestrians is approaching, Walking Boss. We assess they are not a threat. Repeat, no threat."*

Sergio nodded. A cluster of five or six people came around a distant corner. Just from the shapes, they appeared to be too young. Maybe high school age; definitely not the killer. He worked alone and was likely mid-twenties to mid-thirties. The group scattered, a few walking off towards an apartment building, and two others heading across the street and down the next block. Within a few minutes, he was alone again.

The breeze picked up. Sergio shoved his hands in his pockets. The conscious thoughts of trying to appear vulnerable had faded; now his feet were tired enough to actually move slow without making an effort. Little by little, the dull grip on his stomach eased, until he began to think maybe the sergeant was right. Nothing would happen, and it'd just be a long night.

He took a deep breath. It actually didn't require effort. The tension in his shoulders dissipated.

He was just a solitary person on a walk. Although he wasn't quite that. Every few minutes somebody would crackle in his ear and ask him a question. He would reply by clicking the hand unit.

But in between, he was just a pedestrian. He walked slow, in no particular rush to get anywhere.

The few streetlights in the area cut holes in the darkness. Since a lot of this section of Seminole Heights was still going through the rehab phase, block after block had no lights at all. He considered options he could suggest for his next visit: pretending to be a stranded motorist with a flat tire or dead battery; possibly a jogger—except he didn't want to jog. And other people were doing that anyway.

One thought kept coming back to him.

*If we screw this thing up with any false alarms, we probably screw it up for good. If our killer sees anything unusual and goes underground, the whole thing starts over again.*

That created a different knot in his stomach.

As he turned the corner toward the safety house, one of the other units spoke in his ear.

*"Unit two, Walking Boss, be advised. We have an individual on foot coming into your sector from the next block."*

The SWAT sergeant was next. "All teams, stay alert. Walking Boss, we have eyes on the situation. Try not to make eye contact. Do not make any sudden or threatening moves. Try to remain submissive."

Sergio squeezed the hand unit.

*Click.*

"Copy that, Walking Boss. If they initiate contact, plan to walk away quickly. Bury your head. Try to convey to the other person you are walking faster because you are afraid of them. Copy?"

*Click.*

He didn't see anything. Empty street. Dark houses. Nothing he hadn't seen since his shift started. But the earpiece had a way of delivering inflection. Calm voices weren't so calm now.

*What did they see?*

"Keep your pace, Walking Boss. Slow and steady."

Easier said than done. He squeezed the hand unit.

*Click.*

The knot in his stomach grew. No street lights for two blocks. A cloud of black, highlighted by reflected illumination from the distance. He squeezed his eyes shut, trying to focus on his assignment.

*You are a resident of this neighborhood, out for a stroll.*

"Walking Boss, you should be able to see the pedestrian in a moment. He is across the street and approaching you."

*Click.*

Looking without appearing to be looking, Sergio kept his head low and strained to see. Nothing yet. He returned his gaze to the sidewalk. Weeds and bits of scattered trash went by underfoot. Another head-down glance. Still nothing.

The wind gusted, sending the trash into the street in a tiny tornado. Lifting and dropping a McDonald's hamburger wrapper, the little vortex danced and raged; then, as quickly as it had come, it was gone. The pieces of trash twitched and were still. The chill in the air remained, though. That wasn't going anywhere tonight.

He glanced down the street. In the darkness, a shadow moved. Sergio held his breath. Opposite side of the street. The motion indicated walking. Tall. Probably a male.

*This is our pedestrian.*

Moving his gaze back to the sidewalk before anyone could tell him to, Sergio watched the stranger while keeping his face pointed at the ground. The man walked with his hands in the front pockets of his hoodie. The stride was long but not fast. The pedestrian seemed to intentionally sway his shoulders, as if he was walking up a steep hill.

*When he's closer, let him see you see him, then immediately look away. Head down, submissive.*

The stranger kept coming. Sergio kept walking, his heart pounding.

*What if this is our guy?*

*If it's our guy, he will approach you. Keep walking. Casual.*

The stranger got closer. He was larger than Sergio had originally estimated. Thicker, and taller. Maybe six foot two, maybe a little more.

*Eyes down. Don't act like a cop.*

He'd have to be big to do all that stabbing, to overcome a big guy like Leo.

*But he used a gun to help.*

Sergio glanced at the hands in the hoodie pockets. Could that conceal a .38?

The man looked Sergio's way.

*Eyes down!*

He didn't think eye contact was made, but if the man had seen Sergio looking, maybe that was the time to walk faster.

*Maybe we'll speed up a little anyway.*

On opposite sides of the street, the two men neared each other.

Forty feet away, then thirty.

Sergio's head was humming. *This is how he did the jogger. Right on the street. A shot to the chest and then he started stabbing.*

*The bulletproof vest will protect you from both for a while. Long enough for the teams to get here.*

The SWAT sergeant was in his ear. "Don't speed up your pace yet, Walking Boss. Stay cool. We have eyes on. You are safe."

Sergio forced himself to take a long, slow breath and walk slower without appearing to be trying. Sweat gathered on his forehead.

The man had heavy movements, a clumping kind of stride like someone might do when they were wearing new construction boots that don't quite fit. The stranger stayed on one side of the street; Sergio stayed on the other. The sidewalk turned to gravel and then to mud. Sergio stepped around a big puddle and into the street.

"Hey, bro."

The stranger's voice cut the quiet night like a knife. Sergio didn't look up. He kept his head down and kept walking.

"I got fives and tens, my man. If you lookin' to party."

Drug talk. Could be a street seller and nothing more. And if the killer was watching, what would he expect Sergio to do? Or if it's the killer, what would work best?

Sergio halted.

The sergeant was loud in his ear. "Do not engage, Walking Boss. If it's our guy he's not trying to sell you drugs. Keep walking."

Sergio did not move.

"Walking Boss, do you copy? Please respond."

Sergio turned toward the stranger, keeping his head low and peering upward. He took a step toward the big man.

"Walking Boss, we are not receiving your signal. Please respond."

*His eyes. I want to see his eyes.*

The man crossed into the street, dropping his hands to his sides. Sergio held his ground. Sweat dripped down the side of his head and into his ear. To wipe it free might draw attention to the earpiece. He let it go, taking a step toward the stranger. "What kind of stuff you got?"

"Walking Boss, do not engage. Do you read me?"

"Just the basics right here. Fives and tens." The stranger pointed to the hoodie pocket. "But I can get something else if you want."

The shadow of the hoodie kept the man's face dark, but his features were coming visible. The

158

man's teeth were yellow and his eyes were red. Could be a drug addict or could be a killer.

"Walking Boss! Do you read me?"

The red eyes moved forward. "What you want, bro?"

The way he said it made the hairs on the back of Sergio's neck stand up. The sneer, the thickness of the voice, like he dreamed it. He fought to not react, holding his breath. His racing pulse throbbed in his ears as a drop of ice cold sweat trickled down his back.

*It's not him. It's not him. It's not him . . .*

"All teams prepare to engage. Command, ready all units. We have a situation."

Images of the victims came to him. The trucker, stabbed so many times his torso looked like hamburger. The eyes of the jogger, staring away at nothing.

Sergio swallowed hard, forcing himself to speak. "Well, I didn't . . ." he cleared his throat. "I'm just out for a walk. I didn't bring my wallet with me."

The stranger smiled, glancing up the street. "That's okay, bro. How far you live? We can go over there and do business at your house."

"Walking Boss, disengage!"

"What you say brother? Take a walk? Where do you live?"

His breath came in short huffs, like he'd just run a mile. The icy sweat seemed to stream down his back. He balled up his fists, readying himself, but forcing himself to sound calm. "No. No, I think I'm good."

The sergeant's voice strained in the earpiece. "Alert! Alert! Alert!"

The stranger put a hand on Sergio's shoulder. "Let's walk to your place and I'll get you all fixed up."

He reached for the hoodie pocket.

"Alert! Alert! Alert!"

Sergio stared at the stranger's hand as it inched toward the pocket, almost as if everything were happening in slow motion. The hand disappeared up to the wrist, the fingers grappling with an object inside. Seizing its target, the hand slowly started to come back out.

"Hey." A loud male voice pierced the quiet, coming from behind the stranger.

Sergio jumped, his stomach surging. The stranger peered over his shoulder.

The badge barely flashed in the dark, but the far-off street lights cast enough light to send the message. The undercover officer's belt held his badge; his voice held the stranger's attention. "Tampa PD."

The stranger let Sergio go. "Hey, I wasn't—"

"I know. You weren't doing anything. What's your name?"

The big man slouched. "Simon."

"Okay, Simon, I work vice in Seminole Heights. I got your name, but it's the end of my shift and I'm tired. I don't feel like spending the next three hours at the station doing paperwork on a small fish, so you're gonna walk today. But If I see you around here again, I'm running you in, you got it?"

"Hey, man, we're cool." He held his arms out, backing away. "Dude looked lost. I was just trying to give him some directions."

"Simon, it's time for you to go. Simon says go home."

"Wow, first time I heard that."

"Well my originality runs low when I work late. Get moving."

Simon walked away. The officer turned to Sergio. "You okay?"

"Yeah." Sergio nodded, rubbing his sweaty palms on his pants. The heat of embarrassment burned in his cheeks. "Yeah. I'm just fine."

## CHAPTER 18

A tractor trailer rolled through the parking lot of Dilger and Conteras' Lakeland warehouse, sending up a dirty, gray-white cloud in its wake. In the dusty front office, Jerry Contreras stood with his hands on his hips, glaring at Tyree. "Are you a cop?"

"No."

The old man narrowed his eyes and leaned his head back, staring down his nose at Tyree. "You look like a cop."

"I'm not a cop."

Jerry frowned.

"I'm not!" Tyree held his hands out. "What does a cop look like, anyway?"

The old man returned his hands to his hips. "Like... you."

Sighing, Tyree brought a hand up to massage the bridge of his nose. "Look . . ."

162

The words were about to leave his lips—*Mrs. Dilger said I wouldn't have any trouble*—but they sounded like a whiny grade schooler ratting out a bigger kid on the playground. Not exactly the authoritative persona he had in mind after the hour-long drive from Tampa. He wanted to interview the employees and have a look at the books. It seemed simple enough.

*And if he's the manager, the employees will probably follow his lead.*

Tyree had done this a million times as a deputy. Why was this one different? Because it was a friend and her father? Or because he wasn't fully comfortable in the role of private investigator yet?

Didn't matter. The clock was ticking. Like the duty officer at Tampa PD said, bodies were piling up. Cut to the chase.

"You knew Mr. Dilger and the family for a long time."

Jerry pulled a rag from his pocket and dabbed his forehead. "That's right."

"Can you think of anybody who would want to harm them?"

"Aside from every competitor and a bunch of hacks from the other political party?" The old man shoved the rag back into his pocket and put his foot up on one of the chairs, resting an arm on his knee. "Well, they want to beat him in business, but I don't know that they'd wanna put the man six feet under, you know?"

"Right."

"But if they did, doesn't that mean the rest of the family is in danger?"

Tyree cocked his head. "What do you mean?"

"There are four family members that run this whole company, and half of them became dead recently. If that's not a coincidence, the other two should get some kind of protection. Bodyguard or something."

"The police didn't say the family was targeted. I figured it was like you said. A coincidence. Just some bad timing, with that serial killer."

"Yeah. And the police are never wrong."

\* \* \* \* \*

"Bodyguard? You're as bad as the police." Mrs. Dilger sounded horrified. "You're investigating the situation surrounding my husband's death."

Tyree held the phone to his ear while poring over the Lakeland ledgers at Jerry's desk, scribbling notes on a pad with a pencil. Every few minutes a tractor trailer rolled by, making conversation impossible—and sending another cloud of dust over the parking lot where his Harley was parked. It was almost as if a gray snowfall had happened since he got there. "Did the police suggest you needed protection?"

"Yes. I refused. I can take care of myself, and so can Susan."

Tyree shook his head. "Well, Mr. Contreras had a good point. The family might be in danger. It could be something as simple as a competitor trying to get you out of the way so they can—"

"No fruit shipper is going to resort to killing people."

"It might not be that kind of competitor." Another truck drove past the office. Tyree pressed the phone to his head and plugged his other ear with his finger. "It might be a Colombian drug lord who wants a shipping company to run product to the States. In either case, you and Susan could be in danger."

"That's just Jerry and his wild imagination, Johnny. Besides, we Dilgers know how to use a gun."

"Yeah, I remember that cannon you said you carry. Still . . ."

"Fine." Mrs. Dilger huffed. "If it will make you feel better, you can be our bodyguard."

"What? No, I didn't mean me."

"Why not? You just said we need one, and you're certainly qualified. Plus, you're already working for us. Why not be our bodyguard as well?"

"One reason is, bodyguards kind of hang around with you all the time, so unless you and Susan are going to lock yourselves up in the house or sit on the back of my motorcycle while I go investigating for you, it's not gonna work."

Mrs. Dilger sighed. "Okay, you can be Susan's bodyguard. Get her back and forth to places she needs to go, and keep an eye on her while you do your investigation. I'll stay here and get one of the off-duty police officers to watch me. Fair enough?"

"It's just for a little while. I don't want you to feel like you're a caged animal or something."

"I won't. Anything else?"

"No." Tyree leaned back in the chair and tossed the gnarled pencil onto the big ledger. "From what I see, the employees loved Henry. Nobody looks squirrelly. I went through the bank statements, though. The cancelled checks aren't here. Should they be?"

"Those will be here at the house. Why?"

He flipped a big page of the ledger. "There is a series of checks for about ten thousand dollars every month that don't tie to any receipts. It's almost like a mortgage payment. And when there's no check cashed that month, there's a withdrawal from the bank in the same amount. Any idea what that is?"

"No."

"No offense, but that's a little odd for a business that isn't doing anything funny."

"We push over a million dollars worth of produce transactions through the port of Tampa every month. Ten thousand dollars isn't necessarily a lot of money compared to that. But, come to the house tonight and look at the cancelled checks. If you tell me the check numbers, I can pull them for you."

"No, I'll do it." He stood, closing the ledger and tucking it under his arm. "Who balances the books for stuff like that?"

"Henry would have, or one of the girls if Henry wasn't—" Her words caught in her throat, her voice dropping. "If Henry wasn't around."

## *CHAPTER 19*

"You do not disobey my orders! When I tell you to reply, Detective, you reply. Do you understand?" Red faced, the sergeant pointed at Sergio with one hand and held onto the bench seat in the van with the other. Veins stood out on his neck.

His cheeks burned. "I understand, Sergeant."

"You can't *want* it. That's not how it works. You have to wait for it. If you go after the perp too hard on a sting like this, you mess everything up and scare him away. We went over this."

"I felt like I had to talk. I felt like doing anything else would—"

The sergeant raised his voice. "You are not receiving me, Detective. If that was the serial killer, you're a dead man right now—because you weren't listening to my instructions. Do you understand?

Sergio looked down. "I understand."

"If you were on my squad . . ." the sergeant gritted his teeth and balled up his fist. "You'd be *off* my squad. I have run dozens of these surveillance interaction operations, Detective. Dozens." He breathed hard, his big fist falling to the bench as he jutted his jaw out and stared at the rear window.

The street lights of downtown went by, throwing odd-shaped light patterns over the walls of the van and across the faces of its occupants. Chatty and nervous on the way to the drop site, they were all silent now.

The sergeant wiped his face with his big hand. "I know you just want to help, Detective Martin. We want to catch this guy as bad as you do, and I don't have the manpower in SWAT to create the presence the mayor is demanding. And I appreciate what you were trying to do back there. Honestly. But it's my job to return you alive to your boss at the end of the shift. I'll scrub the op before I let one of my team get taken out by a perp. It's not worth it."

"I get it. Won't happen again."

"It *cannot* happen again. My people trust me because they know we bring everyone back, and we do that by staying inside the rules we establish for the operation, alright? We can't have wild cards turn the whole thing to crap because someone got an itch. The perps are enough of a wild card."

His cheeks burned hotter. "I'm with you."

The van went over the speed bumps of the parking garage without slowing down. The SWAT sergeant was out of the van before it even stopped moving.

Carly followed Sergio, grabbing him by the arm. "Let's go get a drink."

Harriman came forward with a cell phone. "Lieutenant Breitinger wants a word with you first."

The reaming from Breitinger seemed to last longer than the operation had.

"I understand, sir. I got excited and let myself get carried away. It won't happen again."

He lowered the phone from his ear and stared at it. Carly took the phone from Sergio's hand and gave it back to Harriman. She eyed her partner. "How about that drink?"

He shook his head. "I'm not much in the mood for . . . I don't think I'd be very good company right now."

She snorted. "When were you ever? We don't have to go to a bar. Kyle and the boys are camping. We'll go to my place."

"Thanks, but I don't—"

"Yes, you do. Come on. We'll have a few drinks and it'll help you unwind. Otherwise you'll be up all night thinking about this crap. Might as well think about it out loud. Maybe together we can shake something loose."

He looked away, sighing. "I don't know. Did they take the jet ski?"

"Yeah. Come anyway."

\* \* \* \* \*

Carly poured a glass of red wine for herself and opened a Heineken for Sergio. Crossing the kitchen to the living room, she handed him the bottle, then plopped onto the opposite couch. After sliding her shoes off, she grabbed a pillow and dropped it onto the coffee table, crossing her feet on it.

"Thanks." Sergio raised his beer to her.

Carly nodded, raising her glass. "You bet."

He took a sip from the bottle and set it on the table, resting his hands on his knees.

After swirling the wine around in her glass, Carly took a long drink. She closed her eyes and let her head ease back into the couch cushion. "Okay, what happened out there?"

Sergio shrugged. "I got ambitious and—"

"I heard what you told the lieutenant. Now I want the truth."

"That is the truth."

"Hey." She leaned forward. "It's me."

Her eyes stayed on his, not like an angry wife or an upset mother, but like a friend and partner who needed to know. Who deserved to know.

"Okay, I froze." Sergio glanced around the room. "I wanted it to be our guy so I could take him down, or maybe just get the thing ended, but also . . . I was thinking about Franklin. And the victims. I was thinking about a lot of stuff."

"Well, there's the problem."

"I wasn't focused."

She wagged a finger at him. "You were *trying* to think."

"Thanks."

"That's not what I mean and you know it. I mean you're a good cop and you were analyzing things when you should have been in the zone and reacting."

He stared at the beer bottle. "Maybe."

"Not maybe. Let me ask you this." She sat up, pointing a finger at him with her wine glass hand. "Did you think it was our killer? I mean inside, on a primal level, where we just react, did you think it was the guy?"

"I felt like . . ." He took a deep breath and let it out slowly. "I thought it could be something bad, but, no. On a gut level, I didn't think I was staring our serial killer in the face."

She sat back. "I've gone through a few doors with you, Marty. I won't be worried when we go through the next one, and don't you be. What happened tonight, that could have happened to any of us. Tomorrow's my turn. But tonight, if I'm wearing the wire and approaching that guy, I'm thinking it's our killer. I'll be ready to unload my magazine into him if he asked for a cigarette."

"I wasn't that bad."

"That's right. You weren't. So drink up. We live to fight another day."

"Tell that to Breitinger."

"I did." She swigged her wine. "He gets it. He told me you were off your game tonight and I told him you'd be back on it tomorrow when it's my turn."

"When did you have time for all that?"

"You took a while to get out of that surveillance gear."

"What did he say?"

"He said maybe the operation needs to slow down."

"It can't slow down! It's been—"

"Chill, partner. I told him it can't slow down, too. We have zero apprehensions and a lot of victims. Slowing down is not the answer."

Sergio eyed her. "So now what?"

"Well." She folded her hands across her abdomen, securing the wine glass between her fingers. "He said I should take you out and get you drunk. So, cheers."

Sergio took a gulp of his beer. "I should drink here more often. Kyle likes the good stuff."

"Kyle sticks to wine."

"Well, I appreciate you buying good beer in case I stop by. Last time I was here, you made me drink Bud."

"I didn't buy it. You gave us that last Christmas, as a present. I finally put it in the fridge yesterday."

"How'd you know I'd be coming?"

"Christmas is coming, Marty. There are these things called Christmas parties. I knew somebody'd drink it."

He took another gulp. "You'll need to get more, because I'm going to drink the whole case."

She swirled her wine. "That'll be difficult. You only gave us a six-pack."

## CHAPTER 20

Tyree pointed at the desks in the Dilger's home office. "May I use one of these computers?"

"Let's work over here." Mrs. Dilger stepped toward the kitchen, her frame sagging under the depression she fought. She carried a laptop and several big envelopes. A uniformed police officer sat in the foyer.

"Sure, the kitchen will work fine." Tyree followed her across the living room, equal parts happy and impressed that she'd gotten security so quickly. Taking a seat next to her at the kitchen table, he typed on the keyboard. "I want to show you something, but first—can you tell me where you bank, personally and for the business?"

"Oh, we have an account at Citrus Bank, one at the Bank of Tampa . . . one at FSCU—the dock workers credit union. Our Lakeland office uses First Federal Bank of Lakeland. That's it."

"And you are a signer on all those accounts?"

"Yes," she said. "As are the girls."

"The statements from those financial institutions come here to the home." Tyree brought up a website and turned the screen to Mrs. Dilger. The smiling faces on screen welcomed users to a bank's home page. "But your Lakeland subsidiary office deposits everything locally and then transfers the money to your big account in Tampa. Why?"

"Habit, mostly. Henry was a dinosaur about certain things." She pointed to the wall phone. Several pencils rested on top of it, and the phone's long cord dangled almost to the floor. "He and Jerry set up that account decades ago. When we grew, they wanted to keep as many local relationships as possible. It's always helpful to have friends."

"Dilger and Contreras is a prestigious account, too."

"Yes, but Henry knew people could buy their produce from any supplier. Long-time friends appreciate the service, but they really value the relationship."

"Working for an investigative firm allows me to access certain personal records not available to the public." Tyree reached over and clicked a second tab. Mr. Dilger's credit report appeared on screen. "Your husband had a few bank accounts that show a Lakeland P. O. Box as their mailing address. I'm guessing since they're not any of the financial institutions you just mentioned, you don't know about them. Which means we're not going to find the cancelled checks in that stack of envelopes, either."

Mrs. Dilger glanced at the large envelopes she'd brought to the table, then folded her hands and put them in her lap.

"Ma'am, I don't want to embarrass anybody, especially you." He swallowed hard. "But one account takes out ten thousand dollars every month, and as a partner in the business, if you don't know about it, well . . ."

"What do you think it means?" The words were spoken plainly and without emotion, an informational question like *What time do you close?* that a shopper might ask at a shoe store in the mall. Simply information, nothing more. But the body language spoke volumes. Mrs. Dilger lowered her head, her eyes not looking at the screen, as if not wanting to see the information there. She stared down at her hands, her shoulders slowly lowering from proud and respectable to . . . sad and worried. The delicate façade had evaporated once again.

A lump welled in Tyree's throat. He had agreed to help this family, not inflict pain on it. Another gray area Frank hadn't mentioned.

He reached out and took Mrs. Dilger's hand. "This could mean a lot of things. Some guys like to be flashy with money. I'm sure a shipping business might want a little cash around to grease any local union reps who are thinking about a costly dock workers strike."

"I didn't ask you that." Her eyes didn't move, still staring at her lap. "I asked you what *you* thought."

"Gambling or drugs would be the obvious choices. Or blackmail. None of those seem to fit. But I do know one thing."

Tears welled in her eyes. She blinked a few times, lifting her head and facing him. "What?"

"I don't think Henry was trying very hard to hide this, so I don't think it's necessarily something bad—so don't you start thinking that. Dinosaur or not, a bank account is easy to find. The setup with a P. O. Box is sloppy. You'd have seen it if you ran a credit report on him. Mr. Dilger never struck me as sloppy."

"He wasn't." Mrs. Dilger wiped her eyes, a bit of life coming back to her voice. "Now, take the girls. Sherry took after Henry in that way. Everything buttoned down. Whereas Susan—"

The front door slammed.

"Speak of the devil." Mrs. Dilger jumped up from her chair and grabbed a tissue from a box on the buffet table, turning her back to the dining room entrance as she wiped her eyes.

"Johnny!" Susan strolled into the room, toting shopping bags and smiling wide. "What are you doing here? I didn't see your motorcycle."

Tyree stood. "I parked around back."

"Are you staying for dinner?" She hugged him. The chilly night air clung to her jacket as she gave him a long squeeze.

The bright blue in her eyes was as dazzling as ever, but rimmed with red from crying. People grieve in different ways, and the anger she'd demonstrated the other day told him she was wrestling with the tragedy of losing a sister and a father. How she and her mother managed to get out of bed and function was a testament to their resolve.

"Actually, I'm sorry. I was just about to go." Tyree turned to Mrs. Dilger. "Ma'am, how late would Jerry be at the warehouse?"

Susan lifted her shopping bags onto the table. "Jerry works late, but he'll answer his cell even if he's not at work. Why? What's up?"

"I'd like to talk to him in person," Tyree said.

Susan cocked her head. "I thought you talked to everyone this afternoon."

"I did, but I have some things to follow up on."

Mrs. Dilger chuckled, still dabbing her eyes with the tissue. "You have to stay or take her with you, Mr. Bodyguard. Those were your rules."

Susan rushed to her mother. "Oh, Mom, are you okay?"

"It's nothing." Mrs. Dilger turned away, fanning her hand and dropping the tissue into a small waste basket. "You know it—it comes and goes, the emotions. At the oddest times, sometimes." She sniffled and took a deep breath. "I'm okay now."

"I do know." Susan hugged her mother. Mrs. Dilger closed her eyes and smiled, gently rocking the last remaining member of her family in her arms.

"Are you my bodyguard, now?" Susan faced Tyree.

Tyree shook his head, gathering his things. "Since there's a cop here, you can stay with your mom. Besides, your hair would get all messed up riding on the back of my motorcycle."

"I don't know." She stared across the room to the home office. "I could use a distraction. We all could."

His phone buzzed in his pocket. Pulling it out, he read the name on the screen. Harriman. "Can you excuse me while I take this?"

Susan lifted her shopping bags. "Come on, Mom. I'll show you what I got for the office." The ladies left the room as Tyree slid his finger across the phone screen.

He pressed the phone to his ear and turned his back to the Dilgers. "Hey, what's up?"

"I got an address for you on the boyfriend's apartment in Lakeland," Harriman said. "You got a pen?"

"Yeah. Hold on." Tyree snatched the pencil from on top of the old wall phone and pulled one of the big bank envelopes toward himself. "Go ahead."

"Twenty-two ten Eldorado Drive, Unit 142. It's an apartment near Westside Park. The manager's name is Perkins. He'll let you in. Got anything for me?"

"Maybe." Tyree glanced over his shoulder. "I'm at the Dilger's right now.

"And?"

"And I'm *at* the Dilger's."

"Oh, can't talk, huh?"

Tyree nodded. "Not until tomorrow, probably."

"Got it. Okay, later."

As he ended the call, Susan reentered the room. "Are you going to let me come with you?"

Tyree shook his head. "It's way too cold to ride on the back of a motorcycle tonight, and your hair would get all messed up."

"I need to feel like I'm doing something for them." She gazed at him with those sad blue eyes. "We can take my car. Then you won't get wet, either."

He sighed. "I'm not getting out of this, am I?"

She put her finger to her lips. "I want to help find out what happened to my dad and sister. Will you let me?"

He scratched his chin stubble. "Okay, sure."

"Thanks. Besides." She shrugged. "Mom said you're the one who made the rules about us needing bodyguards. Let me help you work the case. I'd like to be involved. I think I need to be. For Mom."

He shoved his hands into his pockets. "Okay."

"Thanks. I'll go get a car and you can tell me everything on the way to Lakeland." She turned to go, then wheeled back around to face him. "Hey, Mr. Bodyguard, do you have a gun?"

"Not yet. I'm permitted so I'll be picking one up soon."

"You won't be much protection until then, will you?"

He shrugged. "Well, I just became a bodyguard a few hours ago. It's not like I had this planned, so . . ."

"That's okay, you can borrow my old gun." Susan winked. "Mom just bought me a new one, remember?"

"Will we both be carrying?"

"Yep." She rounded the corner and disappeared from his sight. "Twice the protection."

\* \* \* \* \*

Tyree held his collar tight around his neck as he stood in front of the Dilger home awaiting Susan's convertible BMW to pull around. Instead, when the driveway became illuminated by headlights, a red Corvette drove up. Susan lowered the window and smiled at him. "Hop in."

"What's this?" Tyree asked, stepping toward the vehicle.

"My car."

"I thought you had a rag top." He ambled toward the back of the car, admiring its sleek lines as he headed to the passenger side.

"Wait, you drive." Susan undid her seat belt and climbed over the center console, falling into the other seat.

Tyree stopped. "You sure?"

"Yes." She grabbed the seat belt and buckled it. "I'm old fashioned, like my dad. You drive. Please?"

"Okay, sure." He went to the driver's side and got in, letting the knob on the side of the rich, leather seat ease him back far enough so his knees didn't bang into the steering wheel. The Corvette sat low to the ground. He'd be looking up at every other car on the road.

"The BMW was nice, but this is better." He ran his hands over the steering wheel, then grabbed the gear shift and dropped the car into drive. The Corvette purred as it cruised down the long driveway and onto the street. "So, just a BMW and a Corvette? Or do you have a different car for every day of the month?"

"Well, not for *every* day of the month, no."

"That . . . sounds like a lot of cars for one person."

"Daddy said we're allowed to have one expensive vice—but only one. His was golf. He had probably twenty sets of golf clubs for himself, maybe more. And he bought a set for each of us, too. But my expensive vice was cars."

He chuckled. "I'd say yours won."

"You'd be surprised. A membership at some of those clubs is over a hundred thousand dollars."

"Good grief, I am in the wrong business—again. So how many do you have?"

"Cars? None for long. I don't really hang onto them." She shifted on the seat, tucking a leg underneath herself and facing him. "That's really my vice. I kind of buy a nice car and drive it for six months, then I get bored with it."

"Huh. That doesn't seem like you. And I bet your dad loved that—selling a car so quickly after buying it, you lose a ton of money." He smiled at her. "Maybe you should just rent them."

"He complained about it a lot, yeah. 'Big waste of money, Susie Q.' I knew a dealer, though, so it wasn't too bad. I mean, it was bad, but not *that* bad." She turned her face to the window. "Well, yes it was. We argued about it a lot."

The long ribbon of paved asphalt of interstate stretched out in front of him as he pulled onto the interstate. He glanced at Susan. Light from passing cars showed tears in her eyes.

Her voice warbled, the tears silently gliding down her cheeks. "When I was a kid, he used to let me go with him on sales calls. Just me and him, in his old sedan. It's funny, the stuff that makes a special memory. It's not Disney World or the stupid awards or the cars. It's parking at a little lake by the side of the road and sitting on the grass and having a picnic between sales calls. Just me and my dad, eating sandwiches we got at a gas station. The sun was so bright, it reflected off the water like the pond was filled with diamonds. We walked all the way around that pond, holding hands and looking for fish. It was the best day." She sniffled. "I'm sorry for getting so emotional."

"Don't be. That's the stuff you're supposed to think of. That's what he'd want."

They drove the next few miles in silence, the darkness allowing the daughter to finally grieve. The tears were steady and strong, but no more words accompanied them. She just let them fall.

It must have been a lot, to suddenly lose two family members and also have to turn right around the next day and keep the family business running. Sure, managers like Jerry could help—and were helping; everyone pitched in. But that was a temporary fix. Over the long term, the work of the business would fall to Mrs. Dilger and Susan, whether they wanted it to or not, and if her father was planning on handing things over to the daughters and retiring, his death put Susan's workload through the roof and shattered her mother's post-work dreams. Or they could sell, which didn't seem to be in the family's plans, but with the loss of the business' primary driver, it might come to that anyway.

It wasn't fair, and the people in such circumstances were allowed to distract themselves from the pain of such a tragic loss by having an extra glass of wine or going shopping or helping look into the investigation. It gave them purpose again. The stressors and headaches and decisions about the business would all still be there in the morning.

After a few more miles, Susan stopped crying. Reminiscing a little more about the family might be risky—he didn't want her to cry again—but other good memories have a way of coming to the surface once one breaks through.

"So you went on sales calls?" he asked. "I thought Sherry did the sales."

"Ha. Dad's philosophy was, train hardest at what you're worst at. That way you have no weak spots."

He nodded. "So having you do the books . . ."

"As much as it seemed like a constant punishment to me, Dad insisted it made the company stronger. 'Can't be sloppy, Susan. Learn to run a tight ship for the day when . . . when you and Sherry take over.'" She lowered her head. "Who knew it'd be so soon?"

"Hey, listen, why don't I take you back, huh? I need to check out the boyfriend's apartment anyway. I don't know if you wanna see any of that."

She straightened up. "Oh, yes I do. Don't worry about me. I'll be all right."

Tyree glanced at the dashboard clock. It would be almost eight when they got to Lakeland. The apartment manager would let them into the crime scene, and maybe they could still talk to Mr. Contreras afterwards. Jerry seemed like a night owl anyway.

But it was equally tempting to call the whole night off. Getting something to eat suddenly seemed like a much better idea.

* * * * *

The Corvette's guidance system got them to the apartment quickly. A decent-looking place with a tall iron fence around it, the building's pleasant façade and big swimming pool didn't hint at the horrors that had happened within its walls.

The paper sign posted on the door to apartment 142 said it was a crime scene.

*For access, call manager.*

Tyree called the number on the door and went back to the car. Mr. Perkins arrived a few minutes later.

"Stay here," Tyree said to Susan. "I don't know what it looks like inside."

She opened her door. "I'm coming."

"Please. Let me look first, then I'll bring you in. I promise."

Frowning, she shut the car door.

"This way," Mr. Perkins said, walking toward the quaint apartment.

As they stood at the door, the manager dug into his pocket. "Quite a mess inside." He slid the key into the lock and put a handkerchief to his face. "You ready?"

Tyree took a deep breath and nodded. "Yep."

His training sergeant once said a good cop never gets used to a bloody crime scene, and that was a good thing. Tyree had agreed at the time, and had called upon that advice on many occasions since. He wanted the horror of one person's brutality to always stay evil in his mind, and he never wanted it to become normal. Somehow, that helped him keep his balance when he'd been a cop. Today, he'd need it again.

When the door opened, the putrid stench of stale blood hit him. It permeated the room, reeking like a broken refrigerator with old hamburger meat inside that had turned from pink to gray to green, then pooled into a festering pus. Tyree recoiled, not wanting to inhale the awful smell. He held back a cough, afraid he'd vomit if the stench was allowed to get too far inside his lungs.

"Takes some getting used to," Perkins said as he stepped over the threshold. "I put BenGay on this handkerchief."

"Yeah, sorry. It's been a while." Tyree rubbed his nose and swallowed hard, following the manager inside.

The small apartment looked like something from a disaster movie set—one that had been used for the tornado scenes. Furniture was tipped over; trash and papers covered the carpet. Everything that could be smashed or broken appeared to be on the floor. Amid the debris stood numerous marker tags from where the crime scene investigators had collected evidence and taken a photograph.

Through the living room was a short hallway that led to the bedroom. The manager flipped the wall switch. Brown-red stains were everywhere.

Here is where the real crime scene was. The floor at the foot of the bed was thick with dried blood, so dark and mottled that it was nearly black.

Dried flecks of blood appeared on nearly every surface of the room.

Tyree brushed past the manager and took a careful step into the bedroom. "Can you tell me about the guy who lived here?"

"Just what I told the police. He wasn't here much, but when he was, he was loud. I think this was just a party spot for him and another guy, and then sometimes his rich blonde girlfriend would come over."

"How'd you know she was rich?"

The man shrugged. "He didn't seem like the type to have nice things. Even this apartment seemed like a move up for him, looking at the way he dressed. Women do that to a man. Make them change their old ways. Change from the edgy stuff that attracted them to a guy in the first place. Zack Bischoff was a street hustler, a hood. That girl, she had class. Nice clothes, nice hair, nice car. She grew up with money."

Tyree narrowed his eyes and glared at the old man. "She made quite an impression."

"She didn't belong with him. They were worlds different." He kept the handkerchief under his nose. "But when he was around her, he was a different guy, too."

"How so?"

"He was nicer, for one thing. He'd wave and say hi like he did it all the time—but he didn't. Normally, he would walk past everyone like they weren't there. And he talked classier, too. Acted better. Quieter. Then as soon as she left, he'd hook up with his big friend and they'd start the trouble." Perkins shook his head. "Only lived here a few months, but it was long enough. I was in the process of serving him eviction papers."

Tyree glanced at the small desk in the corner. Burnt pieces of foil littered the surface, along with a glass pipe stained with a yellow residue. "Any name on his friend?"

"No, but ask around. Someone will know that guy. Big and bad, all tatted up and acting tough. Had a mohawk, too. A real crazy looking guy. Stars tattooed on his cheeks and stuff."

Tyree faced the manager. "A mohawk? Like Geronimo?"

"No, like that Mr. T in the *Rocky* movies," the manager said. "An African-American fella, and real big."

"Mr. T was short."

"No, he was taller than Rocky."

Tyree shrugged. "Stallone's short, too."

"Man, what's happening in the world?" Perkins frowned. "I thought Mr. T was at least six foot six."

"More my height. Five ten."

"Huh." He peered at Tyree. "You look bigger."

"Thanks, I guess." Tyree turned back to the dresser. There was a lot of obvious drug use stuff laying around, but then the owner didn't clean up before he left, either.

"No!" Susan's voice pierced the room like a gunshot.

189

"Susan!" Tyree ran to her, putting his hands on her shoulders and blocking her view of the blood-stained bedroom.

"Is this where it happened?" She twisted out of his grasp, her eyes were wide, scanning the walls. Her mouth hung open. "Is this her—is that my sister's—"

Perkins shook his head, stepping forward, keeping the handkerchief to his face. "The police were saying this—that this isn't . . . all this is from the boyfriend."

Her gaze fell to the thick patch at the foot of the bed. "Oh, no!"

She recoiled, backing into Tyree and cupping her hand over her mouth, before buckling over and heaving.

## CHAPTER 21

The killer drove past the empty houses of Seminole Heights, the glare of the midday sun bouncing off a new metal roof on a rehabbed bungalow. He squinted into the glare and reached for his sunglasses. As he slipped them on, he slowed his vehicle, observing a man walking along the sidewalk.

He cruised up behind him, maintaining a distance. The man walked with a lumbering stride, keeping his hands in the front pockets of a hoodie.

The killer put down the passenger window and eased the vehicle a little closer. Cold air rushed through the car, rustling the pages of the newspaper on the passenger seat.

Ear buds kept the man from hearing the car right away. He finally glanced over his big shoulder and stopped, a wide yellow smile crossing his face.

"'Sup, bro? You looking to buy?" He approached the vehicle. "I got fives and tens today. More back at the ranch, you know?"

The killer stopped the car and stared at the man.

"Hey, bro, if you be needin' I can supply. What can I get for you?" He pulled out his ear buds and leaned onto the car frame, his hands gripping the vinyl.

"I'm not buying today. I'm just passing through."

"You just be taking a Sunday drive, keeping the streets safe for humanity."

"That's right."

The dealer smiled. "What about keeping me in business, bro? You my best customer. I can make you a deal on that ice you like."

The killer glanced up and down the street, eyeing the bungalows and the piles of construction trash. "Yeah? How much?"

"It's been slow. I'll make you a good deal. Simon says fifty for the small bag."

The killer glanced out his window, away from Simon. "Pass. Maybe next time."

"Not sure there'll be a next time. Not out here." He patted the vinyl of the window frame. "Cops been shakin' dudes down. I almost bagged last night. All kinds of cops been up in here."

The killer shook his head. "What a pain. I hate cops."

Simon chuckled. "Who doesn't?"

Pulling out his wallet, the killer counted out fifty dollars and held it to the passenger window. Simon took it in one hand and rummaged in his hoodie pocket with the other. He withdrew a small baggie and dropped it onto the passenger seat, reaching in to slide the newspaper over it.

The killer nodded, putting the car in gear. "Nice doing business with you, Simon."

Shoving the money into his pocket, Simon turned away. "Take care, Officer."

## CHAPTER 22

Tyree waited while Susan lifted her feet into the Corvette, then he reached over and helped buckle her seat belt. Her hands and legs did the motions, but her face was pale and blank, her eyes not really focusing on anything. As he shut the car door, Tyree glanced at the apartment building to thank Perkins for his late evening help.

The old man was leaning on the door frame, holding his chest.

*What now?*

"You okay?" Tyree trotted over to the door, leaning over to see the man's face. "How we doing over here, Mr. Perkins?"

The old man waved him off, pulling his keys out. He locked the door and leaned on it, lowering his head to his forearm. "I almost had a heart attack when I saw that girl."

"What, Susan? Why?"

"Thought I'd seen a ghost." Perkins turned around, using his BenGay hanky to wipe the sweat from his brow. "The police said she was murdered. The papers, too."

"Oh, that's—" Tyree glanced over his shoulder at the car, lowering his voice. "Her sister is the one that was killed. They look alike."

"Are they freaking twins?"

"No, but in this light . . ."

The man's fingers shook as he dabbed his face with the handkerchief. "Mister, I'm telling you, when I saw her in that bedroom, my heart stopped."

"I'm sorry. I just—I didn't even consider that. I've known them for years, so I guess . . . well, anyway, I'm sorry. You okay? Can I get you some water?"

"Nah." Perkins righted himself and took a deep breath. "I'll be fine."

Tyree nodded. "Listen, you were telling me about the big tattooed guy. The one with the mohawk. Did he come around here much?"

"This isn't that kind of place. The only druggie I had was Bischoff, and I was trying to get rid of him."

"No, I meant, do you think he was local? Like, did he drive a car with out of state plates or did he ever bring a suitcase when he came over, anything like that."

Perkins stepped away from the door, heading into the parking lot. "I don't spy on my tenants."

195

"No, but you're a good manager who keeps an eye on who's parking on your property and using your pool."

"I only noticed Mr. T when he was already here. I'd see them leave in Bischoff's car, that big Caddy of his, and then they'd come back late. They knew this wasn't a good party spot. I always ended up getting complaints and having to bang on the door and threaten to call the police if they didn't keep the noise down."

"Okay," Tyree said. "Well, a guy like that will be on somebody's radar screen. I'll check with the Lakeland police in the morning."

"You know, I read that star tattoos on a guy's face means he's killed somebody. He had the spider webs down the arms and all the jailhouse tats, but it was that star stuff that bothered me." Mr. Perkins stepped closer. His voice was low, but it wasn't steady. The man had something to get off his chest.

"Sometimes it means he's killed someone," Tyree said. "Sometimes it's fake advertising for a drug dealer trying to look tougher than he is. In his line of work, that's a plus. It scares people."

"It worked."

"Not enough to keep you from banging on the door and telling them to pipe down."

"No, but . . ." Mr. Perkins lowered his eyes. "If I'd have been a little braver and stopped their crap a little sooner, that girl's sister would still be alive."

Perkins had been waiting to tell someone that, and the job fell to Tyree. It wasn't a confession, but still required absolution.

The old man shook his head. "Beautiful young thing, nice girl, polite. Her whole life ahead of her, and she's running around with a guy like that."

Sherry wouldn't have been the first rich girl who ran around with a bad boy, but usually that was to spite Daddy. Nothing indicated Sherry had been that way. And by Perkins' own admission, Bischoff was already cleaning up his act when they met.

"That's not what killed her, Mr. Perkins."

"Don't be so sure." Perkins' face looked pained with guilt. "She looked like she had a pretty good life. Now she's gone. In between, that piece of crap Bischoff got into her life. You wanna look into something, look into that."

\* \* \* \* \*

Susan sat up when Tyree opened the car door. "I'm sorry about what happened back there. I should have waited, like you asked."

He shook his head and started the car. "You're not much on taking directions."

She turned sideways in the seat and closed her eyes, resting her face against the headrest. "I just want to go home."

"Home it is then, ma'am." He pulled the car onto the street.

Traffic was nonexistent on the interstate, so the drive was quiet for miles, but pieces of the case bounced around in Tyree's head. It would be interesting to see what the mohawk guy had to say—if anything. He probably wouldn't talk. Posing as a drug buyer might yield something, but that was a stretch. Even Jerry thought he looked like a cop. No way a drug dealer would talk to him. Not unless he had a good reason or no other options.

The best bet was phone calls. The Lakeland police might be able to give him something useful, and Harriman might know more by the morning, too.

But Mohawk would still get followed up on. Something about what Mr. Perkins said rang true to Tyree. Susan wasn't a wild child, and Bischoff cleaned up his act for her. It was hard to believe true love was afoot with a guy like that. What was he after?

Susan rubbed her nose, keeping her eyes closed. "What time is it?"

"It's past my bedtime," Tyree said. "Go back to sleep."

She sat up and stretched. "I wasn't sleeping."

"Good. I wasn't, either."

"Well, that's a relief. I'd hate to see you wreck my new car."

"This is new? How long have you had it?"

"They delivered it today. You've driven it more than I have."

"Really? I feel special now."

"Well . . . you were special before."

"Before I didn't wreck your car, or before I became your bodyguard?"

"Before when we were in school. I always liked you, Johnny. I think you knew that, too."

Tyree stroked his chin. It wasn't uncommon for people in a tragic situation to do irresponsible things to try to connect with life again, and to remember what it felt like to not be sad, but his job was to keep her safe—from herself, if necessary. "You know, you don't really see a friend's kid sister as anything but a kid. And if a kid gets a crush, a nice guy . . . doesn't take advantage of that."

"You were always a nice guy."

"Not always, but I did a good job of fooling a few parents. What about your sister's guy? This Bischoff character? How'd they meet?"

"Chamber of commerce."

"They have a matchmaking service? I didn't know."

"It was a chamber meeting, or so she said. They met and hit it off. She talked a lot about him."

"Your mom gave me the opposite impression. When Sherry called the other night at dinner, your mom called Zack the mystery man or something. From what I've gathered, he wasn't exactly a chamber of commerce kind of guy."

"Sherry knew Mom would disapprove. She told me a few things, but she wasn't being secretive. It was like she was taking her time."

"So she'd know he was the real deal before she introduced him to the rest of the family?"

"Before she let Dad meet him. Dad could spot a phony from a hundred yards."

"Not your mom?"

"Mom has been more than semi-retired for a while. She doesn't know too much about the business anymore, but she still has her contacts. She was never the deal maker or people person. That was dad. He was the deal maker."

"And you and Sherry."

"Kinda. I got us a lot of deals. Booker and Foreman, now our biggest account—I landed that. A few other elephants, too. Sherry worked deals because she was supposed to, not because she was good at it. Like me with the books. If she had her way, she'd have been keeping the records and letting me be down on the docks getting contracts."

"Think Zack was baiting her? Dressing up and playing nice to cash in by marrying a rich girl? Maybe that's why she kept him away. She was still figuring out if he was legit."

"I think . . . I *wonder*, what did she want with him? Excitement? Because doing the books for Dilger and Contreras isn't exactly exciting, I can tell you that. I think he said the right things and did the right things to get what he was after. Money or whatever. I doubt he found religion and decided to change his ways. But what did *she* want?"

"Maybe it was a kind of fling for her. You get to a certain age and you realize you haven't pursued your own path, you've only done what others expected you to do, and you try out something different. A late stage rebellion."

"Are we talking about Sherry now, or you, Johnny?"

"We should talk about whether I'm taking you to your mom's house or your apartment."

"Mom's." She stared out the window. "She can't deal with this alone. Neither can I."

\* \* \* \* \*

Taking Susan to her mother's freed Tyree from bodyguard duty the next morning. The Tampa PD had allowed Mrs. Dilger to hire off-duty officers around the clock, so Tyree could head back to Lakeland whenever he was ready.

He rolled off the couch in Frank's office and dialed Harriman. "We had a deal, but you aren't being straight with me."

"What do you mean? I gave you the apartment address and let you check it out. What did you find on the letter?"

"Bischoff and his friend stink a mile away. How come none of Tampa's finest are looking into them?"

"Who said we weren't? We have a couple of guys assigned to look into Bischoff, but you don't seem to understand we have a panic in this city. The mayor and everybody else is going bananas until we catch this serial killer, so the chiefs are throwing everything they have at it. That doesn't leave a lot of manpower to check out the scummy boyfriend of a dead society girl."

"Man, you are some piece of work."

"No, I'm busy up to my ears, like everybody else around here. I wanna help. The Dilgers are important people—why do you think I let you into this in the first place? Now do you have any new information for me or not? The phones are blowing up around here again."

"Yeah, I have something on the letter, but I don't know what it is yet. I'll call you when I know more."

"See that you do. And next time, remember your manners. I don't have to share information, you know."

"Okay, Dale Carnegie. What about a contact in Lakeland vice, or are you too busy to look up a name?"

"Try Vince Barrings. He's a street cop. If he doesn't know the guy, he knows a guy who knows the guy. And get me some information for my bosses so I can justify taking your calls."

Tyree's phone beeped. Susan's name appeared on the screen. "As much as I'd love to continue exchanging pleasantries, one of my bosses is calling me on the other line. I'll talk to you later."

"Okay."

He clicked over. "Hey, Susan. What's up?"

"I thought you might join Mom and I for breakfast. Ruby made eggs Benedict."

"Man, I am really in the wrong business. I'll have to take a rain check. I'm heading to Lakeland to talk to a vice cop about some loose ends involving your sister's boyfriend."

"Okay. You can tell me all about it at dinner."

"Are we having dinner?"

"Yes. Tonight. Don't you remember?"

"No."

"That's because I just decided. See you tonight."

\* \* \* \* \*

"Yeah, I know him." Officer Barrings blew the steam off his coffee as he stirred it, crossing the lobby to where Tyree stood. "Calls himself 'Big Brass,' but his real name's Lavonte Jackson. Small timer. Runs around the State Street area when he's not locked up."

"Any chance he's at work already?"

"You'll find him at the gym on Clermont. That's where he finds his customers, and gym rats get their workouts in early."

"Done. Thanks, Vince. I owe you."

"Pay me with a collar. We work on commission."

\* \* \* \* \*

Maxx's Gym on Clermont was a real dive, but a lot of Lakeland was that way. One street had mansions; turn the corner and drive two blocks and it was run down mobile homes. One store might have been there fifty years; the one right next door had been three shops in six months. Much of Lakeland was old Florida and the old South, complete with a southern accent that folks in Tampa didn't have.

The dirty red brick building looked a hundred years old, as did the workout fixtures inside.

Maxx's was an old school place, full of barbells and sweaty guys, not treadmills and TVs.

Lavonte and his mohawk were leaving as Tyree pulled up. Switching off the motorcycle, Tyree pretended to make a few phone calls while the big man chatted out front with another muscle head. With a white towel draped around his thick neck, Lavonte flexed and talked, his wet muscle shirt showing off his workout. After a few minutes, Big Brass strutted to a big, shiny red pickup truck and fired up the engine. He put his cell phone to his ear, revved the motor a few times for good measure, then cranked the tunes and peeled out, grabbing a little air as he shot over the railroad tracks.

Big Brass was anything but subtle. The chrome pipes and big tires said "look at me." So did the thumping stereo. Whoever he was talking to on the cell phone either had great hearing or didn't care what Big Brass had to say.

Following the truck out of town to a small warehouse, Tyree wasn't able to be too subtle, himself. Even a blind driver would eventually notice the same motorcycle in the rear view mirror, no matter how far back Tyree stayed.

The truck pulled to a stop in the gravel parking lot of an abandoned feed store. Tyree slowed down and pulled over, watching. When the dust clouds drifted from around his truck, Lavonte got out and went inside.

"Hey, stranger!" Susan's BMW pulled up next to him.

Tyree's head snapped back. "Susan! What are you doing here?"

"You said you were going to the Lakeland police station. I figured I'd meet you and help out."

"You shouldn't be here. You followed me from the station?"

"Yep. You should look in your mirror occasionally."

"Well, I'm sure if you saw me, this guy did, too."

"Who you following?"

"A muscle head named Big Brass. He's a drug dealer with a mohawk. Friend of Zack's, apparently."

"You're kind of hard to miss out here."

"Even more so with you parked next to me. What are you thinking?"

"Hey, I have to do something for Sherry and Dad. Don't be mad."

"I'm not mad, but I'm supposed to make sure you stay protected. How am I supposed to do that out here?"

A pop sounded from the distance. A baseball-sized spider web appeared on Susan's windshield.

Tyree leaned toward the car and glanced at the dime-sized hole in the center of the spider web. "Hey, what the hell?"

Two more pops. Another hole appeared in the glass, and Tyree's headlight exploded.

"Get down! Get down!" He leaped off his bike and rolled behind it, his heart racing. Susan screamed. Instinctively, he reached for his service weapon by his hip. Nothing. Susan's gun was in his saddle bag. He reached toward it as a shot banged off the side of his Harley. Tyree jerked his hand back and hugged the asphalt. The next shot buzzed past his ear.

Heart pounding, his breath sent puffs of dust from the roadway. "Susan! Are you okay?"

"Yes! What's happening?"

"Stay down. You're safe in there. The engine will block the shots." Tyree peeked up from behind his Harley. Big Brass opened the truck door and started the engine.

Jumping up, Tyree flung open the passenger door to the BMW and crouched behind it. Susan lay across the seats with her hands over her head.

"I need to borrow your car."

She waved a hand, not looking up. "Take it."

Big Brass pulled his truck onto the road, pointing the gun one more time. The muzzle flashed twice and the grill of the BMW panged, sending a shot of steam into the air. The red truck squealed its wheels and roared away.

"Crap, looks like we aren't going anywhere in this." He turned to Susan. "He's gone. Are you okay? Are you hurt anywhere?"

"No, I don't think so."

"Good. You did okay."

"Johnny, what's going on?"

"I don't know, but I'm going to find out. Do you have a road service? Like for towing?"

As Susan called roadside assistance, Tyree launched a tirade at the Lakeland PD.

"Now!" he shouted. "And when you get her to Tampa, you don't leave until she's inside the house and in her mother's arms, understand? Or you'll have to answer to me." He ended the call and looked at Susan as she sat in the passenger seat. "The Lakeland cops are escorting you back to your mom's house. When you get there, you stay there. Got it? No arguments. You sit tight until I return." He stormed to his Harley.

"Where are you gonna go?"

"I'm gonna go give Big Brass a new nickname."

\* \* \* \* \*

Tyree drove his bruised motorcycle around to as many Lakeland dive bars as he could find. At the fifth one, he spotted the big red truck in the parking lot of a ratty place called Jimbo's. He rode up to the front door stoop, stepping off before the bike had even come to a full stop. Jerking the key out, he stomped the kickstand down and flung open the front door.

The hazy billiard room reeked of cigarette smoke and cheap beer. Peanut shells lined the floor. Strutting in, Tyree scanned the faces until he saw what he was looking for.

*Mohawk.*

Big Brass was at a pool table in the back, swigging a long neck. When his eyes met Tyree, he stood up. Tyree didn't even slow down.

Lavonte set his beer on the pool table, reaching for a cue stick. "You think you're tough, boy?"

"Nope. I'm just tougher than you." Tyree crossed the last few feet at a run. He heaved the butt of his hand upwards, driving it straight into Lavonte's nose. The impact shot up Tyree's forearm and into his elbow, launching Big Brass' head backwards. Tyree leaned back and shot a foot into the big man's chest. Lavonte crashed to the floor hard, sending his feet into the air.

His hands flew to his face as he groaned. Several rednecks jumped up. Tyree reached back and yanked Susan's .38 out of his belt, aiming it at the closest cowboy with a cue stick. "This doesn't concern you. Keep it that way."

The man set the stick on the table and backed away, his hands in the air.

Tyree turned his attention back to Big Brass, shoving the gun back into his belt. "You and me are gonna have a little conversation." He put one hand on Lavonte's belt and the other on the big man's collar, hauling him to his feet. "Let's go." He half walked, half dragged Lavonte across the room.

The big man held his hands over his face the entire way. "I think you broke my nose!"

"I'm just getting started." He threw Big Brass head first into the front door, banging it open.

The muscleman groaned and slid to the ground. "What are you doing?"

"Venting a little steam. I get pissed off when people shoot at me and my friends."

Big Brass looked up, his face smeared with blood. "That was you?"

"Wrong answer." Tyree launched his foot into Lavonte's ribs, sending the big man rolling over onto his back. Big Brass lay facing skyward, bleeding and gasping.

Tyree stood over him, breathing hard as he put the heel of his shoe into Lavonte's chest. "Listen, stupid. If you don't even know who you're shooting at, why the hell are you shooting at them?"

"If I was aiming at you, you'd be dead right now."

Tyree gritted his teeth. "Am I supposed to thank you? Why were you shooting at us?"

"I don't have to tell you anything, cop."

"You don't have to go home with any teeth, either, dummy. And I'm not a cop, so start talking. Or does ten years for attempted homicide sound better? Because your friends inside are probably calling Lakeland's finest about now."

Big Brass held up his hands. "I thought you were trying to steal my drop. I'm on parole so I fired a few rounds to scare you off."

"Even more reason not to be shooting at people or dealing drugs. Man, you're as stupid as you look. How's your nose?"

"I'll live."

"Not the way you're playing the game." He pulled Lavonte into a sitting position and propped him against the wall, squatting next to him. "Tell me about your friend."

Big Brass spit some blood onto the sidewalk. "What friend would that be?"

"Why are you in business with Zack Bischoff?"

"We sold drugs and did collection work for Carmello."

"That can't be all of it. Carmello wouldn't have people run around Lakeland like it's the wild West."

Lavonte shook his head, wiping blood from his lip. "Bischoff was in over his head. He was trying to swing some deal for shipping out drugs. It didn't work out."

"So a deal doesn't happen." Tyree shrugged. "That's no reason to kill anybody."

"It is when you're supposed to be doing it for Carmello and Carmello don't know anything about it."

Tyree leaned back and rubbed his chin. "So Zack is dead because he was using Carmello's name to 'buy' the company. Carmello didn't know Zack was doing that, got mad when he found out, and now Zack is six feet under."

"In a nutshell."

"Yeah, I guess scamming your boss would limit your upward mobility. But Bischoff didn't have the kind of money to buy a shipping outfit. What was he thinking?"

"He wasn't big on thinking." Lavonte sat forward, wincing. "His whole plan was to do some intimidation work and cause problems until they decided to take him on as a partner for protection. Old-school mafia stuff."

"And you were supposed to be the muscle."

"Hey, he made his plan and it didn't work out. It got him killed. End of story."

"Yeah I guess so." Tyree leaned back and sat on the Harley. "Next time we meet, I won't be this nice."

"My plan is to not run into you again."

"You're getting smarter already. How much money you got on you?"

Lavonte's jaw dropped. "You're robbing me now?"

"Shut up. How much?"

"A few hundred."

"And in the truck?"

Lavonte winced. "Maybe five grand."

"Okay, I'm taking that to get my Harley fixed. And I'm taking the truck."

"What! That truck cost eighty grand."

"I'm borrowing it. You'll get it back tomorrow. Next day at the latest." He held out his hand.

Lavonte reached into his pocket and dug out the keys. "How am I supposed to get around?"

Tyree grabbed the keys. "Try Uber."

## CHAPTER 23

On the way to his office, Tyree passed by his uncle's townhouse. The lights were on. That hadn't been the case since he'd arrived back in Tampa.

*Frank must be home. Wonder if we finally have AC and running water?*

When he opened the sliding glass door at the back of the unit, a thick wave of pungent cigar smoke and raucous conversation wafted out. Across the kitchen, a round table in the living room—accommodated by pushing the couches and end table to the walls—seated five men playing poker. Four of the men were not his uncle; another man, looking grim and dressed all in black, sat on the couch reading a magazine and flipping TV channels.

*I guess the cable's back on, too.*

Tyree stepped into the living room. Upon seeing him, Frank broke out in a wide grin. He pulled a fat cigar from his mouth and spoke to the other men. "Amigos, conheço meu sobrinho!"

Tyree waved at the group and their welcomes of *Ola*. Several didn't look up from their cards. The cigar smoke hung like a cloud over the room.

Frank stood up. "Por favor me desculpe por um minuto." The other men groaned, but Frank put his hands out. "Um minuto, um minuto."

He went to Tyree, slapping his nephew on the back. "Johnny! How are you, boy? How's work going?"

"You should know. Didn't you see the deposits? I made you about twenty thousand dollars."

"That was you?" Frank nodded. "Good. Let's talk outside."

They passed through the tiny kitchen and through the sliding glass door, into a microscopic back yard. Surrounded by a faded wood privacy fence, the entire area was less than twelve feet in any direction—big enough for the neighbor to install a hot tub, and for others to put out a few chairs or a table, but not much good for anything else.

Frank's had a rusty lawn chair.

Tyree put his hands in his pockets, pointing at the house. "Do I want to know who your friends are?"

"No. Argentinians who want to help overthrow Venezuela, but you didn't hear that from me. We're here having a small victory party."

"Did Venezuela undergo some sort of revolution I'm not seeing on the news?"

"In fact, they did." Frank took a big puff on the cigar and blew the smoke upwards. A big smile crept across his face. "We succeeded in devaluing the *bolivar* to the point of hyperinflation, just like what happened in Germany after World War II. Now it's only a matter of time before the whole government goes under."

Tyree shook his head. "*You* guys did that? You and the five guys in there?"

"Yep. Well, no. Not Amir. He's here to—well, never mind about Amir. Anyway, we had some help. But you didn't come here to talk about that. You look lost. What's wrong?"

Tyree gazed at the chilly night sky. A few clouds blocked an otherwise clear view of the heavens. "I'm a little frustrated."

Frank took another puff of his stogie. "How can I help?"

"Nothing adds up so far. Tampa has a serial killer who murdered my friend and her dad. The cops aren't doing anything, but they send me on what's supposed to be a wild goose chase—and instead I get shot at by the partner of a drug dealer—"

"Whoa." The cigar nearly fell out of Frank's mouth. "You got shot at?"

"Yeah. Earlier today. Can I finish?"

"Sure."

"So this drug dealer . . ."

"It's just, you don't seem very shook up after being shot at."

"He—the drug dealer—was . . ."

"I'd be shook up if I got shot at. That's all I'm saying."

Tyree took a deep breath and folded his arms.

"Go on," Frank said. "I'm done."

"The drug dealer is supposed to be this big tough guy, and he falls down and cries like a baby. Meanwhile, I have a bunch of mystery money going out of the Lakeland office—"

"Okay, slow down." Frank laughed. "Be King Solomon—he was the first detective. Did you know that? Before he did that thing about splitting the baby in half. Sherlock Holmes got all his tricks from King Solomon." Frank clasped his hands behind his back and clenched his cigar in his teeth, pacing around the tiny yard. "Let us suppose you are looking at a big jigsaw puzzle that's laid out all over a table. Thousands of pieces. Some fit easily, like the corner pieces and the sides. Others fit together in a little cluster by themselves, but don't seem to fit the overall picture, okay?"

"Okay."

Frank waved a finger in the air. "But! Some pieces seem to be yelling at you to be picked up and placed. Which are those?"

"I don't know. I'm not good at analogies."

"Sure you know. These are the pieces that either don't fit, or they seem to fit too easily—because they're being forced."

"Well, I'll tell you." Tyree leaned against the wall. "I got a tip about the Dilgers' company possibly doing some funny business. That might have some legs."

"Aha." Frank nodded. "What else? What's the piece that's yelling to be picked up, but doesn't even look like it belongs in this puzzle?"

"That tough guy, Big Brass. For a muscle, he sure wimped out quick. He seemed ready to tell me anything."

"Correct! Now—trust your gut. Why doesn't that fit?"

"Because a phony like that wouldn't last ten minutes in the drug business."

"So . . ."

"So it was a set up?"

"Maybe." Frank took a puff on the cigar. "Phony is an interesting choice of words. How'd you meet him?"

"A cop in Lakeland."

"That was the original source?"

"No. The original source was a cop in Tampa."

"And the wild goose chase tip came from . . ."

"Same cop. So he's my problem?" Tyree sighed. "Harriman's connected to the Dilger murders. He's like the number two guy working the case after the lead detectives. Why would he be manipulating things?"

"He might not be," Frank said. "Somebody might be manipulating him."

"Who'd go to all that trouble?"

"Somebody who's involved but doesn't want you to know their secrets. Moses said, follow the money. I'd do that."

Tyree lifted his hands to his face and rubbed his eyes, groaning. "Moses didn't say that, Frank."

"He did, right before he said don't believe everything you read on the internet." Frank pulled the cigar out of his mouth and used it as a pointer, jabbing the air with it as he paced around the back yard. "In any situation, look at who stands to benefit from what happened, or what was supposed to happen. For example, if the murders in Seminole Heights are all by the serial killer, then only he benefits, in his own sick way. But if anyone else can be shown to benefit—" he raised his cigar pointer into the air "—that opens a door for King Solomon to do some sleuthing. Now, who benefits from the death of that trucker? Nobody. The news says his only family is a grown son he hasn't spoken to in years. Who benefits from the death of that jogger? He left a young wife and two small children—who are now wondering how they're going to pay their mortgage. They have a GoFundMe page, for Christ's sake." Frank stopped pacing and popped the cigar back into his mouth, raising an eyebrow as he looked at Tyree. "But who benefits from the death of Henry and Sherry Dilger?"

"Big Brass said the boyfriend was trying to steal the company out from under them."

"Nah." Frank shook his head and waved a hand. "He's your crybaby drug dealer, so it probably can't be whatever he says. In these situations, expect everyone to have a cover story, but when you look into them, one won't hold up. Maybe more than one. Intentionally or not, the Tampa cop steered you toward what his puppet master wanted you to see, but what else do you see?"

"Ten thousand dollars a month going out the door of the Lakeland warehouse operation, and the principles of the company dying off."

"Moses is right again." Frank raised his eyebrows. "Any disgruntled employees there?"

"Not really." Tyree rubbed the beard stubble on his chin. It was his turn to pace. He walked around the little yard, letting the thoughts come to him. "There's a former partner who might want to reassert his claim to the throne. He retired once and blew all the money from his buyout. The deaths of Mr. Dilger and Sherry might make it easier for him to take over the company."

"Hmm." Frank rubbed his chin, settling into the rusty lawn chair. "But the serial killer murdered the Dilgers, so unless that was part of a big smoke screen where a deranged lunatic whacks them to take over the company and then kills a few other people at random to cover his tracks, that's not the picture your puzzle pieces make."

"Go the other way, then." Tyree waved his hand, clearing the mental chalk board. "Ten thousand dollars a month is enough to hire someone to kill anybody you wanted dead, and if you did it *during* a serial killer's murder spree, one that was already happening . . ."

A smile crept across Frank's face.

The wheels continued turning in Tyree's head. " . . . and if you murdered the victims the same way the serial killer did . . ."

"That makes a little more sense, doesn't it?" Frank said. "Now, who—in the middle of all the chaos—would think murders done in the same way as the serial killer *weren't* actually done by the serial killer?"

"The coroner. And the CSI guys."

"And their reports all go through who?"

"The lead detectives, who are too busy to talk to me."

"You know, in the ninth chapter of John, the blind man's eyes were opened, but that didn't make him able to see."

Tyree glanced at Frank. "What? Yes it did."

"Maybe it did, who can remember? I'm sure you know your Bible better than me. I have to get back to my card game. One more thing. Watch your feelings for that girl."

"Who, Susan? I'm not—"

Frank's eyes narrowed. "I saw her. Don't let your feelings get confused."

"I'm not, don't worry. I know how people get in times like this."

"Okay. Now, if you suspect your contact at the police station, go over his head."

"I can try. That puts me back to the lead detectives." Tyree rubbed his chin again. "They're pretty busy."

"Then you will have to let them know you have a piece of information they'll insist on hearing."

"Such as?"

Frank shrugged. "Tell them you found their killer."

"But I haven't."

"It's close enough to get them to return a phone call. You've figured out that all these murders are probably not by the same person. That's important, and it's practically the same thing as finding the killer."

Tyree buried his face in his hands. "No, it's not."

"Well, don't tell them that last part, then. It's still important information. You said they're busy. This will keep them from wasting time on the wrong cases. They'll want to know that."

"Okay. I'll call them first thing in the morning."

"Good." Frank puffed his cigar. "Why weren't you scared?"

Tyree glanced up. "What?"

"When that guy shot at you. Why weren't you scared?"

"I didn't say I wasn't scared."

"Were you?"

Tyree thought for a moment. "No, I don't think I was."

"See? Why do you think it is?"

"I don't know. I reacted the way I was trained to, and then I got a little animated, but I never thought I was in real danger. I was in the moment, thinking about . . . I don't know. Later, when he said he was a good shot, I believed him. It kind of clicked. So I guess I wasn't scared because he shot so many times and didn't hit us. That made me think it was only to scare us, like he said."

"You were using your instincts again. Good. Don't deny talents you were born with, even if others don't have them or it makes you uncomfortable. We evolved from cave men being able to pick out faces in the shadows because it helped us to know if the shadow was a man or a saber tooth tiger, you know? Your abilities are greater than you're willing to remember. Learn to use them again. To trust them."

A neighbor drove past. Through the open fence gate, the car's headlights illuminated Big Brass' pickup behind the townhouse. Frank pointed at it with the cigar. "What's with the monster truck?"

Tyree turned to the parking lot. "Oh. I took that off the guy who shot at me."

"Why?"

"I don't know. Just kind of thought it would help somehow."

"More instinct." Frank chuckled, walking back to the house. "Good! You're learning. We'll make a private investigator out of you yet."

## CHAPTER 24

Debating whether he was hungover or not—and whether he wanted to wake up yet or not—Sergio lay on the bed, staring at the ceiling. The light haze of morning had not crept over the window sill and into the bedroom.

*Probably about 6 A. M.*

He reached to the nightstand and pressed the button on his phone. 5:45 A. M. Throwing back the comforter and sheets, he pushed himself into a sitting position on the bed. His feet hit the cool, carpeted floor. When no queasiness slogged in his stomach and no throbbing pressure seized his skull, he decided a hangover was not imminent, and got up.

His jeans and shirt were folded neatly on the chair.

*She's such a mom.*

Scratching his belly, he got dressed and meandered to the bathroom. Two empty toothbrush holders greeted him there, a bright blue one and a bright red one. In the drawer, a few unopened toothbrushes like kids get after a dentist visit. Several mini floss containers were with them—unopened—and some tiny Crest toothpastes.

*Spider-Man or Superman . . .*

There were two Spiderman brushes, so he used one of those, hoping whoever it belonged to wouldn't be too upset at him using it. He might be "Uncle" Sergio, but that didn't mean he was allowed unlimited access to just anything.

On his way to the kitchen, he glanced at the living room. No empty beer bottles on the coffee table.

He reached past the Cheerios and Golden Grahams in the cupboard, to a box of Lucky Charms. With a bowl, a spoon, and milk, he was halfway through his second roof-of-the-mouth-destroying serving when the front door opened. Sporting a dark gray windbreaker, a sweat shirt, black yoga pants, black running shoes, and very red cheeks, Carly entered the house.

Sergio lifted his spoon. "Good morning. Out getting the paper?"

Panting, she made her way to the table and set down a stopwatch. "Very funny."

"It's still dark out. You should wear light clothing, so you don't get hit by a car or something."

"Thanks, Dad. I notice you wear stuff like that when you run—oh, wait, your only exercise is chasing waitresses."

"And bartenders." He shoveled another spoonful of cereal into his mouth. "And that is a lot more physical than people think."

"I'm sure. How'd you sleep?" She took off her windbreaker and tossed it over the back of a kitchen chair, then bent her arms at the elbows and twisted back and forth a few times.

"Great. Like I was in a coma."

"Good." She peeled off the sweatshirt and dumped it on the chair with the windbreaker. Her black t-shirt showed off her toned torso. She grabbed the dish towel off the refrigerator door handle and dabbed her brow with it, her long, dark ponytail bobbing and swaying as she moved. Leaning against the sink, she draped the towel around her neck and closed her eyes, tilting her head to the ceiling.

"How far did you run?"

"About three miles."

Sergio nearly choked on his cereal. "You aren't even sweating. How long does three miles take?"

She rolled her shoulders, holding the ends of the towel with both hands and keeping her eyes shut. "With stretching and warm down, about forty-five minutes."

"So you went out at 5 A.M.? I think I just remembered why I don't run." Sergio dug into the bowl, scooping up as much cereal as would fit onto the spoon.

"We wake up at all hours for work."

"They pay me to do that. There's a difference."

Carly shrugged, pushing herself off the sink. "I like to stay in shape."

She went to the cupboard, digging out a large coffee can. As he ate, Sergio let his eyes wander over Carly's toned shoulders and back, drifting down to her round butt and long legs. She definitely in good shape. Maybe running wasn't such a bad thing after all. Not many women had a butt like—

She turned around and leaned on the counter. His eyes snapped upwards to her face. She was staring at him, holding the coffee can in one hand and dabbing the towel to her brow with the other. Her high cheekbones were still flushed red from her run, the ponytail still swaying with her every move. She lifted her chin, slowly wiping her neck with the towel, not taking her eyes off his.

Sergio exhaled slowly, leaning back in his chair.

"All finished?"

He opened his mouth but didn't speak. She came forward and took his cereal bowl. "All finished?"

Sergio swallowed, nodding. "Yeah."

Carly put the bowl in the sink and went back to making coffee.

Running a hand over his chin stubble, he thought about asking to use Kyle's shaver and possibly even grabbing a shower, but decided against it. She'd have said yes, but . . .

She slid the pot under the coffee maker. "Long day, today."

"Long day every day, lately."

She pulled a coffee cup down from the cupboard. "We're meeting the new members of the team. Breitinger granted our request to add people."

He sat up. "Did we get twenty?"

"Almost. Ten or fifteen start with us today, I think. Mostly newer officers. More are coming next week."

"We could use fifty."

"This is a start. At least we won't be stuck on phone duty."

He held his hands up. "I take it back. If it gets me away from those phones, ten is a dream come true. What time are we doing that?"

"Eight."

He jumped up, heading for the door. "I'll be there. Thanks for breakfast. And for holding my hand after yesterday."

"Hey."

He stopped, turning to her.

"Don't think about yesterday anymore. It's officially history as of this morning. What happened in the past doesn't live on unless we allow it to. Let it be over, okay? For me." She cradled the cup, her voice softening. "Tonight's my turn."

The house suddenly seemed very quiet. She turned the coffee cup over in her hands.

*World's Greatest Mom.*

On the street, a van drove by, accompanied by the rhythmic thump of newspapers hitting driveways. As it passed, its motor faded into the calm of the blue-gray predawn.

She glanced at him, a few strands of dark brown hair framing the corner of her eyes. "I need you focused, helping keep me safe."

He nodded, opening the door. "I will be."

## CHAPTER 25

Tyree grabbed his phone and slid his finger across the screen without even opening his eyes. "Tyree here."

"Good morning, John," Harriman said. "I have a nice juicy nugget for you. You got anything for me?"

Tyree grunted, sitting up on the couch in the office. "Bad breath and a hangover. Let's hear what you've got."

"Tampa General Hospital took an emergency transfer patient in the middle of the night a few days ago. The guy was beaten and left for dead at his apartment and has been in a coma ever since. Guess what his name is?"

"Rip Van Winkle?"

"Maybe this will help. He was originally taken from his apartment and admitted to Lakeland

Regional Hospital, but TGH has a better coma recovery unit, so after they stabilized him, he was transferred to Tampa General. I guess his paperwork kinda slipped through the cracks, but the doctors think he might be coming around. He might be able to tell us who administered the beating that put him in the coma."

Tyree rubbed his eyes. "Coma . . . coma . . . Sleeping Beauty? Snow White? Who's the one that bit the apple?"

"Zach Bischoff did. Big time."

Tyree dropped the phone and jumped up, grabbing his pants and racing to find the keys to Lavonte's truck.

His phone rang again while he was driving. Susan's name appeared on the screen this time. He lifted the phone to his ear. "Hey, Susan. What's up?"

"Well that was a little less friendly than I was expecting."

"Sorry, I got some important news on the case." His eyes darted to the rearview mirror as he debated a lane change.

"Come get me."

"What? I can't. I'm headed to the hospital."

"Are you hurt?"

"No, I'm not going for me. I have to—"

"Then come get me. What hospital?"

He punched the accelerator and swerved into the next lane. Horns blared. "Tampa General, but—"

"You're my bodyguard and we're supposed to be partners on this case. You told my mom I can't go anywhere without you, remember? I have some meetings I'm supposed to go to, and Mom's house is on your way."

"It's practically in the opposite direction." Tyree glanced at the clock.

"I told you, I need to help. For Mom. I'll be waiting outside when you get here—or should we take one of my cars? I still have a few without any bullet holes."

"I still have that drug dealer's truck."

"Think that's a good idea? There could be drugs in a drug dealer's truck."

He cursed under his breath and banged the steering wheel. "Well, when you say it like that, no, it doesn't sound so smart. But too bad. If we get pulled over, you'll have to vouch for me."

"Thanks, Johnny. See you in a few."

\* \* \* \* \*

When they arrived at Tampa general, Tyree showed his identifications to the admitting nurse. His name was on the list to access the patient.

*I'll have to thank Harriman later.*

"You a friend of his?" the nurse asked.

"I'm a private investigator and he's important to a case I'm working on."

The nurse sighed. "He's not how a family member would probably want to see a loved one, is why I asked."

Tyree took a deep breath. "Okay, thanks." He walked over to the rows of seats where Susan waited. "Okay, I'm cleared to go up. Hang out here in the lobby. This shouldn't take long."

"What? No way. You're supposed to be my bodyguard. Anybody could come in here. Besides, we have to stick together. And I wanna see this guy."

"No."

"Please, Jonnny? He might be able to tell me about what happened. He was Sherry's boyfriend, after all."

Tyree rubbed his chin. "I guess I can't leave you by yourself in the lobby."

* * * * *

Tyree hadn't known what to expect when he saw Zack Bischoff, but he knew no one deserved what he saw lying in the hospital bed. Bandages covered most of him; the rest was not easily recognizable as human. Zack's beaten and broken body was a mass of swollen blue-purple bruises, with an occasional patch of undamaged skin. A thin pillow rested under his unmoving head. Wires ran from his arms to machines that beeped and hummed, ending at a screen that displayed a jagged line for each breath, heartbeat, or change in oxygen saturation or temperature.

They were the only things that seemed to move in the room.

Tyree faced the nurse. "How long will he be like this?"

"Hard to say." She glanced at the chart. "He stirred a while ago, which is why we called the detectives. They sent a guy over. He said you'd want a look." She tucked the chart under her arm. "Guess they're hoping to get 'round the clock coverage just in case."

Tyree looked at the patient. "Yeah, I guess."

Susan stepped to the side of the bed, her eyes wide. "You said he stirred. Does that mean he could wake up soon and start talking?"

"It's a long shot, but I've seen stranger things happen. Stirring can be a first step." The nurse moved to the door. "I had a woman in a coma for two years wake up one day and ask for a tuna sandwich." She shook her head and left the room.

The rhythmic beeps and low hum filled the void of conversation, but what would anyone say? Only the slow movement of Zack Bischoff's chest indicated any life at all, apart from the lines on the screen.

"Hard to believe he might wake up and ask for a tuna sandwich, huh?" Tyree whispered.

"Yeah, hard to . . ." Susan gripped the bed rail, gasping for breath.

Tyree went to her. "Are you okay?"

"I think I'm gonna be sick."

He eased her to the chair. "Sit down. Take a deep breath." He took her shaking hand in his. She kept breathing hard, her shoulders quivering. "Can you—stay here. I'll get you a glass of water."

She grabbed his arm as he went to leave. "No, I'm fine. Just a little overwhelmed at such a sight." She closed her eyes and swallowed. "I'm okay, really."

"Let me get you some water anyway. I'll be right back."

Tyree went to the nurses' station. "Where can I get some water for my friend?"

The nurse pointed down the hall. "There's a drinking fountain by the elevator, and the soda machine there sells bottled water."

"Got it." He nodded.

The short walk to the elevators revealed what he'd missed on the way in. A vending machine with sodas, plus one for snacks. Maybe a few carbs would be a good idea, too. He dug in his pocket and pulled out his wallet, slipping a few bills into the feeder. Carrying a bag of pretzels and two bottles of water, he walked back to Zack's room.

Beeping alarms filled the air.

"Crash cart, room one eleven" The nurse's voice echoed through the hall. "He's arrested. I need some help in here, stat! Code blue!"

A blur of hospital personnel poured out from examination rooms, rushing down the hallway. A strange feeling filled Tyree's gut. They were racing into Zack's room.

Susan appeared in the doorway, holding the door frame and clutching her belly.

"What happened?" He raced to her. "What's going on?"

"Oh, Johnny." She sank to the floor, her jaw hanging open. "He just . . . he . . ."

Inside the room, the doctor held up defibrillator paddles. "Clear!" she shouted. The team of nurses stepped away from the bed as she laid the paddles to Zack's chest. His blue-purple body arched upward in a massive convulsion, then laid still again. Attendants called out orders as they scurried around the bed. The wires and tubes jostled from the activity from the staff; Zack's thin pillow lay on the floor.

"No pulse. Stand by."

"Defib on monitor. No blood pressure."

"Ready with adrenaline."

"Administering one hundred CCs of epinephrine."

"We have no pulse!"

"Get ready to clear. Full charge."

"Clear!"

The body jolted upward again, then went slack. Zack's bandaged head lay limp on the bed, his swollen eyes staring nowhere.

"He's still in defib. We're going again. Get ready. Go up to 360."

"Full charge."

"Clear!"

Another jolt. Another round of medical staff staring at lines on a screen that went straight across.

"Do we go again, Doctor?"

"We're going again." She leaned over him. "Come on, buddy."

"Full charge."

"Clear!"

Zack bounced. The alarms rang solid.

"Again, Doctor?"

She stared at the screen, then looked at Zack. The lines went straight across and the beeping had become constant and unwavering. Whatever small amount of life had been in that body, it was gone now.

"No. I'm calling it. We have no vitals, no heart. He's done." She snapped off her latex gloves. "It was a miracle he lasted as long as he did." The doctor took a deep breath and dropped her gloves into a trash can. "Amanda, call Tampa PD. They're going to want an update. Patient expired at nine twenty-three A. M."

\* \* \* \* \*

Tyree eased Susan into a chair at the nurse's station. "Here, take a sip of this." He cracked open the bottle of water and held it to her lips. With shaking hands, she took it from him and drank.

"Did he . . . did you see anything? What happened?"

She shook her head, glancing downward. "Oh, it was awful. His eyes fluttered open and he looked right at me. It was like he'd seen a ghost. He started kicking, and all the tubes and wires were banging around. I—I couldn't speak. I was in such shock. Then I remembered where I was and yelled for somebody to come, but it seemed like forever. I yelled and yelled, and all the machines were screaming and everyone was yelling . . ."

"Okay," Tyree said. "Let's get out of here. That's enough hospital for one day."

## CHAPTER 26

The killer ran his hand over the side of his head, letting the short hairs of his military flat top poke his fingertips like a bristle brush. He turned his face side to side and puffed out his thick chest, stretching the seams of his shirt as he patted his firm, flat abdomen.

*Perfect.*

The low fire of excitement swelled in his gut as he moved into the hallway. He glanced at his watch. A few minutes late, but so what. Gripping his pen, he thought of the knife. He seemed unable to keep the thought of it away these days. Solid. Heavy. How it moved in his hand as the victims kicked and squirmed.

A pang of excitement jolted his belly. The knife had been the perfect delivery vehicle, allowing every twitch of the fading life to convey itself up his wrist and into his arm—into his being, his very soul. Thrilling, at such a glorious moment of exhilaration, as the kicking grew less and the power grew more, dominating and owning them, one by one.

*Perfect.*

He shuddered, forcing the memory to the side. He needed to focus. But walking down the corridor, he grew taller with each stride. The news talked almost nonstop about him. He could not check his cell phone without seeing his exploits discussed on website after website. He was unstoppable, growing stronger each time. He flexed his massive arms.

He was power.

*Except...*

The gun.

*Weakness!*

He shut his eyes and gritted his teeth, pushing the thoughts away. They came like daggers, sending shards of white-hot pain searing into his brain.

*Weakness, weakness.*

*Stop being weak. Stop being so weak!*

He stood in front of the door, drawing a deep breath. In time. The gun will go away in time. Patience.

*Soon. It will happen soon.*

He grabbed the knob and thrust the door open, glancing at the man behind the podium. Several eager faces stared at him from their seats at the long, thin tables, then they returned their gaze to the speaker.

Seats were available in the front row. Tempting. The back row, too.

*Which to choose?*

But there was no time to hesitate, to appear to not know where to sit. Indecision is for weaklings.

The front row would, of course, let him appear more eager, more do-gooder—but it would also cause a slight disruption to the presentation as he moved into a seat. The back row would be the more . . . polite move. That would be better for now.

He stepped past rows of attendees appearing to be in their mid-twenties, and squeezed his big, solid frame into the small space between the table and the rear wall. He sat, resting his elbows on the flat surface as its edge pressed into his abs. This layout was not set up for anyone who worked out.

His gaze drifted over the group. Not a lot of experience, if they were as young as they looked when he walked in. He could float right to the top, if he wanted. Some took notes. Most stared at the speaker. The man wrapped up his remarks and stepped aside for the woman to talk.

The man next to him sneezed. Someone else mumbled "Bless you."

*Sheep.*

The fire welled inside him, his disdain souring in his mouth. He had to fight to not frown. Someone sneezes, someone else says bless you. That's the program. That's what sheep do. Whatever the shepherd says.

The killer smiled. Only he knew what kind of power was truly possible to realize. Not these talkers, getting their authority from a cheap, wooden podium. Stand here and everyone will listen to you.

*Sheep.*

His heart pounded. He knew real power was on the street, and it took what it wanted.

His mind overflowed with images of the trucker, how the fat old man held up his hand and begged as he bled from the gaping chest wound. Heat roiled in the killer's gut, sending a warm satisfaction through his veins.

He moved his eyes to the speaker, but visions of the jogger flooded his sight. He forced himself to look to the podium, barely even seeing the woman as she addressed the assembly. He focused hard, the welling in his stomach surging. She moved her hands in a rehearsed manner, talking from cue cards, lecturing empty-headed attendees from behind the safety of the podium.

He gritted his teeth. He hated her. What did she know, dressed in her silly gray suit and shiny black shoes? Not power. Not what happens when . . .

A surge of adrenaline shot through him.

He saw himself standing over her as she kicked and squirmed, his knife impaled deep inside her abdomen, her wide eyes reflecting the horror she now understood as he let her body drop to the floor. As she gurgled and gasped, he lowered himself to one knee, holding the big, heavy knife up high, letting her see it, letting her know the redness engulfing it was her own blood. The fear inside her burst forth as he brought the blade down again and again and again, chopping and churning through the fabric and skin, through muscles and tendons, ripping her insides, slashing her into sloppy, wet pieces.

He shuddered, remembering the warmth of the thick wetness that brought such exhilaration. He had to know it again. Soon. He took a deep breath to quell his racing heart.

*Soon.*

As he watched, he took her in. There was no power there, only fraud. The irritation surged inside him again, becoming almost uncontrollable. He gripped the edge of the table. A cheap podium and the pretend power that comes from another sheep higher up the line, telling you not to stray from the herd. Stay in line and get a title, a podium, a place to talk to the smaller sheep. Redness flooded his vision as the throbbing in his head grew.

*Play by the rules, sheep.*

He closed his eyes, turning his head away from the others, the anger growing inside him.

*I know. Only I know.*

He wanted it. He needed to have it. The podium would not protect it.

Rage consumed him. If I had my knife right now, I could show everyone—

His breath caught in his throat as a white light pierced his thoughts and rained clarity down over him.

*It will be her.*

Anticipation swept through him. He was a child on Christmas morning, gazing at a tree filled with presents.

*Her.*

*She'll be the first. She will feel the knife with no gun first. No weakness.*

He stifled a laugh, giddy over the brilliant simplicity of his masterful idea.

*How will she twist and squirm when my blade cuts through her?*

Like a puppet on a string, his knife would send every twitch, every gasp, every shudder—straight up his arm and into his soul, to be enjoyed again and again and again.

*Will your podium give you the power to do anything then?*

She continued speaking, her hands moving, her head turning, but her words did not reach his ears.

*No gun this time.*

*She will be the first.*

He nodded, releasing his grip on the table.

*I am ready.*

He leaned back in the chair, his large frame pressing hard against the wall.

*The warm, thick wetness would cover my hands, and everyone would see. You have no power. Only I have power.*

*Only I, only I, only I . . .*

The throbbing in his forehead subsided, leaving a thin sweat behind.

*Soon. Very soon.*

He swallowed hard and glanced at his trembling hands, uncurling his fingers. Red lines crossed his palms. He chuckled, glancing at the table edge.

*Play like a sheep for a little while longer.*

Another deep breath helped drain the tension from his back, washing out of his shoulders and into the air. The hum of the overhead fluorescent bulbs brought everything back into focus.

The talk had ended. The group was leaving the room.

He pushed himself upward in the narrow gap the rear wall allowed between the table and his chair, sliding sideways to stand. The sneezer passed him as the killer slowly made his way to the door, going along with the group—with the sheep—but gazing at the victim he would claim next.

Hot residual satisfaction coursed through his veins. Satisfaction of purpose. The reassuring strength of power directed at a goal.

*Soon.*

She chatted with two men in suits and a few of the attendees. He hated her. And soon enough he would show her how much.

*Soon, but not yet.*

The urge to chuckle came over him. He shook it off.

*Power knows no fear—the power that will soon be forcing her death upon her.*

He stopped walking and watched her. She was not power. She was not authority, she was sheep. She was nothing. A talking *thing*; an *it*. Nothing more.

A tingle went through him.

*It needs to know.*

Several attendees waited around the podium, near to where the two men stood.

It moved its hands, chatting, acting like authority, hiding its lies in its dark gray suit and its shiny black shoes.

He clenched his fists, keeping his hatred inside, allowing the sheep to go first. He noted her ID badge and the name on it—the name of the victim he would soon see on the news; the name that would be splattered all over every TV station the way her blood would be splattered all over her lifeless corpse. A flash of joy shot through him like electricity as he envisioned the matted hair, the still, open mouth—and the dead, unmoving eyes that gazed into the black void, a thin line of red slowly trickling down the side of her face.

He glanced once more at the ID badge, to get the name right, and then smiled and held out his hand.

"That was a terrific presentation, Detective Sanderson."

## CHAPTER 27

When the last of the attendees had left, Breitinger turned to Carly, speaking in a harsh whisper. "Hey." When she didn't respond, he snapped a finger, jolting her from her daze.

Breitinger frowned. "What the hell was that?"

Carly blinked. "I, uh . . ."

"You were fine for a few minutes, then a latecomer walks in and you drift off—and then come back all rigid and flat. What gives?"

"She's just a little tired, boss." Sergio stepped up next to her, taking her arm. "We were up all night working the case. She's okay. Just no sleep. Like me."

"She'd better be okay." Breitinger headed for the door, then stopped and let out a big sigh. "Look, I get it. This serial killer has us all on edge, myself included. Get some coffee. We have a lot riding on this."

Sergio jumped to her side. "Yep. Got it. No worries." When the lieutenant had gone, he faced Carly. "Hey, are you doing okay?"

She shook her head, looking down. "I don't know. He just . . . made me lose my train of thought."

"Who, the big commando cop?"

"He gave me the creeps. And then he wanted to come shake my hand." She shuddered.

"He has something to prove," Sergio said. "And so do you. Keep your spidey sense in check, would you? He's here to help. He'll be answering phones."

"Right." She folded her arms across her chest. "Think that was okay, saying we'd give the phone squad unprecedented access? I didn't run it by Breitinger first."

"He didn't seem to care."

"What do you think?"

"I think if we're lucky, one of these newbies will catch a detail we've been missing."

She frowned. "I hear a 'but' coming."

"But I wouldn't have done it. It's a gutsy move, though, and if it works out, you're a hero to Breitinger and the mayor and everyone else. If it doesn't work out, you're on phone duty the rest of your career."

"They have to know what we're looking at. The public has details, but these guys need to know the inside scoop. Otherwise an important connection might get missed."

"Or leaked. It's a dangerous move. Some cops have been known to tip off the press on occasion. Or they might just brag to their friends about stuff they know that's not in the news. It happens."

"Yeah." She stared at the whiteboard. The names of the victims were still on it from the other day. "The killer practically has us on the ropes. It's a chance we'll have to take."

\* \* \* \* \*

The recruits poured coffee in the break room, chatting amongst themselves. Officer Davenrod grabbed a coffee pot and a mug. "So whose team is the big dog around here?"

Another officer pointed toward the desk the team leaders had gathered around. "None of the team leaders is much beyond us in seniority. They're mostly volunteers, too. But that guy Harriman works closest to the lead detectives."

"Harriman, huh?" Davenrod blew on his coffee. "Thanks."

"Huddle up." Team leader Rodriguez held up her hand. "We'll each be working with five of you, with new teams coming next week for the other team leaders. If I call your name, come with me." She rattled off the names and the group separated, half of them moving with Rodriguez to the other side of the room, to a small cluster of desks. "This will be our work area for now."

"Ma'am." Davenrod raised his hand. "Do you mind if I work with Officer Harriman? We're old friends."

She hooked a thumb over her shoulder at the other group, not looking up from her clipboard. "Makes no difference to me. Have at it. We had someone call out sick. I'll take that one on my roster tomorrow when he reports."

"Thank you."

She narrowed her eyes and glanced sideways at him as he walked off, then addressed her team.

Davenrod walked back toward Harriman's, standing at the perimeter. "Excuse me."

Harriman stopped his speech. "Yes?"

"Sorry to interrupt. She said I was supposed to be in this group."

"Oh. Okay." Harriman scribbled on his roster, glancing at the officer's ID badge. "Okay, Davenrod. Welcome aboard." He turned to the group. "As I was saying, we will be taking inbound calls and categorizing them after we make a preliminary assessment. Go ahead and grab a desk. One of the tech people will be by in a few minutes to explain how to log the calls and most importantly, how to put them on hold without hanging up."

The group laughed. Harriman tucked his clipboard under his arm and went into the break room. Rodriguez was pouring creamer into a cup of coffee. "That guy is a friend of yours?"

"Who?" Harriman asked, grabbing a mug.

She stirred her coffee. "Davenport."

"Daven*rod*. And no. I never met him before."

"Huh. He said you were old friends. Guess some guys can't handle female authority."

Harriman poured a cup of coffee. "I guess."

* * * * *

The killer settled into a chair by a window. "Looks like we're going to be working next to each other for a while. What's your name?"

"Don Archer," the officer said. "I'm hoping this stint will get me some brownie points and help me climb the ladder. What about you?"

"I hear you." The killer nodded. "Can't say I'm fired up about answering phones and logging data, but this serial killer case is pretty interesting. Doing this is like getting the inside scoop. Who knows what kinds of stuff we'll learn, you know?"

Archer extended his hand. "I didn't get your name."

The killer smiled, shaking Officer Archer's hand. "Ken Davenrod."

## *CHAPTER 28*

Tyree climbed into the big red truck and floored the accelerator, flying out of the Dilger's driveway with the wheels squealing. Susan would be safe with her mother and the security detail—again—but some things needed to be added up, and there was only one place to do that.

For whatever reason, the quiet town of Lakeland had turned into quite the hotbed of intrigue lately. Murders, drug dealers getting with socialites, extortion plans, strange payoffs by legitimate businesses—and a lot of people not coming forward about any of it. If Mr. Dilger was paying ten thousand dollars a month to someone, it was safe to bet they'd come looking for their next installment. And as a smart businessman, he was certain to get something in return for his $120,000 annual expenditure. Meanwhile, with Henry Dilger gone,

Jerry Contreras would be in a prime position to launch a hostile takeover against poor Mrs. Dilger.

*Not on my watch.*

He drove straight to Clermont Street in downtown Lakeland, screeching to a stop in front of Maxx's Gym. Jumping out of the truck, he threw open the door to Maxx's and stormed inside.

Big Brass was standing in the back with a towel around his neck, chatting with a few other muscle heads. A large bandage covered his nose and both eyes were black. "Don't come busting in here like you own the place. I will mess you up."

"Yeah?" Tyree smiled. "Like you did the other day? How's that nose? Still broken?"

"Don't press your luck, cop." Big Brass squared up his shoulders and faced Tyree.

"Relax, Lavonte. I'm just returning your truck." Tyree tossed him the keys. "And I'm not a cop."

"Huh. I thought I'd never see it again."

"I need a favor. Come talk with me outside."

Big Brass frowned. "Why would I do you a favor?"

"Maybe because I can still nail two attempted homicide charges on you, plus parole violations for carrying a gun."

"You're in luck." He flexed his arms and yanked the towel off, dropping it into a bin. "I was just stepping out to get a bottle of water from across the street."

Tyree nodded. "Lucky me."

One of the other muscle heads pointed to the front desk. "Max got bottles of water for sale right here at the counter."

Big Brass whipped around. "Who asked you!"

The man shrunk, putting his hands up. "Hey, you right. That stuff across the street is way better."

He followed Tyree outside, squinting in the bright morning light. "So, what up?"

"Like I said, I'm returning your truck." Tyree stepped to the vehicle. "But I need a lift."

Big Brass folded his arms and shook his head. "Get yourself an Uber, chump."

"I did—you. I need you to drive me to the warehouse for Dilger and Contreras."

"Because if I don't, you'll make a call to my parole officer?"

"Something like that. Let's go." He stepped to the passenger door. "You drive."

"Oh, it's gonna be like that? Getting all Miss Daisy up in here?" He walked to the driver's side. "Gotta be putting down the black man."

Big Brass got in and slammed the door.

"You gonna be like this the whole way?" Tyree asked.

Lavonte bobbed his head, firing up the big truck. "Oh, I am just getting started."

"Great. Well, can you talk and drive? Head north to Tahoe Street and—"

"Hold onto your butt." He squealed the wheels and sent the truck rocketing down Clermont Street. Tyree quickly grabbed for the seat belt.

As they approached the Dilger and Contreras warehouse, Lavonte pulled to the side of the road.

"What gives?" Tyree asked. "It's a little further up the road."

"I figured you kept my truck because you were doing some kind of stake out or something." Lavonte put the vehicle in park, resting his wrist over the top of the steering wheel and leaning against the driver's door. "Didn't wanna be recognized on that Harley of yours, so you're going incognito. What's the plan? Fill me in."

"You watch too much TV. I needed a ride. That's the plan."

"Really? That's it?"

"Pretty much. Wanna drive up to the building?"

Lavonte dropped the shifter into drive. "Man, I thought this was going to be way more exciting."

"Maybe the guys inside found a stray kitten, Lavonte. You can have a look while I talk to Jerry Contreras. I've already had enough excitement for one day."

Inside the dusty lobby, a worker paged Jerry Contreras over the intercom.

*Old school is right.*

Arms folded across his chest, Big Brass nudged Tyree. "Think they got drinks here? You still owe me one bottle of water."

"I don't owe you anything." Tyree glanced around. "It's a safe bet they don't make the employees work until dehydration sets in. I think there's a break room down the hall."

"Okay. I'm gonna go check it out."

"You do that." Tyree debated sitting on one of the dusty lobby chairs, deciding against it. Jerry appeared a few moments later.

"Is there a place we can talk?" Tyree held his hand out to Jerry. "I'd like to ask you a few questions."

Jerry folded his arms. "Suppose I don't want to talk?"

Big Brass came back into the lobby, sipping a bottle of water. Jerry glanced at him. "Is he supposed to scare me?"

"No, not at all," Tyree said. "My friend is looking for stray kittens. I'm looking for the recipient of ten thousand dollars a month from this outfit."

Jerry's eyes went wide. "Hey, quiet down. Don't talk about that in here." He moved to the door, waving his hand for Tyree to follow him. "Come on, let's talk outside."

A faded picnic table under an old oak tree provided a place to talk. The big trucks rolled by every few minutes, hauling fruit and other produce to grocery stores around the state, or bringing in new shipments from the docks.

"I don't get it." Tyree threw a leg over the wooden bench seat and lowered himself onto the faded, gray surface. "Why did you and Henry build such a big warehouse operation all the way out here when you already had one in Tampa?"

"Distribution." Jerry took a seat across the picnic table from Tyree, digging a pack of cigarettes from his shirt pocket. "The headquarters of one of the largest grocery chains in the United States is five miles from here. Henry was a smart man. He knew about building relationships."

"So." Tyree leaned forward, resting his arm on the table. "What was the relationship behind the ten thousand dollars a month?

Jerry looked down, shaking his head. He shook a cigarette out of the wrinkled pack, lighting it and taking a long drag. "Look, I know you're helping the family and all . . ."

"Was it extortion? I heard a local drug guy was trying to muscle in on—"

"Oh, that's nonsense. Henry was too well connected to fall for a scheme like that."

In his gut, Tyree didn't really believe blackmail was behind the payments. A blackmailer was unlikely to keep the payments the same, and for such a long period of time. They'd demand an increase in the amount after a while, once the hook was set.

"Okay, so what was it then?"

The old man sighed, his frame sagging. "Henry was a good man. Maybe too good. He helped me, and he helped a lot of other people in the community." Jerry's eyes scanned the horizon, then fixed on Tyree's. "Don't go trashing the man now that he's gone."

"I'm not. I just want to—"

"You keep asking that question, and you'll open up some hurt." Jerry's face turned red. "If you want to help the Dilgers, you stop asking about that and just go back to wherever you came from."

"I can't do that."

"Why not?" The old man slammed his hand down on the table. "What's so important that it's worth ruining a man's reputation over? When he never—when he did his level best to fix a mistake?" Jerry stood up, shaking his head and stomping back toward the warehouse. After a few paces, he turned around. "He was a good man."

"Mrs. Dilger hired me to look into things for her."

"Not for that, she didn't! If you're gonna dig all that up, you ain't gonna do it with my help. Henry was my friend. And his wife, she—she . . . you just go on. I got work to do."

Tyree stood. "Listen, I'm sorry . . ."

"If you care about these people, you go back to where you came from and leave this alone. You aren't gonna like where it ends."

\* \* \* \* \*

Tyree found Big Brass behind the warehouse, surrounded by a few workers. "I'm telling you, this stuff will get you big in half the time." He flexed his arms. "Look at these guns."

"Lavonte," Tyree said. "We're leaving."

He pointed to one of the men as he walked away. "You got my number. You text me and I'll hook you up."

257

Tyree walked to the truck. "Don't make me add selling drugs to your list of parole violations."

"That was vitamins, baby. All legal."

"Uh huh."

"Hey, it's got the same markup as weed and way less police interference. And it's mostly legit."

"Mostly?"

"Well, I cut the stuff after the first round, so they see a result but then they gotta buy more." Big Brass smiled. "It's just business, you know. Speaking of business, how'd it go with the old guy back there?"

Tyree shook his head, reaching the truck. "I don't think he's up to anything. I think he's what he appears to be."

"What's that?"

"A loyal friend of the family and a hard worker." He glanced at the warehouse. "He's no schemer trying to weasel the operation out from Mrs. Dilger."

"No?" Lavonte leaned on the hood of the truck. "How can you be so sure?"

"I don't know . . . Mr. Dilger saves Jerry's life, and Jerry turns around and kills him? Or steals the company back? I don't buy it. From what I see, he's not in a position financially to take over, and he sure doesn't have the attitude of someone who's trying to be a big operator. He's not the guy. He's not where this thing leads."

"Where does it lead?"

"Next, it leads to the bank." Tyree opened the door and climbed into the truck. "Start driving."

"Man." He got into the vehicle. "I thought this was a one stop gig, not an all-day taxi service."

"Just a few more stops, Uber."

"A few!" Big Brass started the truck. "I hope you got some money for gas. This buggy eats it up."

"Sorry."

"Well, start thinking about a place for lunch. Big Brass is getting hungry."

Tyree leaned over and pointed. "It's that little pedal on the floor. You press it with your foot and the car goes."

"Man, you shouldn't mess with people when they hungry." Lavonte put the truck in drive. "That ain't right. Gotta get me a burrito or a chicken bake from Costco. Something."

* * * * *

At the bank, Tyree took his driver's license out of his wallet and shoved the ID into the front pocket of his jeans. Big Brass opted to stay in the truck—under the agreement he wouldn't attempt to do business in the parking lot. He cranked up his tunes and made phone calls while Tyree put his wallet in his rear pocket and went inside.

The bank counter was open air; the kind without the thick glass that had long been used to deter bank robberies. Customer satisfaction surveys indicated people preferred dealing with the tellers face to face without the bulletproof glass, and since most financial theft took place online, the banks complied. This branch had recently been redone. New chairs adorned the spacious lobby, with an old-time popcorn machine next to the water fountain and restrooms. The smell of fresh popcorn and butter filled the air. A few bags rested on the machine's tray, so Tyree helped himself, grabbing a bag and tossing a few pieces of popcorn into his mouth, wondering if he should take some out to the starving Lavonte.

The first teller to come available was a middle-aged woman with short brown hair.

"Ma'am, I need a little help, please." Tyree covered his mouth and coughed. "Excuse me. Got a piece of popcorn going down sideways." He pulled a bank statement out of his pocket and handed it to the teller. "I've misplaced a few cancelled checks and I was wondering if you could look them up for me."

"Certainly." The woman smiled, typing on her keyboard. "No problem at all."

He set the popcorn bag on the counter and reached into his pocket, flipping his phone to silent, then eased it out. Keeping his hand below the counter, he opened the camera app.

"Thank you." He handed her a piece of paper with a list of check numbers on it, then reached into the bag on the counter and put another piece of popcorn into his mouth. "And the lost checks are right here." He smiled again. "I don't know if I could work here with a popcorn machine. I'd be eating it all day long."

"It's a constant battle, but don't you love the smell?" She glanced at the statement and the list, then typed some more, finally scrolling with her mouse. "Here they are. I'll just need to see your ID."

"Of course." He pulled his wallet out of his back pocket and placed it on the counter, eating another piece of popcorn. "I do love that smell. I don't know how you resist it."

As he opened his wallet, he coughed again, knocking the wallet and the popcorn bag off the counter. They landed at the teller's feet, popcorn scattering everywhere. "Excuse me!" he said. "Oh, I'm sorry." He coughed again, harder this time, covering his mouth.

She bent down to retrieve the wallet. "Would you like some water?"

With her distracted, Tyree held his phone in front of her screen and snapped a picture, withdrawing his hand before she stood up. He cleared his throat a few times as he slipped the phone back into his pocket. "Yes. Good idea. Excuse me one second."

He picked up his paperwork and stepped to the water fountain. The teller looked down and moved popcorn debris with her feet.

Tyree stood at the fountain with his back to the teller, pulling the phone from his pocket. A clear picture of the back of a check was on his screen, along with the driver's license of the person who cashed it.

He turned to the cashier. "Ma'am, looks like I didn't bring my ID with me. I'll have to come back." He waved at her and headed for the door. "Thank you for the popcorn."

\* \* \* \* \*

In the truck, Tyree stretched the image to make out the address on the license.

"How'd you get that?" Lavonte asked.

"Everything's digital these days. If the bank cashes a check from someone without an account, they take a shot of the ID, too."

"How'd you know the person didn't have an account at the bank?"

"It was a guess, but it seemed likely. If you're taking that much money from people who don't want it known, you probably wouldn't do it at a bank where *you're* known. Where is . . ." he held the phone closer to his face. "Maplewood Drive?"

\* \* \* \* \*

The neighborhood was on the north side of town; a newer subdivision, with neatly mowed lawns and houses with nice paint. No chain link fences kept big dogs back, and the street wasn't filled with cars that had seen better days.

Tyree shook his head. "This is not what I expected."

"What did you expect?"

"Crappy houses and crappy cars, dirt lawns, peeling paint and fading fences—like a drug dealer's neighborhood." He smiled at Lavonte. "No offense."

"I suppose your place look like the Ritz, all done up nice over in Crackerville."

"Actually, my place is a couch in an office park."

"Then don't be throwin' stones." Big Brass stopped the truck. "Looks like this is the address right here. You want me to come in with you?"

"For what?"

"Backup, dude. In case something goes down. You don't know this area and neither do I."

Tyree glanced at the freshly cut lawn and the butterfly chimes hanging from the mailbox. "I think I'll be all right. You can wait here."

"You sure do order me around, don't you?" Lavonte folded his arms and turned his face to the window.

"I'm sorry. Would you like to come up to the house?"

"What the hell would I wanna come up to the house for?" He held up his phone. "Man, I got business to do. Get going."

Tyree crossed the lawn and knocked on the front door. Nothing about this place said drugs or blackmail or murder. There was nothing sinister about it at all.

The woman who came to the door looked to be in her later 20s or early 30's, just like the image on the license. Also not a sinister-looking type.

Quite the opposite. She looked very middle class and normal.

The woman opened the door, staying half hidden behind it. "Yes?"

Tyree smiled. "Ma'am, I'm a private investigator hired to look into a matter that might involve you." He glanced at the image on his phone. "Are you Lauren Vasquez?"

Her eyes went to the big red truck. "Oh, no!" She stumbled backwards as her face went white. Tyree looked over his shoulder at Lavonte. The man's jaw hung open, his eyes wide.

"No! No!" The woman leaped forward, throwing herself into the door and slamming it shut.

"Ma'am, wait," Tyree said to the door. "What is it?"

Behind Tyree, Big Brass peeled out, squealing his wheels and sending smoke up from the tires as he sped away.

"Go away!" the woman screamed. "I'm calling the police."

"Call them, I don't care," Tyree said. "Just tell me what's going on. Why did you slam the door when you saw that guy?"

"Clear out! I have a gun!"

He frowned, staring at the front of the house. "Yeah, well congratulations." Standing on his tiptoes, he peeked through the little window in the door. The woman was in the hallway, coming at him with a gun pointed straight ahead. Tyree whipped his head back. "Hey, don't start—"

Three loud blasts filled the door with three big holes. Splinters flew everywhere as Tyree leaped off the porch and into the bushes. "Cut it out! I surrender!"

She threw the door open and pointed the gun at him, holding it with two shaking hands. "I'll kill you, I swear!"

Tyree raised his hands. "I believe you. Can you hold off long enough to tell me what's going on?"

"You sure know what's going on." She shifted on her feet, regripping the gun. "You and your friend."

"Who, the guy in the red truck? Lavonte's not my friend. I just met him yesterday. What did he do?"

"He murdered my boyfriend."

Tyree frowned. "Lavonte did?"

"Lavonte, Big Brass—whatever you wanna call him. He did it and you know he did it." She jabbed the gun toward Tyree as she spoke, gritting her teeth. "I oughta kill you right now, and don't think I won't. Y'all ain't gonna murder me the way you done Zack."

*Zack? Zack was her boyfriend?*

Tyree kept his hands raised. "Well, I didn't kill anybody, and I'm getting awful tired of people out here shooting at me. First Big Brass and now you. I'm starting to feel unwelcome in Lakeland."

She narrowed her eyes. "Lavonte shot at you?"

"Yesterday. Does that change things?"

"How come he's shooting at you if y'all are working together?"

"Well there you go, we must not be. Like I said, we just met yesterday. He thought I was trying to swoop in and steal his drug stash out from under him or something. What makes you think he killed Zack?"

She licked her lips, her eyes darting to the ground.

"Look, Lauren is it? My arms are getting tired and I'm kinda getting violated by a broken piece of shrubbery." Tyree winced. "Do you mind if I get out of the hedges and maybe sit on the porch step? You can keep the gun on me."

Lauren regripped the gun. "Okay. But one false move—"

"Yeah, yeah. I'll get up real slow."

"Okay." She shifted on her feet again.

Tyree motioned her away with a hand. "You should stand back a little so I can't try anything, like grab the gun from you."

She stepped back.

"A little more."

She took another step backwards.

He got up, brushing leaves and grass from his clothing. "Kinda new at this, aren't you?"

"I just got this when I heard Zack got murdered." Lauren shrugged, lowering her eyes. "I knew it was all gonna go bad. We was in over our heads. Knew y'all would come for me soon, so I got a gun."

"Well, you got a doozie. That thing put three baseball-sized holes in your door." He smiled. "I'd hate to think of what I'd look like if you could shoot."

Her shoulders sagged, tears welling in her eyes. "What am I gonna do?"

"For starters, you can put that thing away before you hurt somebody." He nodded to the porch step. "Then you and I can have a nice chat."

"I don't know nothin' but what I done told you."

Groaning, Tyree lowered himself onto the step. She sat next to him.

"How long had you and Zack been dating?"

"Just over seven years."

"Long time. So you knew the kind of stuff he was into."

"Sure." Lauren wiped a tear from her cheek. "I knew about him dealing drugs, and cracking heads for Carmello. Some other stuff." She sniffled. "But he was leaving that life behind."

Tyree took a deep breath, gazing at the road. "They always are, but they never do."

She hung her head. "Now Zack's dead, and Lavonte did it. Carmello had him killed, simple as that. Make an example so nobody else gets ambitious."

"Nothing's easy." Tyree pulled out his phone. "If you don't mind, I'm going to sit here and rest a moment while I request an Uber and let my heart settle back into my chest, then I need to go have another little chat with Lavonte."

"Sure. I'll bring you a glass of sweet tea."

"Lauren, if you're innocent in all this stuff, you shouldn't have anything to worry about."

She looked at him with red, swollen eyes. "Is that how it works where you live?"

* * * * *

Lavonte's truck was back at the redneck bar when Tyree found it again. He got out of the Uber, asked the driver to wait, got another *hello* as a reply, and then watched as the car pulled away from the curb and drove away.

"Well, great."

The place was nearly empty, but a few guys were hanging around in the rear corner.

"Man." Lavonte lowered himself over the billiard table, a pool cue in his hand, lining up his shot. "You're like a fly, buzzing around my head."

Tyree made his way to the back of the bar. "A fly on a piece of crap."

Lavonte glared at Tyree. "Why you gotta be like that? I thought we was getting on."

"That was before you left me stranded back at the O. K. Corral." Tyree picked up the cue ball and tossed it over his shoulder without looking. "We need to talk."

Lavonte stood up. "I think we're done talking."

A few of Lavonte's posse crowded around.

"We can talk now," Tyree said. "Or I can take you apart and then we can talk. Your choice."

"You think you can take me?" A smile crept over Lavonte's face.

"I'm willing to bust every bone in both hands trying to find out. What about you?"

Big Brass chuckled. "You talk some mean trash—but can you back it up?"

"We've already been down this road."

"Have we? Maybe I let you take me down when you came at me yesterday. Ever think of that?"

"I did. I think you folded, too." His eyes narrowed. "But I'm still here, aren't I?"

Lavonte stared at Tyree, outnumbered but unblinking and unmoving, then set down his pool cue. "Okay." He motioned to the door. "After you."

As Tyree turned to go, Lavonte grabbed the pool stick with both hands and swung hard at Tyree's back.

Tyree dropped to one knee and lowered his head, grabbing the stick as it went by. He yanked it forward, pulling Lavonte off balance and sending him face first onto the floor. His boys stepped forward, but Tyree stopped them with a glance.

Standing, Tyree took a deep breath and poked Big Brass in the ribs with the pool cue. "Are we going to play nice, now?"

Lavonte lay face down, groaning as he put his hands to his face. "Man, I think you broke my nose again."

Tyree hauled him onto a bar stool, looking at the nose, holding Lavonte's chin and moving his face from side to side. "No, it's okay." He sat down next to him and put his elbow on the bar. "Why'd you skip out on me? Back at Laura Vasquez's place?"

Lavonte's eyes widened.

"Yeah, she and I talked—after she got done trying to use me for target practice. Turns out you two knew each other. Why didn't you tell me?"

"I didn't know that was her place."

"You were partners with Zack for all that time and you never saw his girlfriend's house? Come on. She thinks you killed Zack, too."

"I'm telling you straight, man. I never been there and I never killed Zack. Why would I go to her place if I did?"

Tyree eyed him for a moment, then swung around on the bar stool and rested both arms on the top of bar. "Okay." He reached for a bowl of peanuts.

Lavonte blinked. "That's it?"

"Yep." Tyree shelled a peanut and popped it into his mouth. "You sold me. If you were Zack's killer, you'd have offed me a long time ago. You had plenty of chances. And you'd have definitely done it before driving me to his girlfriend's house in your big red truck."

"Well . . . I did shoot at you."

"I'm not forgetting that." Tyree smacked the peanut shell dust off his hands.

Lavonte put his elbows on the bar. "You're very trusting."

"Let's not push it. We still need to talk. I'm probably the only reason you're still alive."

"How so?"

"For starters, I'm a witness to whatever happens to you—as long as I'm actually with you. Somebody killed Zack Bischoff. It's unlikely that Carmello did it himself. Guys like him delegate stuff like that. It would have been your job, especially with you two being partners. That's what Lauren thinks. On the other hand, if Carmello offed Zack and didn't use you to do it, it's probably because he thinks you were in on the scam—and that means somebody's probably looking for you right now. That hasn't happened because I've been around, and they either don't want a witness or don't want too big of a mess, so they're waiting until I go away. Either way, Carmello's very unlikely to believe your story, whatever it is."

Tyree leaned back and placed a hand on his knee, eyeing Lavonte. "Even if you're as clean as the driven snow and you tell him the truth, he wouldn't know for sure. Would he take the risk of keeping you around? I wouldn't. Now, with the police, you go to jail. But Carmello probably doesn't like his subordinates acting on their own, so whether the police get involved or not, Carmello is probably going to put you in a grave." He leaned forward. "That, or there's something else you can tell me. It all depends on what Carmello's thinking. How long you wanna wait to see what he decides?"

Lavonte's eyes were distant. He shook his head. "He's not a patient man."

"I'm surprised he waited this long. Maybe he knows something I don't."

Big Brass looked around the room and lowered his voice, leaning close to Tyree. "We should probably stick together a while longer—I mean, for your sake. You could probably use some help with this Lakeland case."

"How generous of you, Lavonte." Tyree grabbed another peanut. "As it happens, I could use some help."

"There we go. We'll be partners."

"More like temporary driver." Tyree clapped the peanut dust off his fingers. "Some bozo shot up my ride."

## CHAPTER 29

"**M**an, what a day." Sergio sat sideways in the booth, leaning his back against the wall and crossing his feet on the vinyl cushion. "I have died and gone to hell. Training newbies to answer phones is almost as awful as answering the phones."

"Crybaby." Carly dropped her car keys and cell phone into her purse and set it on the seat. "At least you didn't mess up your presentation."

"Dude, that was, like, hours ago. And you were fine." He closed his eyes and leaned his head back. "Let's just kick back for a few hours and let the alcohol work its magic. What are you drinking?"

"Iced tea, I think."

"Spoilsport. Have one glass of wine."

"Can't. I have to drive. So do you."

"Listen, Mom, I'm having a few beers and a cab ride, okay? Or maybe a ride from that hostess we passed on the way in. But I'm definitely letting today get fuzzed out so I don't think about it all night."

"That's . . . a good point."

The server approached, pulling a notepad out of the short black apron tied around her waist. "What can I get you, Detectives?"

Sergio glanced at Carly.

"Okay, I'll have a Pinot Grigio."

He smiled and sat up. "That's my girl. I'll have a beer and that big, greasy cheeseburger you guys make. You know, the one with the bacon and onion rings all piled on top of it?" He glanced at Carly. "Is that okay, Mother?"

"Two of those, please." Carly handed her menu to the server.

Lowering his head to the table, Sergio said, "Wake me when my food comes."

"Sit up." Carly balled up a napkin and bounced it off the back of his head. "We need to talk. We have a prelim report due, and—" She put a hand to her face. "Oh, crap."

Sergio lifted his head. "What's up?" A group of their phone bank officers walked in.

"Oh, that guy's with them, too."

"Who?" He glanced at the door and saw the phone squad group. Raising his hand, he waved.

Carly grabbed his arm and yanked it to the table. "Don't do that."

"What's with you? And who is 'that guy' that's with them?"

She turned away, opening her purse. "That guy who creeps me out."

"The big guy?" Sergio craned his neck, eyeing the group. "He's—"

"Don't look."

"Geez." He folded his hands on the table. "What a surprise—cops in a cop bar. Look, we're like their bosses. I'm sure they don't want to spend time with us, either."

"Let's not find out."

The server brought their drinks.

Carly took a sip of her wine, her car keys in her other hand. "Let's get out of here." She slid to the end of the booth.

"What? No." Sergio put his hand on hers. "Let's finish our drinks. What's the problem with that guy? So you got creeped out for a second. No big deal. When was last time that happened?"

She leaned back in the booth, sighing. "It happens all the time."

"Really? That's messed up." He took a gulp of his beer.

"I think women get creeped out a lot."

"Well, I'm not saying as a cop I don't have a sense for who's the bad guy in a lineup, but . . ."

She fidgeted, toying with her keys and glancing to the other table where the phone group sat. She shifted on her seat.

"Okay, let's do this." Sergio rubbed his chin, thinking of ways to diffuse his partner's tension.

"Give me a circumstance when this had happened before. Recently, say."

Carly stared at her wine glass, pushed herself back to the center of the booth seat, dropping her keys back into her purse. "I got creeped out the other day when a guy followed me around the grocery store."

Sergio shrugged. "Totally normal. I start to get nervous if I see the same person in the next aisle too many times. I figure they're going to think I'm following them."

"I especially don't like it when they try to chat me up."

"Yeah, that's different, but then it's—they're just hitting on you. In that case, the guy following you around in the grocery store might be thinking you're hot."

"I don't go grocery shopping to get hit on." Carly took a sip of her drink, setting the glass down slowly. "I'm married."

Chewing his lip, Sergio checked his partner's facial expressions. Things were not improving across the table. He needed to lighten the mood. "I think we may be confusing creepy with just everyday, run-of-the-mill, wolfish guy behavior."

"Well." She glanced at Sergio. "I got hit on downtown."

"Dude, I hate to say this." He chuckled. "But as a pretty woman, you should be used to getting hit on."

"Just leave me alone. I'm only walking to the bank."

"Oh, yeah. You are totally baiting them with that walking stuff." He smiled. "And walking to the bank? Come on."

Carly rolled her eyes. "Look, she's a woman and she's walking!"

He sipped his beer. "Partner, I think this may be a combination of you being an introvert and being pretty, and having guys hit on you. Your whole life, you've thought people were stalking you when they just thought you were cute."

"But it gives me the creeps. We should be able to walk to the bank without getting hit on. It's not like I was in a bar."

Sergio sat back, taking another gulp of his beer. "Let's just say you are a little more aware than the average person. So when a guy's checking you out, in what might be normal guy behavior, you notice—and since you notice and you don't like being watched, it bothers you. Maybe it's not creepy as much as it's 'pretty lady gets hit on.' You're kinda anti-attention. It fits."

Carly nodded. "That's fair, I think."

"Good. Problem solved." He drummed the table, glancing around. The aromas of fried foods and grilled burgers filled the room. "Now we can relax and eat—and enjoy the effects of alcohol. Although now I'm wondering how you met your husband. At some point he was checking you out. I hope."

"Probably." Carly swirled the wine around in her glass. "But he looked into my eyes more than anything else."

"But those are hard to see when you're all the way at the end of the grocery aisle."

\* \* \* \* \*

The young waiter spoke to the group at Davenrod's table as the last of the team finished their dinners. "Can I get any of these empty plates out of your way, folks?"

"Sure, thanks."

One of the younger female officers pointed to Sergio and Carly. "You know, the bosses are over there. Do we go say hi?"

Davenrod opened his mouth. "I—"

"No," a male officer said. "They've been over there the whole time. They probably want to be left alone."

"So do I." Davenrod glared at the officer, then wiped his mouth with a paper napkin and raised his drink to his lips. "I see enough boss types at the station."

"Should we send them a drink?" she asked.

The entire group replied. "No!"

"Okay, geez."

Davenrod eyed the detectives, noting how the woman gestured when she talked, and how the man replied. The man was relatively animated; the woman more subdued. She kept her head down and wasn't as visible over the back of the booth. Trying not to be obvious, Davenrod continued taking mental notes on the pair in stolen glances. A female server approached the detective's table and laid a black vinyl folder on it, then cleared away a few plates. The woman detective stood up, slinging her purse over her shoulder. The man stayed behind, reaching into his back pocket and producing a wallet.

"I'm gonna hit the head," Davenrod said, rising slowly. He let the female detective get across the restaurant before he followed. Strolling toward the front of the bar, he was careful not to follow her too closely. As she went out the door, he glanced over his shoulder. The man sat in the booth sipping a beer.

Davenrod passed under a large wooden finger that said "restrooms," and took a few steps down the hallway, them immediately stopped and doubled back to peer into the restaurant. His group seemed occupied with their drinks. The lone man tapped the table with one hand and read his cell phone with the other.

Davenrod walked to the front door and slipped outside. His heart raced, knowing he was moments away from another step.

*Keep calm, attract no suspicion.*

The entrance was well lit, with a bright sign near the entrance of the parking lot and a big light over the bar's front door. Smokers gathered in a darker corner, near a fat line of shrubbery that ran along the far side of the lot and out to the sidewalk. The woman weaved between the first row of cars, heading toward the hedges. Davenrod strolled toward the smokers, keeping her in the corner of his eye and listening for the sound of an engine starting.

One of the off-duty cops held out a pack of cigarettes. "Need a smoke?"

Davenrod shook his head. "I quit."

The officer frowned. "Then what—"

"I still like to get a second hand whiff every once in a while," Davenrod said. "You know?"

"No." The officer blew a long stream of smoke into the air. "Man, that'd drive me nuts."

"Yeah." Davenrod stretched, thumping his belly. "It's all about control."

Across the parking lot, a car's headlights flashed. The woman opened the door to an orange Camaro and got inside. The engine roared to life, the car's headlights shining bright over the group of smokers.

Adrenaline surged through his system. He licked his lips, forcing himself to breathe.

*Here we go.*

Stepping behind the nearest officer, Davenrod shielded his eyes with his hand. The Camaro backed out of its parking spot. When the car lights moved off them, Davenrod walked toward the front door. "Okay guys. Thanks for the memories of my addiction days."

"Any time, pal."

The Camaro rolled over the crushed oyster shell lot, moving slowly as it headed toward the entrance. A bead of sweat rolled down his cheek.

*Move fast, but don't draw attention.*

At the front door, Davenrod gripped the handle and stared into the glass. He held his breath, waiting as the Camaro's reflection headed out of the lot. As it neared the street, it became fully illuminated under the bright sign at the lot entrance.

*Now.*

Davenrod turned, catching the Camaro's license plate number before it pulled into the street. Heart racing, he closed his eyes and repeated the number to himself a few times until it was committed to memory. He took a few deep breaths and wiped his sweaty palms on his pants. It was done. The next step was under way.

He yanked the door open and stepped inside, smiling as the car drove away.

# CHAPTER 30

**D**avenrod pulled open the ziplock bag and eased the item from inside, unfolding the wax paper and letting the object drop into his palm. It was lighter now, and harder. Stained—but that was to be expected. And it had been a little smelly for a while, too, but that had passed. Around the edges on one end, it was rough. On the other end, smooth, more or less.

His passion swelled as he held the object tonight, but not like before.

Earlier—when the trophy was fresh—the feeling was almost magical. A delight to look at, a fantasy come true to hold. It held him spellbound for hours. He could just look at it, not even touching it, and the visions came rushing back.

The stabbing. The kicking.

The warm wetness.

The delightful surprise of the knife, scraping across hard bones and tough tendons, sending vibrations up his arm into his consciousness to stay, igniting his mind like nothing else had before. Satisfying relief and overwhelming ecstasy. He hadn't expected that. He hadn't expected a lot of things.

The puppet-like quality of holding someone's insides, from their very spine, and feeling them move as if you were pulling strings.

Fantastic.

He was surprised, then, that the feeling had faded. The joy of those first nights seemed like it would never go away, like it never *could* go away. But it did. A rose blossom that withered, dropping petals. The feeling grew distant. He never considered that the trophy would lose the magic, and yet here, only days later, the power was nearly gone.

The urge to exert his power over the sheep would grow and grow until he was beside himself.

Night after night, he'd kneeled before it. Holding it in his hand, feeling its weight, the visions rushing back as if he were there again. Touching it would send his heart racing, bringing the ecstasy of the death every time.

But there was no warm wetness, no screaming, no eyes looking out at eternity.

A hollowness. An itch that needed to be scratched, growing into an insatiable pounding urge in his skull that could not be denied.

And so he had gone on the hunt again, enjoying his passion deeply and fully, satisfying the urge that wouldn't leave him alone—and taking another souvenir. One that wouldn't be as noticeable.

From the jogger, a piece of lung.

It was rapture, gazing upon it, but it withered, too. And the stench made it impossible to enjoy; the freezer held it now, but what good is a frozen trinket when the rush comes from its ability to represent what it had been a part of? And it wasn't as satisfying as the first time.

But satisfaction would be his again. That, he knew.

*It was a mistake.*

No, it was a learning process.

*Taking souvenirs was a mistake. They are traceable. They will identify you.*

And that's why we'll get rid of them.

He rolled it back and forth, willing it to bestow the magic it had once contained, but frustrated by its inability to do so.

He also knew he needed more. He had to have more. He was unable to ignore the urges any longer.

He gazed at it, shaking his head. "I've outgrown this, but . . ."

*You can't keep it, you know.*

"I know."

*You shouldn't have taken it and you can't keep it.*

"I know!"

It was time. Time to become powerful again, to show what he was again capable of.

The humming in his head came forward. Far away, but growing, like a long, slow train. He ran to the garage and turned on the light as he raced by, grabbing the tarp that covered the wheel, and throwing it to the floor. Flipping the little metal switch, he ignited its loud electric whine. His hand drifted over the smooth, spinning surface. Lowering himself onto the wooden stool, he reached for the knife, unwrapping it from its blanket. He eased the blade toward the wheel.

*You can't sharpen the blade to a flat point, boy. You have to round its edge.*

He squeezed his eyes closed and bowed his head, gritting his teeth. "I . . . know."

*A rounded edge will not bend and break, dummy. The flat sharp edge will . . .*

"I know, I know, I know!"

The train grew louder, a freight train on rusted tracks, rumbling closer.

*The blade is pure.*

"It is," he said. "It is pure."

*You must be pure.*

He stopped, the blade an inch from the sharpening wheel. "Pure. And powerful."

The rush came over him. He nodded, rising up from the stool, standing in front of the old mirror from the discarded dresser. The train was nearly upon him.

"Pure."

He ran his hand over the stubble of hair that lined the sides of his head, sliding down to his neck and along his shirt collar.

"I must be pure."

With the massive locomotive shaking his entire body, he gripped the knife with one hand and ripped at the buttons with the other, exposing his thick chest. He undid his pants and let them drop to his ankles. His shoes were next, and his socks. Then, kicking the pants to the corner, he slid out of his boxers. He stared at himself, breathing heavily, twisting to see the many belt marks and whip marks that marred his back. Twenty years had faded the physical pain but not the scorching memories.

*What happened to Daisy, boy?*

*I don't know. I took her for a walk like you said, but she's too big.*

*You're just a little coward, is all. And weak. She's almost still a puppy!*

*She's too big. She pulls me down and she bites.*

*You're weak. Where is she? Tell me, or I'll get my belt and tan your hide again. I know you know where she is.*

Holding the knife in both hands, he raised it over his head, then slowly brought it down to rest on his chest.

*I don't know where she is!*

*Those dogs cost a lot of money, you little liar. What did you do?*

He scraped the blade over his left pectoral muscle, shaving away the few bits of hair that had grown back, then dragged it across the right side of his chest. He dry-shaved his abdomen until he was satisfied, a hundred tiny nicks and cuts all brimming and glistening. The mirror reflected no lies.

*What did you do? Where's Daisy? What did you do?*

The welts stung with each whip stroke as the belt ripped into his seven-year-old skin, his crying going unheard and unanswered as his mother stood watching.

Beatings were necessary to get the bad out of him, the weakness. They made him pure.

*His mother pressed his trembling face to the cage as the growling dog scratched and clawed at him.*

*She needs to get to know you, is all. You'll take her for walks after dinner.*

The family "pet"—a huge dog bred for fighting, and one that never missed an opportunity to snap and growl at him from her rusty cage—somehow got tied to the middle of the train tracks, just past the curve near the creek. A few well-placed treats and a dark winter's night was all that was needed. That, and a second leash he stole from the store in town.

In exchange for a beating, the constant snapping and growling—and bites that drew blood and should have gotten stitches—was gone.

Well worth it.

And when they found their next excuse to whip him, or burn him with cigarettes, or make him sleep in the shed, he learned to help them. He could clean his parents' work tools.

Rabbits and other small animals were caught and butchered for meat.

He could clean the guns and sharpen the knives.

The roiling in his gut returned, pushing away the freight train in his head. He stepped back to the wheel and sat on the stool.

*Wet the wheel.*

He dabbed a finger to his bleeding chest and smoothed the blood over the blade, then lowered it onto the sharpening wheel.

Next to him, the wax paper flitted in the breeze from the electric motor, covering and uncovering the dry, severed finger inside.

He sharpened the blade in small circles, thinking over and over about the way he would kill the woman, the images dancing in his mind. They were the only things now that would keep the freight train from coming, pushing it away and allowing the joyful ecstasy to come. It was the only thing that had ever worked, from the first time when he shot his parents as they slept, then butchered them in their bed, fleeing into the night to never return.

He imagined the woman's cries and felt her kicks, holding her from inside like the puppet she was, worthless and weak, a rag doll in a gray suit and shiny black shoes.

A sheep.

Sweat formed on his brow as he slid the blade back and forth over the sharpening wheel. His heart raced, his breathing heavy. He put a finger to his chest, lifted the blade from the wheel, and dabbed his finger across the glistening edge. Pushing the droplets together until the edge was greased, he lowered it back onto the wheel.

*It will know power as I take its life.*

"It will know." He inhaled deeply. "And it will become pure."

## CHAPTER 31

"Hey, Jayda, can you run a plate for me?" Davenrod towered over the assistant duty officer and held out a scrap of paper as she typed on her keyboard.

She held up one finger. "Roger that unit twenty-twelve. Base clear." Leaning back, she pulled a headset away from one ear and peered up at Davenrod. "Whatcha got?"

He handed her the paper. "Some jerk cut me off on Kennedy Boulevard when I was coming to the station. I'd have stopped, but I was already running late."

She cocked her head and narrowed her eyes. "Why not run it yourself?"

"Everybody they assigned to help answer phones for the big serial killer thing had to give up their patrol car. Chief says they need 'em on the street."

Jayda frowned. "That sucks."

"Tell me about it. The peons get the shaft again."

"Mm-hmm. So what's up with that serial killer stuff?" She faced her computer, typing, setting the paper on the side of the keyboard. "Anything interesting happening up there?"

"Not yet, but you'll be the first to know when it does. Right now, it's a lot of crazies calling in." Davenrod slid his hand into his pocket, fingering a second slip of paper, the same shape and size, but blank, and already crumbled up. He wrapped his fingers around it and withdrew his hand. "Man, if I see this jerk again, I might have to give him a tail and see what kind of driver he really is. Maybe a ticket will teach him some manners."

"Not him. Her. And check it out."

Jayda leaned back again. Detective Carly Sanderson's driver's license photo and home address flashed on the screen.

*812 Fish Hawk Lane, Brandon, Florida.*

"I guess you'll want to rethink that tail," Jayda said, smiling.

"I guess so." He chuckled and picked up the paper from her desk, crumbling it up, then tossed the blank one into the garbage can by her desk.

"Or you could try to be on time next time."

"Good point. I'm still not used to traffic around here." He slid his hands into his pockets, letting go of the wadded paper with Carly's license plate number on it. *One step ahead.* "Well anyway, thanks for running the plate."

If anyone checked, the search for the license plate would be from Jayda's computer, not his, and under her login. The scrap of paper—if any of these mooks ever tried to find it, and they wouldn't—would not have any information on it that led back to him.

*One step ahead.* Little details add up to big things, just like they said about phone duty. But he knew there were very few details coming in from the hundreds of calls they were getting every day, and he loved the fact that they were chasing in too many directions, looking at too many wrong leads. It was almost as if—in fact, it was exactly like—other people were doing his work for him.

And whatever accurate information actually got through, he'd be in the phone pool to see it went nowhere. Accurate tips he received himself obviously went nowhere. Finding other tips in the data base was a snap, so he located them and helped them disappear before they were even officially processed. Once the head sheep found him to be a model employee, he could even end up sitting in on meetings and gently obfuscate things.

He was one level away from the people who were actively trying to catch him, and right now he was earning their trust and being a perceived benefit. The sheep always value that crap. Soon he'd be able to move up and directly influence things, if he wanted to.

He held the balled-up paper in his pocket, smiling. Of course, he planned on influencing them a lot sooner than that. Tonight, he'd influence it in a major way.

"Do you ever miss New Orleans?"

Davenrod's stomach jumped. He took a half step backwards, blinking. "What's that?"

"New Orleans," Jayda said. "You said you were from there."

"Did I? I don't member saying that." His mind was on heading straight to the men's room, opening a stall door, and flushing the paper with Carly's license plate number on it. Nobody would look for it there. Then on to the phone before anybody noticed how late he was.

*What was this little interrogation all about?*

"Boy, you really do have a short memory, don't you? It was at happy hour a while ago. You don't sound like New Orleans."

Why was she asking about that? What did she know?

His heart pounded. What detail did he miss? He needed to go, to get to his tiny desk and start logging calls. To act like a sheep and not get noticed in any negative way, so he could step up and lead the team. He glanced at the wall clock over the duty desk. He didn't have time for small talk.

And he definitely didn't have time to give out personal information.

He swallowed hard, trying to act calm. *It's nothing. Small talk. Play it off.*

Davenrod cleared his throat, taking another step away from the desk. "Yeah, I only lived there for a few years." He hooked a thumb over his shoulder. "Gotta run. Late, remember?"

She waved. "Go. I'll catch you later."

He forced a friendly smile as a ripple of uncertainty went through his gut. He rubbed his stomach and turned away, making a mental note.

*Catch me later? Just try it.*

* * * * *

Davenrod waded through the crush of rush hour traffic on the interstate, making his way south to the Brandon area exits. The old GPS indicated it would take another forty-five minutes to get to Fish Hawk Lane, but there might be wrecks or construction delays. He didn't care. His phone app might point those things out, but he didn't want any sort of online history showing he'd driven to the victim's house. Besides, he wasn't in a hurry. The woman was headed into another meeting when he left the station. He had time.

He smiled as he waited among the commuter sheep, the braying lessers who took what bosses shoveled at them. On the floor of the passenger seat, his black gym bag held some basic disguise materials. He planned on waiting in a park or library until it was dark—the GPS said both were within a mile or two of Fish Hawk Lane, and he didn't want to spend too much time in any one place and risk having his car be remembered. Not a lot of disguise would be needed; just enough to confuse any do-gooder citizen, but he still brought a variety: baseball caps, glasses, a wig, a stick-on beard and mustache. Even a rubber Halloween mask—former President Barack Obama, just so the sheep could send the cops on a wild goose chase looking for a light-skinned African American man, maybe one with long hair.

Plus several changes of clothes. A bright red Tampa Bay Buccaneers t-shirt, a blue Tampa Bay Rays jersey, and a black Tampa Bay Lightning windbreaker—all of which had been gifts, and none of which he'd ever worn. In the event that he needed to be seen *fleeing the scene*, so to speak, the mooks would describe him wearing a red shirt and having a beard. As soon as he rounded the corner, he'd be a man in a blue shirt with short hair and a baseball cap. The original disguise, simple as it was, would go into the black garbage bag in his trunk, to be deposited in the dumpster or a park or fast food place on the way home.

He could even switch shirts again if anyone saw him changing clothes, but in a dark car that was a low risk probability.

He smiled and laid his hand over the wheel, gazing into the unmoving traffic.

*One step ahead, just like always.*

Patiently, he moved and stopped, moved and stopped; until the jammed interstate freed up and the cars started moving at actual highways speeds.

Fish Hawk Lane was in a generally nice neighborhood, by Florida standards; several two-story houses on every block, and a lot of one-story houses between them, all with stony, river rock façades and well-tended yards.

He watched the mailboxes on their posts by the curb as they counted down to 812. He slowed down as he approached, but not too slow; 812 Fish Hawk Lane looked like almost every other house on the block. Tan stucco trimmed with stonework of mixed browns, and a dark green door. The whole neighborhood was a cookie cutter house farm: the developers take out all the big oak trees, plop down rows of houses, and then plant little trees around them that will one day be almost as nice as the ones they took out.

It was a perfect place for sheep to live, and he had no doubt lots of sheep lived there.

But he was only interested in one.

812 had a row of purple flowers lining the walk, and a yellow and red FSU banner hanging over the driveway from a holder on the second floor.

A small thrill went through him. This house would be easy to spot, day or night.

Satisfied with his recon, he drove to the park and turned off his car. Young children played on an old swing set, while high school age kids chatted in groups or played games on their phones. He shook his head.

*Sheep in training.*

As the sky grew dark, the children left the area. The park would probably get locked up at sunset. He started his car and drove to the library to burn a little more time before heading back to 812 Fish Hawk Lane.

## CHAPTER 32

The sheep living on Fish Hawk Lane were married. Houses this size were not typically owned by single people. So each house would contain approximately two adults and two kids, a dog here and there, or a cat, or both. One or two cars parked on the street per block, and a few sat in driveways, but for the most part the residents drove their mid-grade minivans and SUVs into their two-car garages, unloading kids or groceries before the curtain of the garage door came down over the much-repeated play.

Davenrod folded his arms, slouching in his car. A variety of shapes and sizes got out of the vehicles, but they were all basically the same.

They drove the same types of cars, had kids roughly the same ages, wore more or less the same styles of clothes, and disappeared into their very same-looking houses.

He was disappointed and reassured at the same time. The sheep here lacked any sense of creativity. Entering a single house on this street would tell him what to expect in just about every other house in the entire subdivision. These details would be helpful when the time came, but would it make for less of a challenge?

He shifted on his seat, glancing toward the gym bag on the floor, now invisible in the darkness. Power was about demonstration. Showing what he was capable of. What good is it to do something if no one knows?

His car became bright with light. Glancing in the rearview mirror, he narrowed his eyes as two headlights moved toward him. He shifted his gaze to the sidewalk as the car came and went, its tail lights glowing red as it passed. The headlights swung into a driveway, illuminating a red and yellow banner flying from the second floor. The garage door reflected just enough light to show the car's orange color, but the body shape of the Camaro was unmistakable.

His stomach rippled with electricity.

When the garage door was three-fourths of the way open, the car pulled in and the brake lights came on again.

Davenrod leaned forward in his seat, heart pounding, straining to see from his vantage point nearly half a block away. The woman got out of the car and slung her purse over her shoulder, then stepped to the trunk, gathered a few things, and walked around the passenger side of the car. Then she was out of sight.

The garage door lowered, ending the show.

He pressed a button on his phone to check the time. In the house, a light came on, then another.

*She's the first one home. Today, anyway.*

The welling grew inside him, a smile stretching across his face. He could do it right now. Anyone would open a door for a package delivery, and with two parents in a house, neither ever knew if the other had ordered something online. Deliveries weren't even made by UPS trucks half the time. Contract carriers in vans or sometimes even regular cars did drop-offs of small items. He gripped the steering wheel, his pulse throbbing in his ears. A nondescript gray shirt and cap would be enough . . .

He chuckled, shaking his head. Once the door was open, game over.

Or game on.

He leaned back in the seat, his jaw hanging open and his hands falling onto his thighs. How would that work? A quick shove of the door, push the sheep into the house, and slam the door shut behind him? Then one shot to the chest, to disable the sheep and—

*No. The gun was weakness.*

The freight train rolled down the tracks in his head, a distant rumbling growing louder. He pushed it away. There would be no weakness this time.

The victim's terrified eyes would say it all, as the door thrust open and he walked in. Powerful. No gun. The wide eyes and gaping jaw as the sheep backed away. His strong steps moving forward, unstoppable, as the shock came over its face, the big knife flashing in the bright light.

A tingle went through his belly, causing him to gasp.

*I could do it now.*

When he pushed his way into the house, would the sheep stumble and fall backwards onto the laminate wood floor of the small foyer? Would it crawl backwards, pleading, wondering if it was about to be robbed or raped or butchered? Would it turn and run, crashing into walls and tables filled with family photos and soccer trophies?

Anger swelled in his gut. The sheep deserved it just for being sheep. And he could do it right now. He reached out and grabbed the steering wheel again, squeezing it hard and gritting his teeth.

*Stick to the plan . . .*

The rush was incredible. Sweat formed on his brow as he wrenched his eyes shut, envisioning the scene as it unfolded before him.

Would anyone hear the screams over the big, blaring flat screen TV? They would be loud in the house, probably harshly so, but outside—past the sliding glass doors and over the hum of air conditioners, across the short span of manicured lawns mowed every Sunday during the game, over the already-fading, contractor-grade wooden privacy fence and into the next house—where *their* TV blared and *their* microwave buzzed—would anyone hear anything?

His breath came in gasps, rapid and short, as the visions cascaded through his brain.

He could do it now. Right now. He could get out of the car and walk up to the door and ring the bell and . . .

*Wait. That was not the plan.*

Another rush welled inside him.

*Would it know?*

When the sheep saw him, when he forced open the door and threw it to the floor, would it know it was looking at the serial killer it had been trying to catch? Would its face be a mix of confusion and realization and horror?

How would the knife feel plunging into it, fully alert and aware, where a bullet hadn't softened its reactions and slowed the—

His car lit up again. Another vehicle approached from behind. He averted his eyes, waiting for it to pass. The tiny trees cast long shadows that shifted from left to right over the neatly trimmed grass.

The front door of 812 Fish Hawk Lane opened. A thin silhouette emerged, dressed in dark, clinging leggings and reflective running shoes. It moved to the curb gracefully, like a dancer. The car passed Davenrod and pulled up to the house, its tail lights glowing as it stopped. The silhouette went to the car, leaning on the passenger door. After a moment, the brake lights went off, but the tail lights stayed on; the car was parking but not shutting off its engine. They were talking.

The street brightened as another sheep arrived home, this one coming from in front of Davenrod and the car at 812 Fish Hawk Lane. The approaching car's headlights lit the other vehicle, displaying a few large dents in its rear quarter panel. Inside, the driver raised a hand to his eyes. So did the silhouette leaning on its passenger door.

He recognized them both now.

*The two lead detectives on the case, being watched by their serial killer.*

The irony made him chuckle. Was a little after-hours case work about to happen, or possibly something a little more in the nonwork arena? No wonder these two couldn't catch a killer. They had no focus, no discipline, if they were playing house instead of working.

No power. They were weak.

Davenrod frowned, anger coming over him. He detested weakness in any form.

He could kill them both now, just by starting his car and stomping the gas pedal, plowing into them at full speed. The wreck would deploy the air bags and might knock the driver unconscious, but it would surely stun him. The impact would break a few bones in the other sheep, knocking it to the ground. From there it would be a matter of a few strokes. A quick jab to the sheep on the grass as it lay trying to figure out what had just happened, then a few thrusts into the limp driver as he slumped across the steering wheel.

There would be witnesses, of course, but in the darkness, what would they really see? Who among these cookie cutter lessers would ever conclude a double murder was happening on their beautiful front lawn?

They'd hear the crunch of the cars; they'd see an accident. They'd see a man going from one person to the other, but the street light on the curve wouldn't allow them to comprehend what they were actually witnessing.

Double murders didn't happen on Fish Hawk Lane.

But it was not the plan. Plans required discipline, and discipline required the power to stick to the plan. An opportunity like this was tempting but fraught with unthought-of details that might land him in the electric chair.

*No. Wait. Stick to the plan.*

He nodded and took a deep breath, letting the thrill of the spontaneous gift pass. Christmas was worth waiting for, and Christmas would come with the knowledge—the vision—of seeing their faces as they understood who was standing over them, killing them.

He shuddered, letting the last of the thrill go out of his system.

The car's taillights lit again and it pulled away, moving slowly up the street. The silhouette went back to the front door, opened it, and laid something inside, then stood under the porch light and twisted. With hands on hips, the sheep swung back and forth, then bent to touch the concrete porch.

The sheep stepped off the porch, then stopped, returning to the front door and locking it with a key from the pocket of its windbreaker. Bounding off the porch, it walked down the street in long strides, the reflectors on the shoes swaying like two fireflies in rocking chairs that were somehow pulled down the sidewalk as if by tiny, invisible horses.

The silhouette stopped under the street light, adjusted its ponytail, then started running.

The killer smiled. Runners were creatures of habit, even more so than other types of sheep. They find a way, almost every day, to feed that addiction. The shiny leggings indicated they were new. Same with the reflectors on the shoes—they were clean enough to reflect well, meaning they were either new or well cared for, either of which indicated a passion for the habit.

That would be the plan.

When she was out of sight, he started the car. The GPS showed there were only a few connecting streets. The silhouette turned right and increased her pace. He drove past her, neither too fast or too slow, but he knew it almost wouldn't matter. After a few seconds, a runner wouldn't even remember a car had passed. Like body builders, they get caught up in the task and zone out.

The end of that street gave way to apartments under construction. Two- and three-story monstrosities that were rectangles with roofs, but without a lot of doors and windows yet. The fancy trimmings were in, though, like columns and porticos around the entries, and accent colored stucco cornerstones like the mansions on Bayshore Boulevard had.

He waited just long enough to see that the silhouette was coming, then circled around to 812 Fish Hawk Lane again. He parked up the street this time, behind a minivan, and waited the forty-five minutes it took for the silhouette to return.

That would be the plan. It was all coming together.

Watch and wait, just like with the others, and when the silhouette came around the corner, spring his trap. Maybe confront it head on, pretending to be another jogger as it approached, then step in front of it and thrust in the knife.

The welling in his stomach churned, sending deep, satisfying ripples through him.

Or maybe surprise it somehow, letting it round a corner in the empty apartment construction site and catch it alone on the street.

He nodded, his pulse throbbing.

*Yes, that would be the plan.*

He sat back, closing his eyes and sighing, letting the electricity go through him and pushing the freight train away again.

Tomorrow night, just after dark, Christmas morning would arrive.

## CHAPTER 33

Tyree stared at the ceiling from the office couch for about an hour before officially deciding he needed to wake up. Grabbing his cell phone, he called Big Brass and delivered the bad news. "I need you to take me back to Lauren's."

"What! The crazy shooter girl's house? Why you goin' there?"

Tyree rubbed the sleep out of his eyes. "I forgot . . . to ask about the money."

"That was the whole reason you went there! What kind of a detective are you?"

"Oh, I guess your first week of being a drug dealer, you did everything right?"

"Pretty much. You give the guy the drugs and he hands you the money. Yep, I nailed it. It's not that hard. Almost as easy as if you go to somebody's house to ask questions about some money, remember to ask questions about the money."

Tyree sat up on the couch. "There were a lot of bullets flying around at the time. I find that distracting."

"I'm not driving all the way to your place again and then back out to her house. Just call her."

"I . . . can't."

"Let me guess, you didn't get her phone number." Lavonte huffed. "You really are terrible at this."

"You wanna play junior detective? This is part of it." Tyree stood up. "I'll see you when you get here." He ended the call, dropped the phone on the couch, and headed for the shower.

\* \* \* \* \*

Lavonte grumbled as he walked from Tyree's office to the truck. "I sure hope you have some gas money for all this nonsense."

"Yeah," Tyree said, following him. "I'll fill your truck using the cash that's left over after you're done paying for the Harley you shot up."

"That was your fault. You should pay for that."

Tyree stopped at the passenger side door. "My fault? How do you figure? You shot at me."

"Because you were sneaking up on my stash. You can't do that."

"You can't just open fire on people, doesn't matter what they're doing."

"Sure it does. As far as I knew, you were coming to rob me and kill me. I was defending myself."

"Try floating that defense in court. Your momma will be visiting you in Leavenworth for the next twenty years."

The two men climbed into the vehicle.

"But you knew you weren't up to anything." Lavonte scowled. "I didn't. That totally makes you wrong."

"What was I supposed to do, announce myself?"

"It would have saved us all a lot of time and trouble, and then you wouldn't have gotten shot at. Which is why the Harley damage is your fault. Pay it out of your own pocket." Lavonte started the car and drove out of the lot. "Can't cost that much. A couple of scratches and a new headlight. It's not like I flattened it with a bulldozer."

"That's still more than a tank of gas."

"I got pain and suffering, too."

Tyree stared out the window.

"My nose had better look good when this bandage comes off."

\* \* \* \* \*

As she cracked opened her front door, Lauren smiled at Tyree.

He smiled back. "Got any tea?"

She opened the door wider. "You must really be thirsty."

"Well, it was good tea. But actually, I forgot to ask you something. May I come in?"

She peered over his shoulder at the big red truck. "Is that one coming in, too?"

"That's your call. Lavonte can stay in the truck if you feel uncomfortable around him."

She sighed and looked at Tyree. "I guess if you say he's okay, then he can come in."

"Thank you." Tyree waved at Lavonte. He hopped out of the truck and came up to the house, following Lauren and Tyree into the living room. She folded her hands and stopped by the couch.

"This won't take long. I was going over the books at the Lakeland office of Dilger and Contreras. There's a series of ten thousand-dollar checks made out to you."

"And?"

Tyree shifted on his feet. "And I was hoping you could shed a little light on what they were for."

"What's money for?" She swept her hands out, glancing around her living room. "Electricity, furniture, car, food . . . mortgage."

"No, I mean, why was he—Mr. Dilger—paying you?"

Big Brass elbowed Tyree, whispering. "Love nest, dummy."

"Paying me?" Lauren went to an overstuffed leather chair, running her fingers along the top. "Is that what you think, Mr. Tyree? That I was Henry Dilger's whore?"

"Uh, I—"

"Because a nice man like that couldn't possibly be mixed up with a cheap girl—is that it?"

"Ma'am . . ."

"Some cheap girls are born and some are made. I guess I'm a bit of both." Lauren shook her head, her eyes staring at the floor. Stepping around the big leather chair, she lowered herself into it, her shoulders sagging. "But I ain't no whore."

Tyree took a seat on the couch, watching Lauren's eyes. The light had gone out of her.

"Do you know what it's like to lose someone and not be able to cry? To not be able to tell people how you hurt inside and at least let them hold your hand and comfort you? To not be able to go to the funeral of a man you loved dearly—and have to pretend you didn't exist?"

He said nothing, letting it come. Each word ripped through her heart, breaking down a barrage of defenses that had been built over the years. Now they came forth into the light.

"Do you know how terrible it is to feel like you have something to hide? To watch everyone else go about their business while you live in the shadows? Those checks were supposed to help give me that, some of the life I was supposed to have." She brought her eyes to meet his. "My father said I shouldn't have to live in the shadows."

Tyree nodded. "Was your father a friend of Henry Dilger's?"

"No." She clasped her hands and lowered her eyes again, her voice falling to a whisper. "My father *was* Henry Dilger."

The breath went out of Tyree. He leaned back on the couch, putting his hands to his forehead and pushing them back through his hair.

"He lived in Lakeland about twice a week with my mother," Lauren said. "Until she passed away last year."

Tyree's hands fell to his side. "Henry lived . . . here?"

"No, at Momma's house. He's not exactly who you thought he was, is he? He was a good man, but he was human, and he had a secret. That look in your eyes is what he was trying to spare all of us from."

"Most guys would have just . . ." Tyree sat up. "An out-of-wedlock child isn't that uncommon these days."

Lauren shook her head. "That ain't quite it. He was in love with two women. From that came his happy Tampa family—and me, over here, with my momma. His other family. The secret one."

"I'm—how did he manage it?"

"When a father can't go on a grade school field trip, you don't think much about it. But he never went with us to movies or out to dinner. He never went to a Saturday swim meet. Momma always said he was working and traveling on business, and as a kid you believe that. It's your normal. But when you grow up, you start to figure things out. Then the rules become clear. You can't visit him at the office. He ain't gonna be there for your graduation. And when you see him in the newspaper with the mayor of Tampa, you can't be proud and tell your friends, because you're really supposed to stay in the shadows." She raised her eyes and looked around the room, tears rolling down her cheeks. "It's a nice shadow, don't you think?"

"He maintained two separate lives?"

"Maintained. That's a good word. I wasn't supposed to know about them, but I figured it out when he closed a big shipping deal and his picture was in the news. Then the goal was just to limit the damage. Stay in Lakeland, not bother the other family, not make a mess of things."

"So they didn't know?"

"You said you knew them. Did you know? Did you, Lavonte? It was our job to make sure they didn't know. We were the shadow people, not them. We learned to lie and make up excuses and look the other way. Kids at school accept that your father is dead or divorced from your mom and they stop asking. In college, nobody cared. After that, you kind of move on and make your own life."

Lavonte leaned on the wall and folded his thick arms across his chest. "Looks like he took pretty good care of you."

"Henry's money paid for Momma. After she died, the money came to me, and I put most of it in the bank. Until Zack saw one of the checks."

Tyree frowned. "Zack saw a payday."

"I loved Zack, but he was headstrong and foolish." She sighed, her eyes distant. "It was a mistake to fall for a boy like that—a big mistake—

but we were young and I loved him. Now he's gone, too. He never should have messed with that Susan Dilger."

Tyree and Lavonte exchanged glances.

"How does she figure into this?" Tyree asked.

"Well, she must've seen one of the checks, because she came callin' just like you did. Zack was there, and when she left, it wasn't five minutes later he was cooking up his scheme."

"To force his way into ownership of the company."

"No, to force the Dilgers to raise the monthly payment. He figured the family in Tampa would still want everything kept quiet like before, so if he asked for more money, they'd pay. I didn't want no part in that, so the two of them met. But it must not have panned out, because the payments never went up and he didn't mention her again."

"She never came back?"

"No."

Tyree rubbed his chin. "Lauren, where did Zack live? Here?"

She glanced at Lavonte. "He should know. It's around the corner from that Maxx's Gym."

"Downtown," Tyree said. "Not out by Westside Park."

"He couldn't afford nothing out there. They expect the rent paid on time. He was too seat-of-the-pants for that."

"That's true," Lavonte said. "That boy was not good with money."

"He was bad about a lot of things. Sometimes I wonder why I stayed with him at all."

Tyree looked at Lauren. "Maybe because he lived in the shadows, too."

Outside the living room window, a finch flew back and forth over the yard, gathering twigs. The butterflies spun happily, dangling from the string on the mailbox.

"I'll tell you this," Lauren said. "Once Momma passed, Henry still called me every week. He'd come out for supper a few times a month, just me and him, and then he'd go to the old house and sleep in the bed he and Momma shared."

Tyree sat back, putting his hand to his chin and taking a deep breath.

"It don't make it right—I'm not saying that—but no one can say he didn't love us. A girl needs her daddy, Mr. Tyree, and he gave me what he could once I came along. Folks can think what they want, but Henry Dilger did a lot of good things for a lot of people. Maybe somewhere deep down, he needed to do all those good things to help live with the lie he created."

## CHAPTER 34

Excitement coursing through him in waves, Davenrod drove toward State Road 60 and the interstate. Every time he'd tell himself to focus on the road, two minutes later he was enjoying images of red-splattered walls and flailing arms. The beautiful scenes unfolded in slow motion as he brought the gleaming knife down again and again, until he was covered in the warm wetness.

He rubbed his temple, turning onto Brandon Boulevard. A surge rippled through him. That would be something, to sit on top of one of them as it lay twitching and gurgling, shoving his hands inside and then pulling them out, gleaming as he lifted his hands to his face and slid them across his cheeks.

He shuddered, trying to keep his speed to the right limit. He saw himself, naked and hot, painting himself with it, reaching into the ragged torso and slathering himself in blood, letting it run down his chest and over his body—

Flickers of blue light invaded his daydream. He brought himself back to the car. The unmistakable flashing of blue strobe lights filled the interior of his sedan. Frowning, he glanced in the rearview mirror. The rack of lights mounted on the car meant only one thing.

*Tampa's finest.*

He glanced at the speedometer.

*Five miles over the limit is a little picky, isn't it Officer Sheep?*

The four-lane road was packed with restaurants and small businesses. Davenrod slowed down, put on his turning signal, and pulled into an empty parking lot. Midford Office Supplies had obviously seen better days. Its interior was dark and its windows were dirty; trash littered the edges of its parking lot. The combination of Wal-Mart and internet had likely shut it down.

*Sheep love a good deal.*

Davenrod waited until the officer approached, making no sudden gestures and keeping his hands on the wheel. The mook wouldn't expect anything to happen in a routine traffic stop, but why take chances? When the cop was almost at the window, Davenrod lowered it.

"License and registration, please."

The cop had one hand on his gun butt and the other shined a flashlight on Davenrod's face. The steel casing and weight of four D-cell batteries in its shaft made the Maglight an innocent-looking but very deadly weapon if necessary.

Anger welled inside Davenrod. He squeezed the steering wheel.

*This is what you do, sheep. You pull over people for going five miles an hour over the limit and you collect your paycheck because that's what's important. You don't fight real crime. You aren't power, you're nothing. You're too stupid to know the guy the whole city is looking for is right under your nose.*

"Sir?"

"Yeah, sorry." Davenrod reached into his rear pocket. "I'm just a little tired. I have it right here." He opened his wallet and displayed his driver's license, holding it up to the officer.

"Would you mind taking it out of the wallet, sir?"

*By the numbers, sheep. Fine job. You keep earning that pay.*

Davenrod frowned and yanked the license out of his wallet, the anger growing inside him. He regained himself and took a deep breath.

*This is not the time for confrontation. Be a sheep.*

He handed his ID out the window. The officer took it, stepped back, and shined the flashlight onto the license.

The flashlight went back to Davenrod's face.

"I'll be right back, sir."

*Yep, check me in the system, Officer Sheep. Standard procedure. Don't wanna get cold out here in the big bad night air. Not this close to Christmas.*

Davenrod glanced at the gym bag. The lights from the parking lot lit it well. Midford Office Supplies couldn't keep their business open, but they could keep the parking lot lights on. Maybe that's why they shut their doors. No business sense.

But it didn't matter if the bag was visible or not; he hadn't given the sheep a reason to search his vehicle, and unless—

The zipper of the gym bag was visible in the light. It was open. Had he not zipped it shut? He leaned forward a few inches. The tip of the rubber mask peeked out from the corner of the bag.

Davenrod leaned back in his seat, gripping the steering wheel. A rubber mask wasn't grounds to search a car, even if the mook saw it. But would Officer Sheep follow that rule, when the whole city was on high alert?

*They weren't on high alert for rubber masks.*

His heart pounded. An odd item like that might start a "probing conversation," appearing casual but designed to draw out inconsistencies in a suspect's replies. Hesitating to open the bag at the officer's request might get a backup called or . . .

He rubbed the back of his neck, glancing in the rearview mirror. Officer Sheep was typing on the patrol unit's computer.

*He can't know any of this from that ID. He'll just chat for a minute, like cops do, and then I'll be on my way.*

Davenrod tapped the steering wheel, his pulse rising.

*What's taking so long?*

He breathed heavily, gritting his teeth. Stupid cop. Stupid bag. Stupid, stupid, stupid.

*Relax. He can't know anything.*

He took a deep breath. Midford Office Supplies wasn't about to fire up their store lights, so the remaining shadows would do just enough to keep the gym bag and the rest of its contents hidden.

The patrol unit's door opened. The officer got out and approached the car again. Davenrod stared in the side mirror, looking to see the hand placement. One hand was on the gun butt; the other held the license. Still standard procedure.

"Sir, do you know why I pulled you over?"

Davenrod gritted his teeth.

*Okay, it's twenty questions time. Shove it, Officer Sheep! I've got things to do.*

Rage welled inside him.

*Get it together. Play along. Be a sheep.*

He let the tension go out of his shoulders. "No, sir. I don't know why you stopped me."

The officer took two paces backwards. "Step out of the vehicle, would you sir?"

*What's going on? What did the computer show? What did he see? It can't say anything!*

Davenrod put his hand on the door lever, pulling it upward. The overhead dome light illuminated the car interior.

His breath caught in his throat.

Now the glint of metal was clearly visible in the gym bag. The mask, the knife, the disguises. Everything. The sides of the soft bag had fallen down while he drove through the neighborhoods of Fish Hawk Lane, revealing all of his equipment to anyone who cared to look.

"Sir, can you step out please?"

His heart pounded. There was too much light. Anyone looking inside could see his tools spilling out onto the floor.

A bead of sweat rolled down the back of his neck, sending chills throughout his system. He had to comply or risk appearing resistant. He had to act fast or he'd appear hesitant and suspicious.

He had to act calm. His hand shook as he held the door handle. He swallowed hard and eased the door open, lifting his foot and inching it down to the ground outside his car. Trying not to turn his head, he glanced at the bag—and cringed. The contents were on full display.

His head throbbed.

*Can't let him see anything.*

He stepped out of the car, one hand holding onto the door. His stomach churned. All his hard work…

"Step back here with me, please."

The trunk? Was he going to ask to see inside? On what grounds? But protesting would get another unit called and the trunk would get opened anyway. Then what would he say?

So what? There's a garbage bag in there. That's not unusual. And resisting might raise suspicions. But what grounds did he have to ask to look in the trunk? And how could Davenrod refuse without appearing suspicious?

He glanced at the car interior. If there had been a second officer, he'd be looking in the windows right now, seeing the tools the serial killer had been using on victims as reported in every paper in Florida.

He hadn't left anything in the trunk. He was sure about that.

But he had been sure about zipping the bag shut, too.

Uneasiness lurched in his belly. He held his breath and stepped to the back of the car.

"Over here, please sir."

*I could kill him. Easy as that, a quick punch to the face, and while he's reeling, grab his service weapon and put two into his chest. Then casually drive away.*

The rage was building. Davenrod balled up his fists.

He'd have the plate number, though, and the ID. If he doesn't report in, it'll only be a matter of time.

But there might not be any other choice.

If he asks to look inside the trunk, unload on him. Step to the bumper and lean over like you're going to open the trunk, then turn around and smash your elbow into his chin. Grab the service weapon with one hand and unsnap the cover with the other before he gets a chance. Maybe even make a joke beforehand, about hiding Christmas presents inside the trunk, then whip around and smash his sheep face. Grab his gun, haul it up to chest level, and let him have it.

Pop, pop.

That's all, then walk away.

The anger crested as he stepped to the rear of the vehicle, Officer Sheep forcing him to end his sheep life, here in front of Midford Office Supplies. The freight train was rolling, coming hard and fast, with only one way to stop it.

He was going to ask to look inside the trunk. Davenrod readied himself. Lean over and then swing back, and catch him off guard. Officer Sheep would be no match for Davenrod. No one would. He stiffened himself, holding his breath and waiting for the right moment to unleash the fury.

The officer pointed to the right rear of the car. "Got a tail light out here."

The rage vanished. Davenrod blinked, staring at the rear of his car.

*Tail light?*

"Oh. I didn't realize." He got the words out before nearly doubling over as the adrenaline left his system. He coughed down the urge to vomit, holding his belly, a queasiness taking over.

*Stupid. Weak.*

"You okay, sir?"

Davenrod swallowed hard, holding a fist to his mouth. Sweat rolled down his face. "Yeah. Probably something I ate. I'm fine."

The officer nodded. "Well, I figured you didn't know about the tail light. Most folks don't—until someone tells them."

"Oh, sure," Davenrod said.

"It's a small violation, though, and being that it's almost Christmastime and all, how about you promise to get 'er fixed and I'll get on home to supper?"

"I—I can do that." Davenrod forced the words out, hoping he didn't sound as puny and weak as he felt. "I'll do it tomorrow. Or this week. Definitely this week."

"Probably just a bulb. Part with three bucks at any auto parts store, and you'll be good to go."

"Sounds fair. Thanks for pointing it out."

"You're welcome." The officer handed the driver's license back to Davenrod. "Have a nice evening, Mr. Bartlett."

## CHAPTER 35

Sergio followed his partner up the stairs, gasping. "Man, this routine is killing me. Tell me why we're doing this again."

"It helps vent the stress." Carly rounded the landing on the second floor and continued climbing. "That's why I run."

He stopped and leaned on the railing, reshuffling the stack of folders he was carrying. "Well, I try to vent the stress several times a week, but with all these long hours, it's been a little tricky finding nice young ladies to vent with."

"Can you behave yourself? We're at work." Her voice echoed off the concrete walls of the station stairwell as she disappeared.

"It's getting hard to tell, since I've practically been living here lately." Sergio tucked the folders under his arm and dug in his pocket for his phone. "Hey, is this a lunch meeting? I didn't eat."

"It might start at lunch time and run through dinner, but I'm not expecting food."

"Sure, why would they feed us?" He tried getting a better grip on the folders, balancing them on his knee as he shouted up the stairs. "What are we up to after this meeting?"

Carly's footsteps stopped. "We update the chiefs and then we touch base with the phone operations. Then we take a stack of case files home and stare at them, hoping some as-yet unseen facts will jump out at us to help us catch this killer."

He marched up the stairs and joined her on the third-floor landing. "And will we be getting drunk during any of this?"

"I won't." She tapped the stack of folders in her arm and opened the door. Office noises and a lot of ringing phones greeted them. She headed down the hallway. "I told you, after I build up a nice big ball of stress in my belly, I'm going to go home and run three miles to let it all fade away."

"And then relax with a nice glass of Chardonnay?"

"Pinot Grigio, but yeah."

"Okay. I may skip the staring at files thing and go straight to the alcohol."

"I'm telling you, exercise helps."

He hooked a thumb over his shoulder at the stairwell door. "Doesn't that set of steps count? My heart is pounding."

Carly gasped, darting into the break room. She clutched her folders to her chest and pressing her back to the wall, closing her eyes.

"Hey, I was kidding." Sergio chuckled.

She peeked out the doorway. "There he is."

"What? Who?"

She moved from the doorway, leaning against the break room wall again. "That creepy guy again. I don't like how he looks at me."

"You don't like how anybody looks at you." Sergio peered into the phone bank area. "Besides, how do you know he's not looking at me?"

"Is he your type?"

"I'm just saying, maybe they're not all looking at you."

"Fine. He's all yours." She went to the table and set her folders on it. A shudder escaped her shoulders.

Breitinger leaned into the room. "Okay, you two. Let's go. I have to update the mayor after this and eventually get home to my wife and family—if I still have one. I haven't seen them in weeks." The lieutenant headed down the corridor.

"Be right there, boss," Sergio called after him. He lifted a mug from the rack by the sink and poured himself some coffee. "Time to face the lions."

\* \* \* \* \*

He answered the phones and logged the calls, went to meetings and even volunteered to update the data in the system again. He was generally a pleasant human being throughout the day.

But all Ken Davenrod could think about was slicing the woman into pieces and bathing in her blood.

When five o'clock came, he wouldn't be the first one out the door—he couldn't afford to be that obvious—but he certainly wouldn't be the last. Not tonight.

He glanced at the clock. Others were gathering their things. The shift was over. He pretended to add items to the data base, thinking about his long drive back to Brandon, where he would sit up the street from 812 Fish Hawk Lane and wait for his Christmas morning to arrive. The thought made him tingle inside. A quick stop by the house for another fake driver's license, stick a different stolen auto tag onto another stolen car, and he'd be on the road.

*One step ahead.*

At the elevator, Archer rapped him on the arm. "Long day, huh, Ken? A few of us are going to happy hour. Wanna come?"

He barely heard it, daydreaming of blood covering his hands and running down his arms, dripping at the elbow and making beautiful red splatters all over the walls and sofa.

He turned to Archer, reeling himself in from his daydream. "Can't. I have work to do."

The elevator doors opened and they stepped inside. Others followed. Archer yawned, folding his hands and stretching his arms out in front of him.

"Come on, buddy. Everybody can see you're putting in the hours, but don't overdo it on the brown nosing. Besides, it's your turn to buy, cheapskate."

Davenrod said nothing, staring straight ahead. This sheep and its stupid comments should be ignored.

The elevator's indicator lights flashed as it descended, and the comment echoed in Davenrod's ears.

*Brown noser.*

Like his work wasn't good enough and he had to kiss up. Like he wasn't strong enough to do a good job. The seeds of anger grew in his stomach.

*This sheep should not even be talking to me . . .*

Davenrod clenched his jaw, the insult gathering momentum inside him.

*It should not even speak to me, let alone dare to call me names.*

Rage welled inside him. He balled up his fists and forced himself to breathe normally. No one could see any outward signs.

*Sheep. Who are you to talk to me like that?*

When the elevator emptied into the parking garage, he walked along side Archer. His coworker walked amiably past the rows of parked cars. "You parked over here today?"

Davenrod glanced around, his temple throbbing. No other people or cars were visible. No security cameras. Red rage washed over his sight as he glared at his teammate. He hated him. He hated the thought of him.

"Where's your ride, man?"

He grabbed Archer by the throat and carried him ten feet to the parking garage wall, slamming him into the hard concrete. Archer's head whipped back on impact. He clawed at Davenrod's thick hands, his eyes bulging and his face turning red.

"I'm not a brown noser." Davenrod squeezed Archer's neck. "Say it."

Archer struggled against the massive hand, veins popping out of his forehead. "Choking . . . me."

Davenrod lifted his coworker off the ground, his heart racing. "Say it."

Snot spewed from Archer's nose as he fought to get air. The words squeezed their way out of his throat, garbled but audible. "You're not."

The rage roiled and churned, a volcano ready to erupt, but he forced himself to think of the woman kicking and writhing as he ripped her guts out and held them up to her dying eyes. Christmas morning would not be compromised. Not over . . . this.

He glared at Archer's vein-filled eyes and purple cheeks.

Davenrod released him, stepping back. Archer dropped to his knees, gasping and clutching at his throat.

"Brown nosing is weakness."

Archer put a hand on the garage floor and gulped air. "You're a nut job, Ken. A psych case."

He frowned at Davenrod, spitting. "That'll cost you your badge!"

"Will it?" Davenrod took a step toward him. Archer scurried backwards, lowering his head and whimpering.

"Let me tell you something." Davenrod put a foot on Archer's shoulder and pushed. The man rolled over onto his back, curling into the fetal position and whimpering like a sick dog. Tears streamed down his face. Davenrod pointed a finger, speaking through clenched teeth. "If one word of this gets out, if anyone says anything, I'll know where it came from. That won't . . . it won't make me happy. And I'll spend all day, every day, in the unemployment line, thinking about who caused me this pain, and I'll dedicate my life to making sure they know how unhappy they made me. Them, their family, their dog and cat." He breathed hard, almost growling. "They'll know—all of them, each and every one—exactly how unhappy they made me. Do you understand?"

Trembling, Archer nodded.

"You are weakness. I see it. Everyone sees it. Weakness."

The desire to leap on him, to pound the sheep's face until it turned to warm jelly flashed through his mind.

*Focus on Christmas morning.*

His rage ebbed like a fading candle, dwindling until it extinguished. Davenrod squared his shoulders and glanced at the bleeding scratch marks on his hand.

*I didn't even feel them.*

They glistened in the light of the garage, shiny and wet.

*I am power.*

He shook his head at the cowering sheep in front of him. "Go home and take a shower. You wet yourself—buddy." Davenrod turned and walked away. "See you tomorrow."

# CHAPTER 36

The woman arrived at 812 Fish Hawk Lane. Davenrod had anticipated there might be some late meetings and some traffic, and he guessed right. She was about thirty minutes later than the night before.

It didn't matter. He was ready.

The plan was as simple as it was effective. Runners were creatures of habit; very few deviated from their running schedule or their running course. He'd wait up the block from her house until she started her run, then drive around the opposite way and intercept her toward the far end of the construction complex.

Empty, dark, and desolate. The sheep would get what it deserved.

A jolt of electricity went through his insides as he envisioned the look on its face. With wide eyes and a gaping mouth, it would see the blade and then see him, realizing in a fleeting moment of terror who was about to hack the sheep to pieces. Its eyes would broadcast the futility, the emptiness, of its life's work.

Such exquisite pain.

To plunge his hands inside while it was still alive, the hot gush of the pumping blood.

Heat rushed over him. He reached out and lowered the car heater.

*Florida. I thought the weather was supposed to be warm all the time here.*

He lowered his window an inch, letting a chilly burst of air through. A car rounded the curve and drove past. He pulled himself upright. It wouldn't be long now. The garage had closed, the lights had come on. The sheep had followed its routine.

*Run, sheep. It's time to run.*

He pressed the button on his phone. Forty-five minutes had passed. He might have to go to the door and deliver a package. A short walk down the street, across the pretty lawn and onto the fake brick stoop, then press the doorbell and—

The front door opened. The silhouette stepped outside.

He held his breath, waiting as the sheep twisted and turned, hands on hips, and bent forward to touch the ground.

Christmas morning was about to arrive.

It locked the door and dashed off the front porch, jogging along the sidewalk to the first turn, then disappeared down the street.

Excitement welled inside him, his heart racing. He turned the key and started his car, dropping the gearshift to drive and following the sheep. The chilly night air sliced through the window as he drove. He reached over and put it up, clicking the heater up another notch.

His headlights illuminated it as he came up from behind. Long strides and reflecting shoes. Shiny, dark leggings and a windbreaker flapping as it moved.

He checked his speed.

*Too slow.*

He pressed the gas pedal and passed the sheep, glancing at it in the rearview mirror as he made his way toward—

The plan came crashing into his brain.

*Stupid, stupid, stupid!*

He shook his head, nearly driving into the curb. The plan was to circle around. Now she had seen his car. Anger gripped him. He pounded the steering wheel, cursing at himself.

*You were supposed to circle around. Stupid!*

He steadied the wheel, keeping his speed, thinking. It wouldn't matter. Runners get lost in their own world. She won't even remember the car passing her.

*That's it. One step ahead. It's fine.*

He drove to the end of the construction site and looked around. No people were present, but that was to be expected. It would be a few minutes before she got here. He had time.

He reached for the bag and put it on the passenger seat. The light from a single street light illuminated his car, allowing him to pick through his tools.

He had the t-shirts, the mask . . .

The knife.

His pulse raced as he looked at it. Lifting the heavy blade, he set it on his lap and admired its gleaming edge in the light. His eyes drifted to the gym bag. Inside, wrapped in a small blanket, was the gun.

*Weakness.*

He fought the urge to take it in his hands. The gun was heavy, too, and spit a small burst of beautiful fire when he shot it at night. Its flash was like a photograph when he shot the trucker, burning the shocked face into his memory forever. Those gunshots had made his ears ring when he fired it in the back of the truck. He wouldn't make that mistake again. When he killed the jogger, it hardly seemed to make any noise at all. No muzzle flash, either, really, so no photograph-like memory. But by then he was envisioning the warm wetness.

*That was much better.*

He reached for it, sliding it from its blanket and cradling the cold metal against his face.

*Power.*

The gun was power, there was no doubt about that. But tonight was about challenging himself.

Taking the sheep would be easier with the gun, but tonight he was going to the next level.

*You don't need the gun.*

He dropped it back into the bag and slid the bag onto the floor.

Tonight, he only needed the knife. No masks, no costumes. Just one sheep and one knife.

He rubbed his chin, scanning the empty apartment buildings. Half built, more or less, they provided lots of cover—and lots of places to work.

What about flaying the sheep on the cold, hard concrete of an empty apartment lobby? Peeling its skin away and gouging out its eyes as it screamed? Or running up behind it as it ran, tackling it and throwing it down on the cold, hard dirt of the construction site, then holding the knife up to its face? Let the sheep see the blade before plunging it in. Fill the sheep with fear before filling it with pain.

He glanced down the dark, empty street. The sheep would be coming soon.

*Time to get ready.*

Near the corner, a stack of roof trusses lay next to a large mound of dirt. That would be his spot. He could peek out from the pile as the sheep approached, waiting for just the right moment, then launch himself toward it like a missile. The force would knock it off its feet. He would wrap his arms around it and throw himself forward, his weight landing on top of it, crushing it and knocking the wind out of it, rendering it weak and confused.

Then he would brandish the knife.

That would bring clarity.

His heart pounding, he opened the door and stepped outside the car, carrying the knife upside down by its handle, but with its big blade to his wrist. If anyone glanced in his direction, they'd see nothing, or see him holding something, but not be able to see what it was.

Not until he was ready for the sheep to see it.

He crept across the street and crouched behind the mound of dirt. It was smaller than he thought. From the car, it seemed as if he could stand upright and watch for the sheep coming. Instead, he had to crouch. No matter; one was as good as the other.

He gazed at the big blade. It gleamed in the light. Tonight, it would take him to a new world.

He peeked out from the side of the mound. Still nothing. The silhouette would be coming soon, though. Patience.

Would it scream? Did he care if it did? The site was empty for blocks. Who would hear? Who would come looking if they did?

No, anyone who heard anything would call the police—at best—and by the time a patrol unit responded, he'd be long gone.

He glanced at his car. The keys were in the ignition, waiting for him to come to it and drive away whenever he was ready. A calm drive north toward State Road 60, displaying different license plates than last time, then a short drive to the interstate. A different ID in his wallet. Nothing left to chance.

*One step ahead.*

He'd be home and asleep before midnight. Except he wouldn't sleep. Not tonight.

He'd take the most precious souvenir of all and bathe in it, painting himself in blood, glistening and glowing. He'd stand naked in front of the mirror in the garage, all red and powerful and triumphant, satisfied and exuberant.

The rush was upon him.

He inched his head along the side of the dirt pile, peering up the street, holding his breath in anticipation of the silhouette.

Movement came out of the dark horizon. The ponytail, bobbing closer and closer with every long stride. He gripped the knife, his heart pounding, waiting for the moment when he would spring out and see the wide eyes and gaping mouth, the gasping as the sheep backed away, the impact of his massive body crashing into the sheep's small, weak one, and the crushing smash onto the ground afterward.

Growing bigger in his sight, he crouched and waited as the sheep came closer.

The ponytail swayed and bounced with each step. Rhythmic, in the chilly night air, just like the strides. The silhouette came closer, arms swinging, legs churning, its breath flowing over the shoulder of the windbreaker in thin white puffs.

As it neared, the mouth became visible. Open, in an O, drawing breath in coordination with the strides. The sounds of the soft footfalls reached his ears. Clad in black running shoes, each step slapped the sidewalk, pat, pat, pat, pat, keeping time like a bizarre, breathing clock.

Pat, pat, pat, pat.

It was all in rhythm. The bobbing hair, the legs, the breath. All moving in turn, playing their melody.

He clenched the knife, holding his breath, pulling his head back just a fraction. He didn't want to be any more visible than was absolutely necessary.

Pat, pat, pat, pat.

It was almost time. The footsteps grew louder. His heart pounded as he waited, squeezing the thick handle of the big blade again and again in anticipation.

*Come, sheep. Come to me.*

The ponytail bobbed, the torso swaying back and forth ever so slightly with each stride.

Pat, pat, pat, pat.

Closer. Louder.

*Come, sheep. Come . . .*

The sheep's steady huffing became audible, sending his pulse skyrocketing. The sheep's foggy white puffs appeared in the cool night air as if forced out by every second or third footfall, accompanied by the faintest of exhales.

Pat, pat, pat, pat.

*Closer . . .*

He inched his head lower, waiting for the sheep to appear on the other side of the dirt mound, where the sidewalk turned right and the distance was shortest. He nodded, licking his lips. Two seconds, maybe less, is all he would need to be upon the sheep, ramming it from the side and crashing on top of it, then holding the knife over its head.

Pat, pat, pat, pat.

*Come, sheep . . . commme . . .*

It was nearly there.

His hands trembled. It was almost Christmas morning.

*Pat, pat.*

It stopped. The sheep huffed loudly, gasping as it sucked in air.

No footfalls.

His eyes darted about. He couldn't look out to learn what had happened. Had he been discovered? What did the sheep see? Fear gripped his gut. He glanced toward his car. It was still where he'd left it, parked along the curb across the road, under the street light. He quickly recounted his cautious steps. The stress grew inside him. The bag of tools couldn't possibly be seen from this far away. What did she see?

*She can't see anything!*

His ears throbbed with the coming freight train, panic overtaking him. What happened? Why did she stop? She can't know anything. The license plates are different. The IDs are different. The tools aren't visible. The whole car—

The car.

He stifled a gasp. The long drive to Brandon had warmed the car, and the cool night air had allowed just enough of a difference in temperature to fog the windows. That meant a warm car and no driver.

And nowhere for that driver to be coming home to in an unfinished apartment building.

He clenched his fists and squeezed his eyes shut until blobs of purple and green cascaded through his brain.

*Stupid, stupid, stupid!*

But what of the sheep? He cocked his head and put a hand on the dirt pile, leaning forward. He had to look. She would be tying a shoe or checking her time, possibly stretching or . . .

*Or what?*

He recoiled. If he looked, she might see him. If she saw him, she might identify him.

Sweat gathered on his brow.

The mask was in the car. She would see his face.

*Stupid, stupid, stupid!*

The freight train rumbled closer. He shook his head, pushing it away, trying to focus.

*Power. Get control.*

*Get the sheep.*

A loud grunt came over the dirt mound. The footfalls came again, fast and loud, the sheep huffing forcefully with each one.

He raised his head over the mound. She was running away, whipping her arms and slamming her legs, sprinting in the opposite direction. In seconds, she was disappearing back over the dark horizon.

He stood up, growling, flexing his large muscles and gripping the blade so hard his whole body shook. Blinding rage seized him, overflowing into a howl as the silhouette fled.

His brain was on fire. The sheep would not ruin his plan.

*The car. She's not faster than that.*

He raced to his vehicle and jumped inside, twisting the key in a fierce crush and roaring the engine to life. He gritted his teeth and slammed the gearshift down, heaved the steering wheel to the left and punched the accelerator. The tires screamed as they spun, sending smoke over the asphalt road. The car launched forward.

The headlight beams swung over the grass and far buildings, swerving onto the road she'd fled on. He raced the motor, grabbing the wheel and leaning close, scanning the road for any sign of her.

In the distance, his lights caught the silhouette as it sprinted down the sidewalk. He stomped the gas pedal. The car veered toward her, gaining ground as the ponytail bounced away.

He nodded, shouting. "You're weakness, sheep! Weakness!"

The freight train came at him harder now, thundering in his head.

*Stupid, stupid, stupid, to leave the car exposed like that. Stupid!*

He flung his head like he was trying to shoo away a housefly, forcing the train from his thoughts. He'd done it right. He was power. Power makes no mistakes.

*You let her see the car, stupid.*

"Stop. I'm not stupid!" He clenched his jaw and pounded the wheel. "Stop saying that!"

The freight train neared. Its vibrations surged through him, shaking him like a dog with a rag doll.

"It was the weather."

*Excuses are the domain of the lessers.*

He moaned, wiping his brow and focusing on the silhouette. The car sped towards her, closing the gap. The sheep grew larger in the windshield. It glanced back, its dark hair flying, its mouth open and its eyes becoming huge in his headlights.

For a moment, he thought about running her down, just driving the car right over her. But he wanted to use the knife. He *had* to use the knife. The knife was the plan. He had waited so long, grown so much . . . *evolved* to the knife, and the knife alone. It would be no good otherwise.

*It would be weakness.*

The sheep could not be allowed to escape, though. Not now. It had seen too much.

He breathed heavily. Stomping the gas pedal again, he sent the car lurching over the curb and onto the sidewalk. The jolt sent him upward, hitting his head on the ceiling and sending his tools all over the car floor. The steering wheel jerked out of his hands as he landed, bounding as he grabbed at it.

The sheep screamed. He swerved the car again, steering toward the fleeing silhouette.

It glanced over its shoulder again, then jumped to the left and bounded over the grassless construction site. In front of her, an empty apartment building.

He spun the wheel, careening the car sideways and sliding himself halfway off his seat. He righted himself and gunned the engine. The wheels sent a stream of dirt into the air. The car slammed and bounced after her. She was less than a hundred yards from the entry. He gripped the wheel, keeping her in the headlights, narrowing the distance between his fender and her feet.

The running shoe reflectors whipped up and down as she raced toward the building. "It's no use," he chuckled. He had her. He slammed the gas pedal to the floor.

The freight train crushed his brain as it slammed his insides.

*Don't kill it with the car! Don't be weak!*

"Shut up!" he screamed, spit flying from his lips. "Shut uuuuppp!"

The stucco walls of the building loomed ahead. Her feet were white in the reflection of the headlights, inches from the front of his car. He laughed, leaning forward and pressing the accelerator a little harder. The ponytail whipped back and forth. Sand and dirt kicked up from her feet and rained across his windshield.

Her foot thumped as the car caught a running shoe. The sheep twisted and fell, throwing itself to the right and out of the light.

He slammed on the brakes, banging himself into the steering wheel. Heaving himself backwards he turned to see the silhouette lying on the ground. A cloud of dust floated over it as its chest lifted and sagged. It rolled over, got to its feet, and ran lopsided along the building. The pale, frightened face turned again and again as it passed the windows of the lower floors. Newly installed glass prevented any escape through the apartment.

He turned the steering wheel and gunned the engine. The wheels sunk in the sand. A jolt of fear shot through him.

*I can't get stuck!*

The car lowered as the wheel found nothing solid to grab.

*No, no, no . . .*

He slung the wheel back and forth, gunning the engine, sending wild sprays of dirt everywhere. A brown cloud engulfed the vehicle.

He cursed, slamming the wheel.

*Come on, come on, come on . . .*

The car crept forward, the whine of the tires deafening as they plowed the earth. As they caught, the car lurched forward and after its prey once again.

The sheep veered right, barely dodging the front of his car. He swerved on the sandy soil, staying on her tail.

*You can't escape. You are weakness.*

The sheep veered left, crossing between some piles of lumber and a tied stack of long, metal pipes. The killer swung his car left, plowing through the small space. The pipes clashed and clattered, cracking the rear window in a metallic avalanche. The plywood screeched as his car pushed through it.

The silhouette limped between two buildings through a narrow dirt alley.

He spit. "That's right, sheep. Keep trying. This car will fit right through that." He gunned the motor and sped after her.

When she cleared the alley, she ran to the right, flinging herself over rows of pipes. He steered the car wide, avoiding the pipes, and smashed sideways into a stack of giant concrete drains. The impact threw him into the car door and shattered the windshield. He grimaced, forcing the car forward as she got further away.

The gun. That would stop her.

He reached for the bag. It slid over the floor as the car bumped and lurched. His arm slammed into the passenger seat. Glancing up, he swerved to avoid a row of potted trees waiting to be installed. He lunged for the bag again, grabbing the corner and hauling it upwards. More of the contents spilled out. The gun slid forward to the far corner of the floor. He raised his head and grabbed the wheel, his eyes darting around to find the silhouette.

She was gone.

*It doesn't matter. Find her and kill her. She's only going one place right now—her home. You can kill her here or you can kill her there, it doesn't matter.*

He pulled the car onto a concrete section of a patio, ramming the gearshift into park. Turning off the motor, he climbed out and listened.

*She can't have gotten away. Not that quickly.*

His gaze moved along the building, dark and cold, the wind sending gusts of dirt and trash along its concrete corners.

*Doesn't matter. In five minutes I can be at her house and kill her and everyone else inside it. When she gets there, she's as good as dead.*

A piece of dark fabric caught his eye. In the headlights, a dark chunk of shiny gray nylon flapped in the breeze, caught on the framing of a rear portico. He reached inside the car and over the center console, grabbing his flashlight as it rolled back and forth on the floor. He snapped it on and stepped toward the fabric, shining the light on the ground. Many new, small footprints in the dirt and sand made a trail. He squatted, holding the light close to the ground.

The tread marks left by the big work boots of the construction workers were very different from what he knew a running shoe tread to be. He traced the path with his flashlight. They went right to the portico, where the fabric hung.

He laughed, standing.

*She's inside, and she can't get out without me seeing her.*

Lifting the flashlight, he shined it on the building.

"I'm coming for you, sheep." He trudged toward the portico. "I know where you are and I'm coming for you!"

He halted himself, holding his breath and listening. After running that fast, the sheep would certainly need to breathe, and—

*What's this?*

A black running shoe lay sideways in the dirt near the portico.

He picked it up and shoved his fingers inside to the toe. It was warm.

He stepped back, eyeing the entrance. "Why did you leave this for me? Is this supposed to be a trap? I walk in and get whacked with a two by four?" Anger welled inside him. He yelled. "What if I just burn the whole place down with you in it, sheep? What about that?"

Scanning the site, he stepped toward the portico and shined the light on the fabric. It had snagged on a framing nail.

*And she tore it, getting out of it to get away.*

The flashlight was sticky in his hand. He tucked it under his arm and held his fingers up to the beam. They were red with blood.

*Mine? Or hers?*

Shoving her shoe under his other arm, he went to grab the light and shine it over his body, but glanced at the building first. "It this some sort of pathetic trap, sheep? As I stop to check myself, I get attacked?"

*One step ahead.*

He backed a safe distance away from the portico, then quickly inspected himself. No serious cuts or scrapes, just a lot of dirt.

The shoe went under the light next. Around the rim of one side, blood had collected.

*She's injured.*

He smiled.

*Sheep. Cold and afraid and injured, with the chilly night temperatures dropping. And with only one shoe.*

"This just isn't your day, sheep." He chuckled, advancing to the rear entry. "But don't worry, I'm coming."

He couldn't help but consider the many makeshift weapons the site provided. Pipes. Rebar. Glass. He had to move fast, but with caution.

At the rear entry, he paused, considering how to best enter. He glanced again at his car. His gun was there, and if he didn't bring it with him now, she might get the idea to grab it and use it on him. That wouldn't be any good. He stepped toward the vehicle.

A loud metallic crash boomed through the night. He flinched, dropping everything and instinctively ducking for cover, putting his hand to his side for his service weapon—and grabbing only his blue jeans.

The rumble of rolling pipes came from the far side of the empty building, the clanging and clashing seeming like it was higher than the ground floor. He picked up the flashlight and lifted his head, singing like a child. "Somebody has stumbled into something."

*She isn't bleeding badly enough to stop running, but she's scared enough to make mistakes in the dark.*

He raced inside, waving the flashlight around until he found a staircase, then bolted up the steps. "I'm coming for you sheep. I'm coming!"

He heard it now, the hard breathing, just like he'd heard it outside on the street.

*The running has exhausted her.*

He squared his shoulders and stood tall.

*Cave men were able to kill prey by scaring it and running after it. They chased and followed, chased and followed, wearing out the faster animals but making up for it over the miles. Then they surrounded the exhausted animal and stabbed it to death with their wooden spears and stone tips.*

"It's primal, you see?" He stepped along the plywood floor. "The hunter and the hunted. The powerful and the lesser, sheep."

The unfinished surface creaked with every step. He halted again, eyeing a mass of metal pipes scattered over the floor. Behind it, more tall stacks of the long pipes, waiting to be installed. He'd passed several stacks outside, too, but thought they wouldn't make a decent weapon. Too long. The sheep discovered that, too.

*So stupid, sheep. Clumsy and stupid.*

He shined the light down the hallway, listening. The sheep would run or die, and it could only hold its breath for so long after such a long, exhausting race. It would breathe. It would have to. And when it did, he'd hear it—if only he could be quiet enough and listen.

His pulse throbbed in his ears. Sweat trickled along his neck and down his back.

There it was. A gasp.

Down the hall, in the far-right corner, he heard it. He clicked off the flashlight and held his breath, easing one foot onto the flooring and then the other, creeping toward her. His eyes took a moment to adjust to the lack of light.

He crept over the sawdust and nails, past thick electrical wires that stuck out of the walls and ceilings, seeing better now. His breath came easily, so it came quietly. He hadn't run several miles and hadn't fled for his life. He hadn't snagged himself on the portico and hadn't injured his foot.

The sheep had done all of those things. All he had to do was be quieter than the sheep, and victory was his.

And he already knew which unit she was hiding in.

He moved along the hallway, flashlight in hand, ready to turn it on and blind her, then bring it down on her head and smash open her skull before gutting her like the others. He'd leave the sheep's carcass for the construction workers to discover, and read all about it in the news. *Seminole Heights Serial Killer Branches Out To Brandon.* That would have people wetting themselves as far away as Miami and Tallahassee.

He stopped.

*There it is again.*

Panting. Hard breaths. They came faintly, bouncing off the hard walls and floors, floating to his happy ears.

He followed the sounds, slow and steady, stepping softly down the hallway.

*One step ahead.*

He reached the end unit, pausing at the doorway. His heart leaped. The breaths were louder now.

*She's curled up in a bathtub or dusty corner, waiting for me to finish her off.*

He raised the flashlight to his shoulder, pointing it forward but holding the handle like a club. His thumb nestled the rubber button on the metal flashlight's shaft, ready to turn it on when he found her.

By the kitchen area of the unfinished unit, he halted again, listening. The breathing came from the far side, a bedroom or bathroom near the front wall of the building. He tiptoed across the floor and into the hallway, the room ahead of him barely visible in the dark night. The scarcest glow of a faraway street light allowed him to make out a shape.

There, in the corner, she sat, gasping and whimpering, pressed against the wall by an open window.

*Now.*

He clicked on the flashlight. Whiteness flooded the room. She narrowed her eyes and raised one hand, shielding herself from the bright beam.

With one eye cracked open, she lifted a rock from a small pile next to her—small chunks of concrete. Grunting, she thrust her arm forward, the missile grazing his shoulder. The flashlight beam jumped with the impact.

He laughed, stepping toward her, his insides brimming with fire. The moment was his.

Her next throw sent a chunk of concrete past his head. He kept the light in her eyes. She gasped, leaning her head back, her tank top exposing her dirty, bare arms. One foot wore a running shoe; the other did not. She squinted in the light, bending to lift another rock.

He came forward, the breeze from the open window brushing his face.

"You are weakness."

This toss bounced past him, rolling across the floor. She sagged, grabbing another one.

*Her strength is waning.*

He chuckled. "I see it. Everyone sees it. Weakness."

Her shoulders heaved as she gulped the air, her face and arms crusted with dirt and sweat, her shiny black leggings ripped and torn. She favored the bare, bleeding ankle, holding her foot off the ground slightly.

"You are weakness, sheep. Just like the trucker. Just like the jogger."

She shook her head, breathing hard, her torso sagging with each breath. She said nothing as she leaned against the wall, reaching down again. The last chunk was the size of a baseball. She cocked her hand back and launched it toward him.

The impact shook his hand and knocked the flashlight from it. Pain soared from his fingers as the bulb went out.

He rubbed his fingers, gritting his teeth. "I took his finger, you know. And a piece of lung from that jogger. Souvenirs for my collection." His eyes began to adjust to the dark again, but she had nowhere to run except right past him, and he wanted that more than anything.

She breathed harder, coming back into view, gasping as she clung to the wall.

"The news didn't talk about that, but you know about it, don't you? Are you scared, sheep? Thinking about what part of you I'm going to chop up and take home?"

She pushed herself off the wall and turned to the window. The hair band had torn out, her ponytail a matted mess that lifted in the gusts of wind from outside. She threw one leg over, then the other, perching on her butt and thrusting her head through the opening.

"Stop!" He raced toward her.

Her hands pushed away, launching her.

"No!" He raced forward, crashing into the windowsill as she dropped out of sight. His fingers brushed the dark hair, but nothing more.

He pushed his head out the window, eyeing the drop. Below him, the sheep lay in a small pile of sand next to the stacks of fire system pipes. She scurried to her feet and ripped at the cords, sending a cascade of metal tubes under the window.

The deafening clash of metal hammered his ears. He stood up and put a foot over the edge and glanced down. It was only twenty feet, maybe a little more, but the sandy landing the sheep had enjoyed was now covered in hard metal pipes. They rolled and clanged, falling at awkward angles as the stack emptied itself into a pile under the window.

He held himself there, his heart pounding. From that height, he could get impaled, or just twist an ankle—but he wouldn't be able to jump far enough to get past the metal pipes.

He pounded the window sill, cursing.

*She can circle around to the car and grab the gun. She could get any of the tools and use them to identify him. Get to the car!*

Scowling, he pulled himself back inside. The silhouette ran, limping and off balance, down to the sidewalk and across the street toward a wooded area on the perimeter.

He pounded the apartment wall. He couldn't risk it. He had to gather his tools and dispose of the stolen car.

He couldn't chase her.

Slamming his fists through the unpainted drywall, he raged and screamed. He shoved his head back out the window, snarling at the night.

"I will find you, sheep! I will find you!"

She raised a hand over her head, flipping him off as she disappeared between the trees.

## CHAPTER 37

Carly held the phone to her ear as she raced through the traffic on Brandon Boulevard. "Come on, partner. Don't still be at happy hour."

Sergio answered. "Is that you, Mom? I brushed my teeth and was headed for bed—but not alone, so this better be good."

Wincing, she pressed the accelerator with her left foot, trying not to let the mud make it slip off the pedal. "You can tell me how good it is when you meet me at Tampa General."

"And when am I—"

"Now. Get moving." She ended the call and let the phone drop into her lap, swerving to avoid crashing into any other cars as she sped to the hospital.

\* \* \* \* \*

Sergio flashed his badge to the triage nurse, smiling. "I'm Detective Martin. My partner is here within your hallowed halls somewhere, but she didn't tell me where. Detective Sanderson. Any ideas?"

The nurse adjusted her reading glasses and consulted her computer screen. "She's in trauma room six, Detective."

Sergio read the plastic wall signs as he passed each room. The door to trauma room six was open, with Lieutenant Breitinger sitting in the corner chair.

"Wow." Sergio stood in the doorway. "I don't want to say I'm not happy to see you, boss, but my concern level just ratcheted up about ten notches. What's going on?"

"Good question." Breitinger stood up. "Carly's getting an x-ray on her ankle. The nurse just said she'll be back here in a second."

"So, she called you, too?"

Breitinger glared at him. "You thought both of us being here was a coincidence?"

"No, I . . ." Sergio rubbed the back of his neck. "No."

A doctor walked in, followed by a tall male attendant pushing Carly in a wheelchair. Her right leg was elevated—raised and swollen, but clean; the rest of her was covered in dirt and mud.

"Hey," Sergio said softly, kneeling next to her. "What's going on?"

She held up a finger. "One sec."

Breitinger went to the doctor, peeking at the chart. "How's her leg, doc?"

"The x-ray was merely a precaution. I don't think the ankle is fractured." He faced Carly. "You have a bad sprain and you bought yourself a few stitches, but you'll live. You three can have the room for a few minutes, then we'll move to a treatment room for the stitches. You'll want to stay off it for a week or so, and take some ibuprofen. Use ice to reduce the swelling."

Carly nodded. "Thank you, doctor."

"Anytime. But hopefully not any time. I prefer you guys in here asking questions of patients, not being patients."

When the doctor left the room, Breitinger turned to Carly. "Okay, you got us all out of bed and over here. What's going on?"

"I hate to ask this, Lieutenant, but can I talk to Sergio alone for a minute, please?"

"No, whatever you have to say, start saying it. You told me on the phone that you had a break in the case."

"Really?" Sergio faced Carly. "You didn't say that to me."

"I said I *thought* I had a break in the case. Please, sir. Two minutes."

Breitinger scowled. "Okay, I'll go wait in the hall. Make it quick."

As the door closed, Sergio leaned on the bed and held up the remote control. "Will you be more comfortable in the bed?"

"I got attacked this evening." Carly lowered her eyes. "While I was running."

Sergio set the remote down, his voice falling to a whisper. "I figured it was something like that. You okay? I mean, leg aside?"

"I'm okay. And it's just a sprained ankle."

"That you drove across town to get looked at. You guys have a hospital in Brandon."

Carly leaned forward. Her face was tense and serious. "Listen to me. I went running like I always do, through that apartment complex they're building. A guy followed me in his car and then got out and chased me."

"Wow. Did you call it in?"

"No, we're going to handle it." She took a deep breath and let it out slowly, her eyes fixed on his. "I think it was our serial killer."

"What?" Sergio's face fell. "How do you mean?"

"I mean . . . I think that's who was chasing me. I think it was our guy."

"Oh, man." He paced back and forth, rubbing the back of his neck. "Why didn't you tell the lieutenant that?"

"Because he'd try to take me off the case for my own safety."

"That's right." He pointed at the door. "And I'm gonna tell him right now, so he *can* take you off the case for your own safety."

"Don't. I want this guy. He's made it personal."

"It's not supposed to be personal, it's supposed to be—"

She pounded the arm of the wheelchair, her face growing red. "You're not telling Breitinger, and I'm not coming off the case. I'm coming to work in a few hours and that's the end of it. Understand?"

"No," he shouted. "You need to understand me. I'm not going to watch you get yourself killed. This guy is a cold-blooded killer. He has all day, every day, to think of the next way to ambush you. And why are we at Tampa General?"

"I—I didn't want to be anywhere in Brandon. I took a shortcut through the woods to my house, got right in my car and drove here. I didn't want to . . ."

"Oh, come on! You didn't want to be in Brandon where you live, or at the hospital in Brandon, because you think he's still going to come after you."

"Yes! He wouldn't think to come here."

"And that sounds rational to you?"

Breitinger stuck his head in the door. "Hey, if you're gonna shout, I might as well come back in."

Sergio threw his hands in the air, storming to the window. "Lieutenant, would you please talk some sense into my partner?"

Against her protests, Sergio spilled the beans. Lieutenant Breitinger's face turned red with each word. Carly's turned redder.

"Okay," Breitinger said. "So Merry Christmas, and you're off the case."

Sergio nodded. "Thank you."

"You can't do that." Carly frowned. "You—"

"Who do you think you are, Carly? You aren't thinking straight." Breitinger raised his voice. "If something happens to you—if the news reports that I can't even protect my own detectives—it tells the entire population of the greater Tampa Bay area that none of them are safe. We will have a panic on our hands on Christmas Eve."

"We do anyway," Carly said. "Right now, you're a police lieutenant in serial killer city. No tourist wants to come here. The shops are all closing at three o'clock because nobody wants to be on the street after dark, and half the people don't wanna be outside after lunch."

"Wait a minute." Breitinger stood up and paced back and forth, rubbing his chin. "Now, wait."

"There's no waiting," Carly said. "I don't care how things look. I want to catch this guy." She leaned forward, resting her hands on her knees. "The public doesn't need to know. We won't tell them. But this guy wants me, sir. So let him come after me. Wire me up and put a cop on every street around my house if you want. If he's coming for me, let him come. Let me be the bait like you have in Seminole Heights—or is there something wrong with me being the bait?"

"Don't give me that." Breitinger frowned. "Are you gonna go jogging with a twisted ankle?"

She glanced at her swollen foot. "Maybe. And there was something else. I couldn't see him very well in the dark, but there was something familiar about him."

"He doesn't need to know it's not her." Sergio stepped to the center of the room. "Maybe we could have somebody else from the squad go jogging in her place. A decoy."

Breitinger narrowed his eyes, but said nothing.

"Get any female officer with long, dark hair." Carly eyed the lieutenant. "I bet we have a few that are joggers. Put her in a ponytail and bring her to my house. Dress her in my running gear. We wait a few hours and let the SWAT teams check the whole area from under cover, and then we roll out."

"*She* rolls out," Breitinger said. "The decoy."

"Right." Carly nodded. "I tell her the jogging route, everything. You fill the roofs with SWAT teams. And she can be carrying. She can wear a shoulder holster and a bulletproof vest under her windbreaker, plus a side piece strapped to her leg—whatever you want. It'll work, Lieutenant. The killer won't be expecting any of that. When she's good and isolated, he'll make his move—and we grab him."

Breitinger sat in the chair, slouching. The red had gone out of his face, but the concern lingered. "I don't see him going into that neighborhood again after what happened. What if he doesn't show?"

"He'll show." Her eyes went to the window. "If he doesn't show tonight, he'll show tomorrow night. He moved his hunting ground from Seminole

Heights to Brandon for a reason. There's no way he's gonna let this slip through his hands."

"'*This*'?" Sergio said. "You mean you."

Breitinger sat up. "How can you be so sure?"

"I don't know. I just am." She faced the lieutenant. "I think it's personal for him now."

Breitinger sat with his hand on his chin. "I don't know."

"Sir?" Sergio looked at the lieutenant. "Can we speak alone?"

"What, I gotta wait in the hall again? No."

"No, sir. You and me. Let's step out for a sec." Sergio moved past him to the hallway. The lieutenant followed. When the door shut behind them, Sergio spoke.

"I appreciate your situation, Lieutenant. Carly's my partner and my best friend. I'd never let anything happen to her." He shoved his hands in his pockets, eyeing the floor. "But frankly, sir, she's right. You and everybody else have thrown everything at this case, and we're still on square one. Now the killer is coming to us. Let him. Let us run with this."

"You're sure?"

"Yep," Sergio said. "And I'm sure about my partner."

Breitinger sighed, rubbing his chin. "You're convinced this is our best idea?"

"Sir, it's not just the best thing we have, it's the only thing we have."

## CHAPTER 38

Sergio leaned against the conference room wall as the SWAT team commander and a group of department heads seated themselves. Breitinger came in, followed by Sergeant Marshall and Dr. Stevens. On the whiteboard were a few diagrams and a bullet point list.

When the door was shut, Breitinger pushed his suit coat back and placed his hands on his hips. "Thank you all for coming in early on such short notice. I'll be brief." He rubbed his chin, glancing at the faces around the table. "We have a chance to catch our serial killer. Maybe only one chance. So here's how this is going to go down."

He pointed to the whiteboard. "Last night while jogging in her neighborhood, Detective Sanderson encountered and was pursued by an individual we believe was our serial killer. Later today, we're going to have one of our undercover officers leave Detective Sanderson's house, dressed in Detective Sanderson's exercise gear, to run along a three-mile course we've laid out." He faced the group at the table. "Prior to that, we need a sweep of the neighborhood and the running route. We'll need Tactical to determine where they can put their people along the course without drawing attention. We need to acquire the appropriate clothes and running gear from the house, or we can buy them at the mall, to ensure a decoy undercover officer jogging that route tonight will be as visually close as possible to Detective Sanderson."

Pens scribbled on notepads around the table. Department heads would need to assess what personnel and equipment they'd need to fulfill the role they were about to be handed.

"We have to implement every step of this operation quickly and without error, and in complete secrecy." Breitinger stared at the board, waving his hand. "We can't check out the house and neighborhood with uniformed officers, because the killer might be watching. Assume he is. That means we can't have people climbing onto roofs of apartment buildings in plain sight, or parking a bunch of vans on the street. Any of that will look out of place."

The SWAT team commander nodded. "My team can go in as construction workers in pickup trucks, staggered throughout the day. We can also access a newspaper delivery van, cable TV vans, garbage trucks—you name it, we'll be it. I can even put an officer in a sweater and a gray-haired wig so we can pretend to be an elderly neighbor walking the dog."

"Commander." Doctor Stevens set her pen down and folded her hands over her pad. "Won't all that activity raise eyebrows?"

"No ma'am. We coordinate with these service companies and city departments on occasion, so it won't be unusual to them, and we deploy our covert ops teams slowly and in small numbers. It won't appear out of the ordinary to anyone."

"Pickup trucks coming and going from a construction site shouldn't raise eyebrows." Breitinger walked to the whiteboard, tapping the bullet point list. "Still, we have to do everything quickly and quietly. Otherwise, there's no point. In order for this to work, the killer must suspect nothing. I want our teams in place now, before he goes back to the house. And in case he's already there, we need to covertly sweep the whole neighborhood first."

There was a knock at the door. Carly peeked in.

"Come on in, Detective." Breitinger grabbed the knob and opened the door. "Let's see how they did with you."

She stepped in, wearing a dark blue police uniform. Thick black utility belt, service weapon holster, chest badge, big black shoes—even a shoulder radio. The works. Her long, dark hair was pinned up in a tight, round bun.

Sergio chewed his lip. If he didn't know she had a badly sprained ankle, he wouldn't guess from watching her. But she didn't walk far into the conference room, either.

Carly closed the door and held her arms out. "How do I look?"

"Perfect." Breitinger said. "Like a regular cop. Try to act like one and don't draw any attention to yourself today. We'll see about getting you some of your own clothes when we recon your house in a few hours. Make Jeffers a list. She'll get what you need."

"Clothes."

"Okay, people. Make a hard list of details we need to address." Breitinger went to the door and opened it. "Report back in an hour."

"Carly," Sergeant Marshall said, standing. "Officer Jeffers is at the duty desk today. I'll be here in the building until five or six tonight. If you need anything, you call me."

As the department heads filed out, Carly stayed behind. "Sir, what about me? What's my assignment?"

Sergio stood by the door, waiting as the others left.

"You stay locked up and out of sight," Breitinger said. "This whole thing depends on the killer not figuring out our decoy isn't you. The best way to make sure of that is to keep you right here in the station. You'll use my office today. It's quiet, and you can get some rest."

"Won't you need your office?"

"Not today. I've got a press conference and a meeting at city hall, plus some sort of goodwill tour here, then I'll be at the command post we're setting up near your house."

She slouched. "Terrific. The whole thing is going down and I won't be a part of it."

Breitinger eyed her, rubbing his chin. Moving to the conference table, he sat down and pushed a second chair out. "Come here, Carly." He patted the chair cushion. "Sit down."

She slowly took a seat.

He put his elbows on the table and leaned forward, lowering his head to make eye contact with her. "You're a big part of this. All of it. You have been since day one. You came up with this plan and you played a major role last night. Nobody's gonna forget that."

"Yes, sir." She stared at the table, her voice a whisper. "Will you call as soon as you take him down?"

"Sure. I'll have a couple of squad cars standing by to rush you out to the scene. In the meantime, you can keep yourself busy working on paperwork. There's plenty of it after last night, and if all goes well this evening, we'll need every I dotted and T crossed for everything we've done so far. That should keep you busy for at least a day." He stood, adjusting his tie and buttoning his suit coat. "Now if you'll excuse me, I've got an 8 A. M. meeting with the mayor, and then I need to dispatch a small army to your neighborhood."

"Okay." Carly nodded. "I get it."

Breitinger patted her on the shoulder and headed to the door.

"Don't worry, partner." Sergio held up his phone and waved it. "I'll be right in the middle of it all, reporting to you every step of the way."

"No, you won't." Breitinger adjusted his suit collar. "If the killer identified her, he probably knows you're her partner. If he sees you in a car somewhere watching the house, he's gonna know something is up—and then he's going to go underground. You're staying here at the station."

"But, wouldn't I be with my partner? I mean, with the decoy?"

"Not after hours."

Sergio crossed to the table and laid his phone on the surface, slouching into a seat. "Looks like I'll be doing lots of fun paperwork all day, too."

* * * * *

Moving a second stack of reports to the side of the desk, Sergio glanced at Carly. He picked up a third stack and dug through it for a moment, then sighed.

Carly glanced up from the computer screen on the lieutenant's desk. "Something on your mind?"

"Okay." Sergio put his elbows on the desk and rubbed his eyes. "It's none of my business, so I'll only ask this once."

She continued typing. "If it's none of your business, why are you asking at all?"

He waved a hand. "I'm assuming you did not inform your husband about what happened to you last night, or what's going on around your house today."

"He's in the middle of a two-week hiking trip through the Tennessee mountains with the boys. If I told him any of that, he'd come rushing right back here, and that would put my whole family in danger. It's better that they don't know."

"Maybe." Sergio rubbed his chin. "I'm going to guess that the lieutenant, with all he had going on this morning, didn't ask about where the other residents of your house are. But he will. Right now, he thinks your husband and kids will be rounded up by our people and shuffled off to a hotel somewhere. Saying they're camping might screw our chances to stay involved in this deal."

"Worse than they are? We aren't even on scene."

He picked up a hand radio. "We're getting info. If you don't tell Breitinger what he needs to hear, we won't even get that. 'Camping' isn't gonna cut it. They could come home in the middle of the day because it rained."

"Not all the way from the Smoky Mountains." She shook her head, continuing to tap on the keyboard. "Not without calling first."

"Yeah, and then you'll say, 'Oh by the way, there's a serial killer at our house, so stay at Motel 6 in Jacksonville until you hear from me.'"

She stopped typing and glared at him. "That's my situation to figure out. They aren't expected home for days."

"I'm just saying, why don't we address it with Breitinger first, before he asks. Maybe we can suggest sending an undercover officer out to Kyle's camping place to keep an eye on him and the boys."

She rolled her eyes. "Or maybe I can tell him they won't need a hotel because they're out of state and will call when they're coming home. It's a thirteen-hour drive, so we'll have lots of notice."

Sergio opened his mouth, but hesitated. After a moment, he shrugged. "Or we can go with that. That'll probably work."

"Okay." She returned to the keyboard. "Now be quiet and get to work."

"Done deal. I have a ton of voicemail messages to check, and a bunch of reports to help file." He stared at the stacks, then stood up. "Right after I grab some coffee."

\* \* \* \* \*

On the way to the break room, Sergio passed the phone duty teams as they were coming in.

Harriman waved. "Good morning, Detective Martin."

"Morning, Harriman," Sergio said as the phone volunteers went past. "Good morning, officers."

"Morning, sir."

"Good morning, Detective."

He waited in the hallway until they came out of the break room, coffees in hand, sauntering towards their desks—and the ringing phones. Soon the small phone area would be filled with officers and clerical staffers, chattering and typing in a furious, noisy haze.

*I do not miss that. I don't even like being down the hall from that.*

When the stream of bodies slowed to a trickle, he went into the break room. "Did you guys leave any coffee for me?"

A shadow loomed behind him. He turned to see Davenrod in the doorway, blocking the morning light as it streamed around him from outside. The big man stared at Sergio, his eyes bloodshot. Scratches lined his cheek.

The hairs on the back of Sergio's neck stood up.

"There's something leftover waiting for you."

Sergio blinked. "What?"

"Coffee," Davenrod said, walking into the break room and grabbing a cup from the shelf. "There's a little left for you."

"Oh. Right." Shaking his head, Sergio released the tension from his shoulders and reached for a mug. "Sorry. Long night. I'm not all here."

"Tell me about it."

"Yeah, you have a few scratches." Sergio pointed to Davenrod's face. "What's that about?"

"Bumper cars with a friend. Got a little out of hand."

"Looks like it."

Davenrod shrugged. "You should see the other guy."

Sergio dumped cream and sugar into his mug, hurrying to the door. "Have a great day, officer."

"You, too, Detective."

Sergio headed down the hallway to Breitinger's office.

*Man, that guy is starting to creep me out, too. Hope I'm not stuck here all day with him.*

# CHAPTER 39

"Phase one is complete." The SWAT team commander's voice crackled over the radio. "The neighborhood has been swept and all units report it is clean. Ready to start phrase two on your go, Lieutenant."

"Roger that. Stand by." Breitinger looked at Carly as she sat at his desk. "They don't see anything. The decoy is ready to go into your house. Okay?"

"Yes," Carly said.

He put the hand radio back to his face. "Go ahead, Mockingbird. You are cleared to access the residence."

"Ten-four, Base. We will have eyes on momentarily. Stand by for visual."

Breitinger reached across Carly's shoulder and pointed at the computer screen. In the lower left corner was a pair of small brown binoculars. "Click that. The password is 'easy go.' All one word."

Sergio got up from his chair and stood next to the desk as she clicked the image. Six black boxes appeared, dividing the screen.

"When they go live with the cameras," Breitinger said, "you'll be able to see the main ones on that. Number six is officer Jenifer Perez."

Carly leaned back in her chair. "She's the decoy?"

"That's right. Your car came here last night. That means she—you—were here. Your car goes home this morning, where you get a little rest. Then you come back to work for a few hours and go home at your regular time."

"Like she's working a case?" Sergio said. "We checked out a crime scene, came back to do reports and start our investigation, then go home?"

"Right." Breitinger nodded. "That's what you've done for days. Anyone watching would figure that's normal. Except our guy, who knows what happened. He'd think you ran somewhere for protection, but I doubt he followed you to Tampa General and then here to the station. Even if he did, it still fits the plan. And when he sees our decoy go home as you tonight, without squad cars and cops everywhere, he'll think his target is vulnerable. Even if he thinks the house is being watched, when she goes running it should prove too tempting. We're tracking every car that goes in and out of your neighborhood as of an hour ago. If he sticks his nose in there, we'll see it, and if he's already there, we'll grab him as soon as he tries to make his move."

Carly sighed, leaning forward and putting her elbows on the desk. She massaged her temples with both hands. "How do they check the cars to make sure who's legit and who's not? I mean, you can't pull over every neighbor of mine and flash a badge."

The commander's voice came over the radio. "Base, you should be receiving our video signal momentarily. We are ready for insertion."

"Hold that thought," Breitinger held a finger up to Carly and spoke into the radio. "Go ahead, Mockingbird."

The computer screen flickered as the images came online. Carly's home was visible from several angles, as well as a view from somewhere on the jogging route.

Breitinger's gaze was on the screen. "We will have guys on every rooftop in the apartment complex and hidden in a few other places along the way."

Image six came on. From three angles, the computer showed an orange Camaro pulling into Carly's driveway. From camera six, the house came into view over an orange dashboard.

"Check it out." Sergio leaned forward, watching the car come to a stop like a video game.

"Sunglass cam." Breitinger beamed.

The other boxes on the computer showed a dark-haired brunette in bare feet get out of the car and walk slowly to the house, slinging her purse over her shoulder. Her leggings and tank top were strewn with dirt.

"The muddy clothes are a nice touch," Carly said. "Even I would think she was me."

"Yeah. The car, the hair, the way she put the purse on—you totally do that." Sergio leaned over Carly's shoulder. "If I didn't know better . . ."

Her eyes darted over the images on the screen. "The SWAT people asked about stuff like that. They—" She gasped. "She's not limping."

Carly wheeled around to face Breitinger.

"We figured we'd go with a small sprain. That way she can run tonight. She's got it wrapped, though. For appearances."

Carly pursed her lips. "Think our guy will buy her running on a sprained ankle?"

"Do you run when you have a small sprain?"

She turned her eyes back to the screen. "Yeah."

Camera six unlocked the door and entered the house. The box on the screen darkened momentarily as the door shut behind her, then readjusted to the interior light of the home. Officer Perez headed up the stairs. Several people came into view at the top.

"Those are some of our sweep team members," Breitinger said.

"How am I doing, Detective Sanderson?"

Carly turned to Breitinger. "Is that her?"

He nodded. "You can respond to officer Perez over your hand-held unit there. The red button lets you talk. Press the red and black buttons at the same time and it will stay on like a speakerphone."

Carly picked up the radio. "We should probably be on a first name basis, Jenifer. After all, in a minute you'll be going through my underwear drawer."

Perez chuckled. "Yes, ma'am. You said left side of the dresser, top drawer. Slacks and tops in the closet."

The camera entered the master bedroom.

Carly pressed the red button again. "At this point, I'd like all my fellow officers to avert their eyes."

Sergio folded his arms and faced the wall. "Man, you are no fun."

Pressing the red and black buttons, Carly set the radio on the desk and looked at the lieutenant. "What next?"

"We figured after a rough night, any sane person would want to take a shower, grab a bite to eat, and catch a few hours of sleep. Maybe make some calls or get on the computer. After that, head back to the office."

She nodded. "Sounds about right. What does the decoy—Jenifer—do instead?"

"Watch the surveillance cameras or play poker with the other team members stationed in your house," Breitinger said. "She'll get back here around noon, driving your car and followed by two undercover units. Meanwhile, the SWAT teams will move into place throughout the day. It will all be very boring, so I recommend you use that time to get some shut eye."

"Speaking of which, Detective Sanderson—I mean Carly." Jenifer's camera viewed a large master bedroom window. "Would you usually pull the blinds when you nap?"

"Uh, sure," Carly said. "Wow, you guys think of everything."

"That's their job." Breitinger buttoned his suit coat and straightened his tie. "My job is going to press conferences and holding the hands of nervous politicians. I think I'm even giving a tour of a real, live police station to some grade school kids later this morning. So I'll go do some of that and then head to the offsite base. Tactical is setting up operational command in a vacant dry cleaning business near your house."

Carly sat up. "Sir, I . . . I just don't feel like I'm *doing* anything. I'd like to be more help."

He held up a hand, shaking his head. "You'll be guiding officer Perez this evening when she goes jogging, and you'll be assisting the entire operation from here. You can see and hear everything from this office."

Sergio folded his arms and slouched against the wall.

"Lieutenant?" Harriman was at the door.

"Come on in."

"Tactical is ready for you downstairs, sir. They have forty uniformed officers ready, a dozen undercover units, and the covert SWAT teams, all staged and ready. The sergeant said you wanted to go over things one last time before he begins deploying them."

"I guess I'd better go see him, then." He glanced at Sergio, then Carly. "Stay in the station, you two. Preferably in this office. You'll be a part of things, but from right here."

# CHAPTER 40

Sergio yawned. Jenifer had turned off her camera for the long period of down time, and staring at Carly's house was less interesting than watching a sloth play golf.

He rolled his shoulders and stretched his arms, then collapsed into his chair. "Wanna play cards like the people in your house?"

Carly sighed. "No. Can't say I'm thrilled with them being there."

"Think you can sleep? I can go sit in the break room or get on a computer at a vacant desk somewhere. Or should I get us some more coffee?"

"Ugh." She leaned back and rubbed her eyes. "I don't think I can sleep, and I don't want any more coffee, but if you're going to go get some, I'll walk with you. I have to get out of this room for a while."

"We could work on the reports."

She stood up. "Not a chance."

"That's my girl." Sergio jumped out of his chair. "Maybe they restocked the vending machine."

"Don't get filled up on crap. You're buying me lunch today—from somewhere nice, too. Not pretzels or potato chips."

"Why am I buying you lunch?"

She opened the door and limped down the hallway. "The day SWAT does a stakeout that broadcasts your underwear drawer over the internet, I buy you lunch."

"That's fair, I guess." He followed her down the hallway. "Are we talking Burger King nice or Chili's nice?

"Not even close."

"Oh, Red Lobster nice."

"You're getting warmer."

She hopped into the break room and put her hands on the back of a chair, exhaling sharply. "You know, my foot didn't hurt much this morning, but it's really making up for it now."

"Are you allowed to slam a few more ibuprofen?"

"The doctor said I could take—"

Yelling came from down the hallway.

"No, it's not a lie!" A man shouted. "He threatened me."

"What!" Another man yelled. "He threatened me! He—he's turning it all around now."

Sergio grabbed a coffee mug. "It sounds lively out there this morning."

The argument grew louder. "You're full of it, man. You're lying and you know it!"

Sergio glanced at Carly. "Think we should intervene?"

She nodded, stepping gently toward the break room entry. He set his cup down and joined her. Carly leaned on the wall while Sergio stuck his head out. Instinctively, his hand went to the service weapon on his hip.

A small cluster of people had gathered in the phone team area. In the center of the group, several men were shouting. Archer faced the break room, stammering and sputtering, his cheeks a bright crimson and his tie sideways across his chest. The other stood with his back to Sergio, but was much larger than Archer.

*The only guy that big on phone duty is Davenrod.*

The big man shouted and pointed as some of the phone team clerical members backed away from the ensuing melee. Other officers rushed forward. An HR lady, clipboard in hand, moved away from the two men, her jaw open and her eyes wide.

*Looks like somebody didn't like the idea of getting written up.*

Forcing their bodies between the two men, the other officers managed to push them apart. Angry shouts were made and fingers got pointed, but it seemed the disagreement was ending as quickly as it had begun.

Sergio had seen a few of these before, twice at crime scenes and another time in the office, when passions had run high over a detail or strategy that later amounted to not much, but at the time seemed like everything. Cops might get loud, but they generally knew better than to throw punches—at least at work. The downtown YMCA boxing league benefitted from more than a few grudge matches, and nobody could ever say whether a black eye was from the alley behind a bar or a Police Athletic League football game.

With three fellow officers between him and the big guy, and more on the way, the red-faced Archer seemed like he wasn't going to swing on anyone.

Sergio spoke over his shoulder to Carly. "Looks like they have it under control."

"Yeah, well, it's still our investigation, so we need to have a talk with everyone."

Archer yanked his arms away from the officers holding him, pointing at the bigger man. "You're a nut case, Davenrod. A psycho."

"You are weakness." Davenrod turned away from him, sneering. "I see it. Everyone sees it." He pushed his chair away, sending it crashing into a desk.

Sergio crouched at the break room door. "Getting some rest will be harder than I—"

Carly's face was white. She pressed herself to the wall, trembling. Her mouth hung open.

"Dude, what is it? What happened?" Sergio dropped to his knees, looking at her foot. "Did you mess up your ankle?"

Her chest heaved as she gripped the wall. "It's him."

"What?" Sergio stood. "Who?"

Pale and gasping, she stared at Sergio. "The killer. That was his voice. He said that to me, that phrase about weakness." She pushed off the wall and unholstered her gun, holding it to her chest with shaking hands.

"Geez." Sergio pulled out his weapon, his heart racing. "Are you sure?"

"One hundred percent." She gritted her teeth, sliding toward the hallway, wincing with each step. "He said that exact phrase to me when he was chasing me through the apartment. It's our killer."

"Carly, it's—it's Davenrod saying that out there." Sergio swallowed hard. "I know you've had issues with him. Maybe—"

"It's our guy. Nobody else would say that out of thin air." Her voice quivered. "If you don't believe me—"

"I believe you." He gripped his gun and lifted it to his chest, frowning.

*We can't be wrong about this.*

Sergio sprung the release for his gun clip, ejecting it into his hand. He checked it; plenty of rounds to do the job. He slid it back into place with a click. "Let's move."

She inched forward, favoring her good foot as she peered into the hall. "We'll just get him on the floor and put the cuffs on him. We'll sort the rest out later."

Sergio moved in front of her, whispering. "I'll go in and to the left. You go right." He slid toward the break room entry, straining to see out. Davenrod pounded his chest and gestured toward the other guy. Sergio leaned back, exhaling slowly, his finger moving alongside the trigger of his weapon. "Remember, if it's really our guy, he's a deranged serial killer and he's carrying a loaded gun. Don't take chances. If he blinks funny, take him out."

"Right," Carly said. She popped her gun clip and checked it, then slapped it back into place.

"Ready?"

She nodded.

Sweat brimmed on Sergio's forehead as he contemplated his next move. He'd be pointing a loaded weapon into a room full of people, half of them armed. He pulled his badge clip off his belt, to display to everyone in the room. Gaining immediate control would be crucial.

His pulse thumped as he glanced at Carly.

"One . . ."

Visions of chaos ran through his head. People running and screaming.

"Two . . ."

He took a deep breath and put his hand on the door frame.

"Three!"

Sergio leaped into the hallway and aimed his gun at Davenrod, raising his badge. "Everybody down! Davenrod, hands in the air."

Carly jumped from the break room, moving to his right. Her gun pointed at Davenrod's torso. "Officers, keep your weapons holstered and move from my line of fire."

Every eye in the small, crowded space turned toward the detectives, then screams and shouts erupted. Support personnel dashed for cover, ducking and crouching behind desks and chairs. Uniformed officers reached for their weapons as they scurried for shelter.

Carly shouted, waving at them. "Holster your weapons and move from my line of fire! We are apprehending a murder suspect."

A cop grabbed his gun and pointed it at Sergio. "Put your gun down!"

Sergio raised his badge. "Lower your weapon!"

Amid the melee, Davenrod turned and smiled.

Carly advanced, her gun leveled at Davenrod's chest. "Hands in the air!"

The cop widened his stance, moving his gun from Carly to Sergio. "Drop your weapons! Do not advance."

The rear door of the phone room opened. A young lady and a uniformed officer led a string of children by the hand.

*The kids' tour.*

Sergio shouted. "Get those kids on the floor! Everybody down!"

The lady screamed. The children panicked, running everywhere.

Carly limped forward, her gun still on Davenrod, grimacing with each step. "Get down! Get down! Get down!"

Sergio moved to the left as other cops pulled their weapons. "Holster your weapons, you idiots! Move out of my line of fire!"

They aimed at the detectives.

"Put down that gun! Put it down!"

"Lower your weapon!"

Davenrod crept slowly toward Carly. The HR lady cowered on the floor in front of him. Behind him, several children stood screaming while others crawled under desks. Cops shouted at them and at each other.

"Get those kids out of here," Sergio yelled. He glanced at Davenrod as the big man stepped toward Carly. "I swear, Davenrod, if you don't stop, I will shoot you!"

His arms at his sides, Davenrod continued advancing toward Carly.

Sergio dropped his badge and put both hands on his gun. "Stop, Davenrod!"

Carly balanced on one foot, gripping her weapon firmly. Her finger slid over the trigger. "Don't do it. I will fire on you."

"No, you won't." Davenrod said. "Too much background. You can't risk hitting one of those kids." Behind him, adults raced for cover and children cried to get out. "Whereas I—" he pulled out his gun "—have an unobstructed target. Just you."

She backed up, moving unsteadily, her weapon still on him. "Stop. Get on the floor!"

"No way." He raised his gun. "Sheep."

Carly dropped to one knee as Davenrod fired. His shot exploded into the wall beside her, sending a cloud of white into the air. Chunks of plaster hit her shoulder and face. She leveled the gun at his chest and squeezed the trigger. His shirt ripped apart at the shoulder. He recoiled sharply, his hands flying into the air.

Sergio fired a shot, striking Davenrod in the waist.

Davenrod spun around, groaning and flailing. He staggered toward the rear exit, grabbing at the cowering children.

"Stop!" Carly held her gun on him, brushing plaster from her eyes. "Stop! Stop! Stop!"

He turned, yanking a screaming child by the t-shirt. Holding the small girl in front of him, he lifted her up as he stepped backwards toward the exit. The others fled away as he approached, running through Sergio's line of fire. "I don't have a clean shot!"

Carly closed one eye and fired over Davenrod's head. He laughed, raising the child to cover his chest.

"Don't let him get away!"

Officers behind the madman raised their guns.

"Hold your fire!" Carly shouted. "He has a kid. Hold your fire."

The killer laughed, backing toward the stairwell. The girl screamed, flailing in his massive arms.

"I've got you." She kept her gun trained on him. She cringed, stepping forward with her injured foot. "I've got you."

"You have nothing." Davenrod reached backwards for the door with his gun hand. It slid over the door knob. "You are weakness, sheep. I am power."

He grabbed at the knob with two fingers, but it didn't move. He couldn't hold his weapon and turn the door knob with the same hand. The knob slipped from his grasp. He growled, raising the crying girl and grabbing behind him at the door knob, his gun bouncing against the door frame.

The door flew open. Breitinger appeared, lowering a phone from his ear. "Sorry I'm late kids. Our tour can now continue."

Davenrod whipped around, dropping the child and raising his gun at the lieutenant. Breitinger flinched, grabbing the killer's arm and raising it skyward. The big man laughed, forcing their arms downward and bringing the gun to the lieutenant's head.

Carly put her cheek to shoulder, staring down her arm and across the barrel of her weapon as it pointed at Davenrod's big, thick back.

Sergio raced toward the grappling men. "Guns down, guns down!" Cursing, Carly lowered her weapon and limped after him.

At a full run, Sergio dropped his shoulder and rammed into Davenrod's ribs. The killer groaned, crashing through the door and into the stairwell. Davenrod's gun clattered down the steps as Breitinger fell forward into the squad room.

With his arms wrapped around the killer, Sergio churned his legs and sent Davenrod into the steel railing above the stairs. The door slammed shut behind them, echoing through the stairwell. Davenrod raised a fist and hammered it into Sergio's neck and back, dropping Sergio to his knees. The big man reached downward and raised his foot, pulling a massive knife from an ankle holster. He drew it to his side, its serrated edge gleaming in the light.

Sergio stood and tried to force himself out of the big man's grip. The knife slashed through Sergio's leather holster and into his hip, sending white hot pain up his side. The impact knocked Sergio toward the steps. Cringing in pain, he reached for the rail, but Davenrod's massive fist got to him first. The thundering blow threw Sergio forward, and the floor disappeared out from under his feet. He crashed onto the steps and tumbled to the bottom.

Carly heaved the door open and leaped into the stairwell, her gun at arm's length, ready to shoot at whatever she saw. She glanced at Sergio as he lay on the steps, then whipped around to find the killer.

Dripping sweat, Davenrod gripped the knife, his shirt bloody and torn. Carly widened her stance and leveled the gun at him. "Put it down, Davenrod. It's over."

"No chance." He gasped. "I've been saving this for you." He stepped toward her, brandishing the big blade. "Come and get it, sheep."

"Drop it!" She took a step backward, gritting her teeth as she neared the top of the steps. "Now! Put the knife down!"

The killer inched forward, blood dripping from his side, shaking his head and smiling. "Yours will be so much sweeter than the other two."

"Stop!" She limped backwards. "Stop or I will fire!"

He raised the knife, his red eyes looking at her gun. "You are weakness."

"Drop it!" She lifted her bandaged leg and lowered it backward onto—nothing.

Her arms flew outward as her foot came down hard on the first step. She crashed into the wall as the killer raised his knife and groaned, lunging toward her.

Her shoulder to the wall, Carly gripped her weapon with both hands and fired. The gun bucked in her hand. A puff of red mist burst out of Davenrod's neck.

She pulled the trigger again and again as the killer's chest exploded in red, his massive body jerking with each impact. Davenrod howled in pain, lurching backwards and crashing into the railing. His thick torso went over the railing, sending him crashing to the floor.

Grimacing, Carly kept her gun aimed at Davenrod and grabbed the stair rail, hopping down the steps toward her partner. "Sergio!"

He lifted his head and waved her off, pointing his gun at Davenrod. "I'm okay. Get the suspect."

Panting, she bolted down the steps, her gun leveled at Davenrod as he lay unmoving on his back. Blood oozed from the sides of his mouth. Dropping to one knee, Carly shoved her gun under Davenrod's chin and glanced at his hands. "No weapons."

Above her, Breitinger shoved open the stairwell door, his gun drawn. "What the hell's going on?" Cops poured past him and into the stairwell.

"We got our guy," Sergio said, gasping and lowering his gun. "She got him. Carly got our serial killer."

Davenrod wheezed, blood pouring out of him.

Breitinger shouted over his shoulder. "Call for an ambulance!"

As Davenrod tried to lift his head, blood poured down his cheeks. He coughed, laying his head back on the concrete. "Weakness."

"What?" Carly leaned toward him.

Davenrod stared blankly at the ceiling, the holes in his chest gurgling with each shallow breath. "The freight train . . . is gone."

Sweat brimmed on the forehead of the killer, his words weak and distant. He shuddered, releasing a final breath into the dim stairwell. "Thank you."

## CHAPTER 41

**B**ig Brass started the engine and pulled away from the butterfly mailbox. Tyree slumped in the passenger seat, staring out the window.

"Well, Miss Daisy, where am I taking you now?"

"I don't know. Just drive around."

Lavonte nodded, turning the corner and heading toward downtown Lakeland. There was no squealing of wheels, no blaring of music, just the sound of the truck motor as block after block of new subdivisions rolled by.

Old Lakeland was changing, slowly but surely.

"Let me buy you a beer," Lavonte said. When Tyree didn't say no, Big Brass headed to Jimbo's.

At the bar, Tyree slid out of the truck and followed Lavonte to a booth near the back.

"You've been moping since we got in the truck," Lavonte said. "What gives?"

Tyree folded his arms on the table and laid his head on them. "Jerry Contreras warned me. He said I wouldn't like where those checks took me." He sighed. "I sure can't go back to Mrs. Dilger with a story like this."

"She hired you. Don't you think she has a right to know what her husband was up to? What you found out on her dime?"

"She's not paying to be humiliated and have her husband's memory desecrated."

Lavonte shrugged. "I don't wanna stick my nose in, but . . ."

"Why not?" Tyree peered sideways at Big Brass. "It's such a prominent nose these days."

"It's not really your call, what to tell her—is it? What does *Detectives For Dummies* say about this?"

"It would say she gets whatever information I turn up." He dropped his head back onto his arms.

"It does, huh? Well, it probably doesn't say how she gets it. Maybe type up a report about this Lakeland stuff and seal it in a brown envelope and hand it to her. Then give a big ol' hint she doesn't want to know what's inside. She can read it or burn it, that's up to her, but you'll have done your job."

"That's . . ." Tyree looked up. "That's not a half bad idea."

"I told you it could be dangerous in that house, but Big Brass had your back."

Tyree stood up. "Let's go. I need to get back to Tampa."

"Calm down. I need to get some chicken wings first." He waved at a waitress. "You like 'em hot or Chernobyl?"

"Medium."

"Lightweight." Lavonte turned to the waitress. "We'll have a pitcher of beer and fifty hot wings."

Tyree sat. "Fifty?"

"How many you gonna eat?"

"Like ten, maybe."

He turned to the waitress. "Better make it sixty, then."

\* \* \* \* \*

In the flickering light of the WFLA newscast, the flaxen blonde reached across the nightstand and picked up her phone. Seeing "Harriman," she slid her finger across the screen. "Hey, baby."

"Hey, lover. Am I going to see you tonight?"

"Hmm." She grabbed the remote and lowered the volume on the TV. "I think so, yes. You deserve a reward for all the hard work you've been doing."

"Maybe we can reward each other. You've been through the mill lately."

"I really have, baby. I need somebody to make it all better." She pouted, tapping her finger on her lower lip. "How about I go run my errand and you come over to my apartment after? You can tell me all about the new developments in your big case."

"How about I swing by now? I just happen to be in the area."

"Can't, baby. I'm not at my apartment and I have to run my errand." She rolled backward onto the decorative pillows of her bed, sweeping her blonde locks out of her eyes. "But I'll see you after, I promise."

"Where's the errand? Maybe I can meet you there. I'll be off the clock soon."

"It's all the way out in that nasty warehouse in Lakeland."

"I'll meet you at the warehouse, then. As soon as I get off. How's that sound?"

"Aww." She sat up. "Really?"

"Absolutely. See you in a bit. Love you."

"Okay, baby. I love you." She ended the call and jumped out of bed, strolling downstairs. "Mom, I'm heading out to the warehouse."

Her mother glanced at the clock. "At this hour? Why?"

She shrugged, holding up her cell phone. "Johnny just called. He said he needs to meet me out there for something."

"Well, okay, Susan." Mrs. Dilger smiled at her daughter. "Drive safely. It's supposed to rain."

\* \* \* \* \*

"You know, there's a saying." Lavonte brushed the raindrops off his face and started the truck, turning on the windshield wipers. "If you don't know who the sucker at the poker table is, you're the sucker."

Tyree glared at him. "And that's relevant how?"

"I've been thinking about our case. Zack's been killed, we don't know by who, but it's a strange coincidence him going belly up right after one of his girlfriends turned up dead. And the girlfriend's father dies the same night. What ties all that together?"

Tyree stared out the window. "If anything tied it together, I wouldn't be driving around Lakeland getting shot at."

"Oh, please." Lavonte put the car in drive and pulled away from the curb. "You haven't been shot at in almost six hours."

Tyree's phone rang in his pocket. He pulled it out and answered. "Hi, Frank."

"Hello, Johnny. How's the case coming?"

Lavonte mouthed the words, "Put it on speaker."

Tyree nodded and pushed the speakerphone button. "Funny you should ask. Things are pretty bad."

"Yeah, it's a crappy business," Frank said. "Can I help?"

Tyree shook his head. "If it's a crappy business, why do you want me working in it?"

"Because you'll be good at it, believe me. You're a thinker, and that's half the job. Now, what's got you stumped? Sometimes talking it out clears the logjam. Last I heard you were looking into whether Henry Dilger was cooking the books for his company. Was he?"

"No, but that led me to looking at checks, and the checks led me to . . ."

Tyree's hand dropped to his lap, his jaw hanging open.

"Uh huh." Lavonte smiled, turning onto Main Street. "I see we got something cookin'now. Go with it, brother. What you got?"

Tyree sat up, holding the phone close to his face. "Frank, the checks were always going to lead me to Lauren—that's Mr. Dilger's illegitimate daughter. My tip at the Tampa PD said there might be funny business going on, but that means looking at the books—which means finding those checks. If they knew about the checks—then they already knew about Lauren and her mom."

Frank laughed. "Well, whoever 'they' is, that's a heck of a coincidence if they didn't already know."

Lavonte gripped the steering wheel. "My daddy used to say, there are no coincidences. There's just the sucker at the poker table don't know he's being played."

Tyree raised an eyebrow. "Am I supposed to be the sucker in this scenario?"

"If the shoe fits," Frank said. "Who sent you to Lakeland?"

"A cop." Tyree returned to staring out the window. "He's not part of anything, Frank. He's working on the serial killer investigation."

"The killer that murdered Mr. Dilger? Another coincidence."

"Want another one?" Lavonte asked. "Zack's girlfriend. They started dating about seven or eight months ago."

Tyree shook his head. "No, Lauren said they'd been together for like seven years."

"Not Lauren Vasquez, Sherry Dilger—Susan's sister. Zack had been dating Sherry for less than a year, but right before that he set himself up with a nice apartment over by the park. Got a new car, too."

"He was getting ready to make his move." Tyree rubbed his chin. "Zack's pretty central to this thing."

"He might be in the middle of it," Lavonte said. "Zack wasn't smart enough to be at the center of anything, and he's dead now anyway. Beaten to death by a mysterious stranger. So that means either Carmello started laying out hits all over the place, or—"

"That's not right," Tyree said. "Zack wasn't beaten to death. He died in the hospital after having a seizure. I was there."

Lavonte's jaw dropped. "*You* were there when he died?"

"Yeah, he had a . . . well, she said he had a seizure. Nobody was in the room but Susan."

"Susan Dilger?" Frank said. "Get the hell out of here."

Tyree grabbed his forehead. "Wow, maybe she took him out."

Lavonte looked at Tyree. "That little bitty Dilger girl took Zack out?"

"No, not like that. He was already close to dead in the hospital. It wouldn't have taken much at that point—a few seconds with a pillow over his face—but maybe. And if Lauren was telling us the truth, Susan knew Zack from before."

"Johnny," Frank said. "Are you listening to yourself? She knew him, she was in the room when he died, and her sister and father died a few days earlier. That is a lot of coincidences."

"And she had me run down to the police station for them a few days after the murders to insert myself into the case. Her officer friend was busy and couldn't help, but lo and behold, another helpful cop steps in and agrees to work with me."

Lavonte frowned. "In my experience, cops ain't that helpful."

"Is this even possible?" Tyree shook his head, clearing the gathering cobwebs of confusion. "All the links lead back to the Dilger family. Follow the money, right? And look where it took us. To the Dilgers, or someone who's controlling them. I don't see who that could be. They're pretty rich and powerful."

"So," Frank said. "Do you think Mrs. Dilger found out about the Lakeland family and had her husband killed?"

"That gives her a big motive. So does finding out about extortion from Zack." Tyree whistled. "Wow . . . I can't believe it, but—"

"Yeah, she did it." Lavonte pounded the steering wheel. "Sure wouldn't be the first time a rich angry spouse hired a thug to take out a cheating husband."

Tyree faced Lavonte. "And either way, Mrs. Dilger could have paid some scumbag in Lakeland to do Zack—she's had connections there for twenty years. But the killer messed up and didn't kill Zack, just put him in a coma. Maybe Susan got overwhelmed at the hospital and finished the job with a pillow. Who could blame her, with her sister and father's killer laying there helpless? And Mrs. Dilger got me involved to make sure nobody else started looking into it. She was real big on confidentiality, that she didn't want to read about stuff in the news. It fits." Tyree ran a hand through his hair. "I don't see her doing it, but it fits. I mean, I've known these people for years, but . . ."

"Hell hath no fury," Frank chuckled. "But this is what I was talking about, Johnny. You have a gift. I've seen it. You have to unbury that sixth sense you've been ignoring all these years. If you don't . . . good grief, boy, you may wind up dead. People play for keeps in this business."

Tyree stared at the phone, letting Frank's message sink in. Then he laughed. "No. This is crazy. I know these people. They aren't the type to hire a hit man. We're getting carried away. We're overlooking something." He held the phone up again. "Frank, come on. They had me over to dinner when I got back in town, for Pete's sake. They didn't even know I'd be here. I ran into Susan at the airport by accident."

"Unless Susan reads Facebook," Frank said. "You posted about coming to Tampa to work with me—you even mentioned your travel dates. Can't be that many flights to check."

"Frank, Susan was white as a sheet at the hospital when Zack has his seizure. She couldn't smother him. She was practically collapsing herself."

"Maybe not. I'm just saying, the next time they invite you to dinner, think about taking a food taster."

Tyree stared out the window.

*Was it possible? Susan hadn't seemed strong-willed enough to take anyone out, but in a moment of weakness could Mrs. Dilger have hired someone to . . .*

*No, it wasn't possible. He'd known this family for years.*

*Still . . .*

"Frank, I gotta go," Tyree said, ending the call.

"What now?" Lavonte asked.

"Now I think I go visit the Dilgers." He scrolled through his phone contacts. "Turn north when we get to I-275."

\* \* \* \* \*

Mrs. Dilger met Tyree at the front door. "You got here quickly. Are you on your way to meet Susan?"

"Not at the moment. I need to talk to you." He shook the rain off his shirt as he entered the house.

"I'm sorry, ma'am, but this may be a little difficult for you."

She clasped her hands and silently led him to the living room. They sat on one of the big white sofas, where just a few days before the world was light and sunny, filled with jambalaya and memories of good times. Now, even with every lamp on, the light room carried a darkness.

*When I mention the secret Lakeland family, her reaction will tell me everything I need to know—and if she wasn't involved in anything nefarious, I'll be destroying her entire world.*

"I'm sorry, Ma'am." Tyree swallowed hard. "What I have to tell you, I just . . . I couldn't put this in a report and hide it in an envelope and walk away, leaving you to deal with. I felt I owed it to you to tell you directly." He cleared his throat, searching for the words. "I looked into some checks in Lakeland. Large checks, and some cash. Paid on a monthly basis for quite some time."

Mrs. Dilger nodded, her hands in her lap. "We ran a business for many years, Johnny. There was always an occasional odd expense in Lakeland, but businessmen in the shipping business do things. And men do things."

"Yes, ma'am, but . . ."

She looked away, tears welling in her eyes. "If gratuities were needed to grease a port officer, Henry said I was better off not knowing—for my own protection. I heard him do it once in a restaurant. He said occasionally things needed to be done, and if something bad happened, I couldn't reveal what I didn't know." She sniffled. "You try to live a respectable life, run a respectable business, but sometimes . . ."

"And if it wasn't a bribe to a port official? If it was something else?"

"I guess I'd rather focus on the good things than be shown proof of bad things." She raised her eyes to his, tears rolling down her face. "Maybe I prefer to pretend those things don't exist, rather than have them shoved in my face. What would it change? Does that make me a bad person? Or weak? Things—indiscretions—they tend to . . . run their course. When they're over, and things are normal again, what is the benefit of confronting it? Who gets harmed once it's over?"

Tyree took a tissue from a box on the table, handing it to her. "You knew about Lauren and her mother?"

Mrs. Dilger nodded again.

He sighed. "Then the harm gets done to you, ma'am."

"Acknowledging the damage of an affair doesn't erase the damage, John. Whether it's a short-term thing or a long-term thing."

This was no killer. She hadn't hired a hit man or anything else; she'd decided to quietly live with the uncomfortable knowledge about her husband and his secret. Mrs. Dilger and her family were exactly what he always thought they were. Friends. Good people.

He couldn't decide if he admired her, or pitied her, or both. In her own way, she had been strong in ways few people could. He wasn't revealing news after all, merely confirming that the secrets would remain secrets—and maybe that there was nothing else that would come to light to cause more pain.

It was, after all, her call.

"I hate to ask, but blackmail might play a role in all this, and if, well . . . the fewer blackmail options out there, the better. So . . . would there be any other family indiscretions someone could find out about?"

She took a deep breath, her voice falling to a whisper. "Henry gave me reasons to wonder at times. I gave him reasons to wonder at times. Every marriage has moments where the partners wonder. What they do about it—or don't do—is what allows them to stay married. Can we leave it at that?"

"Sure. Sorry."

"Is there any reason this has to leave the room?"

"None that I can think of."

A smile forced its way over her lips. "Thank you, Johnny."

He put his elbows on his knees, looking into her red, swollen eyes. "Ma'am, I've known you a long time. I want you to know, when I see you tomorrow or next month or next year, this conversation will not be what I'm thinking about."

She reached over and took his hand, squeezing it gently. "You're a good boy."

He sat with her, holding her hand and saying nothing, handing her tissues until the tears stopped falling.

"Now I should talk to Susan." He stood. "Is she here?"

"What?" her jaw dropped. "She said she got a call from you—that you were meeting her at the Lakeland warehouse. That's why I was surprised to see you here."

"Then I'd better get out there." Tyree headed for the door. "There are too many funny things happening in Lakeland these days. Besides, I'm supposed to be her bodyguard. Can't very well let her run off to an area where a murder took place."

He bolted out of the Dilger house. Racing through the rain, he grabbed the passenger door of the big red truck and yanked it open, jumping inside. "Back to Lakeland."

"What!" Lavonte yelled. "Man, you sure like wasting my gas." He started the engine.

There was a sharp rap on the passenger window. Mrs. Dilger opened the door, rain matting down her hair. "Move over. I'm coming."

Tyree shook his head. "I don't think it's safe—"

She climbed into the truck. "If my daughter is in danger, I'm coming. Now, move."

Tyree opened his mouth to speak. Mrs. Dilger lifted her giant Magnum revolver and shoved it into her purse.

"I guess you'll be safe enough with that cannon along." He faced Lavonte. "Let's go."

## CHAPTER 42

The rain whipped the windshield of the big red truck. Tyree slapped his hands on his knees. "Come on, man. We have to go faster."

"You wanna drive?" Lavonte leaned forward, hugging the steering wheel. "I can't see squat, and I don't want to roll this thing."

Mrs. Dilger put her hand on Tyree's shoulder. "Johnny, if we wreck on the way, there'll be no point in going at all." She glanced at Lavonte. "Get us there as fast as you can, but safely, mister . . ."

"The name is Big Brass, ma'am."

Mrs. Dilger recoiled. "Am I actually supposed to call you that?"

Lavonte glanced at her. "Uh, you can call me Lavonte."

"Thank you, Lavonte."

Taking a deep breath, Tyree leaned back into the seat and tried to relax. This was definitely not a killer sitting next to him. He knew that now, and was a little embarrassed about thinking anything otherwise about her—or any of the Dilgers. He'd known them for years and had been friends with them, and now he needed to help keep them safe.

But an uneasy feeling gnawed at his gut. Whoever killed Mr. Dilger and Sherry was still out there, and Susan might have been lured to the warehouse to meet the same fate.

*Why did she go?*

The same reason anybody would. Because it was the place she'd been going since she was a little kid. Nobody's afraid to go to their own house, and nobody's afraid to go to the office they've been working at for twenty years. The same reason Mrs. Dilger didn't hesitate.

*But that doesn't mean I have to be reckless about Mrs. Dilger's safety.*

Susan had already plunged ahead, but if someone was lurking at the warehouse to harm them, Mrs. Dilger didn't have to be taken to the danger.

"Ma'am, Lavonte and I can handle this. There are lots of busy, well-lit fast food places along the way. We should drop you off at one. No one would think to look for you there."

Mrs. Dilger's eyes didn't leave the road. "No chance."

411

"Yeah, I figured you'd say that." Tyree rubbed his chin. "When we get there, I need you to stay in the truck, and stay down. If some other car pulls up, be invisible on the floor. It'll be dark enough to hide you. If you think you're in trouble, lay on the horn."

Lavonte nodded. "We'll come running."

"If any other car pulls up," she patted her purse. "They'll be the ones in danger."

Lightning flashed in the distance, illuminating the streaks of rain that pelted the truck. The low growl of thunder followed, rumbling on forever. Gusts of wind batted the vehicle as it sped down the highway.

Lavonte nudged Tyree, lowering his voice. "Who do you think we might run into out here?"

Tyree shook his head. "Hard to say. Could be anybody, but the guy I wonder about is Harriman. He's tied to all the cases, so he has access to things only the killer would know. Seems like he'd also be in a position to stage the killings."

"Mark Harriman?" Mrs. Dilger huffed. "Nonsense. I've known his family for years."

"I don't know. People close to a rich family can get tempted like anyone else."

"Why would he do such a thing?" She held her hands out. "His family has money. *He* may not, but they certainly do. Besides, he's a police officer. He could have taken up a lot of other professions if he was after money."

"Maybe he threw in with Zack and intended to take over the company through intimidation tactics,

412

and things got out of control. Cops make for a good muscle. Especially if there's a secret the business owners don't want known."

"That's just very hard for me to believe."

"I understand, ma'am, but . . . no one can know everything about another person's family."

She turned and stared out the passenger window.

"Here we go," Lavonte said. His headlights lit the warehouse in the distance. Susan's car was visible. "How do you want to play it?"

Tyree unbuckled his seat belt and leaned forward, peering through the glass. "I only see one car—Susan's convertible. That may not mean anything, though. If it's a setup, I doubt the killer would park right in front." He rubbed his chin stubble. "Stay parallel to the street when you drive onto the lot, so your lights don't shine in any windows. I'll go in the front, you head around back. There's a door near where you were peddling your vitamins. Make sure nobody comes in or out." He faced Mrs. Dilger. "Ma'am, you stay in the truck until I come for you—no matter what. And all of us had better be ready to run at a moment's notice. Remember, if it *is* a setup, this guy has killed a few people already. Three more won't matter to him."

Big Brass cut the engine as they approached. The truck rolled onto the lot, stopping in the corner farthest from the street light. Reaching under his seat, he withdrew a .38.

Tyree eyed the gun. "Just like the killer's."

"And yours," Lavonte said.

Raindrops pinged on the truck bed. Tyree stared at the warehouse. "Ready?"

Lavonte inhaled sharply. "Yep."

"Okay, let's go."

Lavonte opened his door and jumped out, running around to the side of the warehouse.

"Remember," Tyree said as he slid out into the rain. "Stay low, and stay in the truck. No one knows you're here."

"They will if you keep talking to me." Mrs. Dilger held up her Magnum. "I'll be fine."

"Right." He eased the truck door shut and ran to the warehouse entrance.

The faded, dingy awning kept the rain from soaking him as he looked inside. A few interior lights were on, in the hallway and some of the offices. With his .38 raised, he gritted his teeth and reached for the door. His heart pounded as he wrapped his wet fingers around the metal knob and got ready to give it a turn.

*No telling what's waiting on the other side of this door.*

He threw the door open and leaped inside, leveling his gun and pointing it at the hallway. He glanced left and right. The room was empty. Reaching back, he pushed the door shut and stepped over the dirty floor, his .38 leading the way. One set of muddy tracks went ahead of him—ladies' sneakers. He held his breath, listening for any noises.

Nothing. So far, it looked like Susan was still alone.

*Lucky break. If the killer isn't already here, maybe we can get Susan out before he shows up.*

Rain battered the office windows, casting a rippled look to anything outside, as if he was viewing it through a waterfall. He couldn't make out Lavonte's truck or Mrs. Dilger. Pressing himself to the hallway entrance, he peeked around the corner.

Empty.

He swallowed hard and lowered his gun, flicking the rain off his hands. If Susan wasn't in danger, he could call out to her. If she *was* in danger and he called out, he'd invite the wrath of the killer down on his head.

But if she was on the wrong end of a bad situation, seconds counted. He couldn't worry about the down side. Interrupting the situation and having Big Brass as his backup would have to be enough.

"Susan?"

The word came out louder than he intended, blaring through the quiet office, as much a statement as a question. He grabbed his gun with both hands and raised it to his cheek.

"I'm back here, Mark." Susan's voice was cheery and light.

Tyree raced across the hallway, stopping at Jerry's office. Susan sat behind the desk, looking over some folders. He stepped into the room.

"Susan, are you okay? I think you're in danger. We need to get out of here."

Her jaw dropped when she saw him. "What are you talking about? Why are you here?"

"I think somebody's on their way." He went to the desk. "Maybe to kill you. Come on, let's go."

Susan's face was one of complete surprise. "What do you think is going on?" She reached into her bag and pulled out the .45 her mother had given her.

Tyree nodded. "Good girl. Always be prepared."

Susan stood, gathering her things. Holding the gun and a purse strap in one hand, she shoveled everything into the bag with the other.

Tyree glanced at the front door. "Your mom said you got a call to meet me here."

"Yeah, well, I knew Mom would let me go by myself if I was meeting you." She slung the bag over her shoulder, holding her gun at her side and leaning toward the hallway. "Who do you think is coming?"

"I'm not sure." He lowered his gun and eyed the front entrance, stepping toward the office door. Turning to her, he frowned. "Coming here alone was dangerous."

Susan gripped her big gun tightly and swung the heavy barrel at Tyree, catching him on the side of the face. He spun around, dropping his gun and throwing his hands out as he crashed to the floor.

"Johnny, you washed out of college, you washed out of the sheriff's department—but you decided to stop being a screwup *now?*"

The room swayed back and forth as Tyree tried to get to his knees. Pain ripped through his head. He pushed his face off the floor, his ear ringing like a siren had been set off.

Putting a hand out, he gripped the door frame and hauled himself onto one knee. He spit, dark red splattering onto the swaying floor as he pieced it together. Susan met Lauren. She knew about Zack. She knew about Sherry and Zack dating. "It . . . was you?" Blood gathered in his mouth. With them gone, she stood to take over the company.

Tyree's stomach lurched as a wave of nausea hit him. "You—killed your own father and sister, and tried to frame your sister's boyfriend."

"I didn't frame anyone. Zack killed them. The cops will eventually figure that out."

"Why set up your sister's boyfriend?"

"Why not? He was the perfect bait for her. Decent looking, but a serious bad boy. After he and I had been having fun for a while, I gave him the idea: help me muscle them out of the company, and then take over with me. He saw big dollar signs and went for it."

"They didn't exactly get *muscled* out."

"Whatever, he's gone now. Cops don't look too hard into a drug dealer that ends up dead."

Tyree dabbed at the blood crawling down the side of his face. "Just couldn't be happy with a slice, you had to have the whole pie."

"You think that tramp in Lakeland should get our money? And Sherry—she didn't do squat."

"So the serial killer provided a good cover and you took them out."

"I keep telling you, Zack killed them."

"What's the difference? Zack killed Henry and Sherry, then you killed Zack—and that erased the trail back to you."

"Did I kill Zack? Maybe you did, Johnny. You were in town. Doesn't matter who killed any of them—the serial killer, Zack . . . As long as they're all gone and I'm not on the hook, I don't care how the police say it went. You know, your fingerprints are all over the gun that was used to kill my father and sister. So even if they don't pin the murders on Zack, I still have a backup."

"Talk about sloppy. That's your gun, remember? You gave it to me."

She shook her head. "Sorry. It was Zack's, originally. What can I say? I'm not as sloppy as everybody says."

Still on one knee, he shook his head. "You can't blackmail me, Susan."

"I don't intend to. I'll just say you surprised me out here all alone—and attacked me—and, well, I guess I just had to shoot you." She cocked the gun and pointed it at Tyree's head. "Say goodbye, Johnny."

The front door opened. Mrs. Dilger stepped into the office, her big gun held high. "Johnny, I've waited long enough. Where's my daughter?"

Susan frowned at Tyree. "You brought my mother?" Glancing at the door, she called out. "Back here, Mom."

In the time it took Tyree to figure out what was happening, Susan's mother had crossed the lobby. He scrambled to his feet. "Mrs. Dilger, stop!"

Susan pointed the gun at her mother.

Tyree lurched forward and batted Susan's arm as the gun fired. The blast filled his ears as he and Susan hit the wall.

Mrs. Dilger flew backwards and dropped to the hallway floor.

Susan threw an elbow into Tyree's jaw, sending his head back and dropping him to his knees again. She stepped away and glared at her mother. "One down."

As Susan leveled the gun, Tyree raised his hands and lunged forward. Another shot fired. He and Susan hit the floor with a heavy jolt. He scrambled for her gun, grabbing it from her hand as he rolled off her. He pushed himself away and got to a sitting position before he realized she wasn't moving.

A large red stain spread through Susan's shirt, seeping between her breasts and running down her side. In the hallway, Mrs. Dilger lowered her gun.

Big Brass burst through the back door. "Tyree! Where you at?"

"Back here," he called out, getting to his feet. "Call 911! We need two ambulances!"

Lavonte ran down the hallway, stopping at Mrs. Dilger as he pulled out his cell phone.

Tyree stood over Susan. Her eyes stared upwards at nothing, unmoving, as the blood seeped out of her and onto the dusty floor. When he put his fingers to her throat, there was no pulse.

"Take it easy, ma'am." Lavonte pulled his shirt off and held it to Mrs. Dilger's side, mashing his phone to his ear with his shoulder. "It went right through. It's gonna hurt like hell, but you ain't gonna die."

Stepping to them, Tyree wiped his forehead as Lavonte gave the operator the address to the warehouse. Tyree lowered his head. "I'm sorry."

Mrs. Dilger winced as Lavonte applied pressure. Closing her eyes, she let a groan escape from her lips. "You have nothing to apologize for, Johnny. She was going to kill you." Glancing at Susan, tears welled in Mrs. Dilger's eyes. "She . . . took everything from me."

Shaking his head, Tyree whispered. "She's gone, ma'am."

Mrs. Dilger looked away, tears streaming down her face. "I suppose so. I kill what I shoot at."

Tyree leaned against the wall and closed his eyes.

The front door banged open. "Susan? What's that truck doing here, baby?"

*Harriman.*

Tyree pushed himself off the wall and stormed into the lobby, balling his fist. Harriman was still in uniform. He cocked his head. "What are you doing here, John?"

Tyree gritted his teeth and grabbed Harriman by the collar, throwing him up against the wall. "Time to come clean. Tell me what you know!"

Harriman slid to the floor, pulling his service weapon. He pointed it at Tyree, lifting himself from the floor and backing away. "What's going on? Where's Susan? Why are you here?"

Tyree pointed at him. "Put that thing away before I make you eat it. How long have you been seeing Susan? What did you tell her about the serial killer cases?"

Harriman rubbed his neck. "Why, are you jealous?"

"Because you got her killed, you idiot."

"What?" He lowered his gun.

Tyree grabbed the weapon and twisted it backwards, trapping Harriman's finger in the trigger guard. Harriman howled and let go as Tyree shoved him back into the wall. Pinning Harriman's neck with his forearm, Tyree leaned in hard and cut off Harriman's windpipe. "Tell me right now. Did you tell Susan confidential details about the serial killer? Things that weren't in the paper?"

Harriman choked out his words, clawing at Tyree's arm. "Maybe. A few things. She liked hearing about it."

"She was using you for information, moron." Tyree released him. "She asked about it to cover her tracks."

Harriman fell to the floor, coughing and gasping. "Where is she?"

"She's on the floor in the back office." Tyree breathed hard, reeling in his anger. "She bled out from a gunshot wound."

Harriman looked up at Tyree, his face turning white. "You . . . killed her?"

Tyree spit blood onto the dirty floor. "We both did."

"No!" Harriman staggered to his feet, scrambling to Jerry's office.

Tyree walked up behind him, seething.

"No, no, no, big fella." Lavonte reached over Mrs. Dilger and grabbed Tyree's hand. "He ain't worth it."

"He screwed up," Tyree growled. "He needs to pay for it."

"He's paying right now, man," Lavonte said. "Can't you see?"

Harriman sat at Susan's side, cradling her head and sobbing.

*He was in love with her.*

Tyree stepped back, watching the grown man cry.

*She slept with Zack and Harriman and tried to bait me, too, but Harriman didn't know any of that. He was in love.*

"I got this," Lavonte said. "Why don't you get yourself some air? Flag down the ambulances."

Tyree nodded, picking up Mrs. Dilger's weapon. He crossed the lobby and went outside, the cool air brisk against his skin. In the glow of the street light, he stood in the rain, holding the two guns. One had killed two family members and helped fuel a city-wide panic. The other had ended it.

He stared at the big gun that had taken his friend's life. After a while, the sounds of sirens came from the distance.

## CHAPTER 43

Frank pushed the elevator button and stepped back. "So, Johnny, since you've been back in town, have you met anyone that didn't end up in the hospital?"

Tyree winced but said nothing.

The ride in the hospital elevator was quiet, with just the bell signaling their arrival to the fourth floor. A nurse scurried past as the doors opened.

"Why won't you tell me why we're here?" Tyree asked.

"If I did, you wouldn't have come." Frank stepped out of the elevator and strolled toward the hallway. Farther down, a woman on crutches entered an examining room.

"This way," Frank said over his shoulder. A few paces later, Frank stopped and knocked on the examining room door. "Are you ready for us?" He pushed open the door and held his hand out to Tyree. "After you."

Lieutenant Breitinger stood in the center of the treatment room. In the bed behind him was Sergio, and next to the bed, on crutches, was Carly. Lavonte stood by the window, smiling.

"Frank, Johnny. Thank you for coming." Breitinger shook their hands. "I think you know these people, John, but Frank—these are Detectives Carly Sanderson and Sergio Martin. Over there is Lavonte Jackson."

Frank smiled, folding his hands in front of him. "Nice to meet all of you."

"I'd have done this at the station," Breitinger said. "But I wanted Carly and Sergio present, and as it turns out, they were both here."

"I put the nix on that." Lavonte waved a hand. "I ain't big on going to police stations."

"No problem," Tyree said. "What's this about?"

Breitinger cleared his throat. "The department appreciates your efforts in the serial killer case. You may have felt like you were doing a minor role by checking out the Dilger leads and keeping us informed through Harriman, but your work turned out to be significant. Getting a second killer off the street will allow a few million Floridians to sleep better tonight. That's a big deal. There won't be any official citation, but a lot of people wouldn't have done what you did. So, thank you."

Lavonte stood up straight. "It was a team effort, you know."

"I gotta admit." Tyree shrugged. "There were more than a few curve balls."

"For us, too," Sergio said.

"I can't say I was expecting our serial killer to be a cop." Carly propped her crutches against the wall and lowered herself into a chair. "Or for somebody like Susan Dilger to use that as cover for her plans."

Breitinger shoved his hands into his pockets. "A raid on Davenrod's Tampa home produced quite a few unregistered guns and a box of fake IDs. I have a feeling they'll be part of some unsolved crimes from New Orleans. We're running that down now." He glanced at Lavonte. "In any case, you gentlemen did some fine work." Turning back to Tyree, he nodded. "Also, I heard about what happened to you in Texas. If you ever decide to get back into law enforcement, Tampa PD would be proud to have you on our team."

"Thank you, Lieutenant. That means a lot to me."

Lavonte crossed the room and clapped Tyree on the back. "We did a great job, partner. What's our next case?"

Tyree bristled. "Us?"

"Yeah, we a team now." Lavonte lowered his voice, leaning close to Tyree. "Besides, I can't go back to work for Carmello after spending this much time with the police."

"Think he'll just let you walk?"

"I think so, if you explain it properly and we don't end up leaning on him."

"Okay, sure." Tyree shrugged. "Why not?"

Breitinger gave Tyree a half smile. "I guess you won't be joining the force, then."

"Actually." Frank put his hands on Tyree and Lavonte. "That brings us to our next order of business. Mrs. Dilger wants to fund our little operation. We need to go talk to her—she's recovering on the next floor up." He waved to the room. "Detectives, Lieutenant—thank you for this honor."

Amidst the thank yous and goodbyes, Frank ushered Tyree and Lavonte out the door and into the hallway.

"Mrs. Dilger wants to sponsor us?" Lavonte asked.

"Yep." Frank nodded. "Never hurts to have a rich benefactor supporting a new business."

Tyree stopped and faced Frank. "I have a favor I might ask of her, too."

"What's that?"

"There's a girl in Lakeland who lost her family." Tyree scratched his chin stubble. "It might not matter how it came about, but the ones who are grieving aren't the ones who did anything wrong. One day, Mrs. Dilger might like to get to know the rest of her family, since it's all she has left. And maybe help somebody else start living out of the shadows."

A smile crawled across Frank's face. "Think she's ready for that?"

"I don't think anybody's ever ready for something like that." Tyree turned and continued down the hallway. "But I know two people who are grieving alone that probably should be grieving together. They both lost their families."

* * * * *

In the examining room, Breitinger stepped to the door. "Okay, you two. Heal up quick and get back on the clock."

As the door clicked shut behind the lieutenant, Carly hauled herself onto her crutches and moved to Sergio's bedside. He pushed himself up in the bed and grinned at her. "Check out the big bad serial killer catcher."

"Yeah, yeah…"

"Think you'll get your picture in the paper?"

She shrugged. "It was a team effort. So if they put in mine, they put in ours."

"Deal."

"How are you feeling?"

"Well . . ." He leaned on his side and put his hand over the bandage on his hip. "The holster and belt took most of the blow, but I needed a couple of dozen stitches. That earns me a week's bed rest and then I'm back on duty. What about you?"

"Same," Carly said. "I re-injured my sprain taking Davenrod down, so they want me to stay off it for a while. I'm gonna fly to Tennessee and meet the boys, and spend a few days in a hotel eating room service and looking at scenery out the window."

"Yeah?" Sergio leaned back on the bed. "Well, if you're gonna be out of town, I guess there are a few waitresses I'll be calling back."

She shook her head, moving to the door. "You're supposed to rest."

"You do bed rest your way, I'll do it mine." He reached for his phone. "See you next week."

# THE END

Carly and Sergio will be back
in
*DOUBLE BLIND BOOK 2*
## *PRIMARY TARGET*

### Note to Readers
*If you have the time, I would deeply appreciate a review on Amazon or Goodreads. I learn a great deal from them, and I'm always grateful for any encouragement. Reviews are a very big deal and help authors like me to sell a few more books. Every review matters, even if it's only a few words.*

*Thanks,*

*Dan Alatorre*

# ABOUT THE AUTHOR

 International bestselling author Dan Alatorre has published more than 22 titles in over a dozen languages.

 You'll find action-adventure in the sci-fi thriller *The Navigators,* a gripping paranormal roller coaster ride in *An Angel On Her Shoulder*, heartwarming and humorous anecdotes about parenting in the popular *Savvy Stories* series, and an atypical romance story in *Poggibonsi.*

 Dan's knack for surprising audiences and making you laugh or cry - or hang onto the edge of your seat - has been enjoyed by audiences around the world. And you are guaranteed to get a page turner every time.

"That's my style," Dan says. "Grab you on page one and then send you on a roller coaster ride, regardless of the story or genre."

**Readers agree, making his string of #1 bestsellers popular across the globe.**

His unique writing style can make you chuckle or shed tears—sometimes on the same page (or steam up the room if it's one of his romances). Regardless of genre, his novels always contain unexpected twists and turns, and his endearing nonfiction stories will stay in your heart forever.

He has also written illustrated children's book and the popular writing guide *A Is For ACTION.* His dedication to helping authors of any skill level is evident in his wildly popular blog "Dan Alatorre - AUTHOR" at DanAlatorre.com

Dan's success is widespread and varied. In addition to being a bestselling author, he has achieved President's Circle with two different Fortune 500 companies. Dan also mentors grade school children in his Young Authors Club and adults in his Private Critique Group (also at DanAlatorre.com), helping struggling authors find their voice and get published.

Dan resides in the Tampa, Florida, area with his wife and daughter.